Peter Prendergast was born in Dublin in 1964. He attended St Paul's College Raheny, and graduated from University College, Dublin in 1985.

He lives in Dublin with his wife and three children.

This is his first book.

WHEN KINDNESS FAILS

Peter Prendergast

When Kindness Fails

For Anne, Conor, Méabh and Clare

Fondest Regards

Peter

Vanguard Press

VANGUARD PAPERBACK

A CIP catalogue record for this title is available from the British Library
ISBN 1 843860 52 X

Vanguard Press is an imprint of Pegasus Elliot MacKenzie Publishers Ltd.
www.pegasuspublishers.com

First Published in 2003

Vanguard Press
Sheraton House Castle Park
Cambridge England

Printed & Bound in Great Britain

Dedication

In memory of my parents

Canice and Angela Prendergast

Acknowledgement

The author would like to thank the people who helped him in the preparation of this book. Stephen Corrigan found the time and patience to explain how burglar alarms work and had the ingenuity to imagine the circumstances under which they might not.

Donal Moriarty's careful reading, not only enabled me to improve my book immeasurably, but also helped me to understand exactly what sort of novel I had written. Likewise I am grateful to David Belbin, to Steve Klaidman for his loyalty and advice, and to my friend Ian Blackmore who brightens every working day.

To my mother, Angela, for her care and love and encouragement. To my siblings, Terry, Kathy and Canice, who always help me laugh through the tough times.

My children, Conor, Joe and Orla ensure that mine is the happiest of households but most of all I owe thanks to my wife, Trish, for her unyielding belief in me and her unending support through the writing of this and other books.

1991

Prologue

Right from the beginning Joe Faherty had seen the danger of staying in the house all day. The longer you hung around at home, the harder it was to go out. Unemployment drained a man's spirit. It took away his confidence and then pretty soon he'd be asking himself, Do I really want to work again?

Joe kept busy. He organised a schedule and stuck to it as though it was a regular work routine. At twenty to eight each morning he rose and made the breakfast. Once Stella had left he started into the housework. Two mornings a week, he did the washing, the following day he ironed. Three times a week he trekked to Superquinn. In the afternoons he went through the newspapers, called the jobcentres and did a tour of the local businesses to see if they needed anyone.

Whatever else, it gave the day a structure.

Monday today and Dublin mild and grey in August, he laid the paper out on the kitchen table and opened the appointments page. He started with the As – accountant, actuary, advertising executive, a porter, architect. On to the B's – bar person, book-keeper, butcher's boy. He telephoned a pallet making company in Drogheda; they were looking for someone under thirty. He made a coffee and skimmed the rest of the paper. Through the afternoon, he watched the television and waited for the early edition of *The Evening Herald*.

Just after four, Mel Barnes all the way from Buffalo NY said, "What've you got to offer me, Joe?"

"Nineteen years selling experience, that's what I've got, and references that show that I always beat my quotas. I'm a salesman. Apart from a year working as a security guard, it's what I've been doing since I left school."

Old Mel seemed to like that. "Well, you sure sound like the

kind of guy we need, Joe. It's a gem of a product we've got here – The Gut Grabber Bodywarmer. You know this system?"

Joe took a breath. "I've a feeling I'm going to find out."

Then the catch. There was always a catch. The way it worked Joe would buy twenty of these Gut Grabbers from Barnes and sell them on at a profit of less than six quid on each one. Then he could get his friends in on the act as well. Pretty soon he could become an agent.

It wasn't a job at all. Nothing surer than he'd end up with twenty of the fuckers sitting in the attic.

"I need something with a basic," he said and he hung up.

Stella was home just after six. A pot of Bolognese was simmering on the cooker. She kissed him on the cheek and said, "Hello love," and they went through the possibilities.

First there was the environmentalist job; some group needed someone with selling experience and Joe had plenty of that. The second he wasn't so sure about. A London hardware company was looking for someone to co-ordinate sales in Dublin.

"A hundred quid to get there," Joe said. "It's a lot to be told, 'Thanks for coming!'"

"Less than eighty if you go with Ryanair. And you can stay with Louis."

"I'm not too keen on that bit either."

"You'd rather pay another hundred for a hotel?"

"I'd rather not go at all."

"You've got to push yourself, Joe. Nothing for nothing in this world."

And that was the end of it. There were things he wanted to say – this job was out of his range, for instance – but was this the right moment? All prepared, his points nicely in sequence, he wanted to tell her that there was nothing wrong with selling for a living. It was a decent, respectable job. The stuff didn't sell itself after all. A salesman needed to know when to push and when to lay off. He had to be able to recognise what a customer needed and then sit back and let the customer convince himself that he needed it.

On top of which, it was all he knew how to do.

Later, he decided. He'd let her know exactly what was

bothering him. He'd explain it to her and then he'd tell her it was a waste of time applying for jobs he hadn't a chance of getting.

In bed that night he went through it. It was called The Peter Principle, he said. A salesman showed promise, so his company gave him responsibility for a few particular products. Then pretty soon, he wouldn't be selling any more. He'd be the area manager, then a bigger regional manager, and once he evened out and became only average at what he was doing, they'd lose interest in him.

The point being: If you were good at something, if you had a talent for it, why not stick with it?

Stella laid her magazine down and turned to face him in the bed. "A loser's attitude," she said, "if ever I've heard one."

"It's been six months now, Stel. I can't get any job, let alone something better than what I had."

"You think I haven't noticed?"

"What I'm telling you is that I'm not proud. Whatever I have to do to keep this house and what we've got here, I'll do it."

"You've just got to get back into the workforce," she said. "That's the first step."

Which was true, he knew it. It was simply a matter of finding something, anything, and then he could move on from there. The trick was to remain positive. And there was the environmentalist job, wasn't there? A result with that and he wouldn't have to go to London; he could settle back into a proper routine, get his finances straightened out. He wouldn't have to stay with Stella's nutso cousin and whatever way you looked at it, that was a bonus.

Stella rolled over to go asleep. "Know something, Joe?" she said, "You used to have more drive. It was part of why I fell for you."

What could you say to that?

"It's been a long day," she said. "I'm the one with the early start in the morning."

1

Paddy Benner took one look and thought, Christ this guy's a bruiser – 6'3" anyway, maybe more, with a whopping pair of shoulders on him and a tattoo on either forearm. The Irish bars in London were the same as the others; keep playing long enough and there'd be someone along to fleece you.

Paddy racked the balls. "That's a good straight cueing action you've got there," the guy said. "You've played before all right."

After three frames he said, "Jesus, some days you just can't get it together. How about a little side bet just to see if that improves things?"

Paddy watched the act. It was part of the fun, the act, either studying or putting one on and this character wasn't bad, groaning and swearing and rubbing his palms against his jeans. Nodding when the black ball dropped and saying, "Nothing wrong with that finish, mate, you're on fire here tonight."

Then slowly upping the bet. From one pound to two and then to a fiver and they'd been playing for an hour when he really began to apply the squeeze.

"Listen," he said. "I don't know what's gone wrong but I've got a feeling it's not coming back. Or maybe I'm just a little out of my depth here, I'm not too proud to admit that. How about we go for twenty a frame and give me one last chance to pull even?"

"Twenty sounds high for me," Paddy said.

"Hey, that's okay. Fair's fair. No sweat. Your decision."

"Well, just a couple maybe.

"That's the spirit. You're a top bloke, you know that? There's plenty others who'd just take the money and run."

And that was when this bruiser really began to play. A slight alteration on his bridging hand and his cueing action was suddenly smoother. A new stance and all of a sudden he was easing the ball around the table. He produced two eight ball clearances in a row. He finished one frame with a swerve shot followed by a double cross. Even Paddy was clapping. Clapping and watching and biding his time – same as always. He miscued occasionally; he screwed up on position; he potted the cue ball two frames in a row. He hardly spun the ball at all. But, two hours later, as he moved to the bar with a two hundred and forty quid in his shirt pocket, he felt a pull on his shirt sleeve.

"You're a jammy fucking cunt, you know that?"

"I don't really know what happened there." Paddy said.

Paddy sat at the bar and ordered a pint. He'd sip it a few minutes and look embarrassed to have taken the money and then, once people had stopped staring, he'd go take a leak and off out the side door.

Two hundred and forty quid for two hours work – it was good money. Maybe things were picking up, Paddy thinking this, then feeling a tap on his shoulder. He turned, sighed and gave a slow shake of the head. What was it about him that attracted folks that no one else wanted to talk to? This one had a fat moony head, looked as though he could lose a few pounds all over. Slow, simple and soft, the bottom lip hanging with a slight quiver…

"What can I do for you?"

"How much did you take off Sudds Donnelly?"

"That's between me and him. I don't think it'd be fair to say."

"You mind buying us a pint?"

Paddy almost burst out laughing. What was he – The Salvation Army? "I don't think so."

"Didn't mean to bother you," the guy said and off he went, in and out between the tables trying to scrounge a free pint. Paddy settled back in the stool and looked around. The first rule of hustling was to get the hell away as soon as you could. But there was a second rule as well – you always stayed in character until you were a safe distance from the mark.

He watched the simpleton do the rounds wandering between

the tables, trying to scrounge a pint. The walk was a slow lurch, feet never leaving the ground, the same simple hopeful look each time he asked. Some laughed. Some insulted him. One poured the dregs of a pint over his shoe.

Thick as shite, someone said.

What's the height of stupidity? another said.

It was interesting to watch people's reactions. Groups were the worst. A guy on his own would just look away but someone trying to impress…

"Give that fella whatever he's drinking, will you?" Paddy said.

"You'd be better off somewhere else," the barman said reaching for the glass. "Maybe you know what you're doing and maybe you don't but either way, don't hang around here."

Thirty seconds later, the simpleton was sitting across from Paddy – big vacant eyes, pint of lager in hand.

"Thanks," he said. "My name's Tim."

"That's terrific, Tim, but just because I bought you a pint doesn't mean I want you to sit with me."

"There's somethin' I want to ask you. Tomorrow we could go hustling and earn the big money. After you and Sudds I'm the best in town. Good potter, good safety game."

Paddy smiled. "I'm not a hustler," he said. "I just hit lucky back there."

"No," Tim said. "I've seen you before. You were in *Moran's* in Cricklewood and you won money there."

Paddy didn't recognise him, wasn't sure how he could've missed a guy like that. But he remembered *Moran's* alright. A whole night wasted battling against a punter he should have left alone. It was unavoidable, the way you'd pick the wrong guy from time to time. "There's plenty better than us knocking around," he said.

"We'll be partners. You and me. What d'you say?"

"I think you're off your rocker."

The fat moony face dropped. "I'm an ace potter," he said. "But sometimes I'm not sure what shot to play. You and me, we'd make a partnership. You tell me what to pot and I'll pot it."

There was no shaking him off. Moony brown eyes staring and on he went about the folks he'd taken money from. Some Paddy had heard of, guys who could've beaten this joker using the wrong end of a shovel. Tim and Sudds Donnelly played together a lot. Paddy left a fiver on the counter and moved towards the toilets, knowing Donnelly was watching, and he was conscious of the knife he carried in a sheath taped between his shoulder blades.

Donnelly stayed put.

Lucky for you or lucky for me, Paddy thought, and moments later he was jogging down the street.

2

"You looking for work?" Harry Fynn asked.

There was never enough Sudds Donnellys in a working week so Paddy was up early the next morning.

"Depends on what you've got." he said.

"A peach. Armed maybe, but I'm telling you it's a sweet one."

"That's not my thing," Paddy said. "You know that."

"Yeah, well it never hurts to look, does it?"

They drove for an hour in Fynn's brand new Nissan jeep. Fynn was a jeweller, late forties maybe, overweight, a man with charm. His trick was to sell a couple a necklace and he'd be so nice about it – knocking a little off the price, going to no end of trouble on the fittings – that the relationship would take off. Sure, he'd say, I'd love to drop by but only if I can give you a free evaluation. Fynn was experienced enough to case the house properly from the inside. Each of the previous three summers Paddy had spent a month in London, taking off as soon as the job was done.

One thing you could always rely on with rich folks: anything going for free and they'd jump at it.

They did a tour of the house Fynn had targeted, then it was back to the room over the jewellery shop. From what Paddy could see this was a non-runner. Detached house in a nice residential area; low walls and not much cover; a good solid alarm system linked to the cop shop by the phone line. In the bedroom there was a safe which would take the guts of two hours to get through. On top of that, there were other little caches but Fynn hadn't a clue where they were.

"By my reckoning," Fynn said, "your cut's a hundred and thirty grand if you bring me back what I want. That's just on what they showed me. There might be more."

Paddy liked the sound of that all right but still the job looked risky.

"I'll come out again in a day or two and take another look," he said. "But don't hold your breath."

That evening Paddy came out of his guesthouse and Tim was sitting on the wall opposite, stuffed into a royal blue suit. Bill Weberniuk in the seventies maybe, or one of those Oompaloompa guys from the Willy Wonka film he'd watched every Christmas when he was a kid.

"How'd you find out where I live?"

Tim pointed across the road. "The barman in *The Four Provinces* lives over there."

Paddy looked the length of the road, then back again. "He told you. Just like that."

"I asked him."

"Handy fella to have around. How many other people'd you ask?"

"Just the other two barmen."

"Anyone else want to know where I'm staying?"

Tim shook his head. "Just me. Listen I was wondering…"

"No, I don't want to go hustling with you."

And the face dropped. You just had to laugh really. "We're friends aren't we?"

"Not the sort that play pool together, we're not," Paddy said.

Business was slow. For every Sudds Donnelly there were days spent slogging away trying to find a mark. Sometimes you'd spend an hour or longer working a guy and then as soon as you pulled even he'd want to pack up and leave. What could you do? An ordinary joe, wife and three kids at home, with his wage packet in his back pocket and he tells you no, he's finished now – what was there to say except, Fair enough.

But at the beginning of each week, there was a rent bill.

Paddy took an 1986 Toyota Starlet from a side street in Kilburn. He drove out to Downs Leaze and parked maybe half a mile from the house. He walked at a nice easy pace, the length of the road and then in a loop back to the car. Then he drove around the area, made a rough map of the way the roads interconnected, and checked it against the city map he'd bought two hours earlier. He was working backwards. Find the best escape route first and take it from there. Paddy didn't know what Fynn was on about; as far as he could see there was nothing sweet about this set-up.

He went through the possibilities, the three ways he worked.

One – go in while the folks are at home, take whatever they leave lying around.

Two – get in, set the alarm off, and get out again before the cops arrive.

The only real possibility was the third one, or a variation of it at any rate. Often with this PhoneWatch business you could set the alarm off, hide and watch the rozzers check the place over, then go in before someone comes to reset the alarm.

But that wouldn't work either. The area was too exposed.

He lit a cigarette, sat in the car and stared out at those nice big houses. A hundred and thirty grand was twice what he'd taken on any other job.

The following night, Tim was on the wall again, same blue suit.

"Know something?" Paddy sighed. "I'm sitting there on an empty bus, minding my own business, thirty free seats all around me and next thing some punter plonks his arse into the seat next to me. Always happens. Hi, he says, I'm Bill. Hi, Bill, I say, and how are you today? And that's where I go wrong. What I should say is, Listen Bill, I'd just as soon sit on my own. But I don't and Bill starts telling me his life story. Any idea what the attraction is?"

Tim said, "Thanks for the pint."

"Pretend it never happened."

"And the fiver."

"I'm regretting it already. But you know what I'm going to do, I'm going to double it. I'm going to give you a tenner. Buy you off. You get your tenner and you leave me alone."

"I thought we could go play pool."

"A tenner, that's five pints. Easiest money you'll never make."

Staring at Paddy's shoes, "I suppose so."

"That's the boy! Plenty of other people to latch onto." Paddy slid a tenner from his pocket, crumpled it into a ball, pretended to bite the pin from the grenade, lobbed it out of the trench to land at Tim's feet.

"That money I took off your mate Donnelly," he said. "I bought a shotgun with it. You're on this wall tomorrow and I'm going to shoot you in the leg. You got that?"

Tim looked up. "It's not your wall. I can sit here if I want."

"Both barrels, Tim," Paddy said. "Right on the kneecap."

The next evening, Paddy said, "You're tenacious, Tim, and that's a good quality in a pool player."

"I *am* a good player."

"I have my doubts."

"You've never seen me play."

"Don't have to. I'm an experienced and talented professional. I know these things."

Tim said, "You're wrong."

Paddy shrugged. "Okay, so I'm wrong. Now scoot the fuck on home, will you."

Fynn's take on things was that it'd be better all round if Paddy took the job since otherwise he'd have to get a couple of lads to stick a Magnum 57 into the old dear's mouth, see if that jogged her husband's memory. A shame, he said, to put a lovely couple like the Byrds through a trauma like that.

"That's what I like about you, Harry," Paddy said. "You're a Christian, nothing else to be said about you."

"What I like about you," Fynn said, "is you're a thief. I'd like you a lot more if you'd get your ass in gear and figure a way into that house."

Paddy was thinking how he wanted to get out of London. Eight years now he'd been on the move, zigzagging his way through North America and across Europe. North in the summer, south in the winter; that was the system. Just following the warmth. The easy life, playing pool, earning enough to get by and then whenever the funds were low, return to London and see if Fynn had anything going.

"You go out to Downs Leaze yesterday?" Fynn wanted to know.

"Drove all around the area."

"And?"

"I still don't like the look of it."

"That's too bad. But there's no hurry on it."

Paddy was going to say more. Tell Fynn how a hundred and thirty grand could set you up for a while. Let you open a small business maybe, or just give you a bit of breathing space while you sorted a life out for yourself.

But why should Fynn be interested?

"I'll give you a call in a week," he said.

Whatever else, it was time to get out of London.

All the places he never wanted to see again and London was right there at the top of the list. He'd first visited when he was a kid – twelve, maybe or thirteen, he couldn't remember – over on the boat with his old man to see QPR play Chelsea. Only the old man couldn't make it to the match. Some last minute business had popped up which involved a chunky redhead so Paddy went alone. He walked right into a group of Chelsea fans who broke his arm and his ribs and his nose and his cheekbone and who danced on his head and who spat on him as he lay whimpering.

That was London for Paddy Benner.

Sometimes, he thought of going to watch Chelsea. Twelve, thirteen years later, sure, but maybe he'd be able to pick out one of the boys. Treat him to a little of the cold steel he carried taped between his shoulder blades.

But what was the point in that?

Now he was driving a blue Nissan Primera, big powerful car, around Kensington again. He was thinking about the hundred and thirty grand, a good chunk of money all right, enough maybe to buy a small business. A bar maybe, he thought. Some place sunny, with a garden where people could sit under umbrellas and stick a hand in the air if they wanted him. Sling us over a few beers there, you big fuckhead, they could say and he'd say, Coming right up, folks. A little humility, a little honest labour, exactly what he'd spent a life trying to avoid.

It had to be better than this.

He parked and sat quietly in the car, a few streets away from where the Byrds lived. In the flicks, the heist man would always call in the alarms expert and he'd find a way in. Anything was possible, it seemed. Only an alarm system was on the inside and the burglar was on the outside and he couldn't get at the controls without setting the whole thing off.

Cutting the telephone lines, that was a possibility.

The only other was to talk his way in.

A runner, maybe, but he'd need someone else. A driver as well most likely.

Later that evening Paddy found a peach of an investment banker. They were in the Topaz Pool and Snooker Hall in Croyden, Paddy thinking how the smell of a pool hall was the same everywhere, the banker thinking, Yeah, I can take this guy, no reason why not.

It was interesting to watch sometimes, the other guy, full of confidence early in the game. The hook was already into this one – all swagger and purpose, moving around the table, a man about his business. Give him an hour and he'd have fallen to pieces. Beating himself, most likely, Paddy wouldn't even have to play. Pride and stupidity, that's what it was most of the time.

How much longer can you go on like this?

Behind the counter the owner was watching a boxing match; some French guy, old for a boxer, taking a hiding from a Mexican. Paddy liked the French guy, identified with him. He was just what the promoters needed, tough enough to stay standing so the crowd could get their money's worth, not quick enough to damage the prospect. Just standing there taking a beating. Thirty-six years old, knowing that if he goes down he's not going to get another fight.

"You want to shoot or not?" the banker said.

Thirty-six. Ten years older than Paddy.

Now Paddy was shaking his head. "You're too good for me," he said.

The banker was too stupid to be surprised. "You had enough?"

"Everyone loves a winner, don't they?" Paddy said, laying the money on the table.

Paddy watched the fight to the end. He watched the French guy stagger from the ring. He watched the coach put a towel around his shoulders and lead him away. Paddy walked back towards his guesthouse wondering if the French boxer had ever thought he'd be a champion. He wondered if he'd ever loved to box just for the simple joy of it.

On the wall opposite his guesthouse Tim was waiting.

"Hi, Tim," Paddy said.

"I lost your tenner."

Paddy strolled straight past him. "I guessed you probably had. You want a burger, it's this way."

Tim jumped down from the wall. "You serious?"

"Never joke about food with a fatty. It's a good rule of thumb."

Now Tim was jogging to catch up. "I thought we might play some pool then."

Paddy could hear the footsteps behind him. Ridiculous, he thought, hooking up with the likes of this clown. "Let's get the food first" he said. "Then we'll see what's what."

3

When Richard Hamilton got a call from Harry Fynn telling him to drive two hundred miles to London he said it better be worth his while or else he'd be sticking an expense bill onto the next job.

He liked that, the way he'd said it: jokey but letting Fynn know he wasn't anybody's lackey.

He set off before the early morning rush hour in the eight year old Ford Escort he'd bought with his last score. On the outskirts of Birmingham he picked up Paul Malik who had been in on that job. Hadn't that been a sweet one! Get the details from Fynn, walk in with a pair of baseball bats, smash the living shit out of the crockery and pretty soon the old couple were throwing the stuff at them. Three and a half grand, easy as you like. Would it be too much to hope for the same this time round?

Smart, he thought, the way Fynn always used people from out of town. Cut down the risk since a burglary investigation stayed local.

But there was a problem with this set-up. He had to spend two hours in a car with a Paki. In the old days a Paki set up on your street corner and you firebombed him right back out again. No messing about. Nothing personal but fuck off back to wherever you came from. Now they were speaking Urdu in the schools – hard to believe but it was true – an English kid goes out in the yard to play and he's listening to all this jabber going on around him. Malik wasn't the worst Paki in the world, maybe – as far as Richard knew he wasn't on the dole and he wasn't selling any lettuce on the street corner – but that didn't mean he wanted to spend two hours in a car with him.

"Into the back," he said as soon as Malik opened the door.

"What's wrong with the front?" Malik said.

"You know how far it is to London?"

"It's like that, is it?"

"In or out. Take your pick."

"Oh, I'm in all right," Malik said jumping inside. "Chance of a lift in a quality automobile like this..."

Paul Malik sat in the back, kicked some old magazines under the passenger seat. He settled himself, looked out the window at the passing buildings, the dull grey outskirts of Birmingham. Lovely, he thought, the way some people just couldn't hold it in any longer. First time working together and Hamilton had been on his best behaviour. Not friendly, no, but not hostile either. But now the cards were on the table, a sleeveless T-shirt and a swastika tattooed onto the upper arm. Another ignorant moron, that was all, and maybe he'd get what was coming soon enough.

"Not much legroom back here," he said. "This a Mini?"

"What was that, Paki?"

Pretending he hadn't heard.

Malik said, "What am I doing back here?"

No answer.

"Not that it's not comfortable. But I thought you'd want me up front."

"You stay right where you are. That's your spot all right."

"So we're not mates?"

"One job, that's all we've done. Get through this and that'll be the end of it."

Malik sat back in the seat and laughed. From this angle it looked like Hamilton was going bald. Just a little spot now but give it a few years and there'd be a big tax disc on the top of that head. Malik slipped a diamond ring from his pocket, big enough diamonds, four of them set along in a row. "Thought maybe you might like to know where I got this." He dropped the ring over Hamilton's shoulder, let it fall into his lap.

"I'm trying to drive, for Christ sake."

"Just look at the goods."

Hamilton located the ring between his legs. Didn't bother looking at it. "Okay, Paki, so you boosted a ring. You want an award?"

"You know who I lifted it from?"

"What do I care where you got it?"

Smiling, Malik said, "I held it back last time round. Just to make sure old Tubbser's on the level and what d'you know, that little beauty's worth eleven grand."

Now Hamilton was looking at the ring, taking his time, the way he liked to. Eleven grand for a single ring. They must've brought Fynn maybe twenty rings, say nothing of the other stuff. Necklaces, brooches, bracelets – the lot. One of those bangle things, Christ, you'd need a month in a gym before you put the bloody thing on. "You saying the little cunt stiffed us?"

"That's what I'm saying. Old Tubbser must've creamed a good whack off the top."

Hamilton wanted time to think, get it straight in his head. No doubt about it – if one ring was worth eleven grand then his three and a half was light. "You got an idea on this?"

"Sure. But first you'd better pull over."

"What for?"

Malik could see Hamilton reach across to the passenger seat to his pack of Rothmans, flip one into his mouth – and miss.

"So I can climb into the front," he said. "About time the Paki was bumped up, don't you think?"

Fynn had said to Paddy, "Seven times I've used these boys and they're solid. Not the most subtle in the world but they get the job done."

Now Paddy was sitting in a leather upholstered armchair above Fynn's jewellery shop, looking across at the two: a mallethead with a swastika tattooed on his arm and an Asian, Pakistani most likely. "Some combination you've pulled out of the bag here, Harry", he said. "A dirty great Nazi and an immigrant, for Christ sake."

Malik said, "Who's the immigrant?"

"Well someone back along the line was. What's the story? You not afraid romper stomper here's gonna jump on your head as soon as your back's turned?"

Malik was sitting back in his armchair, one leg across the other knee. Weighing things up. Paddy watched him sitting here now, nice and calm as though he'd done this before. "Richard's okay. What he does in his own time's his business. He holds his end up on the job and that's all I care about."

"I've nothing against Paul," Hamilton said.

"You not notice he's black?" Paddy said.

"I know what colour he is."

Paddy turned slightly, looked Hamilton in the face. Maybe this was the one to worry about. It could happen all right – plan to the last detail and then find yourself getting screwed because of some racial thing. "What's the story with that swastika?" he said. "Your National Front pals, they'll be chuffed to know you're working with a…" He turned to Malik. "Where're you from anyway?"

"Birmingham?"

Paddy sighed. "How about Grandad? Where was he from?"

"Karachi. Know where that is?"

To Hamilton: "Hear that? A Paki. Why don't we just kick the shit out of him right now? Keep us occupied for a while and then we can forget all about this."

Hamilton straightened in the armchair, fourteen stone of him maybe, a big pair of shoulders and wavy fair hair. "You got a problem with me?"

"I've a problem with that thing on your arm."

"Yeah, well no one's got a problem with Malik as long as he stays off Social Welfare."

And that was it. What was there to say? Paddy lit a cigarette, said nothing for a while. It was a complication, sure, but there was always one, wasn't there? Here was the funny thing – apart from the swastika, Hamilton looked okay for the job. Tall and good looking, somewhere in his mid-twenties but you could knock a few years off that with a shave and a haircut.

He was the only candidate Fynn knew in the right age group.

In or out, the time to decide. You had to be careful, sure, but wait for everything to be perfect and you'd never make a penny.

Paddy said, "We bring back what Harry wants and it's worth a hundred and thirty grand. I get an even ton of that.

Anything else, he'll buy as well. I take half of that and you two split the rest."

He watched the reaction, Hamilton's eyes wide open at the figures, Malik's telling nothing.

Malik said, "You really think you're taking a hundred grand?"

"That's the offer. Take it or leave it. I do the work, get us in and through the safe. All you've got to do is drive. All he's got to do is stand next to me. You're not exactly skilled labour."

"We'll talk it over. If we're not back in twenty minutes, we're out of it.

Walking down Tottenham Court Road, past the rows of electrical shops, Paul Malik was thinking of how he needed a break. For six years now he'd been on the scam, credit cards mostly, and what had he to show for it? He'd done two stretches – six and eighteen months apiece – and now he had a pregnant girlfriend in tow. He worked the hotels mostly, all decked out in a suit and tie, checking the jackets left on the back of chairs in the conference rooms. The trick was to take only one card and hope it wasn't noticed. The other trick was to bin it before it showed up as stolen.

Six years; two stretches. Maybe he was going the wrong way about things.

The thing about credit cards was there were three ways you could get caught. Stealing it in the first place, that was a risk, and then you had to buy something with it. As if that wasn't enough, then you had to move what you'd just bought. Three steps, all with a risk, and it wasn't as though the rewards had been great.

If nothing else, this showed Paul Malik that he'd been hanging around with the wrong people.

It was time to move up in the world, he'd been thinking that for some time now, but the question was, Which direction? A skilled burglar, sure: he'd have the chance of taking a good score. But what if you didn't have those skills? Then you took a gun in with you, stuck it in the guy's ear and said, Let's have! That was the best way, the one that always worked. He'd never heard of it not working. But get yourself caught and you were looking at seven to fifteen.

Which was why this set-up seemed so sweet. If he'd hand-picked them, he couldn't have done any better – a burglar and a neo-Nazi fuckhead stupid enough to carry the gun. All he'd have to do was sit in the car and see what panned out.

"That bloke doesn't have much time for you," he said to Hamilton.

"Who, Tubby?"

"The other one."

Nodding, Hamilton said, "Anyone calls me Romper Stomper, it's not going to be him. See the way he looks at you?"

"That's why he does it. To see how you take it."

"Oh, I can take it all right. Doesn't mean I'll take it from him."

Malik wasn't sure about this Paddy character. The way he played one off against the other. Having a go at Hamilton, then watching to see how everyone else was reacting.

"We'd better be careful here," he said. "We say, yeah sure, you take what you want, and he'll know there's something up. But give him too much grief and he'll want someone else. Like he said, he's the one with the skills."

"You think he's in with Fynn?" Hamilton said.

"How do you mean?"

"Trying to do us."

"Maybe he knows it and maybe he doesn't but there's more than a hundred and thirty grand's worth in that house. We'll say we want the extra split three ways. Even shares."

Hamilton was plodding along, staring at the footpath. "Know what I'd really like to do?"

"What?"

"Romper stomp his fucking head in for him, that's what. See what the lippy bastard says to that."

It was Gerry O'Neill, an Irish guy living in Boston who'd first told Paddy about the Mormon scam. He was good value describing it. A nice suit and tie on, Is Jesus in your life, he'd ask the guy on the doorstep. Or else he'd want to know could he and his chum roll on through to share a line of the bible with whoever was inside.

All it was – a way of blending into the surroundings while the cops looked the place over.

Now Paddy was in the passenger seat of Fynn's jeep. What he liked about the two in the back, they were cheap. Mutt and Jeff maybe, but get yourself an experienced burglar and he'd want almost half. And how many burglars, after all, did you need to break into a single house? All Malik had to do was drive. All Hamilton had to do was stand up straight, keep his mouth shut and help carry out the score.

If ever there was a flat rate job, this was it.

When they asked for a higher split, he looked at them, You serious? But he gave it to them anyway. A Nazi and a Paki running around in the background, it was a dodgy enough combination without them grumbling about their cut. Sure, he told them, why not?

Moving through Clerkenwell now, staring past a row of level grey buildings, Paddy began to explain things. Speaking evenly, making sure there were no misunderstandings. "Richard and I just keep going" he said, "until we get to the house we want. We know the folks are out and we've got to make sure the keyholder for the alarm's out as well. We just bang on the window to set the alarm off. Then we head on."

"And suppose someone stops you?" Malik said.

"No one pays any attention to an alarm these days. Someone hears the wailing and they don't think, Oh that's my neighbour getting rifled. They think some dipstick's set off his alarm."

"You're taking a chance on it," Malik said.

"It's no risk. We get stopped we just say Yeah, sorry about that, we knocked against the window and set off the alarm. Harry says there are sensors on the windows."

"Hear him out," Fynn said.

"So we just keep on the round," Paddy said. "With this PhoneWatch business, the first thing the alarm company does is ring the house. If the owner's there with the right password, that's fine. If not, they ring a named keyholder who goes and checks the place over. If neither of those are home, they call the cops. You usually get between six and twelve minutes before the cops arrive. Less if there's a squad car in the area."

"How far's the police station from the house," Fynn asked.

"Five minutes maybe. Three in an emergency. I'd say we'll have company in about six to seven minutes."

Malik said, "By which time you and Richard have moved on up the road."

"That's right. The cops arrive and we're ten houses away. Maybe more unless someone invites us in. But there's not much chance of that – those Mormon boys get their teeth into you and they'll be beating your door down for the next six months. So we wait until the cops check the place over and hoof off with themselves. Then we double back and go in."

"What if the filth go in and turn the alarm off?" Hamilton asked.

"They're not allowed to. Trespassing. Otherwise they could just bang on your window and in they go for a dekko about the place. All they can do is look around the outside and, if everything seems okay, that'll be the end of them."

"So you're hoping no one sees you walk into a house you've already been in," Malik said.

Yes, he was right: that was the moment. The same as with any other job, there was always one when you held your breath and prayed to Christ no one was watching. But there was another problem here. To get through the back door all Paddy would need was a slim piece of metal called a tension tool, one with a feeler pick on the end of it. But what about the safe? The way you got through a safe was by peeling it, one layer of the steel door and then the next. Two hours work maybe, and you'd need a lot more than a tension tool for it.

"We'll have to go back to the car," Paddy said. "I'll need tools and we'd be best off bringing a metal detector for extra stashes. Harry says not all the stuff's in the safe."

"What sort of safe is it?"

"You know anything about safes?"

"No. But what if it's something you can't get through?"

Paddy shrugged. "If it's just an ordinary steel safe then I should get through it. A floor safe will take longer. But the real problem here is that Richard and I are going to show our faces.

As far as London's concerned, you can keep my share of it. What about you, Richard? You happy to stay out of London for a while?"

Hamilton was interesting to watch now. His turn to ask the questions. Sitting back in the seat, more confident now, he wanted to know why Mormons? Paddy told him it was because they all looked the same. No one noticed the colour of a Mormon's eyes; the average homeowner said, Fuck off with yourselves there, lads, and shut the door again.

"So you ready to stay out of London?" Paddy asked

Hamilton shrugged. "Never liked the place," he said.

4

At first Paddy would feel guilty about keeping him waiting. Tell the big simpleton to wait in a pool hall and he'd say yeah okay, but then you'd find him on your wall again the next night. Just sitting there, legs dangling, his gaze empty like a baby's.

Nowhere else to be probably.

They started in the pool halls around Kilburn, Paddy offering some gentle coaching, trying to change Tim's cueing action. One smooth movement, that was all you wanted, head and bridging hand dead still. See? Nothing to it, Tim, once you relax. But no, old Tim had to smash the balls. A big jerk of the elbow and whack! the cue ball was racing up and down the table. It was funny the way he did it, his tongue stuck into the corner of his mouth like a five year old writing a letter. But funny wasn't going to earn anyone money.

"You're choc full of shit, Tim," Paddy said. "Telling me you could play this game."

Still a deal was a deal. Those big sad cow eyes, you couldn't just send him away. So Paddy picked him up each evening around six. The rules were simple: genuine suckers only, never for more than a fiver a frame. It was a question of minimising the losses. But the problem was how to organise the game. They tried playing doubles but with only one shot in four, the frame was too hard to control, especially with Tim slapping the cue ball around like a lunatic.

Finally, Paddy said, "We're getting fleeced here, Tim. Any ideas on how to stop the rot?"

"It's all my fault," Tim said. "I won't bother you any more."

"Fair enough. It's been nice knowing you."

Tim took his head out of his hands. "I'll do better tomorrow, Paddy," he said. "I promise."

Tim listened closely while Paddy explained how to hustle.

First of all, you worked off a float: five hundred quid usually but down to an even ton with Tim in tow. Lose that and you walk away. Don't offer your watch, don't make a run to the bank. Someone takes five hundred from you, chances are he'll have your watch as well, so you just shake his hand and let him go. Think of the float as a prop, that was the trick, not your money to spend at all.

Then you learned how to choose a mark. Go by profession, that was a rule. Guys in suits, they were usually good – bankers and lawyers and insurance executives. Cash carriers, Paddy called them, young professionals on the way up, too proud and too stupid to say, Shit pal, you've beaten me. Punters like that chased their money, but you didn't find them often enough.

Just a couple of simple pointers to start with.

Paddy explained them slowly. Got all that? Tim said, Yeah, he was ready and took the thirty quid. Paddy sat back and watched and would you believe it, the big melon managed to choose the one guy in the poolroom that Paddy would have avoided. Half an hour later, he was back again.

"Nice work," Paddy said.

"I think I picked the wrong one," Tim said.

All you had to do was sit back and let the boy talk. Tim would have a slip of paper in his shirt pocket. Every now and then he'd sneak a peek and then, twenty seconds later, another topic would be lobbed into the conversation.

Drivel mostly but it was funny the way he did it.

Truth of the matter was that Paddy had begun to enjoy the company. Spend enough time on your own and even the likes of Tim was a welcome distraction. If he lost a few quid along the way, so what? Buttons, that's what hustling was most of the time, a fiver here or a tenner there. All you needed was sixty quid a day to keep you ticking over while you waited for the big score.

Five mornings in a row Paddy lifted a car with tinted windows from one of the nearby car parks. He'd sit patiently across the road from the Byrds, just watching, seeing if the job was a runner. Watching the husband leave for work in the morning, then tailing the wife to see if she had a routine. On Monday morning, he followed her to the nearest Oxfam, then along a route to Kilburn and back into Croyden. Staying a safe distance behind, stopping when she stopped to hand covered plates into doorways. Meals on wheels, a weekly commitment most likely.

Maybe things were shaping up…

One night, in the Kings Inn in Tottenham, Paddy cracked it. Nothing planned, just a moment's inspiration, two jokers facing him looking for an easy few quid.

He grabbed Tim's face in his hand, pressing the cheeks between thumb and forefinger. "This guy look normal to you?" he asked. "We want odds of five to one for him."

"You his manager?" one of them wanted to know. He didn't look up to much but his pal had a flashy new two-piece cue.

Paddy lifted the cue, studied it. "This is a beauty, all right," he said. "Either of you care to use it, I'll give you the same odds."

That was the new system. All Paddy had to do was win at a faster rate than Tim was losing and they were making money. Use Tim as a prop, that was the secret: don't think of him as a hindrance.

They earned forty quid that night. Peanuts maybe, but it was better than getting fleeced.

"Twenty each," Tim said.

"You still owe me thirty from the other night."

"Oh!"

"Oh! is right. I look like a charity to you?"

***

This new system, it was a good old laugh.

The way Paddy looked at it, he'd spent too long telling lousy players they were good. Shot! he'd say to some Sammy Spud and the guy would look up and nod, Yes it *was* rather brilliant, wasn't it?

But not any more. They found a couple of punters wearing England football jerseys in a bar in Croyden.

"That pretty much sums up English sport," Paddy said when one of them missed his shot.

"You say something?"

"English sport is one sorry mess," Paddy said, grinning. "Tennis, rugby, footy – the lot. Pick up a paper any day of the week and there's some tosser waffling on about crappy coaching structures. You want to know what the real problem is?"

The two boys looked from one to the other. "Go on," one of them said. "Enlighten us."

"I hate to say it but you're the most untalented fucking race I've ever come across in my life. It's in the blood. There should be a handicap system. Make the other team run around with a rucksack full of rocks, maybe. Or if it's tennis, you could make the other guy play with a breadboard or something. Glue it to his hand."

One of them, big good-humoured guy, stood up to his full height. "You like to stick in the boot, don't you?" he said.

"Certainly try my best. You want to play?"

"Set them up, champ."

And that's how it worked: Paddy would goad them into playing. All good-humoured, pick a topic, any topic. But there were quieter times when he just talked. Spend your life conning people and you were reluctant to open up about how you did it. Let the other guy find out the hard way if he wanted to.

But now with the sense that this part of his life would soon be over, Paddy felt as though he was unburdening himself.

Where most hustlers went wrong, he explained, they tried to win too quickly. Four, five frames an hour, that was as fast as you wanted to go. Let a frame open up and you might have to show too much to win it. So you closed things off. You covered the pockets, left the cue ball resting against the cushion. Just sitting back, letting the other guy beat himself, that was the secret.

Could Tim understand that? Maybe, maybe not. With Tim it was hard to tell sometimes.

Because most people – Paddy's old man, for instance, a pro golfer who'd never quite made the grade – actually wanted to lose. Amazing, yes, but it was true: a big part of them was just begging to throw in the towel. Take a guy who's been playing for eight hours solid, Paddy said. He's tired. His eyes hurt. He wants to go home and climb into the scratcher. Three more frames, he reckons, that's all it'll take. Anyway he's so far ahead that the other guy must be dead on his feet. Just keep going, he tells himself, nice and easy. But it's not easy, it's never easy when you're playing for your own money. He loses the frame, and then the one after. It's then that it occurs to him that he's not going to bed. His chance has gone. And here's the crazy bit – it's a comfort to him, all along he'd known what was going to happen. He's happy now. The pressure's off and his eyes don't hurt as much any more. He can settle back and lose, just like he's used to doing. He can even complain about the shitty luck he's having: it's so much easier than taking those last three frames.

But of course Tim didn't really understand. He was sitting there in the corner of *The Betsy Trotwood* in Clerkenwell with the same vacant expression on his face.

"Stop me on the spot now, Tim, if I'm boring you." Paddy said.

Tim shook his head. "These are the best days ever."

"You don't get out much, do you?" Paddy said.

Friday was comics' day. The comics weren't like they were in the old days, Paddy thought – when Roy Race was banging them in from all angles and Billy Dane was mislaying Dead Shot Keen's boots – but Tim seemed happy with them. He had his own sequence: *The Beano*, *The Dandy*, *Judge Dredd*, *Tiger and Scorcher* and *The Beezer*. It was fun to watch him: tongue stuck into the corner of his mouth, pint going flat on the counter. You'd have thought he was reading *War and Peace* from the look of him.

But then one Friday, Paddy saw him lumbering up the road. No comics under the arm this time but there was a dark red row of stitches across his forehead.

"What the hell happened to you?"

It took a moment for Tim to catch his breath. "Went to The Four Provinces this afternoon," he said, "and we were playing World Cup winners. We made a goal and the others'd throw beer mats and I'd head them into the goal."

Paddy gave a slow shake of the head. "Someone chuck a brick at you?"

"It was Sudds. He threw an ashtray."

"I can see how that'd be an easy mistake to make."

"It was really funny, Paddy. Everyone was laughing."

"Maybe you'd want to stay out of that place, Tim. You want to go to an Irish bar, there are nicer ones."

"But it's where my friends are."

Paddy looked across at him. "If they were your friends, Tim, they might treat you a little better. You ever think about that?"

Sitting in a stolen Toyota Carina one morning, Paddy started thinking about his theory of winners and losers and the way some folks were just so used to losing that you couldn't get them to do anything else. Tim was the first person he'd explained it to. Keeping on the move, after all, didn't lend itself to serious conversation. The old man would have been interested, Paddy thought, only he might have recognised himself; or maybe Aoife Brennan whose picture he still carried in his wallet and who had been interested in the psychology of pretty much anything. But that was about it, Paddy considering this when Jesus, the alarm in 27 Downs Leaze began to wail. He wasn't sure what set it off, a bird most likely, but it saved him the trouble of doing it himself. Paddy watched an old guy emerge from five doors away, a retired colonel type with a stiff backed walk. Now he knew who the keyholder was. A minute later, the alarm was silent and he drove away.

Tim wanted Paddy to meet his family. His mother and father, that was all; Tim's sister was married and living in Germany.

"You really are fucking bonkers," Paddy said.

It was all he'd need. Tim's old dear taking his hand in her clammy mitt, rattling on about how wonderful it was for Tim to have a friend. The old lad puffing on his pipe, Tell me more about this hustling business now, Patrick, hmmmm…

But Tim had an uncle who lived nearby and they ran into him one night in a local pub.

"Some way to make a living, that is," he said. "Cheating good honest folks out of their money."

He was just standing there, holding his pint, waiting for a reaction, a chubby guy, just like Tim.

"It's an offer," Paddy said. "I ask if you want to play and you say yes or you say no. No one's twisting your arm."

"But you're pretending you're no good."

"Of course I am and that's right there in the offer. Some punter comes up and asks if you want to play, there's a fair chance he's a hustler. That's what you're betting on."

"How do you do it?"

"Do what?"

"Pretend you're no good. Just keep missing?"

Into his third pint now, feeling talkative, Paddy said, "I can put a jerk into my cueing action. Two actually. One makes me look like a complete spud, the other's the one I use most of the time. I look like a pretty good amateur, the kind most people might beat if they really put their mind to it."

"So that's the level you're trying to pitch to?"

"You have to decide how good the other guy is and play to a level just above his. People think you feed him a few frames and then start walloping him. But it's not like that at all. The best way is to take more and more of the tight frames as the night goes on."

Tim's uncle was nodding now. "That's how you don't get rumbled."

"Slow and easy, it's the best way."

"Ever get the shit beaten out of you?"

"Over a pool game?"

"When someone copped you were hustling them."

"Not so far. I've been lucky. Twice I've dropped a bundle on purpose. Got myself into a situation that looked like turning nasty so I just let the money go. Cheaper in the long run than having some fucker take a baseball bat to you."

"What isn't?" the uncle said. He was a talker, just like Tim. Maybe it was in the blood. He drove lorries for a living, London to Newcastle or Sunderland mostly but every Monday night he did the Holyhead run: over on the ferry to Dublin. Paddy was welcome to a lift if he ever felt like a trip home.

"You took your life in your hands tangling with Sudds Donnelly," he said. "He works as an enforcer for Ron Sanderson. Him and his brother, they're a bad pair. You ever hear of Sanderson?"

Paddy shook his head.

"Underworld guy. Hides his money in construction. Only he has these two and a few others to do the dirty work. If anything the brother's worse. Quick with a knife. They've both been up on murder charges but the witnesses wouldn't testify."

Paddy whistled gently. "He's always in *The Four Provinces*, is he?"

"Most of the time. I go there every Monday night with a gang of truckers. Anyone who isn't driving. Every time I'm there, he's there. Bumping into people, waiting for them to back down. Or else trying to hustle a few quid."

Paddy sipped his pint. "Why does Tim hang around there?"

"Same reason he hangs around you."

"Which is?"

"You don't ignore him."

Paddy nodded. That was it, all right. Push the guy around, treat him like shit and it was okay by him. As long as it was attention of some sort. Throw an ashtray, laugh, pour a pint over his shoe. Anything was better than being ignored.

Then he was back at Paddy's shoulder, setting the pints on a nearby table. He had news. He hadn't wanted to say anything earlier because he thought Paddy was still angry over business with the ashtray. But Sudds Donnelly wanted a rematch. Same table, twenty quid a frame, just like before. What a game it'd be, Tim said, the two best in London.

Paddy looked to the uncle, laughed back at Tim. "Sorry, Tim," he said, "but I think I'll pass on that one if it's all the same to yourself."

5

"You think you'll be able to help us, Joe?" Evelyn Jones asked.

"I think so," Joe Faherty said. "I'm a good salesman."

"And what is it that makes a good salesman?" Eoin Jones asked. It was a husband and wife team.

"The most important thing in selling is not to push too hard. A customer likes a product, then he's going to buy it anyway. If not, he won't. If he's in between all you can do is make sure he knows about the product's good points. Sure, you could probably push a few but later on, maybe when they're in bed that night, they start worrying about the money they've just spent. Bad purchases weigh on people's minds. They hate to think they've been taken for a ride. So the next time you're trying to sell them something, they don't want to see you. Being pushy is bad policy in the long term. You sell less. If I get this job, will I be selling memberships?"

Evelyn nodded.

"How much?"

"Twenty pounds. For that we post them all the relevant leaflets and posters and any publications we bring out. What do you think of the price?"

"It depends on what you can offer the product for. A lot of people, even if you got their attention at the door, would baulk at twenty. No one wants to shell out twenty quid on a doorstep. Fifteen would be a good price. On a doorstep, twenty sounds a lot more than five up from fifteen. That's my opinion anyway."

Joe was on a roll. Already he'd been waxing on about the ozone layer, the greenhouse effect, the reported aftermath of the Chernobyl and Three Mile island explosions, the Sellafield workers and the danger of burning fossil fuels – all the things he'd gone through with Stella the night before. Then there was

Greenpeace, CND and ENFO and how it was now left to the people to protect themselves. Waffle, sure, but it sounded okay coming out of his mouth. Tossing out suggestions now – a family rate or maybe organising a system of environmental education through the schools. Bullshit, that's what he was giving them – twenty-four carat stuff. But were they complaining?

"We'd like to create a hypothetical situation," Evelyn said. "Say for instance that I open the door to you. I live in a nice area and there are two cars in the driveway so it's pretty obvious that we're not short. It's a big house. Anyway, I tell you I don't want to take out membership but I offer you five pounds as a contribution. Give us your answer."

A fiver, Joe thought, well you'd just have to take the money and run, wouldn't you? But that wasn't the answer these folks were after.

"Well," Joe said, "First of all, I'd thank them…"

"No, Joe," Evelyn said. "Sorry to stop you but I want you to pretend that you're on my doorstep. You have to speak directly to me. I'm the woman of a house and it's a wealthy house. I'm willing to donate five pounds but I'm not interested in taking out membership."

His gut began to turn, Joe sitting there, his mind blank.

"Well, thank you for your contribution," he said after a moment. "With your permission I'd like to take your name so we can send you a written acknowledgement. But to be honest, this is about more than money. Our finances are tight of course but most important to us is the size of our membership. I have to ask you to reconsider for a couple of reasons. Firstly, the greater our numbers, the more political clout we have. Our voice is stronger. And secondly, from your point of view, you have the chance to invest in the quality of your children's future. Because that's what we're talking about here – your children's future. As a member you'll receive all brochures, so the educational aspect is very important. Education about what's happening to the environment should be around the house. It's a lot better for our brochures and leaflets to be available for kids to read in their own time, instead of making them listen to lectures at school. I'm very grateful for your contribution but I ask you to reconsider joining our group."

All this delivered with a perfectly straight face. When he was finished, Eoin turned to Evelyn. "Well, would you be tempted to take out membership?"

"I'm not saying I would or I wouldn't," she said. "I couldn't say that for certain. But I'd certainly rethink my decision." She turned to Joe. "That's an excellent answer, Joe," she said.

Eoin stood up and stuck out his hand. "We still have some others to interview," he said. "We'll let you know as soon as possible. We don't want to keep anyone waiting."

"Thank you both for your time," Joe said.

Two o'clock by now with the workers on the way back to their offices and Waterstones doing a healthy lunchtime trade. In his pocket, Joe had a fiver. A treat for himself maybe? A good thriller to while away an afternoon or two, or a bag of Oatfield's Chocolate Emeralds. Or maybe even a Big Mac. He wondered if there was a free exhibition somewhere to fill the day. He clapped his hands together and smiled and thought how some days you were hot and there was damn all anyone could do about it.

He crossed O'Connell Bridge, his coat buttoned against the breeze and the clank of the blind beggar's tin ringing in his head. He'd begun to feel sorry for himself, he knew this. You could talk all you wanted about staying upbeat but, well it wasn't easy. Stella had stopped loving him, this was a fact: first the respect had gone and then the love. She was impossible to please these days. He bought her a copy of *Hello* and hurried to the Number 11 bus stop.

On the way home he laid out his plan. The love had disappeared gradually so why should it return any more quickly? The sequence would still be the same – first the respect, then maybe the love. He'd have to wait it out. He'd be patient. She could have as long as she wanted; it wasn't as if he'd ever think of going anywhere. And the interview, at least there was that to think of…

When Stella arrived home, the magazine was sitting in her place, the best china and glasses were out. The meal was ordinary enough – chops, potatoes and carrots – but he'd prepared melon boats as a starter. She hung her coat on the end of the stairs.

"You got the job?"

Joe smiled. "They still have others to interview but it couldn't have gone any better."

"So what did they say?"

"They'll get back to me in a few days."

Stella sat down, slid the magazine aside and started on the melon.

"I was full of ideas," Joe said.

"Sorry, Joe," she said. "I don't want to get my hopes up. You understand that, don't you? I'm happy for you but I don't want to get my hopes up."

Joe felt good. Each afternoon he spent an hour in the library. He read about rats the size of cats in Chernobyl. He learned about chlorofluorocarbons, forest clearance, aerosols and fermenting rice. There was even an article on flatulent animals. He studied Ireland's record regarding greenhouse, gas and CO2 emissions. Then on Friday afternoon, the letter arrived. Twice he read it, his gut churning. What the hell had happened? It was the perfect interview so how could anyone else have done better? He could have made money for Eoin and Evelyn and the rest of the miserable fucks.

"Oh Jesus," he whispered.

He lay on the couch and opened one of his books on the environment – a big hardback job, tricky to manage while lying down. He lay staring at pages eleven and twelve, his stomach gently heaving, until the book finally slid from his grip to the floor. It was an effort to shift himself from the couch but he managed and cooked what he'd prepared earlier. Sitting at the table, he waited for Stella to arrive home at six. It was seven before she returned.

"Can't wait for dinner," she said. "We've news to celebrate."

"Oh?"

"We closed the Vendorf deal today. Everyone out to the Trocadero tonight."

"Fancy."

"Only the best."

"And what'll that cost?"

"Won't cost us a bean, dear," she said. "All on the company."

Stella's eyes were glazed; he knew she'd been drinking.

"I made dinner," he said. "Maybe you should eat something now."

"Don't fuss."

He followed her into the bedroom. She took her time, laying the clothes out on the bed, inspecting them for marks or creases. She put on a blue and white pin-striped silk blouse, a navy skirt with a slit up the back, high heels. She studied herself in the mirror, turned to one side and then the other.

"Needs do as needs must," she said.

"I didn't get the job," he said. "The environmental one. I got a letter today."

She turned to face him, her eyes still slightly glazed. She stared a moment, then smiled emptily. She picked up her moisturiser from the dresser.

"I'm sorry, honey."

He smiled out of the side of his mouth. "I was sure I had it," he said.

"Well, you can never be sure, can you?"

He watched her go through the routine of putting on her make-up. She had sharp precise movements. After using each, she placed it into a navy leather handbag. She pressed the perfume bottle against one wrist, rubbed it against the other, then dabbed her neck.

"We've worked hard on this deal," she said. "There's nothing like when a plan comes together."

"I'm happy for you, Stel."

A horn tooted outside. "That's Louise," Stella said. She picked up her jacket and handbag and went downstairs. Joe followed her to the landing and leaned over the banisters.

"I shouldn't be late," she said.

"Stella… love… things'll change. You know that, don't you?"

"Sure they will," she said. "This Vendorf deal, that's a good sign, isn't it?"

And then she was gone. The house seemed much emptier than before she arrived. Joe had had it with Fridays. He'd been canned on a Friday; now he'd been refused a dead cert on a Friday. He switched off the oven. After pouring himself a beer, he made his way back to the couch and began to play with the remote control. Flick! and on came Brookside; flick! and it was gone again. He went through the channels and settled finally on a western. Nothing like a good western, he told himself, you knew where you stood with a western. Goodies and baddies and the baddies got it in the end. No fucking environmentalists and Jesus, you couldn't get a better start than that.

Next up was a French film called *Betty Blue* about some failed writer guy and his girlfriend. Only the girlfriend was off her rocker. Whatever about Stel, this woman was certainly tricky to live with. At one stage she decided she wanted to move so she burned down the house they were living in. Jesus, Joe thought, talk about drastic action. But she was a beauty, there was no denying that. And she really loved the writer guy. Joe sipped beer and had a cigarette every hour and followed their journey from the country to Paris and back again. He ate cold and tasteless chicken and poured himself another beer. Transfixed, he sat smoking and drinking until the late news came on. It was half-eleven.

"Damn you, Stel!" he said.

At twenty to twelve, the phone rang.

"Joe, honey, it's me."

"Where are you?"

"The Trocadero. I wanted to call."

He said nothing.

"We're finished with the meal but the drink's still flowing. I think I should stay."

"It's late, Stel."

"I don't want to spoil the party, do I?"

"You leaving won't spoil the party, will it?"

"Listen, I have to wait for Louise."

"I can come in and collect you," he said. "I don't mind."

"I've the car keys in my bag. Don't wait up."

"Stel..." he said but the line was already dead.

He went back to the couch and opened another beer. He was beginning to feel drunk: the figures on the screen were blurred, their voices indistinct. He pressed number eleven and watched the tangled mass of the scrambled movie channel. He thought of going to bed but stayed put, picturing himself deep in the screen, much younger, sitting on a hold-all, a background figure in a train station. He calls to a girl and asks her for a cigarette. She's wearing a denim jacket, T-shirt, jeans and brown ankle boots. He looks into her face and hey, it's Betty – beautiful, nutty, volatile Betty with her hair hanging down over one side of her face. She hands him a cigarette, lights it and slides another behind his ear and it's only as she withdraws it that he notices her nail varnish is jet black. They smile at each other. She disappears into the throng and he wonders where Zorg – that was the writer guy's name – has got to. Maybe he's Zorg, he thinks.

The telephone rang again.

He twirled the glass in the palm of his hand and checked behind his ear for the cigarette. After six or seven rings, he answered. "Stel?" he said but all he could hear was laughing and shushing and then more laughing. He heard a crash like someone had fallen over, then the laughing escalated and someone said, Get a job, and the group seemed to break down into helplessness and then the phone went dead. Joe held the receiver, curved over the palm of his hand, for almost five minutes. He could hear his own breathing. Bedlam maybe, but there wasn't a man in the world who couldn't have picked his own wife's laugh out of it.

It was after three when the key turned in the door and Joe woke. The television hummed: he flicked it off and, his eyes heavy with sleep, looked to see her, smudged mascara around drunken eyes, no more than traces of the eyeliner remaining. He said nothing. He was staring her down, he knew it. His gaze was fixed.

"What the hell are *you* looking at?" she said.

She lurched to one side. The wall held her upright. "Well?" she said.

Joe raised an eyebrow.

"WELL?"

She lurched again.

"What the fuck gives you the right to sit there with that look on your face. Eh, Mister?"

She grinned drunkenly.

"I earn it," she said. "I sure as hell have the right to spend some of it. Just every now and then. I mean to say! I must at least have that right, for Christ sake."

She was still talking as she moved away up the stairs. Joe heard her fall, pick herself up, stumble to the bedroom and land on the bed which was almost directly overhead. He smoked another cigarette. A short time later, he undressed her, hung her clothes in the wardrobe, slid the night-dress over her head and pulled the sheets up under her chin. He wasn't angry, he didn't know what he felt. He slid into the bed next to her.

What now? he was thinking

London, he reckoned. Three more days and he'd be on his way to London.

6

Richard Hamilton said, "When a white man makes the Nazi salute what he's doing is showing an open hand. He's saying: I'm here, I'm standing up for what I believe in, and I've nothing to hide. That's what the open hand's telling the world. But you take your average nignog and look at him shake hands, all that tricky shit with his woggy pal. Those hands down at his side, what he's saying is, Please give me a hand out, I'm too fucking lazy to work."

Listen to this, Malik thought. The two of them sitting next to each other in Hamilton's car, Malik smoking, Hamilton tapping on the steering wheel and doing the talking. A nice reasonable tone like he was speaking at a board meeting or something.

Unbelievable.

Already Hamilton had screwed up the surveillance. How hard could it be to follow an old guy walking his dog and remember the route? The problem was, it seemed, there were too many roads to remember. First Hamilton had tried to remember each one but after a while a new one was knocking an old one out and then they seemed to get mixed up together. Primrose Drive or was it Avenue and then by the time he got back he wasn't sure if it was primrose or some other flower.

And then as soon as he sits into the car, straight into the Aryan shit.

He said, "What you and this Irish prick don't understand is the importance of simplicity. I've a system going with this mate of mine back in Durham. Everything kept nice and simple, that's the secret. One of us goes into the bank and marks an old dear's back with chalk and then the other picks her off as soon as she comes out. Twenty-two jobs we've pulled so far and you know how many times we've been caught?"

Malik said nothing, just stared out the window.

"You see, where most muggers go wrong, they go for the bag first. Do that and you end up in a tugging match and by the time you've got the bag free some fucker's down the street after you. No, what you do is you deck the old dear first. Just ease up next to her, one hand on the bag and bang! She's on the ground and you're on your way to the back of the motorbike. That's how you get caught – wasting valuable seconds trying to release the bag. You know why I'm telling you this?"

"Why?"

"Just so you know you're in with the big boys now. No handouts here, Pak."

Malik sighed and turned away again.

The next day, Thursday, it was Malik's turn to follow the keyholder. Through the back roads of Kensington as far as Notting Hill Gate, up to Earls Court and then back around home again.

When he got back to the car he said, "I was thinking about what you were saying yesterday. About being in with the big boys now."

Hamilton was sitting back in the driver's seat, pleased with himself, it seemed. "That's where the readies are."

"Fynn tell you much about me?"

"He said you lift wallets. Sell the credit cards."

"That's right. Small time stuff. No disrespect or anything to you and your pal but I doubt you're exactly creaming it from the old ladies coming out of the bank."

"We do all right."

"A hundred grand?"

"No. But you'd be surprised. Especially in the summer around holiday time."

Malik reached for his cigarettes on the dashboard, taking his time. The likes of Hamilton, you were better off working him slowly. Nothing but a pile of wet cement between those ears, he'd need time to take things in. "Fynn's got a mouth on him. He told me about this Paddy guy. He's a creeper. Usually goes into people's houses when they're at home."

"I wouldn't mind catching him getting in my window."

"Well, that's just what I'm saying. He used to do this creeping business around America. It's one thing doing it here but over there some fucker could step out with his brand new legally held shotgun and bang, you're dead as a fucking dodo. It takes a hell of a nerve to do that there."

"Maybe he brings a shooter in with him."

"Fynn says he doesn't."

"So what's the point?"

"The point is, you think he'll just say: Oh well that didn't work out, maybe I'll have better luck on the next job? I'm telling you, it's right there in the eyes. You were the one noticed it. The way he looks at you. He's going to start searching for us. To him we're just a pair of clowns along to make up the numbers. You think he'll take getting stiffed by us? The first thing he's going to do is go to Fynn and find out how to track us. Fynn'll tell him since he'll think he's been stiffed as well. How does Fynn get in touch with you?"

"Phones a bar I go to."

"Same here. Even without those phone numbers all Paddy'll do is go to Durham and see if he can find a National Front meeting. Remember he said something about that? You ever go to meetings?"

Hamilton was quiet for a moment. "Maybe."

"Well, give it a few months and you'll get into your nice new car and there's a gun stuck into your ear. Then as soon as he's finished with you, he's going to come looking for me."

"You said he doesn't carry a gun."

Malik gave a soft laugh. "He comes looking for us, you can be damn sure he'll carry one. You were the one who said it. We're playing with the big boys now."

For Paddy the real beauty of a Mormon was that he had all day to talk to you. A Mormon didn't have to go to work or he wasn't rushing home or off to the flicks. No, a Mormon was happy to sit as long as you wanted. He'd pray for you. He'd open his bible and read to you. A Mormon cared. Only for as long as your soul was up for grabs, maybe, but still he cared.

Most folks, they gave the Mormons the bum's rush. No thanks, they'd say, I'm not interested, or, We're happy with our religion in this house. But not Paddy Benner. What Paddy said was – Roll on through, boys, I'm in the mood for a chat.

The secret to dealing with the Mormons, Paddy had found through experience, was to go on the offensive. Bombard them with questions. Ask them about their homes and if they were lonely and how they felt going around all day getting booted off doorsteps. Ask if they ever got pissed off with each other. Ask them if they liked football or music or if they were allowed to watch telly. Tell them to pick a topic, any topic…

Problem was, your average Mormon only ever wanted to talk about God.

"You and me, lads" he'd once told a couple of clean cut young men in Kansas, "we're the pariahs of society. I'm a thief and you lot are fucking pests. No one wants us within miles of them."

Oh yes, the Mormons were a good old laugh. Especially if you weren't hanging around for the follow up visit. But Paddy had never imagined that his conversations with them might someday prove useful.

Now he was in Camden Public Library revising what the boys had told him through the years. About how the prophet Joseph Smith had hoofed off out into the woods for an old think and the three stages of glory you could expect after you popped your clogs. About the one true path to heaven…

Why not? he was thinking. These days it seemed as likely as anything else.

Malik had his speech prepared. About how this Paddy guy was a drifter, just wandering around Europe, then back to London to see if Fynn had anything on.

A guy like that, who was going to miss him?

But he didn't have to say anything. As soon as he got into the car Hamilton said, "It's him or us. We're going to have to do him."

Do him – like they were in the Mafia or something. The

same reasonable matter of fact tone, like he was reading a shopping list or reciting his Aryan shit.

"I know," Malik said. "I've tried to look at it from every angle now and there's no other way. We take his money from him, he'll find us and he'll kill us."

"In with the big boys, eh?"

"You said it!"

And then they were silent. With the likes of Hamilton you had to let him think everything was his idea. Hamilton would have his own thoughts, for what they were worth, and Malik intended to hear him out. Just listen, say, "Yeah that was a good idea all right, but what about this?" The beauty of it was that the escape routes Paddy had marked out would take them through the centre of town. Pull a gun on him as they were driving along and he'd know he was going to be killed. What would you do, Richard? Some fucker's got a gun to your head and you're driving in a built up area. You think you'd let him take you somewhere quiet? No, you wouldn't. You'd take a chance the same fucker wouldn't want to shoot, especially if he's got a hundred grands worth of stolen jewels in the car so you wait your chance and you crash the car. Grab the driver, hope you don't get banged up too badly and run like hell.

Wait and see what happened to the two who crossed you, then go looking for them.

"We're running out of time," Malik said. "We'd better get things organised."

A couple of businessmen this time, all the way from Cardiff. The printing trade, they said. No more abusing the punters, Paddy decided, especially as Tim was actually winning.

They asked what Paddy did for a crust and he told them he hustled pool. He explained the system. How Tim was crap and would lose slowly since it took him all day to decide which ball to play and how Paddy would win quickly because he'd been hustling for years and just about made a living at it.

"Here, watch this," he said and he cleared the table.

"Say you had somewhere in the region of a hundred and fifty grand," he asked. "What sort of business would you go into?"

It was interesting to listen to. Guys like this, they could bore the fuck out of you explaining how they made their money. But this was okay. A pub, they said, you'd need more capital for a pub. And restaurants were a disaster; fifty percent of restaurants went under in the first year. The trick, apparently, was not to overextend yourself. You held back some capital and you got out before you lost your furniture. Beyond that, they said, it was a matter of luck and finding a niche in the market.

Get out of England, they advised.

Paddy showed them the best way to hold the cue, explained how to go about clearing a full table. This was twice now in the past couple of months that he'd let a mark walk. A banker first and now a couple of businessmen, Paddy's bread and butter, and yet here he was talking about the importance of keeping your head still and your eyes level. It wasn't conscience, no, but what was it? Tiredness, maybe. Or could it be that he was losing a little of the killer instinct you needed?

"I was hoping one of you might have a hot tip for me," he said.

"If you've got a hundred and fifty grand from hustling pool," one of them said, "maybe you should think about sticking with that."

The other option was to wait until they got to Fynn's place and kill Paddy Benner there. Which would leave Fynn with a dead body, see how he'd like that? He comes up with the job, he gets no money and a stiff on his living room carpet for his troubles.

Then of course you could do Fynn as well which was even messier. Plenty of people had seen them about the area.

No. Paul Malik knew he'd have to be patient. He'd let Hamilton come up with it himself. The only place to kill Paddy Benner was as soon as he opened the safe. One shot into the back of the head. Then, Richard, you take his wallet and any other signs of identification. Then you roll him over and you empty the gun into his face.

Let the coppers figure that one out. A faceless body at a

burglary scene. One that no one's going to report missing.

It was just a question of letting Hamilton come up with the idea.

Hamilton said, "Whoever does this, he'd want to be getting a bigger share to make it worth his while, wouldn't he?"

Paul Malik nodded. Maybe they were getting there.

Two days after he'd let the businessmen walk, Paddy didn't feel so charitable. The previous night, they'd taken the guts of a hundred quid and then when it came for Tim to buy his comics, he was broke.

"You lost your money again," Paddy said.

Tim was looking at his shoes.

"You're a fucking cretin," Paddy said.

There was no need to ask what had happened. Tim had gone back to *The Four Provinces*, blowing about how he and Paddy had fleeced a couple of salesmen.

And of course Sudds was there, ready to take his money from him. Orchestrating the ridicule. What's the height of stupidity? someone would say. Thick as shite. And then when the money was gone, he'd be begging a free drink and maybe someone would pour what was left in his glass over Tim's shoe.

Stupid, Paddy knew, to let it bother him so much. It wasn't as though Tim was ever going to change.

But still he said, "You go find Sudds and tell him if he wants to play he can bring five hundred quid to *The Four Provinces* tonight."

Tim looked up. "I'm sorry, Paddy," he said.

"What're you apologising to me for?" Paddy said. "I'll be the one with the money."

At eight o'clock Paddy walked into *The Four Provinces* and there was a crowd waiting for him. Why wouldn't there be, a grudge match like this. Tim and Sudds and a gang of dense looking fuckers and what had to be Sudds's brother – a slightly shorter version but with the same eyes and forehead.

Tim's uncle was watching from the corner with a gang of his trucker pals.

"Fifty quid a frame," Paddy said. "First to five hundred's the winner. Why don't we each leave the money behind the bar so there are no arguments later?"

He told Donnelly he could rack the balls since he lost the last time round.

And they started.

Simple pool, the same as before – seven balls each and call your pocket on the black. As close to a lottery as you could get in sport. Paddy preferred the American games – straights, bank, nine ball, one pocket – where the better player won every time he needed to. But you walk into a place and you play the local rules; Paddy was well used to that.

An uneasy quiet settled over the room. Since he'd left the States Paddy had missed the pool halls, where a guy that wasn't playing could drink at the bar or play on a pinball machine or bet on the day's races. In Europe you'd find the same faint radio music, the same cigarette smoke, the same crack of hard glossy balls hitting each other. But even with a crowd, the atmosphere was different. The standard was too low. In America you could find a game between two guys who knew each other's games backwards, who couldn't be bothered hustling for a hundred dollars, who played each other twice a week and never spoke otherwise. You'd run into one of those games and you'd stay because they were beautiful to watch. This crowd, all they wanted was to see someone lose money.

He set about beating Donnelly. There was no jerk to his cueing action this time. No reeling him in, no feeding him early frames, no subtle shift in the balance of power. This time it was different, Paddy just easing his way around the table, nice and gentle, never losing position.

No one clapped when he potted the black.

"They broke open for you," Donnelly muttered.

Paddy looked across and shrugged and then he really started to play. It was a lot of things: the mean ugly sneer maybe or the thought of Tim begging for acceptance, but nothing to do with any insult Donnelly could throw his way. Your opponent called you lucky and it was the sign of a good hustle. But there was something about Donnelly that made Paddy sick. Just the look of him standing there with the cigarette hanging from his lips. He was the sort of punk hustler Paddy had despised for years. A big dangerous thug who'd cause you trouble if you ran into him in the wrong place.

Paddy cleared six balls to finish the second frame.

It was simple, remarkably simple. A kid's game, this type of pool. Small table, big pockets and Donnelly's nerve draining with each ball. Paddy didn't say a word. He just continued on, taking one frame and then the next. It felt good. No deceit, no tricks. Just potting the balls like he used to do when he was a kid.

After the fourth frame Donnelly had thrown in the towel.

And then when it was over Paddy stuffed twenty quid into Tim's hand and told him to buy himself a few pints.

"I'm going away for a while," he said. "If I'm not back in a month or two, I'll call you or write. Maybe you can come and visit."

Tim was too shocked to speak.

Paddy turned to walk away and he heard Tim say he'd come too but Paddy just shook his head. It was sad leaving him like this, and he'd miss the big fucker, but there was no better way to do it. Anyway, what did Tim think was going to happen?

He could feel the eyes watching him as he walked out the door. He heard Tim call his name again. As soon as the fresh air hit him, he started running.

7

There were times, Joe Faherty thought, when Stella's cousin Louis Marks could come across as being pretty much an ordinary guy, the full shilling so to speak. Like now, Joe telling him how his marriage was going through a bit of a rocky patch, Louis sitting there at his kitchen table, nodding every now and then. Joe telling him that his own pride was part of the problem. He liked to be in control. He was used to being the breadwinner because that's what happened to a seventeen year old if his old man keeled over on his way to the park one evening. He forgot about college and got himself out into the workforce, especially if he had a younger sister who had serious prospects. Yeah, Joe said, it was easy to get into the habit of thinking of yourself as a provider. You liked the feeling it gave you. And then when the rug was pulled out from under you…

Louis listening and seeming perfectly normal until he said, "She screwing around on you yet?"

Joe shook his head. "I hope not."

"You sure?"

"Who can be sure about anything?"

"Now you said it!" Louis stood up to leave. "Sooner or later it's going to happen – you know that, don't you?"

They were sitting in a cafe now on the edge of Kensington, Hamilton lifting a pack of Rothmans from his trouser pocket, a nice dark blue jacket and tie on, his big Nazi head looking just like a Mormon's. "I might get used to this," he said. "Might get to like spreading the good word."

Paddy stretched across and swiped the cigarettes. "You're a beauty, you are," he said. "What happens if someone invites us in and I'm there spouting on and the lady of the house starts thinking, Why's this Mormon smelling of smoke? That's a bit on the funny side, she'll think. And here's another funny thing – that alarm's going off. One suspicious thing and people shrug and mind their own business. Give them another and they're off to the phone. Or what if the cops decide they want to frisk us and they find a box of smokes?"

Hamilton said, "I thought no one was going to invite us in."

"Maybe we'll be a hit. We might have thirty converts by noon."

"I always have a smoke before I go in."

"Not today you don't," Paddy said.

He wished the minutes would pass. The waiting was the worst, imagining what could go wrong. Now he wanted to concentrate on the future. Spain maybe, a slow train moving south, watching the countryside as it passed, the burnt earth and the white houses brilliant in the sunlight. Find a nice little town and take it from there. Pleasant thoughts and he was just getting into them when the phone rang.

A moment later, Hamilton was back.

"Time to boogie," he said.

They were moving at a steady pace now, small rucksacks on their back, just like the Mormons alright. Neither spoke. The wind had risen overnight and all of a sudden England had turned cold and grey and rotten. Tall houses on either side, elegant redbrick houses with long driveways. Tickets for Wimbledon, dinner at the golf club, rich folks driving big cars into the city and back out again…

Two streets away, Malik was sitting in a stolen BMW. He'd watched until both the Byrds and the retired colonel guy three doors away had left. Then he'd called the coffee shop on the car phone. Everything was in place and all that was left was for Paddy and Hamilton to hold their nerve.

No answer in the first house.

In the second an old lady appeared with a purple rinse in her hair. "We're with The Church of Jesus Christ of Latter Day Saints," Paddy said.

"Not interested," she said and bang went the door.

They turned and moved back up the driveway. Overhead, it looked like rain. Hamilton said it was cold as a witch's teat and Paddy said it was a grand head of purple hair that woman had and Hamilton said what had that got to do with anything? Paddy wasn't sure, it was just a question of looking natural in case anyone was watching them. "The small things in life," he said. "Learn to appreciate them, Richard, and you'll be a happy man."

The houses were numbered in twos along each side of the road. Two down, eleven to go before they reached Number 27. No one wanted them around. People just shook their heads and said they weren't interested. One said she was a Catholic and happy to be one: another said, "Sorry, I don't give at the door."

Three houses in a row there was no answer.

An old lad stuck his head out the upstairs window and shouted, "Whatever you're selling, I don't want it."

Next door the curtains twitched but no one came downstairs.

And then they were turning into the driveway of Number 27, Paddy's nerves easing now that they were in motion. A little shiver of excitement, that was all, same as he always felt on a job. The Byrds kept their garden tidy: a nice neat lawn on one side of the driveway, a flowerbed on the other. The downstairs curtains were drawn.

Paddy walked to the door and knocked and waited, and then he moved to the dining room window and slapped the glass once. The alarm wailed. Jesus, the noise of it! They moved back up the driveway, walking at the same even pace. There was no reaction from any of the neighbouring houses. Nothing apart from the empty road and the wind and the trees and a few parked cars: just another quiet neighbourhood, Paddy thought, where your alarm could go off and no one would give a damn about it.

Number 29 was empty.

A short, stocky guy stepped out of Number 31, early forties, maybe, and not an ounce of fat there.

"The Church of what?"

"The Church of Jesus Christ of Latter Day Saints," Paddy said. "I wonder could we come in and share a line of the bible with you."

The stocky guy looked from Paddy to Hamilton and then back to Paddy. Then he looked to the alarm box high on the wall two doors away, a strong blue light flashing from it.

"That was me, I'm afraid," Paddy said. Keeping it cool, speaking nice and slowly, looking him in the eye. "I wasn't sure if the bell was working so I tapped on the window. I never thought it'd set the alarm off."

The guy looked back to Paddy. "You've no business knocking on anyone's window."

"I'm well aware of that, Sir, and I'm terribly sorry about it. You know, Sir, Jesus is in each and every one of our hearts."

"Get the fuck off my doorstep," he said absently and he stepped back inside.

A cop car turned onto Down's Leaze, and by now they were at Number 35, Paddy looking at his watch, thinking, Six minutes, not bad. A nice rich neighbourhood like this, of course they'd shift themselves.

They turned into another long driveway and slowed the walk slightly. They'd gone through it all before. How they'd keep going, just stay in sight as though they hadn't noticed the coppers. A woman's voice came from behind the door of Number 35 telling them she wasn't interested.

Number 37 was empty.

An older woman, late sixties or so, said she'd no interest in religion. Paddy shoved a leaflet into her hand and told her he'd pray for her.

Still they kept moving at the same steady pace. Paddy knew the routine. Two coppers most likely, checking the place over, looking to see if the doors or windows had been tampered with. Then they would disappear again. At least ten more minutes before the alarm reset itself. Paddy knew he could be inside in less than two.

Louis Marks had taken to sitting in the spare room waiting for his wife to come home. He'd sit on the edge of the bed and watch the quiet road, nice and patient, just sitting and waiting, chewing Doublemint all the while. It was a sign of betrayal he was looking for. Nothing as obvious as another man letting her out of a car, or a goodbye kiss – she was much too smart for that – but maybe a dreamy look as she appeared into his line of view. The signs were there, he was sure of it. All he had to do was put his finger on them.

You couldn't live fifteen years with someone and then not notice her distance herself from you. The way she'd smile and shrug and say, No there's nothing wrong. The way she'd shake her head slowly and then move off into the other room.

He slid another stick of Doublemint from the pack and began to chew. And here come the Mormons, he said to himself, the charge of the God brigade. Stella's husband, Joe, was downstairs; he could deal with them. It was maybe the only perk to having a cheating wife, the way you could spot all the people you didn't want to answer the door to while you were tearing your guts out waiting for her to come home. He laughed at that. Then he laughed at the way Derek Stark in Number 21 gave the two boys the heave-ho.

At least he wasn't losing his sense of humour.

He considered following her. Just for a day or two maybe. Not spying exactly, just a little gentle surveillance until he found out who the other man was. Tail her to work, sit in a coffee shop across the street and see who she was having lunch with.

Arm himself with facts before he confronted her.

Then he began to laugh. Some pair of dopes, all right, the dozy Mormons had just set off the alarm in Jim and Flo Byrd's house. Yes indeed, he thought to himself, it was hard to believe just how chronically stupid some people were.

Just what Paddy didn't need, the guy who stepped out of Number 41 was Irish, a good thick Dublin accent on him.

"What happened?" he said, laughing, "A couple of those Yanks get their teeth into you? Beat you over the head with the bible and drag you into a truck."

For the first time in years, Paddy felt himself stuck for words.

"I thought all you lot were Yanks," the guy said.

Finally, Paddy said that Mormonism was the world's fastest

growing religion and the guy was laughing again. An Irish Mormon, he'd never heard the like.

"Hey," he said, "I was reading a thing in the paper about the Mormons there the other day. How you've all got secret names to identify yourselves when you go to heaven and you can't tell anyone what it is. Only some geezer stuck his onto the Internet and then a few others did and it turns out half the world's Mormons have the same names. It's going to be pretty confusing up there if you don't mind my saying."

Paddy hadn't a clue what he was talking about. "Sir, maybe we could discuss this inside. I'd like to read you a line of the bible."

"Don't think so somehow. My wife's cousin owns this place. I'm over for a job interview." Then after a moment: "But hey, you could give me a visit in Dublin. If you've got the time, that is."

"Perfect," Paddy said. "Someone from our church in Dublin will be in touch with you."

And then the squad car sped away again. Paddy took the address in Dublin and on the way out, he explained it to Hamilton, how the guy was most likely stiffing a friend, setting the Mormons on him. A hanger, he said: find some clown no one else wanted to talk to and leave your best pal stuck with him.

They walked back out the driveway, turning left past the houses they'd already visited. A man and a little girl emerged from one of the houses and drove away. Paddy felt the nerves in his stomach again. It was the same every time – first you'd be scared shitless you were going to make a mistake and once that passed you worried about becoming complacent.

They turned the corner and Malik was waiting, sitting behind the wheel of the black BMW, smoking and smiling, everything under control there, boys?

Paddy and Hamilton left their rucksacks in the boot. Malik handed them each an identical one.

Paddy looked down to check the strap, tugged it once to make sure. And it was then that he saw it. Just out of the corner of his eye. He'd missed the initial look Hamilton had thrown Malik but Malik's expression changed suddenly. Just for a moment and then it was gone again. A brief look of shock, telling Hamilton not to fuck around. Telling him to shut up. Telling him to stay in character.

Jesus Christ. It was something from which Paddy had been excluded.

Which could mean only one thing…

Louis Marks watched the two Mormons throw in the towel and said, "Adios, boys. Happy hunting tomorrow."

Then he made a list.

Baked beans on a Tuesday. Fifteen years they'd been married and he'd never once got baked beans on a Tuesday.

New shoes.

Wearing different lipstick to work.

Throwing out the old lipstick to throw him off the scent.

Laughing about him with her friends when he wasn't around.

Five little beauties. He numbered them one to five and then added number six, the way she'd been working late. Then he laid out six Doublemint wrappers along the windowsill and looked out the window, everything quiet now, the Mormons gone, nothing left but the breeze and the trees and the empty road.

It was time to make decisions.

A private detective or not – he considered the question, the pros and cons, whether or not he himself was up the job. He could picture it. A nice second hand jacket on, staying a safe distance behind; slipping into a doorway if she turned around. But maybe he was too emotionally involved. A job like this required a cool detachment.

It was hard to decide.

Patience, he told himself. Collect the facts.

Then the two Mormons reappeared. You just had to laugh: some guys just didn't know when to give up. Still with the rucksacks on their backs only the bigger squareheaded one was carrying something in a black plastic sack. A whopping great bag of bibles maybe.

Dopes, Louis Marks thought to himself. Bill and Bert and a bagful of bibles.

Then he watched them turn into Number 27. Jim and Flo Byrd's house; they'd already visited that one, in fact that was the one where they set off the alarm. He laughed and lay back on the bed: it just kept getting better. Then he bounced back into sitting position. Watching them now, almost at the house, the big squareheaded one looked nervous, but the other, he was a study. Cool as a breeze, as if he hadn't a care in the world, just strolling around the side of the house and out of view.

Jesus, the cheek of it.

Louis Marks moved to the phone by the bed. He felt as though something important was going to happen.

Paddy was tempted to use his jemmy. Just ease it out of the rucksack and crack Hamilton on the back of his fat head…

Was there nothing the big cretin could do without screwing it up? All he had to was stay in character, just shut up and look like a Mormon. But first he wanted to smoke in the cafe and now he'd screwed up the cross by signalling behind Paddy's back. Which if nothing else showed that you got what you paid for. Peanuts and monkeys, he'd known that, but he'd never expected the cross. It was some fucking world, he thought, where you couldn't even rely on a neo-Nazi and a Paki not to team up against you.

Still he had two hours. Not even these two clowns were stupid enough to make their move before the safe was opened. Time to think and figure out where they were going to make the cross. Time to go through the route in his head.

Malik must have a gun back in the car. No point in working a cross without a gun. Unless they intended chucking him out of the car as they were driving along. He traced the route in his mind, right back through the centre of town…

A pair of cowboys like this, they weren't easy to predict.

But first he had to gain access to the house. The back door was a bitch: even with the key you'd have trouble opening it. Paddy tried his tension tool with the feeler pick and nearly broke it. Then he tried to loid the lock with a piece of cardboard but no joy there either. Which left brute force. He wedged the jemmy between the door and the jamb and waited for the crack.

The alarm drowned out any sound.

They moved inside, the sound of the alarm easing slightly as the door closed again, but still like having your own private drummer inside your head. The kitchen had a style to it, a small island in the middle of a chessboard floor, a rail of copper pans and kitchen utensils overhead. The smell of a cooked breakfast was still in the air.

The alarm box was under the stairs in a downstairs toilet. In ten minutes or so it would have reset itself and then when Paddy and Hamilton were leaving they would set it off again. The rigmarole would be the same. One phone call to the house and then another to the keyholder. The keyholder would take a look and see the damage to the back door and then he'd be off to the phone. The coppers were third on the list. No matter how quickly they moved there would still be six minutes to make it back to the BMW.

Paddy checked the downstairs. There was a beam sensor in the living room which Fynn hadn't noticed. Paddy unscrewed it and readjusted the angle so that the beam would shine on the top corner of the room. Then he rescrewed it again.

They divided the house between them. Hamilton took the downstairs, Paddy took the upstairs. On the landing he tugged the plastic sack from the metal detector and pointed it to his watch. The light flashed.

"And beep to you," he said.

He began in the bedroom, starting in one corner and moving along the walls and there it was alright, a heavy black safe set into the wall behind the dresser. Then he started checking the room for any of the caches. You could never tell where folks hid their money. On his last trip to London, he'd found three grand stuck into the vacuum cleaner. First he checked underneath the mattress. He ran the metal detector over the mattress itself. Then he slid onto his back and checked underneath the bed. Two pairs of shoes, side by side. His and hers.

Methodically, he moved through the rest of the room, starting with the wardrobes. The noise was murder. He could feel it thump inside his head. He flung the clothes from the dresser – underwear and socks mostly – onto the bed. In the bottom of the drawer he found an old wedding photograph. He left it as it was.

Then the alarm stopped ringing. Thank Christ for that! Now he could think, settle down to peeling the layers of steel from the door of the safe and figure out how these two clowns were going to try to cross him. He had an idea already of what he'd have to do. One thing for sure, the best of the jewels wouldn't be going into the black canvas hold-all lying next to the safe.

Richard Hamilton was looking forward to telling Malik all about it.

The shooting, Paul? he'd say. Yeah, I'll tell you about it in a minute. But guess how many tries the dozy fuck needed to get through the back door.

Let the Paki drag it out of him.

He started his search in the kitchen, reaching in under the sink, tossing what he found back towards the centre of the room. Then he stopped a moment and slipped the revolver from the rucksack Malik had handed him. It was a small snub nosed thing with a blue tint to the steel and a brown plastic handle. It was lighter than he thought it would be. He tucked it in at the back of his trousers and stuck his head back under the sink again.

The funny thing was that Malik wasn't sure if he, Richard Hamilton who had twenty-three jobs behind him, would have the nerve for it. Looking at him with his Paki face, thinking, Richard knew, that there was a hell of a difference between mugging old ladies and putting a gun to a guy's head and blowing him away. He liked that, the sound of it, *blowing the guy away*, just like in the movies, when someone gets in your way and it's you or him and you know for sure he's going to be the one to go down.

Like Malik said, this Paddy bloke would be coming after them if he got the chance.

But now he wanted to think of just how the moment would be. He'd have to say something. Let him realise what was happening and then, Bam! Just a second to think Oh sweet Jesus, those two guys have outsmarted me and now I'm fucked.

But he wasn't sure what to say.

You really think you're taking a hundred grand out of this, you thick fuck?

See this? Who's the Nazi fuckhead now?

Yeah, he thought, that was better. Let him know he wasn't dealing with any dodo.

Then he heard the siren at the end of the street. He felt something catch deep inside him.

Louis Marks watched and waited and chewed Doublemint. A clear head was needed. There were only two rational possibilities.

Maybe one of the fake Mormons was banging his wife. She was the victim of a sophisticated gang of burglars, being used for information about Jim and Flo Byrd's house.

Or maybe neither of the fake Mormons was banging his wife.

He couldn't make up his mind.

The evidence was there but it was far from overwhelming.

He took the six Doublemint wrappers from the windowsill, tossed four over his shoulder and placed the remaining two back again.

He buried his head in his hands, still chewing. He eased his breathing and watched some more. He rolled the Doublemint flat and stuck it to the roof of his mouth. Outside there seemed to be an immense stillness. Then there was a moment's clarity. It was so easy, he almost laughed. A trick, that's what it was, a simple illusion. It wasn't the background to the situation that was important, that would be revealed in time, but rather how he dealt with the situation as presented.

Two fake Mormons, a cheating wife and a police car on the way.

A moment later he knew what he had to do. A no-lose situation, he told himself. At best he would confront the guy who was banging his wife, at worst he would foil a robbery and show her that he wasn't a man to be trifled with.

He stood up from his spot at the edge of the bed and moved downstairs.

He stepped out onto his driveway, shut the door behind him. Then he began to jog. Amazing, he thought, how clear things could become once the voices stopped. His breathing regular now, he was moving well. Two good sized driveways to run. A steady jog was required: the last thing he needed was to be out of breath by the time he arrived.

Then suddenly the alarm switched itself off. He laughed aloud. Those treacherous Mormons, he thought. It was too late though, he was onto them. At his own gate, he looked towards the end of the road and smiled. A squad car had turned the corner.

On he went. It was best to follow the same route as the burglars had taken around the back. In the side passage, the voices began. "No," he said quietly.

He was in control now. It felt good to be calling the shots again. What sort of a man wouldn't protect his family? he asked himself. Turning out of the side passage, he stepped into the back garden and suddenly the alarm began to wail again as the bigger Mormon appeared through the back door. Louis stopped dead. The noise of the alarm killed the voices altogether, and he was left with nothing but the bigger Mormon and himself and the cold morning air. Everything seemed serene. The bigger Mormon standing still, then reaching behind his back. Louis Marks smiling, just standing here now, letting the guy know he'd been rumbled. From the trembling hands Louis Marks doubted that this was the one who'd been handling his wife.

"Don't move," he said and smiled.

The words died away in the din of the alarm. Then the gun appeared, and the guy was shouting but you couldn't hear a thing with the noise above.

Louis Marks's expression turned gentle. "It's all over, son," he said and he moved forward to take the gun away.

Richard Hamilton shot him once in the face.

8

Paddy watched it unfold before him, Hamilton drawing the gun from the back of his trousers and firing once into the guy's face, the guy buckling at the knees, then falling backwards. He'd been shot through the nose. His legs twitched for a moment and then they stopped.

Oh sweet fuck…

He watched Hamilton scale the back wall, and then a female copper was checking the body. Then she was scaling the wall, Paddy watching all this from the downstairs window, too scared to move in case the movement attracted attention. Just standing there behind the curtain and then out to the front window.

The cop car was gone.

One chance to run. Take it or leave it.

Paddy was out the front door now, running at full tilt, turning left away from the direction of the police station, hearing sirens coming from all directions and then, when a door opened across the road, he was running down the driveway.

He shouted at the lady to get back in the house. Then before she could close the door, in behind her.

"One of your neighbour's been shot," he said. He told her not to open the door unless she was looking at a uniform. A woman, sixty maybe, unable to put a sentence together, just stammering and nodding and Paddy was in her kitchen now, asking where her garden backed onto, not listening to the answer.

Then he was in a lane, composing himself, letting his breathing slow. He could hear a siren get closer, on its way to cut off Hamilton maybe. Now it was time to walk away. Nice and easy like any other punter, one foot in front of the other until he hit the main road. A question of nerve, that's what it was. There'd be squad cars coming from all directions and he'd try to walk through them. Maybe, if his luck held…

He saw the blue flash at the top of the road.

"Fuck it," he whispered.

Malik had it figured out, how to cross Hamilton. He'd bought two identical 22mm Berettas from a dealer in West Bromwich, one of which was tucked into the back of his trousers. It was an uncomfortable feeling, having the gun there, pressed between the small of his back and the car seat. But he didn't want to be unarmed if Hamilton was carrying. Big Nazi shithead like that, there was no telling what he might try.

The first step was to get out of London. Two murders with the same type of gun within a few hours of each other – a smart detective might look for a link. And maybe someone around the Tottenham Court Road might remember an Asian walking down the street with a guy with a swastika tattooed onto his arm. No, the best thing was to get out of London. Tell Hamilton that the fence was in Birmingham and did he want to come along?

You bet he would.

It would bring them onto Malik's home patch. Night time, that was the time to shoot Hamilton. A nice little waste area next to the river and there'd be no mucking about like in the movies. No walking the guy off at gunpoint, waiting for something to go wrong. No, he'd just tell Hamilton that this was where the fence wanted to meet and then as soon as he stepped out of the car, he'd shoot him. Once up close in the body, a good big target you couldn't miss, and then once in the head to finish him off.

Then he'd collect his hundred grand.

Thinking about this when he heard the siren in the distance. Maybe the alarm was just going off now or maybe something was wrong. Either way he could afford to wait. True, he was sitting in a stolen car, but that was a small enough risk. The thing to do was to sit and wait and see what panned out. No need to run just yet.

The squad car screeched to a stop. Paddy stood and stared and then there was a revolver pointing at him and a detective shouting at him to get down. He rolled over and lay on his front.

They were all over him. Shoving his face to the ground, kicking his legs apart. Slapping his back and then his trousers, Paddy feeling the concrete coarse against his face, looking at a shiny shoe, and the smell, something from childhood, the last time he'd laid on uncovered concrete. Just lying there as another copper was shouting at him not to move. Thinking of what to say. Nothing, that was a good start, say fuck all until you had a lawyer in the seat next to you.

Then he felt his wallet being drawn from his back pocket.

The voice said, "He's a fucking Mormon."

Paddy wasn't sure he'd heard them right. No one could be that lucky, could they? He watched the shiny shoe move from his line of vision, too scared to look in case they rumbled him. They should have known he was a Mormon, otherwise there'd be no reason to pick him up.

Then he heard the car door slam.

They were gone.

Paddy didn't move for a moment. Just lying there thinking, What the fuck…Then he was up, resisting the temptation to run again. Walking had got him this far, but he could hear more sirens. Jesus, how many coppers were there in this neighbourhood? And another thing, he couldn't remember which was the best way out. He could barely remember which way Down's Leaze was. He needed a bus – something that was moving where he could mingle.

He started walking – listening and trying to figure out where the loudest siren was coming from.

He was looking for an unalarmed house. He walked quickly towards the next best thing – a house where he was sure someone was home.

Richard Hamilton had no idea who he'd killed. One thing for sure, he wasn't a copper; no way a copper would let you take a gun out and point it at him. A copper would be all over you. A copper would ram your face into the dirt and come close to wrenching your arm off when he was handcuffing you. Only this guy seemed to have something to say. That weird grin on his face, mouthing the words through the sound, and then a little smile when he saw the gun. Maybe he was telling him to give up.

But he could think about that later. What he had to do now was make it back to Malik in the BMW and get the hell out of there. Fifty yards behind the WPC was keeping up. Not gaining on him maybe but no signs of flagging either, a nice easy stride, slowing once to talk into her walkie-talkie.

He wondered where the squad car was.

It was a stroke of luck, he felt, the way he hadn't lost his bearings with the mess that had happened. All these rich streets looked the same with their long driveways and poxy trees everywhere. Take the wrong turn and you'd be fucked. It could happen so easily especially if you had to hop over the back wall and then do a loop back to where the car was.

Only the car wasn't where he'd left it.

He stopped dead. There it was, the simple truth – Jesus, you just couldn't trust a bloody Paki. Loyalty? Responsibility? Fuck, no. The WPC was gaining. Richard started running again. There was no strength left in his legs; he ready to give up when, Christ, it was there, after all – the green BMW. He'd been looking on the wrong part of the street. All he could hear was his own gasping and he put his head down and pounded on.

All the houses were alarmed – why wouldn't they be in a nice rich area like this? Paddy kept a steady pace. The sirens, it was hard to make out exactly how close they were, Paddy knowing that if he was stopped again, he was screwed – just walking and watching and resisting the urge to look behind.

Then there was a possibility.

It was alarmed, same as the others, with the box up high on the side wall. But the car, that's what he was going on. An old Morris Minor – reasonable condition, nothing special.

Maybe it was an old person's car.

He turned in the driveway with his mormon ID in his hand. Feeling the shake in his hands, then composing himself. It took him less than fifteen seconds before the bolt dropped on the door.

He stepped inside.

There were voices coming from somewhere.

He took the stairs two steps at a time, letting his banisters take the weight, sticking to the edge of the steps where they were less likely to creak. On the landing, he paused a moment. The smaller bedroom had an unoccupied look to it.

He stood and listened and then he crawled under the bed.

Paul Malik heard the second siren, then a third and he knew it was time to get the hell out of there. He switched on the engine and checked the rear-view mirror and it was then that he saw Hamilton appear around the corner. Head down, legs pumping and no sign of a bag of jewels. But there was a copper, a woman, fifty or so yards behind. He pulled out a little from the kerb, lined the car up.

He lifted the handbrake and put the car into reverse, and almost missed him. It was the rear-view mirror, the way things always seem closer than they are, Malik holding the thing in reverse, keeping it straight, then putting the boot down. Watching Hamilton stop dead, then try to get out of the way. And bang! on the right rear of the car. He wanted to back up and run over the fucker, finish the job good and proper, but there she was… the copper, the WPC, right behind him. Behind her another squad car was turning the corner. He saw the gun in Hamilton's hand and hit the accelerator. He heard a shot and the WPC was down. Then, as he reached the corner, he heard more shots – eight, ten maybe – but he wasn't hanging around to see what had happened.

9

Paddy lay under the bed thinking: Well things could be worse, couldn't they? A monumental fuck-up, yes, that guy had to be dead, but maybe there was a way out. It was now a matter of patience. It was a matter of lying and waiting and then when the moment was right – once the folks downstairs were asleep – of slipping away. Malik was gone, Paddy was sure of that, foot to the floor as soon as the police sirens started up. But Hamilton, what had happened to him? Maybe he was in the cop shop spilling his guts. Maybe he was telling about Harry Fynn and the Irish guy named Paddy who had organised the whole thing.

Paddy needed to get out of England. Hang around and someone would recognise him. The longer he waited here under this bed, the longer the coppers had to find out where he was staying. He needed money and he needed his passport. He needed to get to his guesthouse before the coppers did.

Still, in a situation like this – patience.

Take the worst case scenario, he thought – Hamilton in the cop shop, Fynn in custody and Paddy's picture on the front of the evening newspaper. What then? He still had to wait – until evening time at least, until the roadblocks were taken down and the door to door was finished. Then he'd move, find his way out of London and keep going from there. Make his way towards the coast and then if his luck held…

The chances were slim.

Another possibility was Tim's uncle. To take a fugitive out of a country just because he'd played a few games of pool with your nephew, it was a big ask. But then again you just never knew.

He woke just after half-one, his shoulder stiff, voices

coming from downstairs. A lady's voice saying, Isn't that awful! A man's saying, No, they hadn't seen a thing. Dead? the lady said. It was a terrible shock, they'd never had anything like this before in the neighbourhood.

Neither had noticed anything strange – apart from the sirens earlier, that was.

Paddy had been dreaming. The details of the dream were vague but Aoife Brennan had been in there. Which was strange; he seldom dreamed of Aoife. Not now, at any rate. He still thought about her – three, maybe four times a day on average – but at night? He didn't think so. Or maybe he just couldn't remember the dreams. He wondered what she was up to. Married maybe, that was one possibility; she'd be twenty-six next January. Or engaged, she might be engaged. She'd have graduated by now, he was sure of that, and leading an entirely different life to the one she'd led with Paddy.

Eight years, it was a long time. So why dream of her now?

Maybe it was the idea of going back to Ireland.

The folks stayed put for the day. Just after midnight, Paddy eased the front door open and slipped outside. He walked quickly, north he reckoned, for twenty minutes; then west for another ten. He hailed a taxi in Croyden which took him into the heart of Kilburn and made his way towards the truck depot. All the while waiting for someone to recognise him.

Would Tim's uncle do him the favour? Paddy doubted it, thinking this when the front page of *The Evening Standard* caught his eye. All about the mayhem in Down's Leaze. Two dead, one critically injured, that's what it said: a WPC fighting for her life. Hamilton, according to the report, was dead – killed in a shoot-out with armed detectives.

Jesus.

No mention of Malik; he must have bolted.

Which meant that the coppers, for the time being at any rate, had no idea that Paddy had been involved. He had time – not much, maybe – to collect his stuff. He could get hold of his passport and make a run for it.

He felt calmer.

Tim's uncle was still the best bet. At least to take him as far as Holyhead. Better than the airport or stealing a car, Paddy turning down the street towards his guesthouse and there he was! That shape, you could pick it out a mile away – big dopey fucker sitting on his spot on the wall.

Now he could explain it to Tim, tell him it was time to move but he'd be in touch. Maybe Tim could come visit.

It was the sobbing Paddy heard first. Then he noticed the way Tim's shoulders were heaving, Paddy running now, knowing this wasn't a set-up, this was real…

On one hand Tim had his sweatshirt wrapped around like a bandage. In the other he held out a thumb – purple, bloodied and detached.

"Oh Jesus, Tim."

Tim pitched forward into Paddy's arms. "Sudds Donnelly's not my friend."

"…He never was, Tim," Paddy said. "He never was."

What had happened: Tim had strolled into *The Four Provinces* blowing about how he and Paddy had fleeced a couple of bankers from Sussex. Two hundred quid, he said, hard cash. The easiest money anyone ever made. And then when the offer came, Sudds wondering if maybe a little challenge might be in order…

When Tim couldn't pay, eight of them dragged him outside.

Paddy had heard the story in the back of the ambulance and now it was his job to explain it to Tim's family. The mother wept, the father quietly stared away. The uncle standing there, Paddy had called him too. Everyone knowing no charges would be pressed. Why would they be? You involved the coppers and you received a visit. The terms would be clear – claim it was all a mistake or worse, much worse, would happen to him.

Paddy led the uncle out of earshot.

"The offer of a lift back home, that still stand?"

The uncle nodded.

"Tonight. I'll need to go tonight."

"This isn't your fight. What happened, maybe it was just a question of time."

"All the way. Onto the ferry as well."

The uncle was pacing back and forth, still agitated. "The customs in Dublin, they're your problem. That's the one that's checked."

"I'll be at the depot in a couple of hours."

Paddy lifted an unalarmed Ford Fiesta from the hospital car park. He drove steadily, just under the speed limit, back towards Kilburn. He needed a weapon – a baseball bat, something like that – only how would you get one at this hour? Try a building site maybe for a piece of wood. He continued on, searching either side of the road when, hey, that was a possibility – a cricket club.

He pulled over in the shadows.

The pavilion was alarmed. To the side of it there was a small shed. Paddy wrapped his jacket over around his hand and punched in the window.

There were no cricket bats inside. But a stump would do. He selected one with a pointed metal tip and made his way back to the car. He checked the address – Tim's uncle had supplied it – and started up the engine again.

He turned on the radio. He felt calm. The city was quiet now; the last bus, the last tube, each shop or cinema barricaded by a metal grille. London had closed down for the night and soon Paddy would be on his way, back to Dublin if his luck held. He checked the directions again. As soon as he hit the centre of Kilburn, the house would be easy to find.

Donnelly's bathroom window, the small one at the top of the bigger one, was open. Paddy climbed the drainpipe with the cricket stump stuck into the back of his trousers. He tied a small hook in a piece of wire, dropped it in the open window and caught the handle of the bigger one.

The window opened outwards.

Sudds didn't live alone. On the windowsill there was a row of shampoos and conditioners and body lotions. Paddy placed each on the other side of the glass.

He climbed inside.

From the snoring, he knew which room Sudds slept in. He checked the others first – no one. He eased open the door of the main bedroom and stepped inside. And fuck, it was dark in here! Heavy curtains, that's what it was, Paddy standing with the stump in his hand, trying to slow his breathing. Standing there letting his eyes get used to the light.

He waited. Slowly, vague shapes appeared in the dark. There were two people in the bed, Sudds on this side which was good.

Paddy brought the stump down on his head. Heard a grunt, a small movement, then struck him again. And then the screaming; the woman hysterical, half asleep, disoriented, kicking at the covers and out of the bed. Paddy caught her by the hair, threw her back to the other side of the bed. He held the metal end of the stump to her throat.

"You want to get out of here?"

And he set to work. Up and down the body using the stump and his boots. It was like kicking a bag of cement. He heard Donnelly's knuckles crack under the stump. He stamped on his face and felt the teeth shatter.

He stopped after a minute and checked Donnelly's pulse.

Then he started up again.

10

Eight years Paddy Benner had been on the move and more than anything else it had been a matter of discipline. Momentum was everything. One step and then another; one place as good as the next, if not you could always move on again. And nice simple rules. Don't let yourself get too comfortable, don't make close friends. Don't acquire anything you can't walk away from in the morning.

No lame ducks, that was part of the rule. No vicious thugs and no simpletons.

But now some guy was dead. Some poor clown who wanted to be a hero, shot in the face by a bottler. Paddy stepped off the boat at Dun Laoghaire and said, How about it, God? He always liked the way people did that, never go to mass and then when they find themselves in a jam, they'd say, Just get me out of this one, God and I'll never do anything bad again.

How about it, God? he said. Get me through here and I'll be a reformed man.

It worked. He sailed straight through customs. A little guy with a sad wispy side part hardly looked at the passengers.

Home finally, he thought. Home and safe and lucky.

Paddy had once been a good customer of the DART. He'd take a nice scenic trip out to where the money was, then spend ten minutes mooching around the upstairs while the folks down below sat through Coronation Street or Eastenders or maybe took notes from The Holiday Show. He regarded himself as another version of the Peeping Tom – more expensive maybe but something along the same lines. Not above listening at the door if there was an argument going.

Once he'd seen an old man watching telly with a small pig

on his lap, the two of them sharing a Choc Ice.

Then on the way home he'd sit back and feel the rocking of the train. He'd feel the satisfaction. He'd picture the victims once the cops had gone – the wife blubbering, the husband playing it tough, explaining how he just wanted five minutes alone with the bastard and then they'd see how many more break-ins there'd be.

Eight years ago now.

The carriage emptied a little at Blackrock. Paddy sat and looked out the window and watched the sea as it passed. He could remember the sequence of stations – Blackrock, Booterstown, Sydney Parade, Sandymount… The train left the coast and moved in towards the city and now the houses were smaller; a dull grey pebbledash instead of the redbrick. Most of the passengers stepped off at Tara Street. He saw no one he knew. Maybe some of the regulars would still be in the pool halls, he thought. Maybe he'd pay them a visit. They could ask what it was like over there and he could tell them how you could practice every day of your life and just about scrape a living. No self pity, no excuses. It's ruthless, he could tell them, but that's what makes it beautiful.

As if they'd understand.

The train moved away again and he stared out the window at the dull green of the Liffey and then out onto the north side. It was like coming out of a tunnel, at first the darkness and the rocking of the train and a few light raindrops against the window. Then the view seemed to open out and on one side he had Fairview Park, empty this morning, and on the other a wasteland stretching out to the sea. Landmarks he'd forgotten but nothing could have been more familiar. The train picked up speed coming into Killester and he closed his eyes and he knew he was finally home.

He stepped off the train at Killester station and made his way through Clontarf. The rain had cleared and he walked slowly. It was a nice peaceful area of the city. The houses were handsome and redbrick and the gardens were well kept. A prosperous area. Not filthy rich like Down's Leaze but not far off it either, the gentle smell of money around the place; cricket and rugby and golf clubs and children on the way to university. The sea on one side, St Annes Park on the other…

He knew each step from the train station. Not much had changed, the same gardens and hedges and the same willow tree along Castle Avenue, up along Blackheath and around by the edge of the park. On Mount Prospect Avenue he spotted an old neighbour but she didn't seem to notice him. He continued on slowly, taking in as much as he could, and it was if he'd never been away, making his way home from school maybe, or returning with someone's jewellery in his pocket.

Just like the old days there was no one home. He rang the bell twice and stood and waited. All the time you could spend visualising your return and you'd never picture yourself coming home to an empty house. He sat on his bag on the doorstep and smoked a cigarette, watching the houses opposite, watching to see if any of his old neighbours came out. He stubbed out the cigarette on the sole of his shoe, shoved his bag out of sight into the corner of the porch and walked away again.

Paddy's mother had died when he was twelve. He could remember being driven home from school by the Geography teacher and the conversation they'd had about football and how it had seemed a strange thing to talk about when something was clearly wrong.

He could remember his father nodding to him presuming that he already knew and then his Uncle Roy holding him by the shoulders and explaining it. Paddy had never heard of anyone being struck by a bus before. A car you could understand, maybe she'd just stepped out in front of a car by mistake, or you could even be hit by a motorbike that came flying around a corner. But buses were huge, impossible not to notice. He'd never heard or read or seen anything on television where anyone had been hit by a bus.

That night he lay in bed and thought it through. All day people had been calling it an accident as though they were trying to get it clear in their own minds. A dreadful business, they'd say. Just like that, they'd say, and they'd click their fingers, what on earth could she have been thinking of?

For months after she died the word *accident* preyed on his mind.

He wasn't sure about accidents, how they happened. Maybe it was because people weren't careful enough. There should be a special group going around stopping accidents before they happened, he decided – maybe the Government could organise it. He'd sign up as soon as he was old enough. He pictured himself in a flash suit, a business card to hand out with a number for people to contact if they thought something bad was about to happen. But he was twelve years old and he couldn't wait that long. So he'd often head out with his ball under his arm and then he'd throw the ball into the hedge and continue on looking for accidents to stop. He stuck to his own area, up and down Mount Prospect and the neighbouring roads and into St Annes Park. He was amazed no one had thought of it before. In a full afternoon's walking he could average maybe fifteen or twenty accidents stopped. People were always ready to fall off ladders, or they were about to put their hands into dangerous machinery or there were kids climbing trees and Paddy would be there to catch them when the branch broke. Old people you had to look after very carefully. A bad fall on a patch of ice and they'd break a leg or an arm.

Then just before it was time to go home each evening, he'd hear the 44A rumbling up the road and he'd see her there always wearing the same green anorak standing on the edge of the footpath. He'd take her gently by the sleeve and lead her away from the road.

"Well, look who it is," she'd say "I was wondering where you'd got to."

Now, fourteen years later, he knelt on the edge of her grave and pulled the weeds from the dry earth. He'd taken the 44A into town and then a 42 out to Balgriffin cemetery and sitting here now on the small stone kerb that surrounded the grave he decided what he'd have to do. First of all he'd let the old man set the tone. There was no point in dredging up the past. He wouldn't stand there and take a whole load of shit either. But why be hostile?

But before that he'd call on Aoife Brennan, see what she

was about these days. Maybe she still lived at home. With Aoife he'd try a little honesty. He'd thought about it often enough, God himself only knew, the best way to approach things if he ever ran into her again. One thing for sure, this was the time to tell the truth. He'd explain things, tell her he just didn't have the words last time round so it was easier not to bother, that it had torn the heart out of him to leave. He'd keep it simple. He'd tell her she'd never been far from his thoughts, that there'd been other women along the way, sure, but no one he'd ever felt attached to. Nice and simple and honest and she could take it or leave it.

All the stuff he should have come out with last time round.

He took one last look at the grave, decided it wasn't a bad old tidying job, and headed away again.

11

Thursday morning, looking at the misshapen face on the hospital pillow, Ray Donnelly was thinking how for the past ten years he and his brother had hung around with rich folks who never lifted a hand. First there was Mohammed Al Jahir, the son of a sheikh who spent his day being driven between Harrods and Stringfellows, typical miserable Arab fuck flashing his Visa Gold card and looking to pay the minimum wage. Ray had learned nothing from him other than it didn't matter how ugly you were; if you were rich enough you could still get laid by some nice looking women. From there they'd spent two years looking after Billy Leaburn. The lesson he'd learned from Billy was that if you stiffed the wrong people there was no one in the world who could protect you. Which had led them to Ron Sanderson who was standing on the opposite side of the bed now wanting to know what the damage was.

Ray Donnelly said, "Broken cheekbone, detached retina, broken nose, four broken ribs and seven of his teeth are gone. His hand is broken and his nuts are the size of tennis balls."

"Someone sure did a job on him."

"Used a cricket stump."

"Where'd he get a cricket stump?"

Donnelly looked up. "Soon as I track him down, I'll ask him."

Sanderson sat into a seat next to the bed. Sanderson paid good wages and he knew his business. The best way to get yourself money, he often said, was to find the people who were making it and ask them for some. Not too much, just a little cut of the profit, enough to make sure no one burned out your premises or your car or took a baseball bat to you when you were closing up some evening.

Ask and you shall receive. It was that simple.

Now he said, "A bank lets some bloke off with a debt and then the next guy thinks, Why the fuck should I pay? We let some clown come near us with a cricket stump and next thing we know there'll be a queue of them down the street."

"You think you have to tell me what to do?"

"You able to tell me who we're looking for?"

"He's Irish and he hustles pool. His first name's Paddy."

"Well, that narrows it down, doesn't it?"

Ray shrugged. He had a starting point. Back in *The Four Provinces* the barman directed him to the Brighton Arms guesthouse and twenty minutes later Ray was smiling and explaining his problem to the owner. He'd had a few beers with this Paddy bloke and they'd exchanged addresses only now he couldn't find the slip of paper. To make things worse he was thinking of taking a trip across the channel before the year was out.

The owner, early thirties maybe but with a gut on him, said: "Love to help you out, mate but you've got to see it from my point of view."

"Which is?"

"As long as a guest keeps to the law, he's got a right to his privacy, doesn't he?"

Ray Donnelly shrugged. "No harm in asking," he said.

He walked back out the gate. What he'd been hoping for was the surname. Once he got that he could set the wheels in motion. Sanderson had contacts all over the city: hotels, bars and pool halls – just the sort of places this guy might turn up. He'd call someone in Dublin and see if they might make a few enquiries.

Ray went out to his car and took a 22 millimetre Beretta from the glove compartment.

"Let's give this another bash," he said as soon as the door opened again. "And this time we'll look at things from *my* point of view."

***

From the front porch Paddy looked inside to see the old grandfather clock and his bag lying against it, the same old wallpaper and carpet. The old man just standing there leaning his shoulder against the edge of the door. Playing things cool, the line already prepared, saying, "Well, you haven't much of a colour for a fella who's been away."

"You going to get out of the way so I can come in?"

"Come on through. I've the dinner ready to go."

Paddy followed him into the kitchen. "Don't like to grumble," he said, "but this hasn't been much of a homecoming so far. I call here first and there's no sign of you. Now I just called on Aoife and her mother gave me the bum's rush. Wouldn't give me her new number. She says it'd probably be best if it was left to Aoife to decide if she wanted to make any contact. Can you believe that?" He looked around. "Hey," he said, "this place has a woman's touch."

"You're on the ball today. Only she moved out last week."

"New presses, all those new saucepans sitting on the hooks over there. That a new washing machine?"

"The old one was knackered."

"What about those shelves?"

"Stuck them up myself."

"Well easy come, easy go, eh? At least she did a bit of work while she was here."

Paddy crossed the room to sit at his old place at the table. The old man looked well. Eight years older maybe but not really looking it, the outdoor life suiting him, and pretty much as Paddy remembered. The same smooth look as when he was living out of bed and breakfasts or mobile homes, missing the cut by two shots on a good day.

Des Benner held up two microwave dinners. "You want the chicken supreme or the barbecue ribs? There's a hot and spicy duck down the bottom of the freezer if you want me to root it out."

Paddy smiled. "I want the chicken."

"That's the one I was going to have."

"Well I'm the guest."

"Chicken it is," Des Benner said and he tossed the package

in the air. He caught it and turned and smiled. "It's good to see you," he said.

"How've you been, Dad?" Paddy said.

"Well, son. I've been very well but I've missed you."

Not counting his mother, Paddy had known three of his father's women.

First there was Lynn Staunton, about the same age then as Des was now, a tiny blonde with huge knockers and a rich husband who played off fifteen. Lynn Staunton with her capped teeth who'd give Paddy a tinkling smile and say, You going to be as good as your father then, Patrick? When the old man ricked his back on the driving range one day the story going round was that he'd fallen off John Staunton's wife. Paddy would pretend he hadn't heard. Then one day John junior pulled Paddy aside and said, "You'd want to start fleecing that old man of yours. Soon as I found out he was porking my old dear, I brought her into town and told her she better think about kitting me out properly." Paddy still didn't believe it. What did John Staunton know about anything, after all? And when he asked about it, his father pulled over onto the kerb and explained how it was a tricky situation being the new pro in a golf club, how you were in the spotlight, what with the place being full of guys who couldn't hit a shit off a rope. Jealousy, he said, that's all it was. If Paddy kept practising every day he'd have plenty of people spreading stories about him too and the best thing he could do was to ignore them.

The second of his father's women that Paddy knew was Judith Flynn who helped out with the club catering twice a week and was between boyfriends at the time. From what Paddy remembered Judith was no more than twenty-three, a tall slim ordinary looking girl who'd never picked up a club in her life. Judith held to the theory that by and large the average golfer was a prick. Which was what Paddy's father liked about her, he said. She was different. She wasn't one of the glitzy airheads you'd find hanging around on a Saturday night or one of the other bunch who'd hack their way through the front nine on a Tuesday and then start grumbling that they couldn't do it at the week-end.

No, Judith Flynn was a real person. She had all the characteristics that Paddy should look for in a friend – and that was why they went out to lunch every now and then.

Twelve years old, his father a sports pro, Paddy was able to believe him.

"No real need to tell your mother any of this," Des would say.

And then there was the chunky redhead in London. Paddy had caught a glimpse of her from the hospital bed. He didn't even know her name or much else about her but still she counted. So that was three that he knew of. Others he'd spoken to on the phone – one as soon as six months after his mother died – but at least Des had the courtesy not to bring them home. Now another had walked out on him.

"Things at the club okay?" Paddy said.

"Couldn't be better. I've the franchise for the shop now and it's going well. Every time some bozo hooks one into the trees, I just tell him I've a driver back at the shop that'll correct that for him. I still get ten percent of the green fees."

"What's a round now?"

"Fifty-five. That's five-fifty for me before a visitor's even hit a ball. I still pick up a few quid in the Pro-Ams. What about you? How've you been getting by?"

"Playing pool mainly."

"You good enough to make a living at it now?"

"Not much of one but it beats working."

"You play in competitions?"

"Competitions are tricky. Get yourself into the top three and you're in business. But spot three guys who can take you and you're better off getting beaten early and seeing what you can pick up in the backroom games."

Paddy told him about it. How he'd started in Boston, moving up and down the East Coast, thinking of Canada but knowing he'd never get back across the border without a visa. Then zigzagging his way up and down the country again before thinking Fuck this, time for a change, but running into trouble before he could do anything about it. From there he'd flown to London. Five and a half years in the States, two and a half knocking around Europe, that was the score to date.

He said, "I even had a few jobs along the way. Notice anything different about my face?"

His father nodded. "That scar on your forehead. You wouldn't really notice it unless you were looking closely. Someone hit you with a pool cue?"

"I got that driving a limo," he said. "This guy I knew ran a limo service only he's not the most organised fella in the world. He finds he's a driver short one day so he drags me out of a pool hall and says he'll give me a hundred and fifty bucks if I pick up this party and take them wherever they want to go. I say, Fair enough. Who's going to stop a limo driver and ask him if he's got a licence, after all? So I head off and pick up this party of eight. They're all stuck in the back and the guy tells me to take off. I ask him where he wants to go and he starts going spare. Turns out it's a surprise sixtieth birthday party only the guy who's birthday it is, he's the one who ordered the limo. He's surprising his guests. They don't know where they're being taken. They're all in the back bored shitless but trying to look like they're having a good time and he's there giving me lackery over it."

"What'd you do?"

"I said, Why don't you whisper it to me. That way we won't ruin the surprise. It's already ruined, you asshole, he says and off he goes about how if he ran his business like this he'd have gone bust inside a fortnight. Tell that to the owner, I tell him and he says, No I'm fucking telling you and *you* tell him. So he goes on a little more and I'm just looking at him trying not to laugh and eventually we step out of the limo and he whispers it to me. Only he hardly says it at all. The rest of the punters are stuck in the back with the windows down and he's right up to my ear and I'm saying, You'll have to speak up a bit there, chum, and he's saying, You deaf, you fucking asshole."

"This guy, he's a pearler," Des said.

"A beauty," Paddy said, nodding. "Right up my street. So he gives me the address and we get into the car. Only I haven't a breeze where I'm going. So I drive about a hundred yards and I open the shutter and say, You'll have to direct me from here,

Boss, and now he really goes apeshit. Starts shouting at the top of his voice, Right everybody, for your surprise you're going to lunch in the Biscayne Hotel, then it's some park or other and then someplace else for cocktails. I don't remember the details. But he's really shouting. He says, now your whole fucking day is ruined thanks to Mick up the front here and the rest of the folks are all saying, Don't worry about it, John, we'll still have a great time. Then the guy leans forward and snarls at me, You needn't think you're getting a fucking cent for this, Mick. So I pull over and say, Everyone out. No way I'm driving anyone anywhere for nothing. I'm due a hundred and fifty dollars out of this and I can't see me getting it if the guy doesn't pay.

"So we all end up on the footpath. He's telling me to get back in the fucking car and I'm saying, Sorry Sir but you've cancelled the contract. I'll just take the car back to the garage. He starts swearing at me some more and I say I'll pass your complaints on to the owner. But he still wants the limo. Where's he going to get another one at such late notice? So a couple of the others start pleading with me to just give it a moment. I say, Of course. Why not? I'm having a whale of a time. So eventually this dickhead says, All right, you'll get your money now get in the fucking car and drive. Sure, I say. Just as soon as you pay me. He can't believe this, none of them can, so I say, Look at it from my point of view, feelings are running high here and you've already threatened not to pay me. You're not happy with the service and you might not pay me at the end of the day. I'd rather see the money now if it's all the same to yourself."

"You're antagonising them now?" Des Benner said.

"I'm protecting my money."

"Okay. Get on with it. I want to know how this ends."

"No happy ending here, I tell you. I say I'm not going anywhere unless I've been paid and they're saying you'll get your money. Then old John says he'll write me a cheque. I ask him if he's got a banker's card and he pulls out a Gold Visa card and says, This good enough for you? 'Fraid not, I say, I can't accept that. But I'll drive you to a bank and you can get some cash out. He can't believe I won't accept his cheque. The real reason I won't accept the cheque is I think he's going to cancel it just after he gives it to me. But at this stage I've had enough of him. So I say, Look chum, what sort of spoiled prick goes and arranges a party for himself and won't tell anyone where they're going. What's the problem? I ask him. Folks not paying you enough attention?"

"And he lost it," Des said.

"Exactly. It was a stupid thing to say but Jesus, I'd had enough of him. And he went for me. He wasn't too tall but he was blocky. He charges me against the wall and I'm trying to get him in a headlock so he might calm down and then this old guy who's in the party steps in with his walking stick and clobbers me right across the noggin. Splits my head open. Then everyone's trying to break us up and then all of a sudden there's a copper in the middle of things. I know I'm screwed then. Driving without a licence. Working without a visa. That's where I made a mistake, I should've just run like fuck. But I tried to talk my way out of it. Few days later I was deported and the guy who owned the limo, he was waiting to get fined."

Des Benner was grinning now. "It's a good story."

"One of my best. Smacked across the head and chucked out of the country, all for trying to be a good employee. Taught me to stay away from work though. From there I dossed around England for a while and then just travelled around Europe. Lots of places you can live cheaply enough."

"Not doing any stealing?" Des Benner asked.

Paddy looked across at his father. Tossing it in, just like that. "Not for a long time now, Dad."

His father nodded. "That was the only thing I worried about. I don't know how I knew but I was always sure you were okay. I suppose you'd been fending for yourself for so long that I knew you were getting by. But I hated to think of you breaking into people's houses. You remember what you called me before you left?"

Paddy nodded. "I told you you were an asshole."

"That's right. You said it was the saddest day in a kid's life when he realised once and for all that his old man was an asshole."

"I was a very wise kid."

"You remember the reason you gave?"

"Because the kid had always spent years denying it beforehand."

"That's right. Because you gave me more chances that anyone. Know something, Paddy? Maybe even an asshole deserves another chance."

Paddy shrugged. "You never know," he said. "Maybe we both do."

12

A man had been murdered, yes, but Joe knew he needed to concentrate on his own situation. He'd just wasted the guts of a hundred quid on a job he hadn't a chance of getting. What was it now – six months? – since he'd been let go? He could remember the MD puffing on a fat cigar and telling them how it was all over: the deathly quiet, then a nervous giggle from the back of the room. Just like that. No mention of who'd run the company into the ground, no mention of the way they'd tried to expand to compete with the big boys in the industry. No mention of a redundancy payment either, just we're sorry and we wish you all the best.

Forty-eight employees sitting in six rows of eight. Joe sitting amongst them, thinking, Well what's going to become of me?

He could remember manoeuvring the car along the icy roads – an odd, detached feeling having come over him – watching the pedestrians shuffle along with short careful steps. At least Christmas was over, that was something. And in one way it was a release. A decision had been taken out of his hands. Something else would turn up, he hoped; maybe something better, maybe even something that would have him rue the years he'd spent selling shampoo.

It wasn't as if it was the most important job in the world after all.

When Stella came home that night she slid her jacket off her shoulders and slipped it onto the back of the chair. She lifted the box of Roses and said, "What's this?"

"Whole company's gone down the tubes," he said.

She hugged him tightly, her cheek against his chest, hands flat against his back.

"This could be the break you needed, Joe," she said. "You never wanted those other jobs badly enough. Employers sense these things. Sure they do. That's why they're employers."

He could remember her stroking his face, and her exact words, how she loved him and how they'd see it through together. Then pushing him away, telling him to look at her. Repeating it, how they were in it together.

He could remember the whole scene and he was thinking about it now, staring through the window at the early afternoon traffic.

It was now six days since Stella's onslaught. She never mentioned it. Maybe she didn't remember, maybe she knew there was no point in going over it again. Joe continued as though nothing had happened. His marriage hadn't crumbled yet. They were still together, living in the same house and if he could turn things around the incident would fade. It was a matter of patience. Some things could destroy you if you dwelt on them so you just had to blunder on regardless.

If anything, it made him more determined to win back her respect.

Anyhow, was she solely to blame? She'd never hidden her expectations, right from when they started going out together. In a pub, he went to the counter; at the cinema he'd always been the first to the kiosk. It was always he that rooted for change at the ice-cream stand. He liked to treat her: she liked to keep her money. Some people were funny about money – he'd understood this right from the start – so maybe it was he who hadn't lived up to his half of the bargain.

Late one evening, he handed her a copy of the CV she'd typed up as soon as he'd been laid off.

"I've picked out some companies around town. There's nothing in the papers and I'm not going to sit around waiting. I made some changes to it."

"Give me a number."

"Think you can manage twelve?"

"Lunch tomorrow, I might have time."

Stella was saying little. Embarrassment maybe, Joe thought, or else she was in shock. Her cousin had been murdered, after all; someone she spoke to on the phone each Christmas and who visited every few years. An eccentric, yes, but where was the harm in that? Now he was dead. He'd run into the wrong place and the wrong time and now she'd never speak to him again. That was the hardest thing, she said: trying to get her head around the fact that he was truly gone. You spoke to someone, you told him thanks for letting your husband stay – and then that was that.

Yes, she said, she'd be heading across for the funeral. It didn't matter where she had to find the money. Jesus, she said, fifty yards from his own home and some thug pulls a gun and shoots him in the face. Louis, the most inoffensive person you could meet; Joe listening and thinking that this was where unemployment really hit home, when someone you loved needed a dig out. Joe had been a good employee. He'd worked hard. He should've been able to take Stella in his arms and say, "Hey, don't worry about the expense." He should've been able to tell her, "Money's only money. Family's what's important."

Stuff like that, it was a comfort to everyone involved.

He barely slept that night. When dawn came he was picturing himself rushing Louis to hospital. He pictured himself winning back Stella's respect.

Half-one in the afternoon, the lunch time throng hadn't moved back to work yet. In the briefcase Joe carried under his arm were the CVs: not quite the whole truth but not far off it either. Just a slight fudging of the facts. He'd signed himself up to a couple of sports clubs – employers loved that stuff, the way it showed a nicely rounded personality – and he'd doctored his Leaving Cert results. Dishonest? Yes, maybe, but being truthful hadn't brought him any rewards so far.

What you had to do was give yourself an edge over the other guy.

Stella had made a good job of the CVs – nicely laid out on the word processor and neatly photocopied. He had picked out seven firms in town, then he'd take the bus out to the industrial estates. A plan was essential to avoid covering the same ground twice. Pushing himself as a salesman hadn't produced anything so far so now he was going to concentrate on the security firms. Soul destroying work maybe, but it would do for the time being.

He started at Parnell Square, with a security firm close to Belvedere College, then moved along by the back of the ILAC centre and on to Bolton Street. On Capel Street, he found a firm he hadn't picked out. The receptionist was staring into space.

"Excuse me," he said.

The receptionist tuned back in. "What can I help you with?"

"I'm here to look for a job."

"Is Mr Reynolds expecting you?"

Joe was surprised. She was the one who should know. "I hope so."

"Who will I tell him's calling?"

"My name's Joe Faherty."

She led him through after a moment. The office was bare enough, as though things were still being set up. And the guy behind the desk, he was a bruiser – someone who'd spent his share of weekend nights standing outside nightclubs. Eyes set close together and a nose that had been reset a few times.

Joe handed across one of the CVs. "I was hoping you'd take a look at this. I'm looking for a job."

"You and a thousand others. What've you got to offer me that they don't?"

"Good looks." Joe said and smiled.

Reynolds smiled back. "Takes more than that for this business, I'm afraid."

"You'll see when you read that. I'm honest and I work hard and I need a job. I don't mind what I have to do."

Reynolds flicked through the pages. "You worked in security for a year. That's not exactly comprehensive experience, is it?"

Joe looked him in the face. "I'll be able for the job."

Reynolds shrugged. "Maybe, but I'm afraid I don't have anything for you at the moment. I've just set up on my own but I've been in the business for years. So anyone I've got is hand picked. But if you want, I'll hang onto this and if anything pops up, I'll consider you for it. I'm not saying what sort of a chance you have but I'll think about you."

"That's all I'm asking."

Joe continued on the round. He'd put on his best suit and his good shoes, but now the shoes were beginning to hurt. Just a slight rubbing on the little toe of his left foot but Jesus, it was enough. He tried to walk differently, pressing the ball of his left foot harder into the ground to relieve the pressure but he couldn't keep it up. Soon he was walking normally again, feeling the skin being rubbed raw.

People were polite. They smiled and nodded and said, of course they'd put the CV on file, but well… times were bad. No one's hiring these days, they said. Two refused saying that he'd be better off trying elsewhere. Another flicked through the pages and said he wasn't qualified for anything the firm might have to offer. As he limped along, it occurred to Joe that he was probably wasting his time and money. Which was a quitter's attitude. One person, that was all it would take – one person to take an interest and things would have turned for him again.

For every refusal there was another firm to try. His original plan had become no more than a vague guideline and he plodded along, reading the lettering along the upstairs windows. His limp became more pronounced. By three o'clock he realised that he was falling behind schedule. Not that it mattered, the dinner was prepared and ready to be popped into the oven. Stella would look after it if he couldn't make up the time.

He took a bus out to the Sandyford Industrial Estate – a pound ten to get there. Three firms accepted the sheets, two refused. He took the bus back into town and did a tour of the Leeson Street area. Another waste of time; it was mostly accountants and lawyers around there. Then he took a 32A out to Baldoyle. The industrial estates, they were the places to try, but the bitchy thing about them was that they were so spread out. Another eighty pence, but at least he'd be able to walk home.

By a quarter to five his toe had been rubbed raw. Stupid, he thought, not wearing his most comfortable shoes. A heavy futile feeling had come over him; chances were that the whole day had been a waste. Still it would be a mistake to give up early. You did that and you didn't deserve to get anywhere. Just when he was sure he was finished he noticed a publishing firm. Schoolbooks, the sign said. One last try, he thought, just in case they needed a salesman.

He limped in and stood in front of the receptionist's desk. She was a pretty blonde woman, late twenties maybe, or early thirties at a push. Behind her, four men were chatting as though they'd packed in for the day. Joe managed a smile.

"Hi," he said. "I'm looking for work. I've a CV made out here and I was hoping someone might take a look at it."

"I don't think there's anything going at the moment," the receptionist said.

"Don't worry, I know that. There's nothing going anywhere but maybe if there's a selling vacancy in the near future, you might give me a shout. I'd appreciate it if you could file this away just in case."

The receptionist appeared confused for a moment. Then she gathered herself and shrugged.

"Well, I suppose so. I'll pass it on to the MD."

Joe headed away again. What would it take? – the guts of an hour? – to walk home. Longer maybe with his foot hurting the way it was. He stuck the briefcase under his arm and plodded on but he'd barely made it to the main road, when it struck him. The sheer stupidity of it! On another day it might have been funny, but today? He had forgotten to keep his master copy. Stella had stored the stuff on disk most likely but he didn't want to ask her to print it out again. If he needed more photocopies, he had to go back again.

Sore feet and he'd gone and made a stupid mistake. Up until now, he'd followed his plan as far as he could, never covering the same ground twice, so at least the pain he was feeling was unavoidable. But this? This was plain stupidity.

The receptionist blinked at him and looked around when she saw him again. Then she took a breath and composed herself. He wondered what was wrong.

"I'm sorry," he said, "but you're not going to believe what I did. I've been walking town all day, dropping those CVs around the place, so I'm a bit addled. I forgot to keep one in case I need more copies." He laughed gently. "You'd think I'd have enough sense to put the master copy aside. I'll have to take back the copy I gave you and then drop another out to you."

Why were the men behind so interested? The receptionist began to fumble on the desk. Why wouldn't she look him in the face?

"I'm not sure where I put it," she said.

Joe laughed again. "Well, it's got to be there somewhere. I just gave it to you a few minutes ago."

She fumbled some more, looked under some sheets. "Yes, I know. But you know how you can mislay things. Maybe you could call back in a little while."

"You're my last call," he said. "I'm a bit stuck for time as it is."

She smiled a helpless smile at him and the four men behind turned away from his stare. What was wrong? Why were these people so embarrassed? He scanned the room and then back to the area behind the reception desk. And there it was… Three sheets sticking out from the top of the a small metal waste paper basket. Just sitting there, his name for anyone to see.

He stood and looked her in the face, his mouth open.

"You just threw it in the bin."

The receptionist turned and glared at one of the men behind. He picked up a sheet and looked at it. "I'm really sorry," she said.

He could feel the stinging at the back of his eyes. "I can't believe you threw it in the bin."

Now, the receptionist's bottom lip was trembling. "It was a mistake. I can't tell you how sorry I am."

When he had the sheets in his hands again, he stood for a moment. Holding back the tears now.

"You got any idea how I feel?" he said and he turned away towards the door.

Walking was murder. By now his right shoe had begun to grate against his heel, so there was no respite on either step. His limp was more pronounced. The sun had come out and his body was covered with sweat.

He tried to think clearly about what had happened. It wasn't easy; between the heat and the pounding of the footpath, his head was spinning. Still, he was sure it was one of those smug fuckers behind the counter who had tossed his CV into the bin. Showing off to the receptionist, most likely, talking bollocks about being able to see the big picture. Something like that. Probably laughed as he did it. It was nothing to do with the receptionist – she'd been mortified – but fuck her, she could always have taken it back out, couldn't she?

By the time he turned down his road, his feet had been rubbed raw. He turned the key in the door and stepped inside and smelled the food cooking. Thank Christ for that, he thought. Coming home to an empty house, he wasn't sure he could have taken that today.

He could hear Stella move around upstairs. He'd set the table earlier and everything was as he'd left it apart from the post which had been brought in from the hall table. He stared for a moment. The gas bill had been left over his side of the table. The rest of the post she'd taken for herself, but the gas bill, she'd left that for him.

Telling him what?

He could barely believe it.

Stella walked in, straight past him and over to the cooker.

"How'd you get on?" she said.

He picked up the envelope. It was no mistake, he was sure of it. Everyone knew the gas bill – the same brown envelope at the same time every month with the same Bord Gais ring at the top.

"Why'd you put this over here?" he said. "You know I can't pay it."

Stella just looked at him and shrugged. "I didn't put it there."

"Well how'd it get there then? You're the one who took in the post."

"I just threw it on the table."

Joe pointed it out to her. "You threw this one over here and the others over there. We've got a postcard from your sister and the rest of the shit in the green corner, and over here in the red corner we've got the gas bill. Maybe there's a reason for that."

She stared at him. "So it's my responsibility now, is it? The gas bill."

"It is until I can pay it again. Right from the start I've been paying the mortgage and the bills and now I can't do that anymore. We have to dip into the savings, for Christ sake."

"Maybe I'm the one who's scraping by while you're the one spending money on cigarettes," she said.

"Is that what this is about?"

"Well, you're the one who's always going on about tightening our belts and organising our finances. Then you waste money smoking."

He could feel himself trembling. "I'm the one spends fuck all around here. You're the one who's eating at *The Trocadero*."

"Don't start bringing that up," she said. "That was paid for. Maybe you'd want to start facing up to some of your responsibilities around here. You're damn right I'm putting money aside. I'm putting it aside so maybe we can have some sort of future."

"And I'm bursting my bollocks trying to get a job so I can pay the gas bill. Until I get one, you can pay it."

He picked up the envelope and flung it across the room. It held its line for a moment, then swerved and dipped to the floor. Stella stared at it for a moment. "Sure," she said. "Why not? Just add it to the list."

She turned and walked away. She stepped out into the back garden and Joe watched her go and then he suddenly began to sob. His breath came in spasms. Gasping now, trying to breathe deeply, knowing he should get out of the room or even go sit at the table and stick his head in his hands. But he didn't. He stood and felt his whole body heave.

Stella came back inside. She stopped and looked at him. Then she shook her head and said, "Crying doesn't pay the bills or put food on the table, does it?"

He struck her. Just once with his fist closed, right on the eye, and he felt the sharp thud, Stella reeling backwards, Joe watching her crash off the table and into a sitting position. Blood appearing now, a small patch over her left eye, then covering one side of her face. She stared open-mouthed for a moment and she began to scream.

"Oh Jesus, Stel," he cried.

Then she was on her feet, running to the door. She screamed something; he couldn't make it out.

"Stel," he shouted after her.

He watched her from the front window, weaving across the road, her left hand wiping the blood away. Straight into Ed O'Brien's. Of course, Joe thought, why not? What was the point in having a copper live opposite if you didn't make use of him at a time like this?

"Oh sweet Jesus," he said.

He went to lie on the couch.

13

The first thing Aoife Brennan said was, "Hey, you got rid of your curls." Paddy said he'd done it himself and she shrugged and said, well she'd seen worse jobs. He wanted to touch her. Sitting there at the counter smiling at him, wearing a white T-shirt and jeans, her hair cut shorter than he remembered it. On the arm maybe. Or kiss her cheek. Butterflies going like crazy in his stomach which was madness when you could have a nice calm edge creeping around someone's house.

There was no ring on her wedding finger. That was a good start.

He'd spent the afternoon wandering around town. Getting off the bus in Marlborough Street, moving through the shopping areas, looking at clothes and shoes, not interested enough to try anything on. Then finding himself doing a tour of the pool halls. Nowhere to go, waiting for the time to pass, all the while wondering – Is she married now?

Which she apparently wasn't. "I wasn't sure if your mum was going to give you the message," he said.

"She told me all right. She said she wasn't going to give me any advice."

Paddy nodded, knowing what was coming. "Then she gave you some."

"She said maybe it'd be better for everyone if I didn't call you back."

Paddy shrugged. "Yeah, well that's mothers for you. Most of them are pretty much nuts but everyone thinks their own is the nuttiest. It's a theory of mine. If you want you can take it and pass it off as your own."

"Thanks," she said. "I might do that."

He smiled at her. "You look great, Aoife," he said.

"You too, Paddy," she said. "Sit down there and tell us all about it."

She wanted him to start right back at the beginning with what exactly had happened eight years ago. The way she remembered it, she'd heard from her mother about Paddy getting picked up by the police. When she asked him what the story was, all he could say was, Yeah it's true all right – nothing more than a shrug when she said she didn't want to see him again.

Then a few days later the charges are dropped and Paddy's gone. No goodbye, nothing.

Paddy said, "I got done because of a guy named Danny Butler. He used to buy the stuff off me only he gets pulled over one night and there's a whole load of stolen jewellery in his car. And of course he's not shy about telling where it came from. So I was pulled in and charged. It was a first offence so I was bailed out almost immediately. But it wasn't just my stuff that he had. A couple of nights before, these two clowns walk into this old couple's house, stick a gun to the old dear's head and sell the stuff on to Butler. One of them was the nephew of the wife of one of the Flynns. You've heard of the Flynns?"

"Sure. Everyone's heard of the Flynns."

"They're not the folks you want to cross. Only Butler doesn't know of the connection when he starts talking to the coppers. Then a few days later his kid goes missing. Just for a day, there's a big search, but the kid's dropped back by evening time. It was just a warning. So Butler retracted. Said he'd bought all the stuff off some guy he couldn't remember the name of. The charges against me were dropped."

"Simple as that."

Paddy nodded. "Mystery solved."

"They couldn't get this Butler guy to give evidence just against you?"

"It was the other two they wanted most of all because they'd really scared the shit out of the old couple. They weren't going to offer him any deal just for me. And there was nothing else to connect me to the jewellery."

"You were lucky."

Paddy shrugged. "Yeah, well two days later, I was pulled in again. There was another burglary only it wasn't me this time. Some fucked-up junkie job only these two coppers said I was resisting arrest and they beat the shit out of me. One of them was a guy named George Costello. I'd never seen the other one before but Costello was a sergeant up in Clontarf. He was one of the ones working on the burglaries and I'd given him some lip when I was being let go."

"You never were one to keep your mouth shut."

"Live and learn, I suppose. I went into town the next day and bought a ticket for Boston. You and me, we were finished and I didn't blame you for that. And Costello didn't look the type who was going to give up on me. My old man was tearing his hair out. And I'd always intended trying my luck with the pool in the States so I just took off. Seemed like the thing to do at the time."

Paddy stopped for a moment, sipped his drink. Sitting here in *The Yacht* with Aoife Brennan, going over old times, noticing things about her again: the way she'd sit on a barstool with her ankles crossed, the simple gold chain around her neck… In all they'd only gone out for eight months, meeting at a friend's New Year's party, all hell breaking loose just before she was getting ready for university.

Eight months, that was all. Now eight years later, he was still thinking of her. "I should've told you, Aoif," he said.

"Which? That you were a thief or that you were going?"

"Both, I suppose."

"A double life, for Christ sake. I should be on *Sally Jesse* or *Geraldo*."

"I'd been stealing for a good three years before we hooked up. I knew you'd have nothing to do with me if you knew."

"I doubt it'd have made much difference in the long run."

Paddy shrugged. "How do you mean?"

"Remember how you were always butting in on conversations. You'd walk right over to some group and say, Well folks anything of interest going on here?"

"I haven't done that in a long time."

"Or else you'd have this dreamy look on your face. Jesus,

Paddy, you used to get bored so easily."

Paddy sighed. "I don't think I was ever bored with you."

"Maybe not. But I always knew you'd be on your bike soon enough. It was just a question of time."

Paddy said nothing; didn't know what to say.

Grinning now, she said, "But enough about you. Let's talk about me for a while."

George Costello told Ed O'Brien there was a stranger back in town. Ed asked who might that be? George said, "The one who ripped off my house eight years ago, you coming or not?"

Ed sighed and put down the phone. It was the last thing he needed. What he wanted to do tonight was call Stella Faherty and see if she wanted to get together; maybe to go through the legal side of things, where she stood in relation to getting back into that house and obtaining a court order. Which was what he'd advised her to do yesterday. Eleven years on the force, you learned one thing for sure: if the wife didn't get a judge to sign something, soon enough the husband would be right back on the doorstep kicking up murder.

That was the way of domestics. They never got any better.

He'd told her it was a pattern of behaviour that seldom changed. She'd nodded and said she didn't really want to take that chance, Ed listening and thinking that what liked most about Stella Faherty was her legs. Nice shapely legs with a good curve to the calf, legs that looked like they never took any exercise and still not an ounce of fat there. What was she? Thirty-one maybe. Thirty-three at the most. A grand healthy woman in her prime locked into a marriage with a prick who used his fists. Maybe she'd be ready for a little diversion. He pictured it – the two of them on the floor with the paperwork laid out in front of them, a nice bottle of wine to ease things along. Just being there when she needed a good neighbour. Seeing how things developed…

Only now he was going out with George Costello to settle some old score. He couldn't even remember the guy's name. Some burglar who'd walked and got a few slaps for his trouble and then the next night he breaks into Costello's house while the family's there and robs the place. At least he had the good sense to take off. But now he was back again. What did he think, that Costello was going to forget? Ed went to change his shirt. Stella Faherty would have to hold for another night and, if nothing else, it might be interesting to see what this burglar guy was made of.

14

The house Stella had grown up in, right next to the Artane roundabout, wasn't much to look at from the front. Friday evening, half past nine, Joe slipped the car keys into a brown manila envelope and started up the driveway.

He'd written her a letter.

First up, he was accepting the blame for what happened. He wanted to lay that on the table as a reference point and no matter what else was said, that wouldn't change. But he had a story too, he wanted her to understand that, and maybe in time she'd be able to see things from his point of view. He described the frustration that had caused him to strike her, the sickening feeling in his stomach as he made contact. No right to ask for forgiveness, he said, but he was asking anyway. Think back over the good times, he wrote, and see if they mean anything.

Stella's father met him at the door. All five foot four of him standing there in his green woolly cardigan, arms folded like he was a night club bouncer.

"Stella won't be coming to the door. Anything you have to say, say it to her solicitor."

Joe said, "I'm moving out today. My sister's flat is free for the time being."

"She's taking a barring order out against you. You know that?"

Joe shook his head.

"Step within a hundred yards of her and you'll have the law down on you."

Joe stepped forward and handed the envelope across. Stella's old man staring for a moment before accepting.

"You're a bully," he said, "and there's not much worse than a bully."

Joe stood for a moment.

"What kind of man hits his wife? You able to tell me that, Joe?"

Joe turned and walked away. Let the old fucker talk all he wanted, what difference did it make?

Paddy thought it impressed her, the reasonable way he could talk about the past eight years. No bullshit about the breeze in your hair or waking up in the morning and following the road.

"It's like everything's accentuated," he said. "You're miles from home with a good size wad in your pocket, a few drinks on board, then you think, Yeah this is the life. But find yourself in a trough and it can take you months to pull out of it. There were times, Aoif, I swear when I'd want to cry with the loneliness."

Aoife said, "I always pictured you on a permanent holiday."

"I used to think of you having a whale of a time over here. Especially when you were in college. Parties every night, that sort of thing. Then after that I kept thinking you'd be engaged or married if I ever saw you again."

"I was."

"Which?"

"Engaged. When I was teaching part-time, the school wouldn't pay me through the summer so I got a job teaching English to Spanish and Italian students. I met a guy there and we started going out and a year and a half later he asked me to marry him."

"Did you love him?"

Looking up now, she said, "That any business of yours?"

"Just curious."

"I liked him a lot. I thought maybe that was enough."

"You ever see Moonstruck?"

"With Cher?"

"That's the one. I can't remember the actress's name but she'd ask the daughter if she loved the guy and when the daugher'd say No, she'd say, Great, go ahead and marry him."

Aoife said. "Olympia Dukakis."

"Could be. She reckoned if you loved someone they'd just

drive you nuts so you were better off hitting the middle ground."

"Cher didn't marry the safe guy in the end. That's what the film was about, not taking the safe option. Only, guess what? I didn't get a chance to take any option. We're meant to be going out to dinner one night and he calls by early and says he's met someone else. A teacher in his own school. I say, that's fine and he says, sorry about that. I say, don't be. Then he potters off out the door again."

"You give him back the ring?"

"Of course. I was angry, sure, because he must've been seeing this other one on the sly. Though you can't blame him if he fell in love. But most of all, I was relieved. It was like we were engaged all right but I could never see us being married to each other. It was one of those things where you think, Yeah this is all right, but then as soon as you're out of it, you think Jesus no it wasn't."

So that was Aoife up to date. Rough details going both ways, Paddy giving her the run through of the places he'd been, leaving out the robberies, but being honest otherwise. Aoife filling in the years. Four in college, two working part-time, then two more as a full-time teacher out in Howth. Which suited her down to the ground, she said. A nice quiet girl's school, it was a damn sight better than some of the places you could end up.

She said one of the worst things about being a teacher was the way everyone had their school stories. "Tell someone you teach English," she said, "and they say, I had an English teacher once and next thing you're hearing all about it. It's something everyone's got in common. They've got some funny story which is always boring as shit and you're stuck there listening to it."

Paddy nodded, sympathising, "What you need is a baseball bat."

"You said it."

"A good clip across the kneecap'd sort all that out. Or else a good swift boot in the clackers. You ever try it?"

"Not so far."

"Some folks, it's the only way they learn. It's the opposite with me. Tell people you're a pool hustler and they just look at you."

She sipped her drink, looked back at him. "You ever feel bad about it?"

"Which? Hustling?"

"Amongst other things."

"Not about hustling, no. The other guy plays because he's greedy. He thinks he sees a sucker and he wants to make on it."

"But it's still a trick."

"Sure. I don't think it's the same as say diddling someone's bank account. Or finding some old dear and telling her you'll tarmac her driveway and six weeks later the thing still hasn't set."

Aoife said, "What about the robberies? You ever think about those people whose houses you robbed?"

Getting right into it now, Paddy thought.

He said, "Sometimes."

"No fun coming home and finding someone's ripped your place off."

Paddy looked away; it was hard to explain. Well into his second pint now, he'd have liked to be going over old times, making her laugh, maybe inching his arm a little closer to hers along the bar… All of which seemed a long way off now. "What I did was I locked it away in a little part of my mind and I didn't think about it." Leaving it in the past tense: not pushing but hoping she picked it up. "Same as most criminals, I suppose. You take some thug who beats up old ladies, you can bet he still thinks he's a great guy."

Aoife nodded. "He ignores the bad stuff."

"Pretty much so," Paddy said. "Ask him and he'll tell you how he looks after his family, which he probably doesn't, or how he's a rock solid friend. A real stand-up guy, as they say in the States. He'd never grass you out. That other business he just puts it aside. Unless he's a fucking nutcase who enjoys it."

"How about you, did you enjoy it? The stealing, I mean."

Paddy thought for a moment. "For a time, yeah, I think I did enjoy it. A lot of the money, I never spent until I went away and then I got stung badly in a couple of pool halls early on and that was the end of it. Easy come, easy go I suppose since it wasn't really my money in the first place. But I never hustled or stole from anyone because I wanted expensive things. I think my main problem is that I'm bone idle. Playing pool hasn't been much of a living but it beats the hell out of working."

Aoife shrugged. "One good thing about you, I suppose. You're never going to embarrass anyone with your success."

"Or my ambition."

"How long you home for?"

Paddy looked along the length of the bar, the place filling up now. "Who knows? I'm starting work with my old man in the morning. He has some hours in the club shop."

Aoife smiled across at him. "Welcome to the real world, Paddy," she said. "See how long you last."

Joe walked home along the Kilmore Road, the blisters bearable now in his Reeboks. His next task was to pack some things. A single suitcase would do, a few old clothes and maybe one of the wedding photos from the wall.

Enough to get by on; leave the rest to let her know he hadn't given up.

Seven years of marriage, he was thinking, and at least four of them had been good. Yeah, it was probably three years ago now when Stella had begun to get edgy, little things at first like when he'd come home and she'd be there with the property section of the *Times* open on the table. Sometimes she'd just toss it into the conversation. Not the really expensive stuff out in Ballsbridge or South County Dublin but more of a step up from what they had, the kind of house you'd need an junior executive's salary to afford. Once, she'd looked up at him over the dinner table and said, 'We ever have kids, I swear we're going to be living on top of each other.'

As though there was some doubt about it.

Which he supposed there was. Looking at it now, maybe she didn't really want to have kids. They'd talked about it, sure, but always as though it was some way off. A girl got married at twenty-five, it didn't mean she was going to spend her twenties with babies on her hip, did it? Still, she'd been saving for a long time now, leaving the mortgage to Joe and a good chunk of the bills – electricity, phone, Cablelink – looking after the day to day expenses but salting the rest away for holidays or emergencies. A small life assurance policy on Joe. She talked a lot about the future. She'd say, When things sort themselves out for us… Or sometimes she'd look at Joe and ask, You ever feel like you're stuck in a rut?

Joe always let it slide. The thing to do here was to get her to concentrate on the small good things in life. A good walk or, if he could knock off a little early, a nice dinner cooked by the time she got home.

Shortly before ten, the light was bleeping on the answering machine inside the hall door.

"Tom Reynolds here," the voice said. "Call me within an hour and you've got yourself a day's work. One of my guys has let me down. I've two others lined up but they're both monsters so you're the only one the uniform's going to fit. But I can't hang around on this so call me at 088-880631."

Joe headed towards the kitchen, the house desolate before him. "Well now," he said, "isn't that just a riot?"

15

George Costello said, “That’s our boy.”

Ed O’Brien watched Paddy Benner emerge from the side door of *The Yacht*, a slim guy with shortish brown hair, wearing a plain blue sweater and denims. Watched him hold the door open for a woman about the same age, Ed beginning settle into the evening now, thinking: If nothing else this might be interesting.

“Who’s the girl?” he asked.

Not expecting Costello to know.

“I think that’s Aoife Brennan. I tailed her a few times to see if she’d lead me to him but he left her high and dry.”

“They look young.”

“Benner’s twenty-six.”

“Which made him what? – eighteen when you had your run-in with him.”

“Old enough to know better than to fuck around with me, I tell you.”

O’Brien shrugged and said she wasn’t bad, maybe Costello could take this Benner guy off and give him another hiding while he looked after the girl. Costello was a tricky bugger to figure out. They’d worked together for six years while O’Brien was in Clontarf, serving time on the routine stuff – traffic duty and burglaries and sporting events – all the while figuring out how to make something on the side. The easiest way was to find yourself a garage owner who might be willing to pay for a little extra business. Just suggest his name every time you were called out to a crash. Same with an undertaker. A decent funeral could cost the guts of two grand, a small percentage of which got you a tidy little earner. Three, four hundred a month if you were lucky.

Only then Costello had gone and finally got himself

promoted and O'Brien had been moved to Coolock, parts of which were bandit country. Costello said the thing to do here was to keep the system going. A detective and a uniformed copper, working out of two different stations, as far as he could see there was no reason they couldn't double the revenue. Fifty-fifty, the same as before, and it would keep them in contact.

There was eleven years between them, Costello's forty-five to O'Brien's thirty-four, Costello thinking that gave him the right to make the rules.

"Well, George," O'Brien said, "you want to handle this any particular way?"

"Just haul him down the station and have a little fun. Let him know we're around."

"What're we bringing him in for?"

"We'd a burglary up on Dollymount Avenue last night. A couple of days after our boy arrives back home."

"And what's that got to do with me?"

"You have any burglaries in Coolock in the past few days?"

"There's always burglaries in Coolock."

"Well then," Costello said opening the car door. "Let's co-ordinate the investigation."

Paddy held the door open for Aoife saying, "That's the thing about sitting up at the bar. Go in at nine and you've a nice comfortable seat but soon as it gets near closing time you're wedged up against the counter and there's a stampede going on behind you." Aoife said, "You want to try *The Sheds*?" Paddy said, "The closer the better." Ready to continue the theme, about how packed pubs were bearable if you'd somewhere to put your pint, but otherwise it was a nightmare holding the bloody thing against your chest, thinking: Jesus, how am I going to light a smoke here?

Good cheerful stuff, hoping to get the conversation back on an even keel.

But looking up, he said, "Oh fuck, here's the coppers!"

And there they were. Good old George Costello, dirty great bullneck that he was and a sidekick Paddy didn't recognise, good looking guy with short dark curls.

He had a sinking feeling inside.

Blocking the footpath, Costello said, "Welcome home, Paddy."

Paddy sighed. "Sergeant Costello." Letting Aoife know this was the guy who'd beaten him up.

"It's Detective Costello now and we'd like you to come down the station," Costello said. "You happy to answer a few questions?"

"In relation to?"

"In relation to a burglary on Dollymount Avenue."

"Sure," Paddy said, "Always glad to co-operate."

Keeping it nice and straight. What was the point in arguing? Last time he'd been picked up by the Gardai, some big galoot had held him while Costello set to work with his fists. But this was different. The other copper, the good looking one, didn't seem primed for anything; just standing there with his hands in his pockets, sneaking the odd look at Aoife. Flexing their muscles, most likely.

He told Aoife he'd call her.

Then he was in the back of an unmarked cop car, picturing the look on her face as he was led away. She'd seemed frightened. Coppers unnerved a lot of people, that might've been it. Or maybe she was thinking, They're going to beat him up again. Either way it wasn't good. A quarter to eleven now, he should've been in a snug somewhere, explaining things, letting her know that he was a different man these days. Not telling her straight out, but talking in a nice reasonable tone about his mistakes so she could see it for herself.

He sighed and swore quietly. Maybe Aoife was on her way home asking herself: Do I really need this shit?

The room they brought him to was right at the back of the station, nothing much here apart from a table, some plastic chairs and a *No Smoking* sign. Paddy tossed his pack of Rothmans in the air and said, "I suppose that rules this out."

Both Gardai just turned and walked out.

Paddy wasn't surprised. The same as the last time. Bring him in, let him stew a while. The only way Paddy imagined you'd be nervous in a police station was either if you were innocent or an amateur. A pro knew the law and he answered whatever questions he wanted to answer. For most criminals, unless they managed to stay entirely anonymous, getting dragged down to the cop station was just another part of the business.

They left him there for fifty-five minutes.

Then apologised for the delay, Costello saying, "Before we begin here I'm obliged to inform you that you're entitled to legal counsel."

"What's this chap's name?"

"This is Sergeant Edward O'Brien from Coolock Station. You want a lawyer or not?"

"No."

"We'll be taping this conversation. You have any objection to that?"

"Be my guest," Paddy said.

Paddy watched Costello set up the tape recorder. It was a tricky situation, this one. Last time around he'd given Costello some lip and got a beating for his trouble. Stupid stuff. Saying, That's a grand ruddy complexion you've got there, what part of the country would you be from then? Making out as though Costello was fresh out of the sticks. Then after the charges had been dropped, he'd looked Costello in the face and said, Nice work, chum. You get me handed to you on a plate and you still manage to fuck it up.

Looking back on it now, maybe he'd deserved a few thumps.

Costello said, "I'm probably one of the few people happy to see you back again, Paddy. Where've you been?"

"Five years in the States. Since then I've been wandering around Europe."

"When'd you get home?"

"Two days ago."

"Which was what? Tuesday?"

"That's right."

"What time?"

"Sometime around eleven in the morning."

"You were somewhere in the region of Dublin Airport at

that time."

"I got the boat."

"From Holyhead?"

Paddy nodded.

"You'll have to speak your answers," Costello said. "For the benefit of the tape recorder."

"That's right. From Holyhead."

"You still have the ticket to prove that?"

Shaking his head, Paddy said. "I don't keep tickets." Knowing Costello had no reason to check the passenger list.

"Did you travel alone or is there anyone who can verify that that's the boat you came back on."

"I was alone."

"Well, Tuesday's the day we're interested in. Where'd you go after you got off the boat?"

"I went home."

"To your father's house on Mount Prospect Avenue?"

"Yes."

"Was your father there?"

"No."

"Did you have a key to get into the house?"

"No."

"Did you enter the house?"

"No."

"What did you do then?"

"I took a bus into town and then another out to Balgriffin cemetery."

"Why'd you go there?"

"To visit my mother's grave."

"And you went alone?"

"That's right."

"Is there anyone who can verify your whereabouts between two and three o'clock on Tuesday last."

Paddy shrugged. "Not as far as I know."

Costello looking across the table now. The other clown raising his eyebrows, Now isn't that interesting… Only he didn't seem interested at all. Everyone in the room knowing that Paddy had been dragged in for the sake of it.

"These places you've been," Costello said. "You hold down a job anywhere?"

"Not if I could help it."

"Any trouble with the police?"

Paddy shook his head. "No."

"You sure about that?"

"I got chucked out of the States, does that count?"

Costello turned to O'Brien. "What do you think, does it count?"

"What were you chucked out for?" O'Brien asked.

"Working as an illegal."

"Well, that's trouble with the law," Costello said and all of a sudden he clicked off the tape recorder. "And there's plenty more of it on the way. You know that, don't you?"

Paddy looked away. Nothing to see through the window but the glow of an orange streetlight.

"You broke into my house while my wife and kids were there. Remember?"

Silence.

"You think I'm going to forget that, Paddy?"

Still Paddy said nothing. He'd have apologised if he thought it might do some good. It was right there in Costello's eyes, the calm even stare: all the fury gone now, a guy who'd waited eight years and could hang on a little longer. For now Paddy knew the drill. Some more questions and then they'd let him go. Just testing the waters, seeing how far they could push.

Paddy sat and looked around the room. He'd have preferred a simple beating. This way he'd be looking over his shoulder, seeing if Costello was there.

Costello flicked on the tape recorder again. "Let's go over this once more, Paddy," he said. "You say you came on the early ferry from Holyhead…"

16

Friday morning, just after eight, Stella was back in her own house thinking maybe Joe wasn't so bad after all. Hit you a dig one day, leave fresh bread and milk for you the next.

But the same Joe was now in the past. Her father had said it and Ed O'Brien, the copper across the road, had said it – No one ever hits his wife just once. A thing like that becomes a habit. He wanders home after a few pints and all of a sudden you're right there in the firing line. Cook him peas instead of broccoli and bam! you're flat on your back again. Their description, not hers; but the principle still held true. Any woman who went back to a man who'd hit her was just asking for trouble.

In the letter he said he'd struck her out of frustration.

That, as far as she could see, was his problem. Her problem was where to go from here. She could press an assault charge, that was one possibility. There were plenty of others she knew who'd think that way. Say to themselves, Hey I got hurt here and damned if I'll be the only one. Only she wasn't that type of person. She was the type who could see the big picture, who could look beyond her own grievances and say, Maybe I'll let that one go.

In the letter Joe had pleaded with her.

Seven years, he'd said, don't they count for anything? Well, they counted for plenty. They were keeping him out of the criminal courts which was probably more than he deserved.

A court order however, Stella thought, that was a different matter. Like Ed from across the way had said, it was a simple act of self-preservation. Would Joe hit her again? It was unlikely. But then again, she'd never imagined him hitting her in the first place. She was on her own now. She was vulnerable. The court order would protect her physically, sure, but from here on in, she'd have to start looking out for herself. Most of their savings were in her account. There was some money in a joint account and she'd move that later today. Go see her solicitor first, then the bank. Or maybe the other way round in case Joe had any funny ideas.

What judge was going to award a house to a man who'd been barred from it?

She wouldn't make it across to Louis's funeral, which was a pity.

Ed O'Brien saw her step out of the car and thought well you had to give her credit. Half-seven in the morning, a dirty great shiner around her left eye and here she was making him feel as though he wanted to run over there and throw her onto the bed. Nice tight pair of jeans on today and one of those T-shirts that only came as far as the belt hooks.

Yeah, he thought, the bedroom, that'd be nice. Or maybe the kitchen. Or there was always the top of the stairs.

By five to eight he was standing on her doorstep.

"I've some stuff you might like to have a skim through. What we were talking about the other day."

Sitting at the kitchen table he told her all about it. About how there were actually four different types of court order. First you had your *Civil Order* and your *No Contact Order*, neither of which would be any use to Stella since one was pretty much for stalkers and the other could only be obtained if there were criminal charges pending. No, what Stella needed was a *Protection* Order. Or maybe a *Restraining Order*. Both being pretty much the same thing: first sign of a violation and Joe would find himself spending a night or two in the slammer. Only with a Restraining Order, you might get child support or maintenance or the family home. Or if there was any extra property, you might get that.

But first of all, you had to file for legal separation.

Just listing her options for her. "Maybe you'd like to come across for a bite to eat tonight and we could go through this properly."

She didn't seem to hear the offer. "The last one," she said, "the Restraining Order. That sounds like the one for me."

Paddy's father said, "Remember the customer's always right."

Paddy said as far as he was concerned the customer knew bog all. Any lip and someone'd be getting a three wood across the top of the conk.

"I can see you're going to be a success here," Des said.

That was the end of the good humour, Des explaining how to work the till, Paddy nodding and thinking, Why the hell hasn't she rung yet? Maybe he'd blown it the night before, all that stuff about how a criminal blocked the bad things from his mind, or telling her how he'd no ambition. Maybe he should've said, The remorse is killing me and I can't bear to think about it. Who knew what was the right thing to say? Eighteen to twenty-six, they were both different people now. He'd wanted to be honest with her. Within reason, of course. No point in telling her he'd come home because it was the only way to get out of England, that some poor fucker had got a bullet in the head because of a robbery that went sour…

There were things he wanted to say to her.

Maybe he should've come straight out with it like he'd planned to. Tell her he'd loved her eight years ago. Tell her he'd missed her ever since.

The least she could have done was pick up the phone.

Look at it like this, he thought: two coppers beat the hell out of an eighteen year old kid over a burglary charge that was dropped. Then, eight years later, as soon as the guy sets foot in the country, he's picked up again. One of the coppers is the same guy. Who knew where they were bringing him? Then his old girlfriend doesn't even call to see if he's still alive.

Well, maybe he was getting his answer without having to hear it.

Fuck it, he thought to himself.

As soon as his old man was gone, he took out a putter and began to roll a few balls along the carpet. Through the past eight years, he'd slept with fifteen, maybe twenty, women – some who wanted him to hang on and see how things panned out, others who were just as glad to see the back of him. The problem, generally, was finding something to talk about. Once he'd even thought about settling down. Four, maybe five years ago now, wandering around Boston with Carla Ancelotti, going through some of his savings but not worrying too much about it. Thinking maybe this wouldn't be such a bad life…

Once, on the way home from a Patriots game, she'd squeezed his hand and said, "Well, who'd have guessed it? Nice Italian girl like me falling in love with a mick." Just like that. It didn't frighten him at all. He was flattered. Terrific looking girl like Carla who could laugh and joke around as well as talk about pretty much whatever you wanted to talk about, who wouldn't be flattered? What frightened him was the way he smiled at her and said, "Well, I love you too." It was the purest deceit. Even in the short time it took to answer he knew he was calculating a lie. Which in a way was worse than the robberies. You broke into people's houses you could say, Fuck it, that's how I make my living. Or, if you were really in the mood for bullshit, you could tell yourself the only real loser was the insurance company.

Maybe he might've loved Carla Ancelotti if he hadn't been trying so hard to remember Aoife Brennan.

The same Aoife Brennan who hadn't even checked to see if he was still alive.

"Bollocks," he whispered and he rolled a Titliest Premier up to the skirting board.

The *Des Benner Golf Hut* stocked the latest line in Callaway drivers. There were Cabretta leather gloves at three for a tenner, Synchron II metalwoods for an even ton and five Scotty Cameron teryllium putters which hadn't been priced yet. There was a good clear view of the driving range where Des Benner was conducting a lesson.

Paddy reckoned you could go nuts hanging around here waiting for someone to come in.

He organised a three hole course for himself. Playing from the front door to the edge of the counter, an easy par three opener through the clothing section. Then he teed off at the counter and shot the other way off the skirting board underneath the driver rack. The last hole was a tricky one, the length of the shop and back again, in and out between the discount baskets and around behind the shoe stand.

He went around in fifteen – four over par.

Jesus, only thirty-five minutes gone.

An hour later he'd sold a Pringle sweater, a small pack of tees and a pair of Adidas golf shoes.

Then she walked in. Standing by the doorway now as he rolled his putt up to her. She stood on the ball and said, "You in the mood to explain what happened last night?"

Paddy felt relieved. His stomach turning suddenly but mostly relieved. "They asked me questions and I answered them."

"About what?"

"About where I was on Tuesday."

"And of course you had an alibi."

"Well actually…"

"Iron clad, no doubt."

"I didn't need one," he said. "It's up to them to prove…"

"And where were you?"

"Tuesday?"

"That's right. Tuesday."

"I got off the boat, dropped my bag home and went to tidy my mother's grave."

"And what'd they say to that?"

"It was Costello who was doing all the talking. The other bozo, he didn't give a shit. He knew it was all a load of cobblers."

She picked up the golf ball and looked at it. Paddy wondered what was coming. She said, "That's the bit I don't understand. Eight years, think how many cases that copper's had in the meantime and then as soon as you come back he drops everything just so he can pick you up. See my point?"

"I do. It's a good one."

"And?"

"You want to know what I'm not telling you."

"I just came here to see if you were all right. Tell what you want. You don't owe me anything."

"I ripped off his house."

"Costello's?"

"Took his badge and uniform and some of his wife's jewellery."

"And that's why he beat you up?"

Paddy shook his head. "No. That was *after* he beat me up. It was the only way I could get back at him so I went into his house while he and his wife and kid were watching the box. I rifled the upstairs. I threw the stuff in a bin on the way to the airport."

Watching her now, he wasn't sure what the look was telling him.

"Jesus, Paddy," she said, "you don't mind my saying so that was a really fucking stupid thing to do."

He stood and smiled at her. It gave him a strange feeling standing there, waiting for her to turn her back. It would be last he'd see of her. Out the door and gone… no point in following her. But watching her now, she didn't seem to be going anywhere. Looking at him funny again, appraising, maybe trying to figure out if he was telling the truth. Knowing it was better to leave but still standing in the doorway.

Then he guessed it. Maybe she was stuck.

Was it too much to hope for?

It could happen easily enough and who knew that better than Paddy did? Hit up with someone when you're young and leave yourself screwed when it came to other relationships. There were people, it seemed, who had the capacity to move on. Mope for a while and then maybe after a year or two, the hurt would ease.

It hadn't eased with Paddy.

Maybe it was because the relationship had never run to any conclusion. Everything fine, then suddenly a bombshell and it's over. No Dear John shit. No explanations.

Aoife said, "What's going to happen with us, Paddy?"

He shrugged. "I missed you, Aoif. Eight years and I missed you every single day."

She looked away and back again and shook her head slowly. "Don't look for any sympathy here," she said. "After the way you hurt me, you've no right to look for anything."

He showed her his golf course. The secret, he said, was to reach your par on the first two holes and let the third take care of itself. She said, “What’ll you do about your copper chum?”

“Sit and wait.”

“That’s it?”

“I’m hoping he’ll run out of steam. I’d be happy to tell him I’m sorry.”

“Only it wouldn’t work.”

“I doubt it.”

“You afraid of him?”

“Sure.”

“That he’ll beat you up again?”

Paddy shook his head. “That he’ll try to stitch me up,” he said. Stranger things had happened, he was sure of it. Come back some night and there he is on your doorstep, a search warrant in one pocket and a bagful of stolen jewellery in the other. What had to be remembered here was that you weren’t dealing with a rational human being. A conviction slips away through lack of evidence and next thing two grown men are in a deserted park kicking the shit out of an eighteen year old kid.

Officers of the law, no less.

No, he didn’t think Costello was the type to forgive and forget.

Aoife said, “I’m in Wexford until the weekend with some friends from the school. You want, you can take me somewhere nice on Saturday with your first ever pay packet.”

He smiled at her. Jesus, just like that.

She said, “If you’re not in jail, that is.”

“Of course. Goes unsaid.”

“I was thinking we might as well run with this thing and see where it leads.”

“Which might be nowhere.”

“Right,” she said. “Nowhere.”

“But at least there’s a chance we’ll able to move on.”

She sighed and moved towards him. “Maybe that,” she said. “If nothing else it has to be better than this.”

Paddy was ready to touch her, ready to take her hand in his and pull her closer, to smell her hair and feel her face against his… when his father walked in. Standing in the doorway now, arms out wide, grinning like a moron. Jesus, Paddy thought, the sheer uselessness of the guy! Big clown moving across the floor to her, grabbing her in a hug, saying how great it was to see her.

Crazy, Paddy thought, the way the old man could do it. A simple gesture of physical affection.

Still Saturday night and she'd be back again.

Des Benner said, "Just dropped home and there was a call for you. Some guy didn't leave his name. Said he was an old school pal and he'd call you back."

Paddy felt his mood swing back a little. Who from school would be calling him?

"You're not much of a receptionist," he said. "Either of you fancy a round on my little course here?"

17

It was the kind of shop, Joe imagined, everyone knows is there, a nice little location just off Grafton Street, but no one bothers going into. Small entrance at the front, opening out once you're inside, a soft carpeted staircase leading up to the second floor. Joe stood by the front door. He was wearing a freshly ironed blue uniform. He was thinking, Who the hell buys fur coats these days?

The fur coat, in Joe's opinion, was about the biggest thing you could get in the line of a luxury item. Yet here was a shop selling them in the middle of a recession. True, the second floor was leather goods entirely but downstairs there was what? …maybe two hundred furs. Coats, jackets, hats and scarves. Joe never saw anyone in a fur coat these days. Wear one in public and you'd be right there in the firing line, some animal rights nut tagging along with a bucket of paint.

That's what the country had come to, he reckoned. It was a question of lobbies and power groups and whoever had the most clout.

Also, Joe imagined, it was a question of employers having it easy. Take his industry for instance. Okay, so he himself had really only sold shampoo, but with minimal training he could sell pretty much anything in the cosmetics line. Hook up his old clients and see if he could branch out from there. But why would an employer bother to train someone when he's already got six resumes on his desk from salesmen who've been selling cosmetics? Why waste time fine-tuning a product when you've got the ready made one at your disposal?

Selling anyway was a matter of consistency.

Truth was, with any group of experienced salesmen there would be little to choose between them. Selling was about increasing your quota by fifteen, maybe twenty, percent each December when the figures were done. Do any higher than that and you could be screwed the following year. So what you were after was a good solid performance. Nothing spectacular. Nothing that might separate you from any other good candidates should you lose your job.

He suspected that this was as far as his luck was going to turn.

He stood in the doorway and waited for someone to take off down the street with a fur coat.

What now? he was thinking

Just after ten, William Brosnan, the owner of the shop appeared.

"There's a couple of scams you have to be alive to," he said. "One: someone grabs a coat and makes a run for it. Two: someone wears an old coat in and a new one out. Three: someone sticks a new coat under an old one and walks out. Four: someone tries to distract you while an accomplice steals the coat." He looked Joe in the face, almost like a threat. "You got all that?"

"Absolutely."

"So keep your eyes peeled."

"Of course."

"Just so we know where we stand. You watch the customers and I watch you. That's how it works."

Yes, it was work and there was a lot to be said for that.

But Christ, it was boring.

From what Joe remembered of security work you got a job that was either dangerous or one that'd have your brain turned to sludge half way through the shift. As security jobs went, this wasn't such a bad one. Regular hours, indoors, no one likely to come through the door with a sawn-off shotgun.

If nothing else it would be a lesson in humility.

No one even asked him his name. Three sales assistants – two upstairs, one down – that was the staff and you'd think one of them might have said "Hello." But no, it was like he was part of the furniture. Straight by him and Well, Gladys, how are you this morning? Gladys, that was one of them. Gladys and Damien up top while bossman William and Deborah manned the downstairs. The four of them standing at either end of the stairs now waiting for a customer, Deborah telling how she was Aquarius which meant she was not quite visionary but not far off it either. William saying he was Capricorn but was thinking about moving across to Leo.

Jesus, did they find that funny!

None with the manners to offer a simple *Hello*.

Still, Joe thought, it could be worse. Colm McCourt from down the road was working in McDonalds. So, this wasn't such a bad old station after all. Standing here like a tulip in a silly blue uniform, hearing Damien tell how he, his sister, his brother and *both* his parents were all Virgos.

Thinking, Well would you fucking credit that?

Just before eleven Deborah disappeared. Ten minutes later she was back with a cardboard tray containing four coffees. She turned to Joe:

"Sorry, did you want something?"

The way Joe shook his head, he knew it unnerved her. Nice and slow, as if he was thinking about something else, something related to her but nothing to do with coffee.

"Fine then," she said and moved quickly away.

He shrugged and looked back to the television monitor that showed the upstairs. It would be interesting to see if he was offered coffee tomorrow.

This job, it gave you plenty of time to think. About Stella, of course, but also about Louis and the way he'd died. It was bizarre, Joe thought, the conversation he'd had with the Irish Mormon, about how he'd thought all the Mormons were yanks and the way the guy had just looked him in the face and said, No Sir, we're the fastest growing religion in the world. The whole thing had an unreal feel to it. What frightened him most was the coldness. How could a man, a murderer, appear so plausible? How could someone pull a gun and shoot an innocent man in the face like that?

A different city, sure. A different country too. But every now and then Joe would feel a shiver down his spine.

They were funny to watch.

Gladys was his favourite, or maybe Deborah, he couldn't decide: Gladys in her late forties, all that make-up doing the trick unless you caught her directly under the light. Everything about her – walk, clothes, expression – telling you here's a woman who knows her furs.

Aah, she'd say, I think that's the one all right.

Or else: Absolutely stunning and there's no other word for it.

What they needed were a few tips. Right after his lecture on courtesy, he decided, he'd help them. Courtesy and humility, they'd be his themes today – sit the four of them down in the middle of the shop and offer a few home truths. Begin maybe with a little question and answer session to get them involved. What is courtesy? he'd ask. Who needs courtesy the most? Set up a little makeshift blackboard and have them come up to write their answers.

Any of you ever been really humiliated? he'd ask them.

Here's a story, he'd say:

Pal of mine gets chucked out of his job because some machine can do what he does faster and he goes to work in McDonalds. Forty-five years of age, with a wife and two kids to feed, so he does it. He puts on that uniform and he eats twenty-five different flavours of shit each day. He cleans up other people's rubbish and empties it into a bin that says *Feed Me*. He sets up those little plastic yellow men and mops in between. And you know what he tells me? He says, I can handle it all, Joe, everything, except when my kids' friends come in. That's the only really hard bit.

The moral being…

Anyone at all?

Joe decided he could wait with the moral, that's what being a teacher was all about. Wait them out. Toss the chalk up in the air a few times and when they couldn't get it, he'd say, let's leave the moral for later and talk a little about unemployment. What it does to you inside. Or what it does to your wife and your kids and your friends. Yes, he'd say, your friends too. Pal rings you, asks if you're going for a pint, what do you say? No can do, that's what you say, and he offers to stump up double but both of you know that only screws up the relationship. Either end of the phone line, sure, but you both know the other guy's embarrassed. Then two weeks later he stops ringing.

The moral, he'd tell them, is that it can happen to anyone.

Even to Deborah, bursting a gut now, Joe watching her and thinking, She can't sell for shit. Her trick was stick the coat onto some rich cow's back and step away with this expression like someone had stapled her lips shut. Terrified to commit herself. Watching the customer's face, ready to gush of course but holding fire in case the customer didn't think much of the coat.

No two ways about it, it was funny to watch.

Only she sold the coat. One and a half grand's worth of fur heading out the door, Joe barely able to believe it.

Jesus, he thought, maybe there's more to this than meets the eye.

Four on the dot and the shop closed for half an hour, Damien saying, Last in goes for the coffee, I believe.

Joe wanted to punch his lights out. Walk over there nice and casual and bury the little fucker into a pile of sables. No problem. Standing there in his cashmere sweater, his flecked trousers and his black patent shoes, treating Joe like a houseboy. Saying, Yeah, we'll acknowledge you as long as you get our coffee for us.

Gladys said, "What's your name by the way?"

Deborah said, "I'm Deborah, it's good to have you aboard."

Walking down the street with William Brosnan's fiver in his pocket, it finally occurred to Joe what was going on. On a building site it was the glass hammer routine, send the rookie across the site to ask for a glass hammer, sit back and wait… Or what was the other one? The sky hook, that was it. Head on over there and ask Ulick Magee for his sky hook and make sure you don't come back without it.

Hilarious, Joe thought.

But at least it was acknowledgement of some sort. The three back at the shop, they'd ignored him. Nothing, not a word. Letting him know what? That there was a system in operation? That there was a pecking order and once that was understood, he could tell them his name.

Jesus, where would you get it?

When he got back, they were sitting next to the counter, a small pack of doughnuts on the ground between them. Five chairs in a circle, Joe's waiting for him. William saying, "Soon as we finish tonight, I'll show you round the place. See what you think of this security system I've put in place."

"Sure," Joe said.

And why not? he thought. It was better than telling the guy he was a prick and finding yourself fired for it.

"Grab yourself a bun there, Joe," William said. "Damien's in the middle of a story."

18

Stella Faherty had been holding plenty of stuff inside. It was in her eyes, Ed thought, as much as in anything she said.

The worst, it seemed, was the way Joe would try to cheer her up. He'd tell her to think of the good things – the nice house that was keeping them warm, the fortnight in Spain every July. Or a good meal. Some days she'd get home and there'd be candles in the middle of the table. Candles and napkins and Joe holding the seat for her. Expecting her to smile. Expecting her to say, Isn't this wonderful! Seven years, she said, in the same shitty three bedroom house and you were expected to look excited if you had your dinner cooked for you.

The problem with Joe, she said quietly, was that the guy was a loser.

No ambition, that was a big part of the problem. No imagination either.

She said, "You probably want to know why I married him. Well, if I knew the answer to that I could open a course and save everybody a lot of trouble. The crazy thing was, I think I panicked. You believe that? Twenty-four years old, not a bad looking girl if I do say so myself and I swear to Christ, I think I panicked. You've got to understand something here – my life seemed to be going nowhere. You grow up in a two bedroom house with four other kids and the first thing you want to do is get the hell out of there."

Ed had already heard that bit. He wanted to move things along. Things were just getting interesting now – nothing like the low-down on a couple of neighbours if you could get it – so who needed another run through her childhood? He hoped this wasn't going to be another Liz Sheridan. Three, maybe four, weeks now since he'd met Liz, her mother's back door having been jimmied,

Ed seeing her as a mousy little brunette but thinking, Well, maybe still waters run deep. Four solid hours he'd listened to her and then, later on, ten minutes spent hammering away on top thinking, Jesus, she still alive? Liz staring over his shoulder at the ceiling like a dead fish.

The first thing Stella had said tonight was, "You've no idea how good it feels to be back in your own bed again."

She said, "I never thought I'd have to spend another night in that house."

Ed sat and listened. Let her talk. That was the secret, he knew, letting them talk, keeping up eye contact and nodding at whatever shit they threw your way. Especially with looks like his. Most women, he knew, would take a look and think: That fella, he's full of himself. So what Ed did, he bought them dinner and he listened. He laughed and made sympathetic faces and about fifty percent of the time he got his rocks away at the end of the night.

Stella from across the road, however, might require a different tactic. By the looks of things she seemed to have had enough of guys who'd hold the door open for you or walk on the outside or tell you how lucky you really were. Now she was saying, "The first few years, they were okay. We looked like we might be going somewhere. Plenty of disposable income. No kids and am I glad I insisted on that? But then you begin to get a feeling. What you do, you marry someone and you're saying to them, Let's set out on a life together and see what it can bring us. It's a journey. You're ambitious. Not just for yourself but for your husband too and your kids if you have any. It's a sorry disappointment, I tell you, when he says – this is it, like it or lump it."

Ed asked if Joe had actually said that.

"Not in so many words," Stella said. "That's what I'm trying to tell you, it's a feeling. Christ knows, it'd be easier if he'd just come out and said it. Then you could say, Either shape up or on your way, pal. But it was sneakier than that. It was like he was stonewalling me. Pretending nothing was wrong, so I'd always have to make the first move. Making me out to be the baddie in the whole affair. That's what weak people do, they blame whoever's next to them."

Ed just stared for a moment: she'd lost him now.

"What Joe lacked most of all was guts. That's all it would've taken. A little guts, a little self-belief. Walk into the boss's office and say, Let's talk promotion or I'm on my way. And if he calls your bluff then so be it. But Jesus it has to be better than letting your life pass you by."

Ed filled her glass. The early signs weren't good – not like with Liz Sheridan where it was just a matter of staying awake and nothing surer than you'd be in the scratcher before long. Stella, though, she was harder to figure. Not disinterested, no, but not particularly interested either; more like there were priorities and finding a new man was down the list.

He was glad he hadn't gone overboard on the meal. Simplicity, that was the message he was trying to put across: a simple gesture of kindness between two neighbours.

When the bell rang he excused himself. Had the night been a little further along he'd have said, Let them come back. He'd done it before with the phone. Sitting with some woman, either end of the couch, and you make eye contact and tell them to keep going with their story.

Jesus, they loved that. So interested you couldn't even drag yourself away to answer the phone.

When he pulled back the front door, he shook his head and said, "And what in the name of sweet Jesus might you be doing on my doorstep?"

"Fighting crime," George Costello said stepping inside. "What else do I ever do?"

A woman with a shiner, no less.

Maybe this was the reason O'Brien hadn't been returning calls. Three calls, three messages and not a dicky bird in return so George Costello stepped inside, happy to be friendly about it, but thinking maybe he'd have to explain a few things to Private Ed O'Brien. Tell him the thing about being a Private was that you were bottom of the shitheap. Tell him next time a detective rings you, you pick up the fucking phone and call him right back.

Maybe he'd come right out and say it now, he hadn't fully

decided yet.

Shiner or no shiner, she wasn't bad. George knew where she'd got it too. The husband from across the road had clocked her one and now Ed was doing his best to move in, buying bottles of wine and cooking what looked like a fish pie. Sitting there with a sincere look on his face no doubt, hearing what a brute the husband was. Which showed how incredibly dim he really was. Two places you didn't leave your dirt – home and work. But try telling Ed that.

George Costello introduced himself and said, "There's a lady looks like she's been in the wars."

"Things've been better," she said.

"Want some advice?"

"The good solid kind?"

"I don't offer anything else."

"Let me guess. You're going to tell me not to go back."

"Got it in one. It'll only happen again."

"Thanks," she said. "That seems to be the popular opinion."

What struck George was that there was no self-pity in her voice. Some women, they got a clip and Jesus, you'd think they'd gone fifteen rounds but this Stella woman just looked him in the face and said, Let me guess… Really saying, You're nuts if you think I'm going back there. She was tough, he could sense it. Sitting here now, nice and relaxed with two coppers, sipping her wine, not showing the slightest bit of embarrassment. Embarrassment or fear or shame, they were the reasons a woman didn't press a charge, the thought that someone might think she'd been asking for it. The worst were the ones who came in screaming and then two hours later they'd be begging you to let the husband go.

She told him she wasn't going to bother pressing charges. "What's the point?" she said. "It was worth it to be rid of him."

"That's what you want to be sure of."

"Well, that's why I'm here. Ed has some stuff photocopied for me."

"On what to do to get an injunction?"

"If that's what I need."

"It is and you've come to the right place. Get yourself a

solicitor and he'll charge by the hour. We're in the middle of a case at the moment but Ed can spare a few moments. This big-time burglar has come back from Europe and we've got him under surveillance. I just dropped by to discuss a few things but I can wait 'til tomorrow. If I can get him to return my calls, that is." Looking over the table, Costello said, "He must've been out buying fish today."

She laughed at that one, a nice gentle laugh showing her white teeth.

"Or else he was in the wine shop," he said and watched the smile fade a little, George knowing he was killing the joke, but having a good time, feeling O'Brien's stare next to him. Yes, this was fun. Letting the fucker squirm a little. Tossing in that bit about the phone calls so he'd know the reason. Deciding if he was going to stay or not, whether or not he'd sit down and finish off that fish pie that looked so nice.

Yes or no, that was the question. Twist the knife or show a little mercy.

"Must run," he said finally.

He gave Ed O'Brien an affectionate thump on the shoulder.

"Ten tomorrow morning we'll be interviewing our suspect. Be there or be square."

Stella said, "He makes you nervous." Ed said, "Well yeah, that's Costello for you, he makes most people nervous."

He wondered if she'd seen it, right there in Costello's eyes. Dull eyes, not much life in there, but watching all the time. Eyes you came across every now and then in Ed's line of business.

Maybe he could explain it to her, he thought. How it was really a question of focus.

Take this Paddy Benner for instance. Here was a man, if he had any sense, would be well advised to beat it out of Dodge. What was the percentage in staying, after all? The thing about Costello was that he was a pitbull; once he got his teeth into something there was no shaking him off.

The night before, they'd had an argument. Right after wasting an hour and a half rousting Paddy Benner what does Costello do only stick his mitt out, same as every other month.

Which by now was wearing thin. The original idea was that they would double their income. Ed would keep supplying the garage and the undertaker and he'd keep collecting every fourth Friday. It was harder to direct the business from Coolock to Clontarf but he was doing okay, just gently suggesting the best way to sort things, waiting for Costello to start bringing in his share.

Ed taking the risks, Costello sitting back and waiting for the end of the month.

Then trying to let Ed know who was boss. A bloke who listens only to his langer, Costello had said, he's not in the best bargaining position. Just tossing it in to let Ed know who had the most to lose. Three strikes and then you were out and Ed had already screwed up twice; once when he knocked off early to suss out another copper's wife, once because he'd bottled it which could happen to anyone. Which was why he'd hooked up with Costello in the first place. Try paying a mortgage in Dublin on a private's salary and see what you had left at the end of the week.

He'd been stupid, he knew this now, always agreeing to make the collection.

"You know this big time burglar Costello was telling you about," he said. "It's just a vendetta against some bloke who burgled his house. Or maybe he didn't, who knows? What I do know is that eight years ago this kid is pulled in for a string of burglaries on what is pretty flimsy evidence, and he walks. So then Costello gets hold of him one night and gives him a couple of slaps. Which could mean anything. I've seen Costello dish out a few slaps alright and I've seen him really lay the boot in when he's in the mood. Then the following night his house is burgled and Costello goes looking for the guy. Only he's disappeared. That was eight years ago and now this guy has popped up again."

"What's he like?" Stella asked. It surprised him; he didn't think she'd be interested.

Ed shrugged. "Very calm."

"That's it? Calm?"

"He came out of *The Yacht* with some old girlfriend and it was as if he'd been expecting us. Just said, Fair enough, when Costello asked him to come down the station. Which made me think he was used to it. But this was different. Most regular criminals, you drag them in and they put up a wall. The hostility, you can sense it."

"What made this one different?"

"He seemed just like an ordinary joe."

"Apart from how calm he was."

"Exactly. Most people find a cop station intimidating. But he just sat there and answered the questions. Very polite even though he knew we were just jerking him around."

Stella shrugged. "What's any of this got to do with you?"

"Nothing. Costello just called and asked me to come along."

"As a favour?"

"I suppose so. We're not even working in the same station anymore. Now I bet he's already rung my Super with some shit about how we're co-operating on a case. Just to get me released tomorrow."

"Why don't you just tell him you're not interested?"

"Maybe it's not that easy," he said.

She was smiling now. "Know what I think?"

"What?"

"I think he's got something on you."

Which was where she'd been leading the conversation. She'd sensed a tension and now she was fishing for the reason. Idle curiosity, most likely. And she'd guessed right. If the scam with the undertaker and the garage came out, who was first in line to go? But that wasn't why Costello's visit had shaken him. You had to know Costello to understand it, the way he sometimes turned the screw slowly. Starting with Stella if he wanted to. Let her know she was just one in a line, that five years ago a copper had been isolated because Ed had momentarily lost his nerve.

That was Costello's style. Say it just to mess up Ed's chances of getting Stella into the scratcher.

He didn't intend giving up on Stella just yet but he had some ground to make up after tonight. "You want to get down to work on these papers?" he asked.

"No hurry," Stella said. "I'm enjoying hearing about the tensions amongst the Gardai."

19

The music started at 1:30 a.m. Joe had slept for an hour but now he was awake again – the different bed maybe – lying here now hearing what sounded like U2 coming through the walls. His sister Jean had told him to expect it. Anywhere between one and two, she said, continuing for a couple of hours and generally knocking off before four.

The house next door was rented to three Engineering students. That was all Jean knew. She guessed maybe they did bar work in the evenings, getting home late and sleeping late when it suited, going back down the country on the odd weekend when it was quiet. At first, Jean said, she'd tried to be friendly. She'd asked what they were studying and they said Engineering and she sat in their living room and explained the situation, how her tenants were having trouble sleeping with the level of noise on the other side of the wall. All she was requesting was a little consideration.

Two days later she asked for the name of the landlord. They said, Why don't you go fuck yourself, Missus!

Which opened the way for Joe's rent-free accommodation. He wasn't quite sure what he was going to clear at the end of the week in the fur shop, but after paying his share of the mortgage and feeding himself, he doubted he'd have much to offer Jean. Not that she'd mind. Jean owed him. Jean had been to college. Four years at Trinity studying Chemistry while Joe supplemented his mother's pension, even putting a little aside for books or so he could slip her a few quid at the weekend. It made him feel good, looking out for his sister. It made him feel responsible. And now she had the chance to do something for him.

On average, Jean said, it took eight to ten weeks to get rid of a tenant. She said, "You've no idea how hard it is. Even the messers, you can't just kick them out."

Now Joe was lying on the bed and staring at the cracked ceiling. Two hundred and ten quid a month for two rooms; let the mortgage payments go and a place like this was affordable. Simple as that. Just let it slide. Only that mortgage payment, it was his one remaining contact with Stella. She'd calm down, he was sure of it, and he needed to be in good shape when she did. The cheque would come through the door letting her know he was turning things around.

The music stopped.

2:05. Not too bad.

Then it started again. What was it this time? Joe didn't recognise the band, some rock shit, thud! thud! against the wall next to his left ear.

He turned over and put the pillow over his head. Then thought, Why not? and reached for his trousers.

It was a young guy, nineteen or twenty maybe, who answered the door. One of those rocker types with long shaggy hair and a leather waistcoat.

"I'm your next door neighbour," Joe said.

"Yeah?"

"I was wondering if you wouldn't mind keeping the music down."

"Bothering you, is it?"

"'Fraid so. Most people are trying to sleep at this hour."

The young guy shrugged. "Okay," he said. "Why not?"

The door was practically closed again when Joe said, "You sure about that now?"

The door opened again.

"What'd you say?"

"I said, You sure about that?"

"You got a problem?"

"Only in as far as you owe me an apology."

The guy was smiling now, leaning against the door jamb and running his fingers through the mop. "You think so?"

"I do actually," Joe said. "But that can wait. My real problem is that the landlady has already been onto you about this. The last tenants moved out since they couldn't stand the racket."

"People move out for all kinds of reasons."

"Then you told her to go fuck herself."

"Must've been one of the others. I'd never use language like that."

Joe shrugged. "I just want to know what the story is. I don't want to be back here tomorrow night so you can say the same thing to me."

Another smug one, laughing now. "You want me to tell you now?"

"It'd save me coming back tomorrow."

"Fair enough," the guy said. "You can go fuck yourself as well."

Joe shrugged again. "At least we know where we stand," he said and he turned away. He felt tired. One o'clock in the morning, why wouldn't he be? – but it was more than that. A month like the one he'd had, it was bound to take its toll. Louis getting a bullet in the head and Stella turning against him which he never thought she would. His CV getting chucked in the bin. The fight with Stella and starting his new job.

Now this.

More than tired. It was though all the fight had left him. The frustration and the anger, they were gone now. All that was left was this tiredness. Forty next birthday and already he had the feeling that his time had passed.

Joe shook his head and trudged back to his new flat. By the time he made it to his bed, the music had been turned up a few notches. He picked up his pillow and blankets and went into the other room.

When Paddy thought of boys being close to their fathers he thought of them attending sports fixtures together. He thought of a football being punted back and forth in the park and then, later on, when the boy was older, long talks about friendships, girls, careers. It was the best a father could hope for, he imagined, that once the kid reached a certain age maybe they could still spend a few hours together. Paddy's earliest memories, when Des was still on the Tour, were of a father who came and went, who usually had a gift but if he didn't, well hey, that was your tough luck. He could remember the feeling it gave him to stand up in class tell everyone his father was a golf professional. He could remember Des saying, "Just you and me, kiddo, that's how it works. Your mother's the best in the world but Jesus, she can get the wrong end of the stick at times."

Other things too. The silences, for instance. Or his mother's smile when Des landed the job in the golf club. He remembered his father saying, "That's where golfers go to die, isn't it?"

Which just about summed it up, Paddy thought. The guy had regrets, he had to. His marriage, for one, but mostly his career, Des moving from schoolboy prodigy to a real championship prospect to a guy who had a reputation for playing a brilliant front nine. All that talent and it still wasn't enough. Paddy would ask him about it someday. They'd sit down together and talk it out. Not the shitty stuff – what was the point in dragging that up? – but there were other things to discuss. Sport, of course, but not just sport. Like how you coped with a regular life once your dream had turned sour.

Not like an ordinary father and son, it was too late for that, but maybe they might get to know each other a little. If things panned out with Aoife, he could hang on long enough for that.

Saturday morning and Paddy had never felt better – the shop to himself since Des was up North for a couple of days playing in a Pro-Am. The first customer wanted a bucket of balls for the driving range. "Sure," Paddy said, "but Des always says that's a mug's game. He says everyone drops their shots on the green so they'd be better off at home practicing their putting on the sitting room carpet."

The customer seemed a good humoured chap, a nice round belly on him sticking out of a bright yellow Pringle sweater. "You Des's son?"

"That's right."

"You want to learn something about golf?"

"I want to learn something about anything."

"Well, most people play to get out of the house. It's not really in my interest to let the wife know I can just as easily play at home."

Paddy grinned. "That's a fair point," he said and he went to fetch the balls.

Paddy was enjoying the work today. He was busy. All the time he'd spent through the week practicing his putting or making sure every bucket had exactly the same number of balls… By half-ten he was being run off his feet.

Thinking, This beats the hell out of hanging around.

Then looking up and seeing Costello and his chum Ed O'Brien walk into the shop. He knew what was coming.

"Officers?" he said.

"Let's go, Paddy" Costello said. "We might as well do this down the station."

Practically shouting it, just in case there was anyone in the far corner hard of hearing. Paddy looked at O'Brien. O'Brien shrugged.

"Nothing we can handle in the back room here?" Paddy said.

Costello shook his head. "We're asking you to come down the station with us."

Paddy picked a club from the rack. "Can't tempt you to this Callaway driver, can I? Come in handy if you need to biff an unruly suspect."

"You willing to come with us or do you want to conduct the interview in front of these people?"

Dead silence. The whole shop listening. "Why not?" Paddy said. "It beats working."

They brought him to the same detention room as the last time, Paddy sitting and waiting and wondering where this was going to end. Costello's game was a simple one: he wanted people to know Paddy was a thief. First Aoife and now the customers in the shop, just jerking him around for the sake of it.

But what next?

Paddy walked to the window and looked through the grille. He could see a few cop cars, two Carinas and an Opel Montego; beyond that the promenade and the sea and then the sky, a clear blue today apart from a few puffy white clouds. He looked at his watch. The shop was closed half an hour now; the old man was losing money. He needed to sort this matter out. Either get

Costello off his back or get a lawyer onto the case. See if a harassment charge calmed things down any. If nothing else, it might be useful to have this on record if he suddenly found himself stitched up.

Or it might just make Costello more determined.

As soon as the two boys came back into the room, Costello said, "You mind if we tape this interview?"

"Go right ahead. But I'd like to get a few things straight first."

"You want a lawyer? You're entitled to have a lawyer here with you."

"No. I don't want a lawyer. I want you to consider something."

"What?"

"That I might be a different person to when we had our run-in last time round. You ever think about that?"

"Sure, I thought about it."

"And?"

"The likes of you won't change. I want *you* to consider something."

"Go ahead."

"That you broke into my house and stole from my family. You never go near a copper's family."

"What about you and some big fuckin' mongo thumping the shit out of me in St Annes Park. You remember that, don't you?"

Costello shook his head. "I don't remember that at all."

"Well, I remember it. I kept thinking, Jesus he has to stop soon only you didn't, you just kept going. I thought you were going to kill me."

"I already told you. I've no recollection of that."

Paddy sighed. It was like talking to the wall, big ignorant prick with that smug look on his face, sitting back in the seat knowing he was in control. He knew Paddy didn't want to lodge a complaint.

"Answer me this then," Paddy said.

"Fire ahead."

"You going to stitch me up?"

Costello shook his head. "Wouldn't dream of it. You know

why?"

"Why?"

"Because that'd be too easy. But when you slip up, which I know you're going to do, I'm going to be there. I might even come visit you in the Joy. You want to know why?"

"Tell me."

"Because that's the way things are. Sure as you're sitting there in front of me, that's where you'll end up. It'd be a shame for me to miss it."

Paddy sat back in the seat. Costello flicked on the tape recorder and went through the rigmarole introducing the interview: it seemed some house on Victoria Road had been ripped off early yesterday morning.

"Friday morning," Paddy said. "I started work at nine and I was there all day…"

20

Aoife sat in the bar in *The Hollybrook Hotel* sipping from a bottle of Budweiser, thinking about Paddy Benner and how she'd be crazy to expect too much from him. Eight years on the hoof and suddenly he turns up again. No explanation as to why, nothing, just straight back into her life, telling her he'd missed her every single day. Which he had no right to do. Not after the way she'd missed him. In different ways at different times, she now supposed: crying herself to sleep for the first few months, which was to be expected, telling no one and feeling as though she was carrying a rock around in her stomach. Then resigning herself to seeing out the year. Since that's what she believed people did – they took a year out and then they came back and picked up where they left off.

After fourteen months she called around to his father.

Then she knew she was wasting her time. Paddy was gone. God himself knew where but he was gone and it was madness, she knew, moping like this. She was young. Her whole life was opening out in front of her. The thing to do was to involve herself in the university. She joined the English Society and the Literary & Historical Society and she went out with Barry Ryan who had a habit of tracing his name on the back of her hand with his index finger. Barry sat next to her in lectures. He spoke earnestly about Chaucer and Wordsworth and what they meant to him. Through the week Aoife studied or did lounge work and then, come Friday, she'd take in a film with Barry or if there was a party taking place, they'd go to that. It was okay. She liked the routine.

Towards the end of the first year she said, "I'm sorry but I need to be on my own."

Leaving her free again. She felt lost. Attending college with seven thousand others and each day her overriding feeling was one of being alone. Alone in a crowd, which was the worst kind, leading her to take up with a rugby player named Stephen Prescott. This was a different scene altogether. Here you stuck on your make-up and got your backside frozen off watching the match. You smiled and you clapped and you sipped your glass of Heineken. It was a miserable time. Always waiting for the end of the night when Stephen would roll off her, and she'd look at the ceiling and think, Jesus what am I doing here?

She could remember a poem she'd written in a tutorial at the end of third year.

Twenty-eight steps to my room:
I count each one now,
Coming home alone.

Twenty years old, her life in front of her, and here she was writing poems about being alone. The next day when Barry Ryan asked if the poem was about him, she shook her head and said, "You never even had a chance, did you?" Same with the others. They never had a chance either. Decent enough guys for the most part, the problem with each being... well, he wasn't Paddy. Which was crazy since she'd never really known Paddy in the first place. Paddy had deceived her. He'd lead a double life and then when things turned sour he'd taken off.

Leading her to ask, Why him?

She had no idea.

It wasn't looks anyway, that was for sure. He'd always been slight and even now at twenty-six he hadn't filled out much. A stick insect, she used to call him. She'd grab him around the waist and say, Pleeeese give a little, it'll help a lot. But his face, she'd loved his face. The face and the curls but mostly the face, the way his eyes would crinkle up at the sides when he smiled. Best was the way he could deadpan it. Big gang of people talking about politics or something and Paddy would start up about how a gorilla had stolen his Choc Ice on the train that morning. She loved the way he'd do it. A nice serious voice and the folks would be looking from one to the other thinking: What *is* this idiot on about?

Time flew when Paddy Benner was around.

He made her laugh, that was a big part of it. He made her feel as though there was something special happening around her.

Still she was wondering: How long did *you* count the steps for?

When Paddy saw the poem printed on the back of a beermat he said, "It's a beauty."

"I know it is," she said. "You know what a haiku is?"

"It's a three line poem."

"Seventeen syllables, a seven and two fives, they're the rules. Guess what the tutor said?"

"He said: How about I give you a good stiff poling on the couch up in my office?"

"No. He said, 'Actually that's not bad.'"

"*Actually?*"

"Can you believe it?"

Paddy shook his head, amazed. "Ever write any others?"

"That's it, the collected works. Produce a masterpiece first time out and where do you go from there?"

Tonight they were sitting as far as you could get from the counter without being blasted out of it by the telly. Paddy had spent the day worrying. First about Aoife and whether her mood might have changed, then about Costello, all the while wondering who was the old school friend who'd telephoned. There was something odd about it. Some bozo calls out of the blue and won't leave his name. Then he seems to give up. If it's worth a call in the first place, why not try again? Why not leave a message on the machine asking Paddy to call him back?

Maybe it was nothing.

Even so, Paddy was carrying his knife once more. It was a butcher's trimming blade. All the days he'd spent playing pool, he'd carried it in a sheath taped between his shoulder blades. He'd never used it. A couple of times he'd been ready to, sure, just ram it into the biggest guy's neck and run like fuck, but he'd always managed to calm things. In a situation like that it was a question of letting the money slide. It was a question of humility, being willing to take whatever shit was being offered and to pay for the privilege.

Paddy felt safer with the knife on him.

Tonight he was carrying it taped to the inside of his leg. The back offered easier access but what about Aoife? She might put her hand on his back. He couldn't risk her finding it. Costello was a tricky one to explain, but a knife?

Now she said, "Sell any golf clubs today?"

"I was doing okay," Paddy said, "until Costello turned up."

"Uh-oh."

"Uh-oh is right. I'm there selling my little heart out and then he barges on in shouting it all over the shop how he wants me to come down the station."

"Trying to embarrass you."

"I think so."

"What about the sidekick?"

"O'Brien?"

"That his name?"

Paddy nodded. "He was there but he's hard to figure out. He just sits and looks like he couldn't give a flying shit what's going on. Every now and then he might ask a question, just for the sake of it, and then he drifts off again."

"He knows Costello just wants to mess you around."

"I tried to explain that I might not be the same person who ripped off his house."

"And?"

"He said he'd nail me if it was the last thing he did."

Aoife sighed. "Well, it was worth a try."

Paddy watched her in the pale light, noticing the freckles across her nose again, the way she'd fiddle with her rings when she was thinking something through. It was a difficult one, she said. Costello was determined. He'd a wasp up his backside and as far as Aoife could see nothing was going to shift it. Paddy needed to protect himself, find himself a lawyer.

The problem being: a complaint might only make things worse.

But then again – how much worse could things get?

"You have to ask yourself," she said, "what's his next step once he gets tired of dragging you down the station. Or once he sees he's not really hurting you. What then? Does he take you back into the park and beat you up again? He says he's going to wait you out but what happens when he gets sick of waiting? Then he's going to think something up."

Paddy didn't say anything.

"How else is it going to end?" she said. "You tell your old man about this?"

"He's up in Belfast 'til tomorrow evening playing in a Pro-Am."

"You getting on okay?"

"With Des?"

"I always liked Des."

"Everyone likes Des. Des is a lovely guy until you need him somewhere he doesn't want to be. Then you might as well forget about him. It's what screwed him up on the circuit."

"I don't get you."

"He was weak."

"When he was playing?"

"Everywhere. But most places, it doesn't show like it does in golf. That's what's so great about sport. Any weakness and it's exposed. There's a ball and a hole and you either put the ball in the hole or you don't. You either hold your nerve or you bottle it."

"And your Dad couldn't hold his nerve."

"'Fraid not. The other day, I was watching him out the window of the shop showing some punter how to do it and Jesus, even now, you've never seen such a perfect swing. But a perfect swing only goes so far when you're a shot behind at the sixteenth. Then you need something old Des never had."

"You think that was what started him with the women?"

"How do you mean?"

"Once he wasn't a champion, then he went off the rails a bit."

Paddy shook his head. "I'd imagine he was screwing around when he was on the Tour. Old Des always took the easiest option. Sometimes that was to hop into the sack with some bimbo and sometimes it was to lose."

He watched her with a beermat now, working it over,

bending it into quarters, then peeling the edges. “You still blame him, don’t you?” she said.

“For Mum?”

“That she was killed.”

“I blame myself for lying to her. Even after we got home from London that time, after I’d had the shit kicked out of me, I told her Des and I just got separated in the crowd. He told me what to say and I said it. I was scared she’d boot him out of the house. But other than that I don’t think about it much any more. Except how everyone thought she’d topped herself. I find it hard to accept that she’d just leave me like that. I worshipped the old man, until I saw through him at any rate, but I was always much closer to her. She was the one who’d be there when I got home. There were two buses one after the other. I think maybe she didn’t hear the second one and stepped out in front of it.”

“Two 44A’s on the same road. Jesus, she was unlucky.”

“I mean, why wait for the second one? Why not throw yourself under the first one?”

“Maybe she thought the second one might crash.”

Paddy nodded. “You’re not being much help here,” he said and watched her grin. “But she was tough, much tougher than Des. That’s where I got it from. I had to learn how to win. Because if I didn’t then I was going to have to go find a job.”

“The way you were brought up, that’s what toughened you up.”

“Maybe.”

“Always coming home to an empty house. Then when Des finally got home, you’d fight with him. Know something? In a way I wasn’t surprised when I heard you’d been dragged in for those burglaries. All that mess at home, it had to show somewhere.”

Paddy lit a cigarette – down to ten, maybe twelve, a day now that he was working – and held it so the smoke wouldn’t drift towards Aoife. This was good: he was getting close to explaining things to her. He knew where he wanted to start. Back with the Accident Run, the way it had led him into other people’s houses, just watching initially, then beginning to lift something small he liked the look of. Or sometimes, if he liked the feel of a house he might just sit a while, imagine what it was like to live there, to have brothers and sisters and someone waiting when he got home. Feeling comfortable with the stealth. Learning the burglar's trade without really knowing it, then finding it easy and beginning to select the houses…

And yes, he still blamed his father.

"This is better than therapy," he said. "A chance to talk about myself and no bill at the end."

Willie Byrnes was Sanderson's contact in Dublin, Ray Donnelly having to make the arrangements over the phone, offering three hundred to find the man in question, Byrnes saying, "Any chance you could make it four?" With a real whiney tone. Ray knew immediately the guy was doped to the gills. What he wanted to say was – "No, let's make it two, how about that, you fucking scaghead?" But he didn't, he just said, "Three hundred, take it or leave it," and Byrnes said, "Times are tough y'know, but if that's your upper limit, well what can we do about it?"

The next day he got a call to say that Paddy Benner was in Dublin alright. Ray hated dealing with druggies. He'd done it before and it always left you with a something nagging at the back of your mind. A druggie was a liability. A druggie had no dignity. You could hear it in his voice, that pleading little whine, and you felt like slapping him and saying, Hey am I the one got you into this mess? A druggie had no self-respect. He had no honour. You could frighten him all you wanted and still he'd sell you out for a little bag of white powder.

Half now, half later: that was the deal.

Twelve noon, Ray had paid over a hundred and fifty and eight hours later, he'd watched Paddy Benner leave the house, considering taking him then, but deciding it'd be better to wait until after dark. Get him indoors, pull the blinds and set to work.

Do things at his own pace.

Make an example like Sanderson wanted.

Then he could worry about keeping Byrnes quiet.

21

The Engineering students left one by one: the Yeti first to go, wearing a leather jacket and a PLO scarf, even the walk irritating Joe who felt like walking out and booting him clear across the road: number two looking like he was off to work – all dickied up in his white shirt and black chinos – half an hour before the last one stepped out into the evening, Joe watching all this from his front window and thinking, Well now, let's see who can go fuck himself tonight.

He felt good. He felt like something had been coming back through the day, yesterday's *What was the point?* turning to today's *Why the hell not*? He'd been up early. Tired, yes, after the racket last night, but with things to do: starting with the laundry – standing over the sink rubbing the stains out of his shirts and vests and underpants – then cleaning and sweeping out the flat, getting it in good working order so Jean wouldn't have to once he'd left. By ten he was hungry. He walked to the supermarket and bought eight slices each of the cheapest cheese and ham. He said it straight out – "Eight of your cheapest if you don't mind," not giving a shit what the guy thought and feeling good about it, knowing that something was happening inside him. He put on his Reeboks and walked into town. When the nice looking lady asked if he'd like to help the Blind Dogs Association, he said, "No thanks, I don't think I will if it's all the same to yourself."

That, more than anything, summed up how he was feeling today.

He walked up and down Grafton Street a few times. Here, there were changes: the nice brickwork paving, new waist high black dustbins you could sit on, old style lanterns every forty yards or so. All that money the Government had been shoving into the Dublin Millenium on show right here where the expensive shops were, Joe moving through the crowd, remembering how in the early days he and Stel would walk this street on a Saturday morning. Back then the atmosphere was different. Back then you could walk past a shop front without having music blaring out at you. Get in by eleven and you could have a nice easy walk, nobody pushing or shoving you or rattling a tin under your nose.

What if he decided: No, I'm not going to put up with you blasting your racket into my flat tonight.

He found a hammer in Lenehan's Hardware Store. As far as he could see it was a good one – a 16oz tubular claw hammer, if you don't mind – retailing at £1.99. In the corner there was a big lump hammer, ideal, but at £28.50 well…? He tapped the claw hammer against the palm of his hand. He liked the feel of it. He liked the way the smooth varnished handle fitted snugly into his grip.

By half two Joe was back in bed catching up on some sleep.

From a quarter past five he was sitting at the front window, watching the driveway below, waiting for first the Yeti and then the other two to leave for the evening. He checked his watch. Give them what? – fifteen minutes? – to see if they'd forgotten anything. Make it twenty to be on the safe side. At 9:30 he stepped out, the night having turned cool, not quite fully dark but what the hell, there was no time like the present…

He noticed the quiet.

He tossed his hammer over the back wall and climbed after it. There was a covering of dew on the grass, he scuffed the soles of his shoes on the concrete before stepping forward. This window or that one, what difference did it make? He swung back and let fly.

Jesus, the noise of it!!!

It spooked him. He stood fixed to the spot for the moment… then took off over the wall again. He tripped on the back step, toppled in through the doorway. Inside the house again, he ran upstairs and sat beside his window. He tried to control his breathing. Telling himself what he needed to do was to stay calm.

He'd lost his nerve, that was all.

All that good feeling he'd had through the day and now his hands were trembling. It wasn't the smash that had spooked him, no, it was the noise of the glass falling. Christ, it was loud. He pulled hard on a cigarette, then thought maybe no one had heard. Yes, maybe he'd be lucky. Saturday night, remember – lots of folks were out on a Saturday night.

He'd give it a few minutes, then he'd go fetch his hammer.

He saw a cop car outside.

Jesus, he thought, how did they get here so quick?

Aoife told Paddy she'd written the poem with him in mind. In the original draft she'd had twenty-seven steps instead of twenty-eight but that was one syllable too many. The other tricky bit was the last line – whether to stick with *Coming home alone* or go for *Returning alone.*

It didn't really matter, did it?

She said, thinking about it now, maybe this was the only way the two of them might have had a chance together. Let him get the travelling out of his system – since she'd always known he'd take off sooner or later – then for him to come back and pick things up again. That way all the memories would be good ones. He'd had his reasons for leaving and maybe, if he'd hung on longer, she'd have become one of them.

What did he think of that?

"Cat got your tongue?" she said and she reached across and kissed him. Just like that. The gentlest touch of her lips, that was all, sliding her hand along the hair behind his ear. She touched the side of his face and smiled.

"Remember the first time," she said.

"Maybe…"

"I had to kiss you then too."

"I was shy," Paddy said.

"Louise Fogarty's house. Sitting there listening to you waffle on, thinking – Jesus, is this guy ever going to make a move?"

He shrugged. "Some things don't change, I suppose."

"I want to take things slow this time around," she said.

"Suits me," he said. "You're the one for the first moves."

She smiled at him. "Nice and slow," she said. "No rush. I don't want to miss anything."

A house like this would cost you what, maybe four hundred grand back in London, big detached place in a suburb where you had plenty of trees and a park close by. Not too far from the city centre either. And a fair sized back garden – Ray Donnelly standing there now, nice and relaxed, taking a little time to get the feel of things. Drawing the tension tool from the belt of his trousers, sliding it into the keyhole and… One sharp click and he was in.

Well now, he thought, that wasn't too difficult.

Into the kitchen now which was really a little annex to a bigger room – one for cooking and one for eating, he supposed – the dining table in a mess with what looked like the cartons you'd get from the local chinkie. Or frozen dinners maybe, our friend Paddy not too keen on cleaning up after himself. Sitting down at the table, Ray shoved some of the shit aside and laid out the tools. First the tension tool, then the Canning hunting knife, a roll of heavy duty insulating tape, and a Browning automatic. The gun you needed in case someone came home unexpectedly. Show a stranger a knife and tell him to keep still while you taped him up, what would he do? He'd scream and run or else he'd come at you. But a gun? A gun calmed things. A gun said – Let's talk this over since you'd already have shot me if you wanted to.

No, the Browning wasn't for Paddy. Ray had the knife and his fists for that.

It was a strange feeling, sitting here in Paddy Benner's kitchen, not a soul in the world knowing he was here. Or even in the country. Not Sanderson and not Sudds – what was the point in telling them? – since all that would happen would be that Sudds would start begging for Ray to wait until he was ready to travel. And when Ray said No, he'd go to Sanderson. Who might say, Yes – you just never knew. What you did know was that in a situation like this one here Sudds would be a liability. He'd be tearing the place apart, pacing up and down the house shouting, *Where the fuck is he?* There was no telling what Sudds would do once he saw Paddy Benner again.

All in all, it was easier this way. Ray would kill Benner quickly – not too quickly, mind you, give him a good beating first – and then he'd make it look good. A decent sized headline with any luck. Fly back to London and collect the early copy the next morning, drop it onto Sudds's lap and say, Jesus, how do you think *that* happened?

He could just picture it.

He walked out into the hall. It was a nice house alright. Last time he'd put someone away, Jesus, you'd want to have seen the place! Dirty little fucking druggie who wouldn't pay his debts and, as if that wasn't bad enough, he gets four grand from somewhere and sticks three of it on a horse. Which, according to Sanderson, was just taking the piss. So Ray and Sudds had to pay him a visit – they'd taped his wrists behind his back and drowned him in the bath – but what stuck in Ray's mind was the state of the place. How could people live like that? Pure slop, that's what it was, one room worse than the other; monster big cockroaches zipping around the place, Sudds having a laugh saying, You'd want to stomp on that big bastard in case he wants to testify. Which, Ray supposed, was Sudds at his best. Just having a laugh: a decent enough bloke when he wasn't looking for aggro…

Ray looked around and, yes, Benner's folks had a few quid put by. There was a big expensive grandfather clock sitting in the hall and right there in the sitting room – Ray could just make it out in the dull light – a smaller clock that looked like it might be antique. Maybe he'd look through the place, see if there was anything that might offset his costs. Later, of course, once he'd finished with Benner. Because that was how you botched a job, you let your mind wander and then all of a sudden the fucker was in on top of you.

Not tonight.

Here Ray intended to keep things simple. Maybe once he had the knife to Benner's throat, he'd tell him it was nothing personal and hey, it'd taken a lot of balls to break in like that and take Sudds on. Tell him he liked his style, the way he'd just walked in to *The Four Provinces*…

He might even ask where he'd got the cricket stump.

Then he'd gut him.

They walked home slowly, Paddy with his hands in his pockets, Aoife linking his arm, telling him No, taking it slow didn't include reefing him into bed just yet. But there was a consolation. She was sharing a house with two other girls – at this very moment entertaining their boyfriends – and maybe he'd like to come inside. Just to say hello. Beer and cold pizza on offer and whatever was left on the video they were watching.

Paddy said, all things considered, he'd prefer a rusty spike up the arse.

Well now, she said, that's a very disappointing attitude. They spent an hour sitting on the wall outside. It didn't seem like an hour – fifteen minutes more like – but that was the thing about Aoife, time just seemed to drift on by without you noticing it. Sitting there on the wall, telling him about college, how for just under a year she'd gone out with Barry Ryan who was in her English class. Barry, she said, was one of the nicest people you could meet. Then she'd gone out with a rugby player named Stephen Prescott who was a nice guy too but dull as fucking dishwater.

Sometimes she'd wished something would happen to Paddy; nothing serious, just enough to bring him back to Dublin.

Later Paddy walked home alone, a light rain beginning to fall. Why had he stayed away so long? Eight full years, it was a long time. Early on, he'd say to himself: This ball drops and Aoife is, at this very moment, thinking of me. Then if he missed he'd make it best of three and if he missed that there was no telling where the game would end. Stupid kid's stuff, but still he did it. The question was: Why not head for home? Pride maybe. Yes, that was part of it. Pride and embarrassment, both of them weighing in there, but mostly it was the fear that Aoife would have met someone else. Which was obviously going to happen. Off to college that September, a whole new life opening out in front of her…

And the longer it went on, the more likely she was to have left him behind.

Only guess what? – she'd missed him too.

It was almost two by the time he turned down Mount Prospect Avenue. He was thinking he might grab another dinner out of the freezer; the chicken maybe, if the old man hadn't already scoffed it. Yeah, he thought, the chicken. Or maybe the canaloni, that wasn't a bad one. Once he dried off, he'd take a look, see how they shaped up…

22

Paddy stepped inside thinking he'd have the chicken or whatever straight from the carton, save on the dishes, when *Ooof,* the breath left him… face down now, then feeling his hair being wrenched and *whap* on the bridge of the nose – Jesus, the pain of it – Paddy scrambling and trying to catch his breath, thinking *Do something now or you're fucking dead…* reaching for the knife and *Whap* again, Paddy not quite sure where he'd been hit, choking back the vomit. Trying to see in front of him. Yeah, there was the grandfather clock, coming into view as he was being lifted, Paddy about to get a look at the guy – boots, jeans and shirt – then Christ it felt like the side of his face had exploded.

The knife, he needed the knife. Down along the side of his leg, almost there now when the pain shot up his arm. He was bundled into a ball like when he was a kid on the footpath in London. Feeling the boots. Waiting for the next one, praying – Please, not the head. Anywhere but the head. Knowing it was Sudds, who else could it be?

He lashed out with his feet – blind panic, nothing else – felt himself being lifted into the living room, reaching for the knife again, then Jesus, his head bounced off the fireplace. He tried to get up, a black gloved fist came down like a hammer, Paddy just able to roll with it this time, then throwing his shoulder into the guy's knees. He crawled on one arm to the window sill. He could taste his own blood. His right arm was numb. He couldn't lift his trousers to get the knife. He tried to stand, felt his legs buckle but then… there he was, standing up. Holding the metal candlestick from the windowsill now, hearing someone laugh. Yeah, that's what it was, Donnelly laughing now.

It wasn't Sudds.

It was the brother. What was his name? Paddy couldn't remember. Paddy heard him say, "You tangled with the wrong folks." He needed to speak – keep him talking while he got the knife out – but Jesus, it was hard enough just to stay standing. The side of his face felt like it was caved in. The face and the arm, all down the right side, Paddy moving out now, watching Donnelly step forward. Go for the knife and this fucker would be on top of him. He watched the guy feint, covered it, then he'd been hit again. An open palm, that was all but Jesus, it still hurt. And again, Paddy slipping this time, down on one knee. He picked himself up. Donnelly was smiling now, having a little fun while he was here.

Paddy stared into his eyes – empty eyes, he thought, like a doll's – nothing more than a slight amusement in there. He swung the candlestick. Donnelly slid backwards and drew himself away, then flicked the back of his hand across Paddy's face and Paddy felt the pain again. A big guy, maybe, but fuck he was quick. Paddy sidled, looking for an opening, and it occurred to him that he was going to die.

"Send my regards to Sudds," he said.

Donnelly moved again, a quick jab before Paddy could even move. He was cut this time, a slow trickle of blood. When it reached his chin, he wiped it away, and felt the itch again. Telling himself to do *something*. But what? – the guy was fucking huge. Throw the candlestick maybe, lean back and bury this bastard right between the eyes. He wasn't even sure if he could lift his arm…

"*He's* asking for *you*," Ray Donnelly said. "Wait 'til he finds out I've been here, he'll be fit to be tied."

Funny, Paddy thought. Killing him and doing a comedy routine as well.

Paddy said, "It's hard to tell the two of you apart what with that inbred look you…" and made his move, bringing the candlestick from over his head, watching Donnelly ease himself away and he felt the pain across his back and that pain merged with the others. Donnelly staring now, eyes cold again. No more chat. He hit Paddy twice, then *bang*, just under the ribs. Paddy cried out and swung the candlestick and once again he made no contact.

The blood in his mouth, it was a strangely familiar taste from childhood. He looked across at Donnelly, thinking how calm the guy looked, just standing there, swaying slightly, watching… Paddy knew he was going to die, and what a funny place to die it was, back home after eight years on the move. He felt okay. He'd put up a fight, hadn't disgraced himself. He'd done all he could and well, maybe there were worse things than dying. He wanted to lie down, just curl up in a ball… Then it occurred that he should at least hit the guy once. Give him a souvenir. He switched the candlestick to his right hand – the feeling coming back now – and then, leaning back, fired the thing as hard as he could. Watched it sail past Donnelly's ear and out into the hall. Donnelly didn't smile. He stared, cold and distant, and took another step closer.

Paddy slumped back against the wall and sidled along it, his arms limp next to his sides. He felt his hip touch the couch. He pulled the corner of the couch from the wall – arms like jelly now – and stepped behind it, using his knees to shove it forward a little. He lifted his right hand and wiped the blood from his face. He let it fall again. He bent down behind the couch, lifted the leg of his trousers and slid the butcher's trimming knife from its sheath.

Donnelly put his leg next to the couch and moved it aside a few inches, then, eyes fixed on Paddy, he lifted it and upended in into the centre of the room. Everyone out in the open again. Paddy could feel his legs buckle, pressed them hard into the ground to stay standing. He was grinning now, not knowing why, watching the guy come closer, trying to remember the name – Rickie or Dave or something. Ray maybe. Yeah, Ray – that was it, Ray Donnelly coming closer now, Paddy watching him slide what looked like a hunting knife from behind his back. Letting the clock run down. Needing him in close.

Donnelly liked to savour the moment.

He pressed Paddy back against the wall, gave a slow nod and drew his arm back from his hip.

"I need you to give that brother of yours a message?" Paddy said.

And brought the knife from behind his back. Calmer now, letting the blade do the work, watching the expression change – the *where the fuck did that come from?* look – feeling the breath being exhaled onto his right cheek: readjusting his grip now and thrusting upwards until there was nothing but wood left on the outside. He heard the hunting knife fall. The life flickered in Donnelly's eyes and then it was gone and Paddy thrust upwards one more time. Donnelly slumped to the floor. Paddy nudged the arm aside with his foot and stepped away.

Paddy fell back into the armchair. His lip was bleeding. His lip and his eye and maybe his left ear, he wasn't sure, his arm hurting like hell where he'd been kicked on the funny bone. He looked at Donnelly, the vacant eyes staring at the ceiling and thought, *Oh sweet fuck.*

He had to stop Donnelly bleeding all over the place. He laid four black plastic sacks on the floor and rolled the dead body on top of them. Then sat back down. Wondering what in the name of Christ he was going to do now. It was a matter of getting a grip on things, straightening out his story for the coppers. Which seemed simple enough – he'd tell how he stepped inside the door and all of a sudden there was some guy kicking the living shit out of him. He'd tell them about the candlestick. Just lay out the details and ask what the hell were you supposed to do when some stranger tries to kill you?

And hear them say – Why carry the knife if you didn't intend to use it?

That was the problem. From what Paddy knew of the law, you'd do time if you stabbed someone with a knife you carried with you. Maybe he could lie – move the body, claim he'd grabbed the knife off the draining board – and maybe they'd believe him. But it was a risk. Sitting for hours answering questions, knowing the next of kin would be contacted, waiting for Sudds to get well enough to travel.

Ray Donnelly had said it himself – *"Wait 'til he finds out I've been here. He'll be fit to be tied."*

Which meant that Sudds didn't know where his brother was.

Already Paddy was trying to piece it together. Old Ray had

decided to settle the score alone. He flies in, spends a few days tracking Paddy down, and waits for his chance. He sees the old man heading away that morning and decides to wait until night-time. Just to be on the safe side. Then he makes his move. He wants to toy with Paddy a while, and ends up with a knife stuck in him. Everything straightforward so far. But why hadn't he told Sudds? To piss him off maybe – could it be that simple? Just an ordinary rivalry between two thugs? Or maybe he'd been scared that Sudds would screw things up.

Either one was likely.

But did anyone else know where he'd gone? A wife, maybe? Or a girlfriend? Maybe he'd told his boss – what was his name? Sanderson – and maybe he hadn't. There was no point in trying to guess. He'd think about that one later: now it was a question of what to do with the body.

Paddy lit a cigarette and tried to smoke it out of the corner of his mouth. He knew he wasn't going anywhere near the coppers.

The old man didn't own a spade. A lawnmower, yes, and various shit you'd never need from one year to the next but something simple like a spade or a shovel? Paddy should have guessed it. He locked the garden shed, looked up at the clear moon and thought, Well no other thing for it.

Already his mind had cleared. He'd drive up the Dublin mountains and give Ray Donnelly a quiet send off – just dig a hole, and toss him into the ground. The sea was risky. He'd seen it plenty of times at the flicks, how a body could wash up on the shore. It was always the same trick – the early morning jogger, the sandy foot sticking up, then cut to the copper arriving on the crime scene. Or sometimes it was a hand. Why the body never floated past a beachful of swimmers Paddy didn't know, but he didn't doubt that the sea sometimes returned the dead. No, the mountains was the place for Ray Donnelly. It was a favourite with the drug boys, Paddy knew this, and well, what was good enough for them…

He locked the front door behind him and set off towards Dollymount Avenue. He felt okay. His arm hurt but he could move it and the cuts had stopped bleeding. He was alive. Bruised, sure, but still breathing, following the curve of Mount Prospect now and thinking about what had happened, about the phone message that tipped him off. Blind luck, that's what it was. Nothing he could put his finger on, no, but enough to remind him that he owned a knife.

It was easy to steal the spade. He climbed over a back wall on Seapark Avenue, slid a thin wire into the padlock and he was inside. He shone the old man's torch into the shed and there they were – two spades and a shovel, take your pick.

On the way back he started thinking how for a while now the luck seemed to be running with him. First walking away from that fuck-up in London then finding a nice untraceable way out of England. Donnelly could have killed him as soon as he walked in the door – wrap an arm around his neck and bring the hunting knife from behind – but he'd screwed around and paid the price for it. The question was – how had Paddy been tracked down so quickly? Directory enquiries, could it be that simple? Maybe Donnelly had found Paddy's surname from Tim – there was no telling what Tim was capable of – or he might've tracked him to the guesthouse he'd stayed in. Yeah, Paddy thought, that was probably it. Get the guesthouse from the barman in *The Four Provinces* and then he had the surname. After that it was a simple matter of picking up the phone. Maybe he'd done the ringing himself – would the old man have mentioned an English accent? – or maybe someone on this side of the water had called.

He knew this business wasn't over yet.

Maybe he'd have to take a flight back to England, he thought, and put an end to it. Climb back through Sudds's bathroom window, stick a pillow over his face and say – there you go chum, this is for you. The thought frightened him, of course it did, but what was the alternative? Sit and wait for someone else to appear? – either Sudds or a contract job, whichever Sanderson preferred. Step out of the house some night and you wouldn't even see it coming. But maybe they didn't know where Ray had gone. It was possible, yes, but if Ray Donnelly had followed the trail to Dublin, why couldn't his brother?

All Paddy had earned was some breathing space.

He'd think about it again later. Right now he needed to dispose of the body on his living room floor, Paddy thinking about this and wondering if there was any Panadol at home, turning the corner and walking… straight into two coppers, one uniformed and one detective. The two boys standing right there outside his gate, another on the doorstep, Paddy feeling his breath go. Paddy thinking, *Oh sweet fuck.* Then thinking, *Jesus, how did this happen?* The uniform nodded and Paddy nodded and Paddy said it was a nice night and walked past, still holding his spade, deciding what was the best route to take. Over Mrs Larkin's side door, maybe, through her garden and into the park.

Maybe he should use the spade, see could he reduce the odds.

Then he heard the one on the doorstep say, "Hey, that's him." Ready to swing only the click of a revolver stopped him. "Patrick Benner," the detective said. "You're under arrest."

Paddy lowered the spade. "This is harassment," he said. "I want to make a complaint."

23

It was all bright lights in the cop shop, Joe trying to remember the last time he'd been in one – getting a form for his driver's licence, maybe – Costello telling him it wouldn't be long now and they'd all be on their way. Giving Joe a little pep talk. Telling him to take his time, make sure he got the right man. Telling him not to feel any pity – yes, it sometimes happened – the one to think of here was the victim's widow and how *she* was getting through the day.

All Joe had to do was give them the nod and they'd take things from there.

Stuff Joe had already been through. It was Costello who had collected him, Costello and another copper, Joe waiting for them to say, Okay then sir, maybe you'd like to come down the station with us. Waiting for them to lead him to the squad car. Only they didn't. They said they were sorry to intrude on a Saturday night and Joe knew right then that he was in the clear. All he had to do was stand in front of an identity parade and pick out one of the fake Mormons. The one with the Irish accent, most likely.

They dropped the uniformed Garda off at Clontarf station.

Then Costello brought him on a tour. Back along the Coast Road, turning left into Clontarf, keeping up the chat and asking what Joe did for a crust. Mink coats, he said, who the hell was buying mink coats these days? Then pointing and saying, "See that house there? That's where our boy lives."

Joe wasn't sure if he'd heard him right.

Costello, for whatever reason, wanted to give the rundown on a guy named Paddy Benner. Benner, it seemed, was an armed robber and yes – what was the point in lying about it? – he could turn nasty if things went bad. Get in his way and it was your tough luck. A dirty little rich kid – look at the house, if you had any doubts – and here was a chance to nail him good and proper. Assuming of course that they had the right guy.

The reason for all this? – just so Joe knew where he stood.

And there was no reason to be frightened. The beauty of this one, Costello said, was that Joe probably wouldn't even have to testify. All they were looking for was enough evidence to have Benner extradited back to England and from what Costello knew there were at least six other witnesses. Let *them* do the dirty work, standing up there in the courtroom. No, all Joe had to do was let them know if Benner was their man and then he could walk away from the whole thing.

Two things stopped people identifying the perpetrator – fear and pity.

"No need for either," Costello had said, "I'll be right there in the same room, leading you through it."

Up front the coppers were silent, the night quiet outside, Paddy staring out the window at the streetlights as they flashed by. The handcuffs dug into his wrists and he felt knackered. He was on his way to prison. He'd make it difficult for them – why not? – but what defence could he possibly have? There was a knife and there was a spade. There was blood and there were fingerprints and there was a dead body lying on four plastic sacks in the middle of the living room floor.

What Paddy needed right now was a decent lawyer.

He needed to file a complaint – yes, that'd be the first step – lay it out for them about Costello's threats. He'd give them the times he was brought in, then ask them to check when the interviews began. What evidence had they to drag him in? Ask for the tape to be listened to and see what that other clown, O'Brien, had to say for himself. Which in itself showed just how desperate the situation was. Still, what Paddy would do, he'd get them to go through the tape, tell them to pause it where Costello had paused it, and explain exactly what had been said.

Would one of you pick up the phone if a copper had threatened to stitch you up?

The Bridewell was busy enough for the time of night. Saturday night business, Paddy supposed, folks getting tanked up and kicking the shit out of each other: one drunk seeing Paddy and saying, "Hey, I know you, you're the fella with the handcuffs." His pal saying, "Leave him alone, he's tied up at the moment."

That guy coming out of the side room there, he looked familiar.

Paddy couldn't place him. A copper maybe but Paddy didn't think so. He didn't have the look. Someone he'd seen recently enough, he was sure of that, but the question was *where*? On the boat maybe? Or on the train coming across the city? It wasn't a customer from the golf shop, he knew that much, but –

Then it hit him, the panic, right in there deep in his stomach. It was the guy from London, of course it was, the comedian trying to stitch up his mate. What the hell was going on? Paddy could see him standing on the doorstep, leaning against the doorframe and asking could they call to him in Dublin.

An eye witness to place him at the scene of one murder.

A dead body on his living room floor for when his old man got back.

"Oh Jesus," he whispered.

Paddy looked around the interview room and slowly shook his head. He was fucked, no two ways about it, well and truly, quite monumentally fucked, looking back to see Costello sitting in front of him now, that same smug look on his face. Costello saying, "What happened to you? Try to hustle the wrong guy?" Costello telling him a story – an interesting old yarn, he said – about this idiot who came up with the bright idea of posing as a Mormon so he could break into this house over in London. Only what happened? – things turned bad. Some brave soul tried to make a name for himself and got a bullet for his trouble and one of the Mormons was shot dead trying to make a break for it. But the question was – what happened to the other Mormon? All the London Met know is that he's early to mid-twenties and has an Irish accent. So they get their witnesses together, they produce a good identikit picture and then they begin to trawl the Irish bars. It's as good a place as any to start. And guess what? They get a couple of hits. Talk about lucky, it turns out this idiot used to work those very same bars trying to hustle pool for a few quid, going by the name of Paddy, if you don't mind. Fancies himself as a pool player. So one London copper gets the bright idea of sending over the identikit in the hope that someone across the water might have a surname to put on the face.

"I only happened to notice it when I came on duty this evening," he said. "You want to talk now or you want your lawyer?"

Paddy looked across the table. "Know what the problem with coppers is these days?" he asked.

"Tell me."

"You'd want to start recruiting a few college boys, that's the problem."

"You think so?"

"You know that career guidance teacher you have when you're in school? That poor bastard's got a hell of a job, has to interview practically the whole school. So what he does, he develops a little system for himself. He gets this brainy kid in and he looks at his results and he says, Hey why don't you be a doctor or an engineer or something like that? And the kid says, Terrific and heads off out the door. Then the next kid's is pretty much middle of the road so he's chucked into the bank or insurance or maybe the civil service. Some mind-numbing shit like that. Then this big fucking moron comes in and the teacher looks across and thinks, Jesus what am I going to do with this one? What *can* you do, guy's fucking unemployable? Look at the results, for Christ sake. Look at the expression. And then, guess what happens? He takes a decky under the table and he sees these huge fucking feet – monstrous big things, size 22 at least. Then he looks across and he sees this tomato red face beaming back at him and all of a sudden the penny drops and he says, Well now, laddie, I think I might just *have* something for you.

"That's you, Costello," Paddy said, "you're an ignorant fucking culchie moron. Anyone ever tell you that?"

Costello was nodding with that same grin plastered to his face. "Keep talking, Paddy boy," he said. "I can't get enough of this stuff."

"Just wanted to let you know," Paddy said. "I'll have that lawyer now, if you don't mind."

So twenty minutes later, Paddy had a lawyer – what was he? twenty-one? twenty-two? – Jonathon Fox who happened to be in the building at the time and could stay a while. Tired, yes, but happy to help, shaking Paddy's hand and saying, Boy, he'd hate to see the other guy. Paddy told him he'd been mugged. Mugged and arrested, both within a couple of hours, sometimes a night just took off, didn't it? Well, Fox said, taking a seat, if Paddy could just tell him where exactly where he was on the morning Louis John Marks was murdered, it might be a good place to start. August 4th, somewhere in the region of 10:40.

Early twenties, he had to be, but stick a bag on his back and you could send him running off to school.

"I was alone in my room, most likely. You know anything about extradition law?" Paddy said.

"Well no, not much."

"Didn't think so. No offence here, pal, but I think I might be better off with someone who does."

"Well, you'll have to pay another lawyer."

"You telling me I can't swap."

"Not with your Free Legal Aid lawyers. Otherwise the whole system would get clogged up. A defendant could keep changing lawyers through the trial and you'd get nowhere."

Paddy sighed. "So it's you and me then. I don't have any money."

"Well, good. We'll see what we can do for you. The evidence here is nothing we can't deal with, certainly not enough to have you extradited. So we'll just get through the identity parade and then you can go home."

"I'd sooner not take that chance."

"You said you were in your room at the time. Were you alone?"

"Yes."

"Would the landlord remember you being there?"

"I doubt it."

"Well, that's not so good. But there's no reason to think the worst here. If you weren't there, you've nothing to worry about."

"I want to file a complaint," Paddy said.

"Against the Gardai?"

"Against that fucking ape out there. Costello. He thinks I broke into his house years ago and now he's harassing me. This is the third time in the past six days he's dragged me in. No evidence, nothing. Just jerking me around and now he wants me to stand in front of an identity parade. How do I know he hasn't already primed this witness?"

"What reason have you to believe he *has*?"

"He threatened me. He said he'd do whatever it took to see me behind bars."

"Well, there's nothing stopping you filing a complaint against him."

"I want *you* to do it."

Jonathon Fox sighed. "Well, that's a problem, I'm afraid. I'm only allowed to defend you on the murder charge. That's how Free Legal Aid works. But you don't need me to file a complaint. All you have to do is go into the Garda Complaints Board on Abbey Street and fill out the form."

"How does extradition work?" Paddy wanted to know. "Who signs the order?"

"A member of the Gardai goes to a judge and requests one."

"In your presence?"

"If you want."

"I want. I want you to be there and request that there is no extradition order issued until my complaint has been dealt with."

Now Fox was smiling. "You really are jumping the gun here," he said. "Why don't we just see what happens with the identity parade?"

"Is there any way I can get out of it?"

"Which? The parade?"

"Yes. The parade. What do you think?"

"'Fraid not. We can object to the people you're lined up with or we can ask that another Garda interview you since you feel persecuted by Detective Costello but the bottom line is that you have to stand up there if you're asked to. All we can do is delay it. And I can't see any point in that, can you?"

Paddy sighed and looked around the room. He could see

one good point and that was enough. "No, he said. "Not really."

Joe was down to his last two cigarettes by the time Costello reappeared, ready to say, Listen you're eating up my time here, how about arranging for some smokes? Only Costello seemed all business. Sitting down next to Joe and telling him that things were moving right along. The Free Legal Aid lawyer was in with Benner now and pretty soon they'd conduct a short interview. Joe was doing great, all he had to do was hang in there a little while longer.

What would Benner say? You could bet your house he was innocent, just like they all were.

"He'll be Number Five," Costello whispered. "Second from the left."

Paddy knew they were just going through the motions, Costello and an older copper coming out with the same old stuff. Where was Paddy on August the fourth between ten-thirty and eleven and could anybody verify that? Did he know anyone by the name of Richard Hamilton? Why did he return to Ireland? They wanted to know where he'd been staying and how long he'd been staying there. And what about the boat home? – when and where had he bought his ticket and how had he got from London to Holyhead?

Paddy answered the questions. He kept his voice nice and even and said that he would be contacting the Garda Complaints Board.

Then it was a matter of organising a line-up. Costello asked if Paddy had any objection to going Number Five in the line-up and Paddy said, "What difference does it make?" He was sweating. Thinking what was the point in being nervous since it was already a done deal and all he could do was wait for this bozo to finger him. But still he could feel it, on his palms and on his back and his feet felt saturated. At one end of the room there was a plain white wall with five men standing against it, Paddy's place reserved second from the end.

Jesus, they didn't even have one of those two way mirror things you'd see on the telly.

On the telly there were always lines on the wall with all the different heights marked and there was always some copper speaking into a microphone, saying: Step forward, Number One. It was always dark with the suspects under a bright light, looking, Paddy imagined, at nothing more than a wall of glass. Probably able to see their own reflections. Here, it was just a bare room, nothing more than a table and a couple of chairs pushed into the corner with five guys – coppers, most likely – standing against the far wall.

He watched the guy being led in. Costello and the older copper and Jonathon Fox, fat lot of use he'd been so far. It was the same guy all right. Roughly the same height as Paddy but broader: mid to late thirties, most likely. Pretty good looking guy but beginning to thin out on top. All each suspect had to do was step forward, turn to either side and step back again.

Fynn and Malik, they'd been the lucky ones.

Paddy stood and waited his turn. What could he possibly do now? Jump out of the line, maybe, pick a number and shout, "It was *him*, I was there and I saw him, the bastard." He listened to the older copper calling out the numbers and it all seemed a little surreal, the whole squad of them face to face in the same room. Just standing and waiting.

Paddy's turn came. He stepped forward, to the left and right and then back again.

Thinking, Maybe there's still hope.

Then thinking, Not a fucking chance.

Then waited some more, waiting and watching the guy's face as his gaze went up and down the line. Thinking, Here goes. Then hearing the guy say, "I can't really be sure, but I think it might be Number Two."

Paddy felt his breathing stop for a moment.

He wasn't sure what had happened, but, Jesus, why give him a second chance?

"See, I told you this was a stitch-up," he said, stepping forward. "Sticking me in with five coppers."

24

Two a.m., Ed O'Brien told a legal secretary named Linda he'd be back before she could drain that glass, and walked straight out the door of *Buck Whaleys*. He was tired – yes, unbelievably tired – tired and bored and hungry and sick of hearing about other people's jobs. What was it with people and their jobs? They were relentless, like Linda here who'd spent a good hour nattering on about wills and codicils and the best way to type a legal statement. Yes, this was Saturday night on the strip; Ed shelling out twenty quid for a bottle of the cheapest plonk, waiting for good sense to kick in. Finally catching that look in her eyes and thinking, *Who the hell needs this?*

He walked to his car, the cool air and the quiet hitting him nicely. He pulled out into the empty street and considered how no one ever asked about his job. Why *was* that? Policework was interesting, wasn't it? You had your dull parts, same as any other line of work, but at least something *happened*. But tell people you were a copper and they wanted to move on to something else. Maybe they thought you couldn't talk about it – as though every single aspect was confidential – or maybe there were things they just didn't want to know about.

Every now and then someone would ask: Are you ever frightened?

And Ed would always say: Sometimes. Which was right, he *was* sometimes frightened. But still it didn't answer the question because the interesting thing was that there seemed to be no particular pattern to where the fear hit. Two similar situations – say a late night call to a shop where an alarm has gone off – in one you're nice and calm and alert but two nights later you're thinking, Jesus something bad's going to happen here. You couldn't put a finger on the reason. A noise or a smell or a funny angle of light. The sound of the wind, maybe – anything could spook you. And once that feeling hit, what you wanted to do was run; run or hide or curl up in a ball and wait for it all to go away.

Ed had been brave plenty of times but no one seemed to remember that.

What they remembered was the time he'd let Garda Sean Linehan get himself kicked into a coma, Ed thinking of this now and still not sure what had happened that night. Maybe he'd been brave until he just couldn't be brave anymore, that was one theory; a simple build-up of pressure, night after night, then *boom* his whole system caved in. Could it really have been that? Linehan chasing an addict named Billy Ryan into the flats on Conquer Hill, Ed knowing Linehan was in trouble but too terrified to follow him in. Hearing the shouts and knowing he had to do something.

Not just scared, paralysed scared.

All of which, mind you, was five years ago. And did it really mean he was a coward? Once he'd had his panic attack, once he'd recovered, he could go back to being brave again, couldn't he? Why not? He'd never lost his nerve before. Only where would he get the chance? Late at night driving into some shitty housing estate, was Ed O'Brien the man you wanted in the seat next to you?

He'd thought maybe a change of station might do the trick.

But no, these days Ed specialised in traffic duty. He stood like a spare tool in the middle of the junction thinking, Why don't I just wave them *all* through and see what happens. He processed complaints, investigated the odd burglary but there was an awful lot of traffic duty. How could you complain? Leave your mate to get the shit kicked out him and you took what you were offered. You took it and said, Thanks very much, and you were grateful for that salary cheque at the end of each month.

He was home by 2:17.

He looked across at Stella's house and wondered if she might be up. He doubted it, everything quiet and dark over there, Stella curled up all alone in the scratcher, which for the time being seemed to suit her fine. It was a trap he'd fallen into before: plenty of people did. They assumed that a woman was automatically ready for a bit of heave-ho as soon as she stepped out of a dead marriage. They thought about the frustration. They thought about the tension and the abstinence and the sudden release. Only it didn't work like that. Women usually needed time to get things out of their system. Even after the lousiest relationships, there was usually a period of mourning.

But was Stella Faherty the type to mourn anything?

It didn't seem so. Already she was looking to the future – pragmatic, that was the word – seeing what she could gain from the whole mess. Seeing if Ed could help her and if he couldn't… well no harm done. She was tough as nails, he liked that. He'd asked her about her job and she'd said, "I type." He liked that too. Her cousin had been murdered recently. She'd given him the details and he'd told her a few things about being a copper – none of the really important stuff like curling up in a ball or the way you felt when the other guys in the station looked at you – but a little about some cases he'd worked on. One murder and one assault over whose turn it was to cut the grass verge out front.

Keeping it nice and simple. No sense in killing the topic.

On the machine there was a message from Costello, saying it was time to get down the station, grab some credit for himself. Paddy Benner was on his way to London on a murder charge.

Ed shrugged. Well, that was one thing off his list.

He looked out the window again. He wanted to see her soon. Maybe he'd tell her more: let her have some of the good stuff and see if she was still interested.

Joe walked home along the Quays, turning off at the Customs House and into North Strand, not much traffic about at this hour apart from taxis. He was used to walking. Stella didn't like to walk; she preferred to lie on the couch and read *Cosmo* or *Marie Claire* or a crime novel and then when Joe would arrive home she'd take one look and say, "Boy, am I glad I didn't go with you!" He tried to explain it to her. The walks were healthy. They cleared your mind. They freshened your body. Most of all, they gave you time to consider things, like now, Joe asking himself why he'd let a murderer go free? Money, that was one reason, but it was more than that, there was also the matter of pride, Joe happy to see he still had some of the old bite left. He was sick of being patronised and he was sick of being manipulated. He didn't enjoy being patted on the shoulder or being told to hang in there, he was doing great.

How much shit, after all, could one man be realistically expected to eat?

It was only when Costello whispered, "He'll be Number Five" that Joe had known what he was going to do, the realisation finally hitting home that, yes, he was being used. In the car he'd listened and thought, *Jesus, this copper really wants a conviction.* And who could blame him? Scum like Benner, they deserved to be behind bars and maybe a copper had to bend the odd rule to get them there. What else could you expect? Yes, up to then it was just a question of pointing the finger, Joe happy to do his civic duty, happy to put his neck on the line and say, "Yeah, it was him." Only Costello didn't seem to care if they had the right guy or not. All he wanted was Benner on a plane to England.

Which, to Joe, was the hardest thing to figure out: if Benner was innocent surely he'd be back home as soon as there was another identity parade.

Had Costello really thought Joe would finger Paddy Benner just because he'd been told to?

The most surprising thing was Benner himself. Christ, he was a piece of work. You'd take him as an ordinary bloke, of course you would, standing there in his check shirt and jeans, nice and calm as though he was doing someone a favour by helping out with the line-up. Your average Joe Schmo looking around the room, his hands slid into his pockets. One pace forward, turning left and right, then back to his spot. Almost daring Joe to pick him out. Then stepping out of the line-up and saying to his lawyer, "See, I told you this was a stitch up, sticking me in with five coppers." No anger in the voice, not a hint of it, just calmly letting Joe know that he was the one suspected.

How could you run another parade if the prime suspect had already been identified?

Jesus, Joe thought, the nerve of it. And the presence of mind. Benner must have been shitting himself – Joe would have been – ready to be shunted back to England on a murder charge. Looking Joe in the face and waiting for it. Thinking, *Christ I'm a goner.* And then as soon as the chink appeared he'd gone for it, his mouth opening in shock at first, just the slightest hesitation, then straight into action. One simple sentence and he'd killed the whole business stone dead, Joe witnessing it and thinking, *Oh yes, this fucker's dangerous all right.* Dangerous and cold and clever. Louis Marks had been murdered, God have mercy on his soul, and if Joe wasn't careful, he might be going the same way. He needed to keep Benner at a distance. Bleed him, sure, but nice and slowly and always at a distance.

When, he asked himself, would he get another chance to acquire the sort of cash Stella might respect?

He was home by 3:15. He'd walked three miles and now he felt good after it. It had been a long day – fifteen hours since he'd bought the 16oz tubular claw hammer – but still he was alert, ready for whatever else might come along. The flat was cool and silent. It occurred that maybe he could use Benner immediately, send him in next door to wreak a little havoc. Tell him to take a good heavy mallet in with him.

He thought this… then thought, what the hell, and climbed the back wall himself.

The hammer was where he'd dropped it, the broken window hadn't been repaired. Joe looked inside and yes, there it was – all the glass still on the lino floor. Was there anyone home? It didn't look that way. He felt unbelievably calm. He smiled and slipped his hand inside to open the catch.

He moved forward feeling the broken glass scrunch under his feet.

The wooden handle felt smooth in his grip.

Yes, he thought, this was what he'd been waiting for – the feeling that he was finally taking control again.

Paddy took the Coast Road into Fairview and from there into town and out again, keeping a nice steady pace, following his line towards the Dublin Mountains, through Rathgar, through

Rathfarnham, and on to where the streetlights ended, turning the heads on full until they showed a small wooded area off to the side. In a place like this the night was as dead as it could be, nothing, not the slightest whisper, pure black apart from the city lights shining away in the distance. He pulled the spade from the boot and began to dig.

This was the easy part. Already he'd stripped the body – maybe the clothes could be traced back to London outlets – and had read and destroyed the contents of Donnelly's wallet. He'd found a gun, a chubby little revolver of some description, stuck in at the back of Donnelly's trousers and a key with a Hertz tag attached. Paddy had never held a gun before. It was heavier than he imagined, a solid lump of steel, Paddy thinking, *Hey this could be just what I need.* But then thought, *Where can I keep it?* Costello was mad enough to turn over the old man's house, of course he was, and what protection could a gun give you if you couldn't lay your hands on it immediately? No, he'd have to dispose of the gun too. Bury it somewhere separate from the body and try to remember where in case of emergency.

The car had been rented in Donnelly's name. Paddy had found it on Seapark Road, reversing up to the front door and heaving the body into the boot. Which he imagined was the riskiest part: you never knew when some nutbag was looking out his bedroom window. Now it was just a question of being careful. It was a question of covering the trail should the body be discovered, predicting what physical evidence the coppers might use and doing what you could to destroy it.

By 4:15 he was patting down the earth, saying, "No more surprise visits from you, pal."

He buried the gun maybe five hundred yards from the body, and drove back towards the city lights. The car was a problem – dump it and the Hertz crew would be on the blower to London. Only what was the alternative? Hand the keys in and he was leaving himself open to another line-up, Paddy thinking Jesus, the last thing he needed was to fuck up now. He'd been lucky, of course he had, luckier than he'd any right to expect but if hustling pool taught you anything it was that luck was spread about pretty evenly. After that it was a question of who took best advantage of it.

He needed to cover his tracks, kill the trail back to Mount Prospect Avenue.

He needed everything neat and tidy: no loose ends for the coppers.

Then he could turn his mind to the witness who'd let him walk.

25

Paddy Benner thought maybe he could give a seminar on lying. Or seminars, for that matter – see could he drag it out a while. He'd lecture on the use of detail. He'd talk about body language and restraint – the ability to trust in your story and let it do the work. He'd teach how best to deal with the sceptic. He'd talk about conviction and about calmness and maybe even offer a few examples – like when Michael Corleone's wife wants to know if he's had his brother-in-law killed and Michael looks her straight in the face and says, No. Just that, a nice simple *No*. It was a terrific lie. One of the best Paddy had ever heard. And if it taught you anything it was the need to match the intensity of the questioner – someone looked you straight in the face and demanded an answer, you stared straight back and told him whatever the fuck you wanted. Someone tossed you a joke with a question behind it, you batted it right back at him with a smile on your face.

Flippancy and over-reaction, both could be a giveaway.

But above all it was a matter of detail, calmness and detail, Paddy describing the scene to the old man, the way two guys, one a teenager and one a little older, had crossed the road and asked him for a light. Paddy knowing something was going to happen, ready to hand over what he had on him when one tried to grab him from behind. He'd taken a few belts with a cosh before he rammed the teenager's head into a wall and made a run for it.

Which was as much as the old man needed to know.

The beauty of Des was that he always had a story to beat your one. A minute later Paddy was hearing about how his father had been robbed coming out of the golf club one night.

"Victims of crime," Paddy said. "That's what we are, Dad."

"Mugged?" Aoife said over the phone.

"I know. What's the world coming to? There was a time when a chap could walk his girl home without being set upon."

"His girl. How quaint."

"I should've let you walk *me* home."

"Quaint and gallant, all in the one conversation. You all right?"

Paddy gave her the same story, about the two bozos asking him for a light, then *whap* from behind. He stuck to the same details, one teenager and one in his twenties – how he'd got a good grip on the smaller one and biffed his head against the wall. What's a cosh? she wanted to know. He told her it was two pieces of wood held together by a chain and it hurt like hell if you got a belt of one.

"What did the police say?"

"I didn't mention it. I'd barely patched myself up and there was a knock on the door and who was it only Dublin's finest."

"At what time was this?"

"Whatever time I got home. Somewhere around a quarter past one."

"Jesus, Paddy, this has gone too far. Costello again?"

"No, it was two other goons. But Costello was at the station when I got there. You know those identikit pictures they use to try to get a likeness, well apparently there was one that looked like me. Or so Costello thought. We had an identity parade."

"At one in the morning?"

"Closer to half-two. Me and five coppers standing in a row and this guy comes in, takes a dekky and says, No he's not here."

"Did you tell them you'd been mugged?"

"No."

"Why not?"

"What was the point?"

"Maybe they might catch whoever mugged you."

"I just wanted to get home and go to bed. I didn't come out of it too badly. My face is a bit banged up but nothing too serious."

There was a pause for a moment. "Paddy, you really have to put an end to this?"

"There was a Free Legal Aid guy in the station, but he said he couldn't bring a charge of harassment. All he could do was hang on to see that my rights weren't violated in the line-up."

"So get someone else."

"I don't need a lawyer to press a charge. There's a Garda Complaints Office in Abbey Street. All I have to is go there and file a complaint."

"I still think you should get yourself proper legal advice."

"I'll see what the Complaints Board have to say for themselves. Then maybe you'd like to meet up in town for lunch and have a ramble around."

"Sure," she said. "Last week of holidays, you know. Might as well get out and about."

They sat at home, Paddy and his father, watching the golf and eating frozen dinners, not saying much for the first while. It felt odd: the old man never stayed in. Or at least he never did in the old days. Paddy could remember waiting for him to come home at night, ready to tell him about the pool halls and about school; ready, if it came to that, to take on serious matters like golf or politics or his own future. Ready, even, to talk of his mother, to fix the old man with a stare and say, "A freak accident, that's all it was." He'd rehearsed it any number of times. "Blame?" he'd say. "Not here in this house." He'd sound adult, forthright. He'd lay things to rest. Then, later on, rather than break that comfortable silence, the old man would switch off the television, give Paddy's shoulder a short manly squeeze – in equal measures a gesture of gratitude and respect – and turn in for the night.

That was how Paddy pictured the scene. For two years he played it out in his mind. Only it never happened. It was never the right moment. Something always seemed to come over the old man when he stepped through the front door. Even now, Paddy didn't know what it was – guilt maybe or defensiveness, something like that – and a silence would descend, punctuated sometimes by the trademark bluff good humour, sometimes by the need to lecture. That was one of Des's methods of communication – the lecture. About clothes or hair or study, always keeping that distance – the one, Paddy thought now, that protected him from his son's gaze, maybe from his forgiveness and the responsibility that might attach itself to it.

Paddy could remember too the routine they'd had after he'd turned seventeen and had dropped out of school. Shift work, he'd call it. The revolving door – Des coming home after work and Paddy on his way out, off to the pool halls or to case a house or maybe to coax Aoife Brennan from her books. At that point he was keeping contact to a minimum. When the old man asked where he'd been he'd just say, "Off on my travels." When asked about school he'd say, "Look at you. If ever there was an ad for an early leaver, it's you."

It was the best way to deal with Des – stonewall him.

But it had taken a while to learn it. Through the previous year they'd taken to fighting. Good fights. Solid rage fights. Des too stupid and confused to calm things, Paddy too hurt and angry to stop. They'd use what they could. They'd swear. They'd search for the arrows and they'd let fly. Paddy would ask his father who he was riding while his mother was lying under a bus. The old man would shout, You're a fucking bum and don't let anyone ever tell you otherwise.

Once he'd said, "Well, your mother didn't think you were worth hanging on for."

And then said, "Oh Jesus, Paddy, I'm sorry."

But Paddy didn't mind. Why would he mind? – he'd been waiting all along for the old man to say it, pushing him to. Because it was true, wasn't it? Of course it was. After the years of bullshit and platitudes and people telling you what a wonderful woman your mother was, maybe it had taken the old man to finally hit the nail on the head.

Or could it be that she really hadn't heard the second bus? There was no way of knowing.

But whatever the case the old man didn't seem to be in such a rush anymore. Slowing down, probably, eight more years under the belt. Or maybe it was because he had Sky Sports these days and some nights Jesus there was nothing but fucking golf on the telly.

They sat for a couple of hours watching the Irish Open.

Every now and then Des would explain something, a technical point. Like Paddy was one of his clients but that was okay.

Then, later on, he said, "Think about these three options. One – you stay in the house and live here. Whatever else about it, it's cheap. Two – you stay in Dublin so you might as well stick around the area. Three – you head off again and that'd be fine if you'd stay in touch. Just call once a week. Reverse the charges if you want."

Paddy looked across, seeing the profile, that was all.

"Take your pick," Des said. "Any of those would be fine by me."

Paddy let it slide. He wasn't sure what he wanted to say.

The copper taking the details of Paddy's complaint was in full uniform: a tubby guy somewhere in his forties, nodding and making sympathetic noises and even asking the odd question. Where had Paddy been picked up? Was it explained to him fully that he was under no obligation to go to a Garda station? Exactly how long had he been left waiting? Paddy answered and watched and wondered about this copper. On the telly or in the flicks, the Internal Affairs folks never got a good showing: they were always the squares in the neat suits. Work for Internal Affairs and you were shit. Rat to them and you were a judas. Apart from that one with Andy Garcia and Richard Gere or there was another with some young guy – Paddy couldn't remember his name – trying to nail Nick Nolte for being dirty.

Here in Ireland, apparently there was no official Internal Affairs section. The way it worked, a team was set up – usually a superintendent and one other – to investigate each complaint and then they would recommend that there either be a hearing or the whole thing be chucked away. Paddy's complaint was down the list but they'd get to it all right.

"I'm not looking for blood here," he said. "All I want is to be left alone."

"Detective Costello will be informed that a complaint has been made against him. He'll be told he's under investigation."

Time to kill. Paddy wandered around town, thinking about

how to sort things out. Three problems – extradition, what was left of the Donnelly clan, and now this witness who'd let him walk – each a whopper by anyone's standards. The witness, he could go to the back of the queue since there was nothing Paddy could do about it until he made contact. And the extradition business, hopefully Miller would be able to manage that one.

Which left Sudds Donnelly.

Paddy didn't like waiting. He'd prefer to fly to London, search out Donnelly and kill him. Find him, stalk him and squeeze the trigger – simple as that. Or else get in close and use the knife. But could he do it? – just walk up to a guy and murder him in cold blood. Why not? Especially if it was a matter of him or you. Paddy had already killed one brother, and well, he couldn't imagine anybody mourning the other. But if he did bump Sudds, where would the investigation lead? One brother gets beaten up, the other disappears and then the first one gets a bullet in the back of the head. Whatever else it would have a nice symmetry. But a copper might learn that a guy named Paddy Benner had some run-in with the most recently deceased and he might feed what he has into the computer. Leading him to Downs Leaze and the nutcase who should be held as an example to other have-a-go merchants.

Crazy, he thought, walking back into a country where he was already wanted for murder.

So he had two choices, the same two as usual – stay or hit the road again. Just pack up and go, back to the pool halls and the burglary, see could he build himself a nest egg. Something to start a life with.

It was attractive, wasn't it? – the idea of drifting back to his old life. Four weeks since he'd stepped off the boat in Dun Laoghaire, and now here he was wandering around town, into the pool halls and out again, feeling the pull. It was the pull of failure, the desire to lose. Just like he'd explained it to Tim. It hit when you were tired and there were hard decisions to be made and all you wanted to do was walk away. And what was stopping him? Aoife, mainly. The old man too, in a small way but mostly it was Aoife and yes he'd miss her but maybe there was no other way.

Twenty-seven next February. He had plenty of time to start a new life.

She linked his arm as they walked. It reminded him of when they were younger and they'd spend the day wandering, Aoife broke, Paddy pretending he was, in and out of the pricey shops so she could try things on and say, "Well, I'm afraid I'm just going to have to think about it now." It was a nice cheap way of passing the time. Women's clothes, they were always a winner but Paddy preferred speciality items. Like hockey sticks. Or panniers. Or saddles. There was a hundred stupid questions you could think up about saddles – the leather, the contour, the type of stirrup that was most appropriate. How best to care for the leather and what sort of guarantee you had on an item like this.

But now Aoife had a credit card in her purse. She tried on a denim jacket and Paddy found himself looking at the alarm system. It was a *Securecam*, whatever that was like, with two surveillance cameras operating way too slowly on the hinges. They both swung to the same side of the room at the same moment which was madness: time it right and you could have one off the hinges by the time the other picked you up. Then it would be a matter of picking the right wall to sidle along and then you were underneath the second one.

Old habits died hard.

"What do you think?" Aoife asked.

"It doesn't matter whether *I* like it," he said. "What *you* think of it, that's what's important."

"What's it like?" Aoife wanted to know. They were sitting in an Italian restaurant on Dame Street, Aoife unable to finish her pizza, Paddy struggling with his spaghetti, especially the shorter strands he couldn't get properly wrapped around the fork.

"What's what like?"

"Burglary. When you step in, what's the feeling like?"

"You thinking of knocking some place off?"

"Just curious."

"Just after I went to the States, I hooked up with this old

timer named Leo Price. Leo knew a bloke who used to get an erection every time he went into a house."

"You serious?"

"Absolutely. You could come home some night and find this clown mooching around your house with a stiffy."

"And that's how you found it – exciting?"

"It's certainly that. Scary as hell too. This guy Leo knew, he was exceptional but the thrill is definitely a big part of it. But it's not the sort of excitement you can enjoy because you never know what's on the other side of the door. There could be some big bruiser with a shotgun pointing at you. You feel a rush but it's tempered until you walk out the door and you're away and safe and then it really hits you."

Aoife was tearing things up again, what was left of her pizza this time. "Where'd you learn it?"

"What? To burgle?"

"To pick locks and things."

"Practice mostly. I only really perfected it when I went to the States and ran into Leo. He'd learned it all when he was in the slammer. He took a couple of courses and by the time his parole came through he didn't need to carry a gun any more. He taught me about locks. And a bit about safes. He wasn't too hot on alarms but I don't think anyone really is. They're too complicated."

"It's like anything, I suppose," Aoife said. "You have to have the right tools."

Paddy nodded. She was right. Some locks took you longer than others and some folks used three or four different locks on a door so you were lifting different tools in and out of your coat. Or you might have to use two together which could be tricky. But if you had the right equipment, it didn't matter what lock was on the door. Once you had a few minutes undisturbed. Yeah sure, he explained, you could get in all right, it was the staying in that was the problem.

She was silent for a moment. "Holding your nerve."

"That's right."

"Hear some noise and your heart jumps."

"That's right too."

"Anyone ever come home on you?"

"At least half the jobs I did, the folks were home when I went in. Slide in the back door, or through an upstairs window, you don't even need to pick a lock. And there's often a lot of stuff knocking around that people put away before they go out."

"Jewellery?"

"Cash or jewellery. Sometimes you'd pick up travellers cheques or something like that."

She stopped playing with the pizza and sat back in the seat. She surveyed him. "You enjoyed it, didn't you?"

"Sure."

"The buzz."

"Absolutely."

"And?"

"And what?"

"Anything else you enjoyed about it?"

He thought about it a moment. "It's hard to explain. You have to have the heart for it. Most burglars aren't particularly violent – professional ones, I mean, not the druggies – and in other areas they're not particularly brave. But it takes a lot of guts to walk through that door, I tell you. A good burglar knows that. He's got something special about him, something most people don't have. And you can't arm yourself. Take any weapon in with you and you're looking at a minimum of seven if you're caught."

"You're talking about courage."

"If you want."

"And ego."

"It's a particular type of ego. A desire to take risks. Or a confidence in yourself to calculate the risk. To case out the job and to see it through, there's a satisfaction in that. After all, that job was sitting there but you were the one who spotted it and pulled it off."

Aoife smiled across the table. "You mind talking about this?"

He smiled back. "You know me. Always happy to talk about myself."

"That's what I thought," she said. "I'll let you know if I

think of anything else."

Walking down Grafton Street, she thought of something. "You never got caught, did you?"

"No."

"Or what about the pool halls? No one ever dragged you into a back room and broke your fingers with a hammer."

"Like in the film?"

"Paul Newman."

"That's the one. No, I've been pretty lucky."

"Well, it's got a nice irony, doesn't it? Here you are doing all these dangerous things and nothing ever happens to you. Then you're walking home back here and you get beaten up."

"I'm glad you appreciate it," Paddy said.

"I've always liked irony," she said. "Once I'm not on the receiving end of it."

The conversation turned to jobs. Working in the golf shop was fine, Paddy said, as long as you kept in mind that it was just a gang of middle class tossers walloping a ball around. The mistake was to take any of them seriously.

Teaching was different, Aoife told him, to what she'd expected. She'd pictured herself collecting assignments, reading and grading them and suggesting improvements, and then when the second draft arrived she'd realise just why she'd chosen the profession. She might even tinker a little more, send it back one more time. Only the second draft never arrived – and thank Christ for that, wasn't there enough to read without getting rewrites? – because that was the thing about English, even the weakest, the real plummers, could fill up the pages. Whatever else, they could certainly do that. It was all over the place, and it was undoubtedly shit, but it was there in abundance, page after page of the purest waffle. And the good ones, what about them? They were more rewarding, sure, and yet there was a sterility to it: they studied because they wanted to be doctors or lawyers or whatever their folks wanted them to be. Did they give a shit about Shakespeare? Would *The Pearl* encourage them to read another book – any book? It was unlikely. Sterile, yes, that was the word. Maybe it was just the school she was in – a nice middle class Catholic girls school – but there was a deadness to the whole thing as though they were all there for a reason but they'd all forgotten what it was and something else had popped up along the way.

She'd thought that she'd be inculcating a love of literature. She'd pictured herself fostering some gifted young writer. But now she understood that a girl who was going to read Shakespeare would read it when she was ready to read it, and if another was going to grow into a writer – a real writer – she'd do it regardless of who her English teacher was. It was that simple. She coached people through exams and tried not to do too much damage along the way.

Still, she was a lifer. The kids were fun, the days passed nicely, and anyone who gave up those holidays would have to be nuts.

"Ever notice how in every classroom scene on the telly the bell always goes?" Paddy said.

Aoife nodded. "I always feel like saying, No hang on here, there's another twenty minutes left. Let them film that if they want to know what it's really like."

Paddy bought her a pair of earrings at a stall in the Dandelion Market. They cost £2.99 and had tiny little half moons.

"You're sure you like them?" he asked.

"I'm sure."

"Because if you don't I can take them back."

"No, I want to keep them," she said. And she did. Twenty minutes later she emerged from the toilets in Arnotts. She turned her head sideways and tapped a half moon.

"See?" she said. "I'm giving them an early run out."

"They look well."

"Of course they do," she said. "Lovely girl like me to model them."

They had tea in McDonalds and caught the seven-forty showing of *Aliens* in the Savoy. Paddy didn't really like space films apart from the old ones where the aliens would take over the human bodies and come across all nice and friendly. Yeah, those ones were the best. Some guy walking down the street only he gets dragged into the bushes and comes out exactly the same apart from a funny glint in his eye. Paddy had a theory about aliens – that they were thick as pigshit. Why not? It was as possible as anything else. All that stuff about them wonking up the earth's computers with their beams or batting away rockets with an electric shield, it was rubbish. They were morons. They were wandering around in outer space banging their heads together. They spent the day grunting and fighting and looking around for some little guy to eat.

He whispered his theory to Aoife and she said, "You're some cretin, you know that?"

Then she whispered, "I want to sleep with you tonight."

They took a taxi home after the film. She led him upstairs by the hand. They made love gently with the housemate just on the other side of the wall and Aoife's eyes filled with tears and then she put her hands over his lips and smiled and kissed him and he could feel her cheeks wet against his face. She said, "I thought you were never coming back."

Within minutes, she was asleep.

Paddy climbed off the bed, put on his T-shirt and boxer shorts, and smoked a cigarette out the window. The night was still lively; in the distance he could hear an ambulance siren. Costello was out there somewhere and so was the witness who'd let him walk. Ray Donnelly was buried up the mountains and somewhere, further away, his brother was looking for him.

Three good reasons to just pick up and run.

But Paddy knew he wasn't going anywhere. He climbed across Aoife and lay next to the wall. He put his arm across her and lay his head on the pillow next to hers.

26

Like most people, he imagined, Joe Faherty knew practically nothing about crime. For thirty-nine years he'd never robbed or assaulted anyone and he didn't know anyone who had. He'd never been burgled or mugged. He'd never even been a witness to any wrongdoing. He didn't know any police officers or criminals and any information he had on them had been gleaned from magazines or books or newspapers. It was a topic he generally avoided. Things like that, they belonged to another world. You could worry yourself silly, he reckoned, and all for nothing, so why bother with it?

Now it was something to consider.

In the space of a couple of hours, he had committed a number of crimes. Breaking and Entering for a start although maybe there was so much time between the breaking and the entering that they couldn't be categorised together. Who knew and who really cared? Destruction of Property, that was another, the tubular claw hammer more than fulfilling its function, Joe having moved from room to room, destroying every item that could possibly be heard on the other side of the wall – the television, the hi-fi, a transistor radio, and even an old guitar he'd found lying in the corner of one of the bedrooms. Alarm clocks too, just for the sake of it. The hoover and a computer that had a compartment for playing CDs. Even the telephone. The television was the trickiest. The screen shattered easily but whatever sort of plastic they used at the back, it was good stuff: three times the hammer bounced off so in the end Joe stood on the kitchen table and dropped the set from over his head.

The feeling that gave him, he could recommend it to anybody.

And between the breaking and the entering, what exactly

was the crime committed? It wasn't perjury, was it? Perjury, as far as Joe knew, only applied to a courtroom. So was it termed 'Obstruction of Justice' or 'Misleading a Police Officer'? It couldn't have been 'Interfering with an Investigation' since he'd never asked to be involved in the first place. Or if there was some wording relating to false evidence…

But then again, who really gave a shit! Whatever it was called, he'd committed it, so what was the point in wondering about it now?

His nervousness had gone. True, he'd dropped his bundle the night before but that was only because it was such a big decision to make – stick to the rules or start hitting back a little. Beginners nerves, that's all they were. It was bound to happen. The important thing was that he'd got away with it: the mistake hadn't cost him since he'd held himself together when Costello and that other Garda called. He hadn't blabbed or confessed anything, and now he was in pretty good shape, ready to think about his next move.

He was lying in bed, thinking about this when a young uniformed copper called wanting to know if he knew anything about a disturbance next door sometime the previous night. Joe led him inside.

"There's always a disturbance next door," he said.

"This was different," the Garda said. "It was vandalism."

"Someone's car?"

"No. Inside the house. You know anything about it?"

"Not a thing. I'm a pretty heavy sleeper if I get the chance."

"A number of items were destroyed."

Joe smiled at him. "I hope the music system was one of them."

"Music system, television – anything that might make noise as a matter of fact."

"You serious?"

"You sure you don't know anything about this? If there was noise coming from the house, you'd hear it more than anyone else, wouldn't you?"

Joe nodded. "Damn right, I can hear it. This really is terrific news. Someone smashed the hi-fi in there, well what I say is, good luck to them."

The Garda checked his notebook. "Was it you that had an argument with one of the occupants, when was it – Thursday night?"

Joe nodded. "He told me to go fuck myself."

"They were his exact words, were they?"

"Did he forget to mention that part?"

"He didn't say anything about it."

"My sister's the landlady here. She's had a big turnover of tenants in the past while with that mob living next door. They don't give a damn. She's trying to get them thrown out but that takes time. They told her to go fuck herself and then when I complained the other night some guy with long hair told me the same thing."

The Garda nodded. "So you don't feel any sympathy for them."

"Not a bit."

"And you don't know anything about what was done?"

Joe shook his head. "Might be one of the old tenants they drove out of the place. And who could blame them, it's hard enough to get accommodation in this city. Or one of the other neighbours, maybe."

The Garda stared into Joe's face and Joe stared back. Then he looked around the room, as if deciding to conduct some sort of search. He took Joe's full name, asked for a home and work number. "If we have any more questions," he said, "we'll be in touch."

"If you do catch whoever did it," Joe said from the doorway, "tell him I owe him a pint. A full night's sleep, that'll be a treat."

And it was that easy. Just like the previous night, because it didn't matter what that copper suspected, he couldn't prove a thing. Would they go rooting around for forensic evidence? It was very unlikely. What with murders and muggings and rapes all over the city these days, who was going to bother about a little case of vandalism? Joe was home free. He knew it and the copper knew it and if those morons next door had any sense, they knew it too.

It felt great.

He was glad it was a Sunday – a nice lazy day without Gladys and Damien and the others providing a distraction. He could lie on the bed and blow rings of smoke at the ceiling and before long, he was sure, things would sort themselves out in his mind. The important thing was to be careful. Starting with his finances. He needed to keep a good tight rein on his budget, resist the temptation to splash out just because he might have found another source of income. What was the word? Prudence, that was it, a bit of good old fashioned prudence. The last thing he needed was to push Benner harder than he intended to, just because he'd become greedy.

He would continue as though nothing had happened.

If Costello reappeared, all he had to do was stick to his story. Just before he'd left on Saturday night Costello had asked him how long he'd spent with the two Mormons and Joe said he couldn't remember exactly but they'd chatted a while. Three minutes? Costello asked. Five? Ten? Joe said he wasn't sure but three sounded about right. Which meant what? Most likely it meant that Benner had instructed his lawyer to check how long each witness had spent with the Mormons. What judge was going to issue an extradition warrant if the witness who got by far the best look at the suspect was quite certain Paddy Benner hadn't been involved?

See? Getting inside Benner's head already, guessing his moves.

Joe felt confident.

Stella had always been interested in crime novels. Other types of book too but crime ones particularly. The old ones were the best, she said, the likes of Agatha Christie and Ngaio Marsh but every now and then she'd stumble across a modern writer and she'd head in to *Waterstones* or *Hodges Figgis* to stock up. Ed McBain was the business. So were Sara Paretsky and Marcia Muller. And there was another guy by the name of Lawrence Block who had been her latest craze around the time Joe had lost his job selling shampoo.

Which had put an end to Lawrence Block. Find yourself

operating off one salary instead of two and crime novels became something of a luxury.

So she'd begun re-reading her favourites which Joe found amazing. He couldn't imagine reading any of these books once let alone going back to them a second time and when he told her so she just shrugged and said, "Well, that's the difference between you and me, isn't it?" Joe read the newspaper and he watched the television. He liked Coronation Street and Brookside or if there was a decent documentary on he'd tune into that. Spend your whole day working, the last thing you wanted was to waste the evening with your head stuck in a book.

When he asked her about it, Stella just said, "It's the only way I can think of to stay sane."

It had struck Joe as an odd thing to say. Sane? – Stella was one of the sanest, most practical people Joe had ever met. Still it was nothing to fret over. Joe didn't mind how she'd just switch into her book for hours on end – that was fine, it was good that she had an interest – no, what bugged him was that she'd never tell him about what she was reading. He'd ask what one was like and she'd say "Not bad." Or "So so." Or "Pretty good." That was all – no elaboration. No indication of what distinguished a good author from a bad one, no hint as to what he might look for if he was to bring one home. And by and large, if she found someone new she'd go on a binge and fill up the collection pretty quickly. Which left Joe waiting for the latest one to come out, anywhere up to twenty quid for a hardback, Stella fingering the cover and saying "Hardbacks are a mug's game. Wait a year and you could get three books for what you just paid."

When she was saying, So-so, what she was really saying was, Why don't you go and read it yourself?

Yes, some things would have to change once he moved back in. There were things they both needed to sort out.

In the afternoon he walked to Clontarf and no two ways about it, it was a nice house – big and detached and on the corner of Seapark Road with a good sized garden. It was just the sort of place Stella would give her eye teeth for. According to Costello the father was a golf pro – Joe thought he recognised the name –

and Benner was helping him out selling equipment in the club shop. Some criminals did that did that apparently, they'd take a job and then when they were asked they'd say, "I'm a working man, why wouldn't I have a few quid?"

It fit with Joe's impression of Benner. It was deceptive how ordinary he seemed, just another guy in his mid-twenties: average height, average looks, nothing to set him apart if you didn't know his history. Which, Joe presumed, made him all the more dangerous. As soon as he got the chance Joe would go see his lawyer and ask would it be possible to have a letter dated and locked away to be opened only in the eventuality of death. He presumed it was possible. In the letter he'd outline what really took place in Down's Leaze, say he was barely back in Dublin when he happened by chance to run into Benner. A simple threat, that's what he'd say, Benner letting him know that he and his family would be killed if Joe said a word.

It would be like a life assurance policy. Just in case Benner decided to come after him, in case he appeared at the door some day.

More ham and cheese and yesterday's bread for tea. Security work a low payer – £112.85 per week after the Government had taken its cut – and Joe's budget was a tight one. Thirty for food, ten for cigarettes, keep another ten for whatever extras might occur. The rest he'd send to Stella with a short note enquiring after her. Nothing heavy, nothing fancy. Nothing that might jeopardise his chances of returning home. Just a few words to let her know she was on his mind, his new address at the top and *Love, Joe* at the bottom.

Then maybe some evening he'd open the door and there she'd be, standing with her hands by her sides, saying, "You want to talk?"

It was a lot to hope for, he knew that. But where was the harm in hoping?

All that quiet coming from next door, it was a joy to listen to. Joe turned in early and lay on his back and tried to figure out his plan. It was hard to know how heavily to lean on Benner.

Five hundred a month? A grand? Two grand? All that Costello had really said was that Benner was an armed robber. But that could mean anything. Did he specialise in banks or in jewellery shops or did he rob private citizens? How much could he expect to make on a job and how often did he work?

Christ, there were a lot of questions.

So pick a number. Say a grand, Joe decided, it was as good a figure as any. Not too big and not too small and now the question was how to arrange payment without meeting the guy. Through the post, that was a possibility. Rent a postal box and drop him a line telling him to have a grand by the end of the week. Tell him to wrap it up good and proper. Tell him to post it off and sit tight and his favourite witness would be in touch in a month's time.

Nice and impersonal, it was the only way to conduct business like this. No arguments, no conversation and hopefully no running into the guy late some night down a dark alley.

27

Stella's sister, Joanne, had a rich psychiatrist husband and a hip to the groove attitude to bringing up her children. A brick creamed you on the back of the head, what you had to do was sit the kid down and reason with him. It was a matter of gentle correction. The idea was to stay positive and preserve the child's self-esteem. A brick was a dangerous object, you explained this, and then when you were finished explaining it you made damn sure you were ready to duck the next one.

Sunday dinner with them was a grim, grim experience.

Starting each week with Stella's mother saying to Joanne's husband, Gerry, how he'd have to excuse the state of the place. You'll just have to take us as you find us, she'd say. It was a theme of hers – the no frills, we're good solid down to earth people routine. If it's fancy French cooking you're after, she'd tell him, you've come through the wrong door. And then her father would start up about what he respected was good solid home cooking, none of that dicky rubbish you'd find in those modern restaurants and Gerry would give a solemn nod and agree. Home cooking was indeed the best. There was no comparison. All this while Joanne was asking one of the kids to please stop doing something and the kid would just keep right on doing it. Gerry had little more than contempt for his in-laws, Stella was sure of it. And guess what? – he was right. All that folksy, salt of the earth shit, making a virtue out of having no class and not even recognising what it was, who the hell could blame him?

Why pay three hundred quid for a dress, they'd want to know, when you could get a perfectly good one in the sales for forty-five?

Why eat out when you'd do better at home?

Why buy a swanky car if you were going to come out some morning and find the bloody thing had been stolen?

These were the lessons that had been drummed into Stella. The other kids too – Paul, the eldest, and Dave and Ciaran who were sweating it out on the sites in Boston these days and Una who sent thoughtful letters home about the way nurses were regarded in Saudi – but mostly it was Stella who got the treatment. Most of all, she'd been warned never to complain. That was the greatest sin, complaining, since weren't there plenty of people worse off than she was and who the hell did she think she was anyway?

All her life she'd been hearing it.

So what was the point in hearing it again this afternoon? She telephoned her mother and said her stomach didn't feel right, a bug maybe or it might have been something she ate. Then she settled into the couch. She opened her book, found her page and then Jesus, who was that at the door? It couldn't be her mother, not even she could cover the ground that fast.

Ed O'Brien was wearing jeans and a plain yellow T-shirt, looking good with a big pair of shoulders on him, saying, "Just a quick social visit."

"You looking for Sunday dinner?"

"Is there one going?"

"Not here there's not."

"Well, I'll have to try somewhere else then," he said and grinned and she led him inside to the living room. The house was tidy: it was easy to keep a place in order when there was just yourself living there.

Ed, sitting into the armchair now, said, "I thought you might like to know that Joe was in the Bridewell last night."

That got her attention. "What'd he do? He didn't hit someone else, did he?"

Ed shook his head. "Remember you were telling me about your cousin who was murdered over in England?"

"Louis."

"Louis Marks?"

"That's right."

"Well, I was out last night and then when I got home there's three messages on my machine. All from Costello. Telling me to haul myself into the Bridewell double quick, that they have Paddy Benner dead in the water for a murder in London. I didn't want anything to do with it, not at that hour anyway, so I hit the hay. But Costello's just been on the phone to say that Benner walked. When he described the case, with the two Mormons trying to bluff their way in, I remembered that it was your cousin. So I asked and yeah, Joe was the witness but he said it wasn't Benner. Apparently, there was an identikit sent over that fitted the description but it wasn't him."

"There was a line-up?"

"That's right."

"Like on the telly?"

"Pretty much. But now the problem is that Benner says he's bringing a complaint for harassment."

"Against Costello."

"And me."

"You were just along for the ride, weren't you? It's Costello who's been bothering him."

Ed shook his head. "Try telling that to a judge. What I'm going to have to do is check the dates and see what burglaries there were around then. Then try to justify my teaming up with Costello and give some reason why Benner might have been a likely suspect."

She thought about it for a moment. "Could you make a few up?"

He was impressed. She could tell from the look he was giving her. "You never know. I'll see what there is and maybe I might add a few of my own. Just to beef it out a bit, you know."

By the looks of things Ed was staying a while and why not? – it wasn't as though she was rushing off anywhere. Let him hang around if he wanted to. The news about Joe being in the Bridewell, it wasn't urgent, but here he was all the same parked on her couch. He'd got the message the other night – how could he have missed it? – that she wasn't about to hop into bed with the first man who asked her. Yet as soon as he had an excuse…

Sunday dinner with the folks, she said, sometimes you just

had to pull a sickie. She told him about how her sister had hit the jackpot on the money front but Jesus, she was earning it living with Gerry. What was it with people and their kids? Did they really have nothing else to talk about? Some days, you'd spend the whole meal hearing about babies or school or toilet training and then once the conversation had finally switched to something else, one of the little turds would come tearing back in and that'd be the end of that.

"It's a nightmare," Stella said.

Ed said it was one of the good things about a job where you worked odd shifts, no need to pull a sickie if you weren't in the mood for something.

"Joe is boring in a different sort of way," she said. "Gerry could nail you on a one to one about his job or a book he'd read and Christ you'd feel like saying, Hey you don't have a gun on you by any chance. He could bore for Ireland, that boy. But Joe was different. Joe just stopped having anything interesting to say. You understand the difference?"

"One's boring, the other's just not very interesting."

"Exactly. With Gerry at least you know that *he's* having a good time. But with Joe it was just like this space had opened up between us and by the time whatever he said had passed through the space, it all sounded the same. You know sometimes if you're at a party and you're left with someone and you just have nothing to say to them. There's no chemistry between you, zilch, not even enough for a conversation but you still say something and the other person says something and it's like you're treading through treacle. It's bloody exhausting. It's almost as if they're making you dull."

Ed smiled. "Or you're making them dull."

"That's right. Or you're making them dull. Well that's how I felt about Joe, whatever he had to say I just felt like I'd heard it all before. Which made him try even harder and that used to annoy me even more. You know what I think?"

"What?"

"I think I might have pushed him to hit me."

She let it go there. She wasn't sure quite what she wanted to say, how much she was willing to reveal. Had she really pushed him to it? Not on any conscious level, that was for sure, since no one in her right mind would want to be walloped across the face. But what about on another level? Take a woman who realises she's been sold a pup but it hasn't really occurred to her to look for a way out. How does she cope? She withdraws further into herself and the more her husband needs some reassurance the less she can give. Or wants to give. Then, with a few drinks on board, it all comes out, the frustration and the contempt, everything that's been building up and after that there's no way back, is there? Which is good because why would you want to go back? Then it's just a matter of pressing the right buttons, waiting for the guy to crack.

Did she feel guilty? How could she feel guilty if she wasn't even sure what she'd intended?

She watched Ed, the way he was sitting there happy to listen. He was another bad bet, she knew this: he was lazy and weak and on a slow road to nowhere. A nice enough guy, sure, but that was as far as it went.

"You hungry?" she asked.

She made him a toasted ham and cheese sandwich and said well maybe this Paddy Benner was bluffing, how many people did you hear say they were going to file a complaint and then you never heard another word? It was one of the good things about her job, she didn't get too many people complaining to her. All she had to do was type and answer the phone and make sure she didn't screw up the computer system. It was a good business to be in, packaging – even in a recession you couldn't send an item off uncovered.

Did she ever think of moving? Sometimes, but never for very long. Especially with all those graduates standing in the dole queue these days.

"The only worry is the money," she said. "Go from two salaries to one and you'd be amazed how fast your savings can disappear."

"You're left with the mortgage now," Ed said.

"That's how it works. You want the house, you get the debts along with it."

"That's one way of looking at it."

"You got another?"

"You've just lost yourself an expense. Joe wasn't bringing anything in but he wasn't starving either. You should have more disposable income now."

She thought for a moment. "Always look at the bright side, that the message?"

He grinned. "Got it in one."

"Must be something to do with that couch," she said and laughed. "Now you're even beginning to sound like him."

Stella was interested in policework. Her interest was academic. She enjoyed the mystery, the way the pieces of the puzzle were presented and you had no idea which pieces were the important ones. Which meant that they were all important. Was policework really like that? she wanted to know. She doubted it – these days it was gangs and rapes and junkies holding syringes filled with blood.

Ed said, "I'd like a change."

She wasn't sure if she'd heard him right. Coppers liked to be out there in the thick of it, she imagined, and if they didn't, couldn't they always get a cushy number behind a desk? It was a line of work where there was something for everyone. But Ed's voice was telling her something else. Tentative, that was the word. Here was a guy testing the waters, seeing what the reception was like before deciding what to say next.

Stella said, "It's none of my business but the first thing you want to do is to get out from under Costello. He sees the chance, he'll trample all over you."

Ed pointed to where she'd left her book. It was an old Ed McBain she'd picked up second hand – six naked bodies found on the ice all shot to hell. "That guy there, he writes about the police, doesn't he?"

"Most of the time."

"Well, you can bet he's not too interested in uniformed coppers."

"You ever read him?"

"I don't read much. And I if I do, I stay away from police

books."

"Well, you're right. If it's a police book the hero's a detective."

Ed nodded. "That's because uniformed coppers deal with victims mostly. You either walk the beat – traffic duty or crowd control – or else you end up processing burglaries or road accidents. That's what it is, hanging around most of the time. Or you might end up in town on a week-end night moving drunks along. Know what the funny thing is? Every copper, when he comes out of Templemore, really believes he's going to make a difference. He actually believes it. He sees himself as some sort of shining knight. Only he goes out some night and breaks up a fight and then both parties turn on him and then there's a crowd calling him a pig and he can feel globs of spit on the back of his neck. Maybe not that scenario exactly but something not too far off it and it lets a young copper know what the job's really like. And then there's the paperwork. The average copper spends his day trying to avoid bloody paperwork. So what he does, he keeps his nose clean and waits for promotion and when it doesn't arrive, he thinks to himself, Maybe next year. Only next year's no good either. But he waits. What else can he do? Patience, he tells himself. And then just when he thinks it might be his turn, he fucks up. He makes a mistake and he knows his chance has gone. He knows it's now a question of putting in the years and waiting for the pension to build. Know what would make an interesting book? One about a copper who watches the clock all day to see when his shift is up."

She was interested now, all right. "That you?"

"Or a copper who likes wearing the uniform but he's had enough of doing the job. You want to hear a story?"

"Sure."

And he stopped there. Losing heart now, she thought, but then he said, "Well here goes," and settled himself in the seat, Stella sitting back on the couch and making herself comfortable. It was an interesting story too, the way he told it. He'd lost his nerve one night, that much was clear, but he couldn't really say why. A build up, maybe, all those nights worrying would this be the one and then *boom* something hit him and he just couldn't move. Another copper getting beaten up, his own friend lying with his face kicked in and there was Ed too terrified to help. And then later, after the enquiry, the way the others would look at him. Did they despise him? Far from it. It was their sympathy that hurt the most, and the lack of respect that went with it. Sorrow too, on everyone's part, his and theirs, since his very presence brought to mind something no one wanted to be reminded of. He made them think of how thin a line they were walking. It was as though thinking about it made it more likely to happen and looking at him made them think about it.

If that made any sense.

A jinx, he said. A specialist in processing reports. That and traffic duty.

"You apply for anything else?" Stella asked.

"Not many people want to employ ex-coppers. You know why?"

She shrugged. "Because they're used to bossing people around."

"That's one reason. But there's a bigger one. Spend long enough in the public sector and people who are running a business, they don't want to know you. They think you've lost the drive that's needed. And they're probably right. Add that to the fact that some people just plain don't like coppers or else they think you're going to shop them for something or other and by and large they just don't want to know you. Or else they think you've been pushed out, that maybe you're not quite the most honest fella in the world."

"And are you?"

"Am I what?"

"The most honest fella in the world."

"I've been around long enough to know that if someone puts a few quid in your hand the best thing to do is to close your fist around it. Especially with promotion prospects like mine."

They watched an old black and white film where Robert Mitchum was a psycho preacher chasing two kids around and searching for some money their old man had stashed somewhere. It was a good one. Stella hadn't seen it before and yes it felt fine sitting there with Ed, no pressure to get things together, just two friends watching the box on a slow Sunday afternoon. Two people with nowhere else they particularly wanted to be. She'd always been curious about Ed. Sometimes, in the early hours, she'd hear someone leave and she'd think why not? – a good-looking fella like that living on his own. He wasn't the brightest cookie in the world, not by a long shot, but he wasn't a complete dimbo either. Which was what she'd once presumed. Sprucing himself up three or four nights a week, then back into uniform in the morning, did he look like the type that was shooting up the promotion ladder?

If push came to shove in a courtroom with Joe, Ed was going to be useful.

"How about a beer?" she said. "A little early afternoon drinking, there's nothing like it."

28

Feng Shui – there were three stages. A ruthless clear out to begin with: any item that was either broken or useless, it had to go. Then you carried out a severe spring cleaning job before filling your place with crystals, chimes, mirrors, candles and a whole load of other shit. An outdoor water feature was ideal, Deborah said, but if you couldn't manage that a picture of a fish would do. You didn't even need your own compass, apparently. Some fruitbar would come into your house and tell you where north, east, south and west were and then you'd start shuffling your possessions around.

The object being: to live in harmony with your immediate surroundings.

Joe almost burst out laughing. but hey, who was he to say anything? Deborah was a nutcase, no two ways about it, standing there with her innocent face telling everyone how she was ready to shell out to have her furniture moved around. Damien, the prick, asking questions but really taking the piss. Would the bath count as a water feature? If you didn't have a chime could you hang a couple of light bulbs out of the front porch? Upping the ante each time until he said something Joe didn't catch and then, of course, they were all having a whale of a time.

Joe laughed too. Why not? Pretty soon he'd have a grand coming in every month; he could afford to be generous.

Deborah was the pick of them. Dim and mad, it wasn't the best combination in the world but there was no malice there. Gladys was a snob and Damien, well… what wouldn't Joe give to stomp on that little fucker's head? William though, he was a study. Every time he opened his mouth it was if he was saying, I own this place and you're just a security guard. Just in case anyone was forgetting. It was in his tone and the way he carried himself. In what he said too, Joe having to listen to a big long rigmarole about the alarm system, what he'd been looking for and how he'd gone about getting it.

"You don't say much," he said.

Joe shrugged. "If I've something to say, I'll let you know about it."

"Well," William said, "there's nothing wrong with that. Nothing at all."

Early Tuesday morning, someone tried to steal a coat. Three grand's worth of sable stuck under some kid's arm, Joe haring down Nassau Street after him, just about to give up when a copper stepped out and into the scene. A squad car took them all to Pearse Street station, the kid saying he wanted the coat for his mother, the copper saying, Well maybe you should save up and buy her one if that's the case.

An hour later, Joe was back at the shop, telling the story.

"Most of the shoplifters," he said, "the coppers know them. But this was a new face which means that he'll probably get a suspended sentence."

"No matter," William said, "it was a job well done."

"That's what I'm here for."

William winked at him. "The secret of success," he said, "is surrounding yourself with the right people. Then you let them get on with the job."

Joe hated it, the way it made him feel. He despised them, yes, so why the buzz when they were telling him what a great job he'd done? William and Damien and Deborah and Gladys, one worse than the other and yet here he was feeling the blood rise to his face. Was he really so desperate for a little attention? Thirty-nine years old and a few words from the likes of these could make him blush.

It made him hate them even more.

Maybe Benner was the man to deal with them, he thought. Get him to come through the door with a stocking over his head, saying, Let's all just have a quick lie down here while my assistant does the necessary. Now that would be worth watching.

He could stick a shotgun into Damien's mouth. Maybe Joe would offer a bonus – or would it be a discount? – if he'd knock the little prick around a bit.

And thinking of Benner – what next? It was time to get moving on that one.

When Deborah was on her way out for coffee, Joe asked her if she wouldn't mind collecting a packet of envelopes for him. Of course she wouldn't! And once she was back would she mind addressing one of them since he'd injured his hand during the chase?

Later he'd get it photocopied, fifteen maybe twenty times, and each time he needed to send Benner a note, he could just stick one on. Or he could get a few of those envelopes with a window in the front. Make it look a little more official.

Yes, he thought. Taking every precaution, it was the only way.

Joe felt the nerves hit again. Could Benner possibly try to brazen it out? Just walk into the Garda Station with the blackmail note and say, There's this guy who says he's going to make up a pack of lies about me if I don't give him a grand a month. He'd have the nerve to do it, there was no doubt about that, but would it benefit him at all? On reflection, the answer was No. A judge might just throw Joe's evidence out and suggest that a witness be flown over from London.

Benner would be mad to risk it.

But still Joe wanted to be careful with the note. Say Benner was caught somewhere with a shotgun in his hand, his place might be searched and the notes would be found. If he kept them that was, and who could tell if he would or not? They could check Joe's handwriting or fingerprints and then Joe would be in the soup as well. No, it was best to be careful. It was a question of making sure that nothing could be traced back to him.

He bought a copy of the *Evening Herald* in the shop down the road.

So far it was going well. He had a Post Office Box and he had the letter drafted to his solicitor. Now it was a question of getting the wording right on the blackmail note. How should he start? The most important thing was to send the right message. Benner needed to know that this was not a man to be fucked with. He needed to be reminded that he'd killed poor old Louis Marks in London and now was the time to start paying.

Who, after all, deserved it more than Joe?

The worst was the loneliness. Joe could remember being at a sales course in the Burlington Hotel one summer and some guy piped up that a lot of people confused solitariness with loneliness. It was a mistake, he said. It came up in the context of overnight stays, how tricky some people found them especially if there were small kids at home. Well, not this guy – he liked nothing better than to eat a nice meal on his own. At the time Joe couldn't understand it. Eating alone – what could be more miserable? And what about those pitiful poor bastards sitting at the counter waiting to see could they nail the barman for a conversation?

Each evening Joe walked for an hour then returned to his new flat. Once a week he took a bus to his mother's and she'd ask how he was and he'd say, "Fine." She'd give him the rundown on the neighbours. They'd have dinner and watch the television – Emmerdale, Coronation Street, Eastenders and Brookside – and then at nine he'd kiss her on the cheek and say good-bye. She'd give him a sad look and a rub on the arm, whatever that was supposed to mean. What was there to say, after all? She never mentioned Stella which was good and he never did either.

Did he miss the telly back in the flat? Maybe, but wasn't it only right that he should suffer? He'd attacked his wife, you couldn't get away from the fact, and now he was paying for it. Lying on the couch, reading the newspaper and staring at the ceiling, it was a miserable existence. But what right had he to complain? The same with Benner, he'd killed Louis Marks and he'd got away with it only to start paying in another way. Maybe he'd run into more trouble trying to pay Joe and maybe he wouldn't. Maybe there'd come a time when Joe would cut him loose, when he'd decide the guy had paid enough and who the hell cared anymore?

It took two hours to make the note, cutting the letters from the newspaper and gluing them to the sheet. He wore rubber washing up gloves to make sure there were no fingerprints.

Yes, he thought, it was the work of a man who was not to be fucked with.

He slid it into an envelope and glued a photocopied address to the front.

Ready to go, he thought.

Friday evening, Joe sorted out his week's wages. He'd been paid in cash which suited him fine and now it was just a question of getting the right denominations so he could split it between Stella and himself. Then he had to think of the best way to package it. He wrote his note, keeping it nice and simple as he'd intended and then wrapped the money in some extra sheets and held them to the light. Nobody would suspect there was cash inside.

Yes, everything going well. Not ideal, no, but certainly according to plan.

Until he received an envelope of his own. Hand delivered by a copper, no less, Joe knowing it was bad – why else would a copper be delivering it? If he made any attempt to contact Stella by mail or by telephone or deliberately strayed within one hundred yards of her, he was liable for prosecution.

"Oh Christ," he whispered.

He stood for minutes, staring at the print and listening to his own breathing. Then he walked back inside and lay on the couch again.

***

"You must have an admirer," Des Benner said.

Friday evening and they were just back from work, the old man saying it was rare enough for anything to come to the house, most of his mail went straight to the club. He wanted to know if Paddy wanted the lasagne or the chicken, he'd go shopping tomorrow, and Paddy said what the hell it was the weekend, he'd take whatever was left. He knew what was in the letter. It was from the witness who'd let him walk, too scared to come face to face and say what he wanted.

In his bedroom, he thought, *What sort of clown cuts words out of a newspaper and pastes them to a sheet?* Was he scared Paddy might track him through his handwriting? Or maybe he was worried about the coppers, as if they'd give a damn about a possible blackmail letter if they got a chance to extradite Paddy off their hands.

The way it was addressed was interesting. Handwritten, but it was almost like a teenager's handwriting – and a photocopy at that. Maybe this guy had got one of his kids to do the address and then he'd run off some copies. But would he be likely have kids that old?

Paddy read the letter twice.

Look at the wording…

You know who this is. Send £ 1000 to PO Box 24642 by next Tuesday or accept the consequences. You will be contacted again in one month's time.

Whoever this bozo was, he'd been lucky to find the word 'consequences'. It was all one word, the type larger and slightly darker than the rest of the sentence. The print looked like it all came from the same paper. It wasn't *The Times*, Paddy knew that much, but after that he was guessing. A lot of the other words, they were pieced together from individual letters but there it was – consequences. The message being: to accept them. As though there was an option.

He must have stumbled across it, otherwise he'd have produced a mix'n'match job.

It was the work of a rank amateur, Paddy was sure of it. Getting some kid to write out the address for him and then going through this rigmarole of pasting letters to a sheet. If he was worried about his handwriting being recognised why not get himself a word processor and printer? Second hand, what would it cost? A few hundred quid at the most which was nothing to a man who was checking himself in for a nice easy grand a month.

Which, in itself, was a joke. Nothing surer than there'd be an increase before long – a holiday or a medical bill or maybe just good old fashioned inflation.

He sighed and looked around the room. Things were clearer now. The wondering was over, that was good, and at least now he had an idea of who he was dealing with.

29

Lawyers were on Joe's list. Doctors too and bankers and accountants; anyone in fact who was likely to charge you just for being in the same room as them. But as lawyers went, Pat Gorman was okay. In his fifties now he had the look of a guy who had his money made and couldn't give a shit if you stayed or not. He charged through the nose, Joe expected nothing less, but at least he wasn't looking down his own while he did it.

He said sorry he couldn't represent Joe, Stella had already been to see him.

"I'm still a client of yours, am I not?"

"As long as there's no conflict of interests."

"It's got nothing to do with Stella. I want to add something to my will."

"Well, that's no problem. We can either redraft or add a codicil."

Joe didn't know what a codicil was but he reckoned he didn't need one. "See this envelope I've got here?" he said. "I only want it opened after I'm dead."

Gorman looked at the envelope. "I see."

"But not if I die of natural causes. You understand?"

Gorman sat up a little straighter. "Have you got yourself into something, Joe?"

"Nothing I don't want to be into. Is it possible?"

"Yes, it's possible."

"Good," Joe said. "That's all I needed to know."

Ed looked through his glass porch door and thought, Of course, why not? – it's the beginning of the month so why wouldn't he be here? Just walk in with his hand out, slide the notes into his wallet. No risk. Ed had been thinking about it again, how he was the one who always did the collecting. Had Costello ever made the collection himself? Ed couldn't remember.

Only Costello didn't mention the money straight away. He brushed past Ed saying, "You know much about this guy Joe Faherty?"

Same as the last time – no invite, no greeting. No fucking manners, that was the problem. What was it Stella had said? – "*The likes of him, he spots you're weak and he'll trample all over you.*" She'd seen it last week, the way he'd just barged on in like he was the landlord and Ed was three months behind on the rent.

Well, maybe today would be different.

Ed felt nervous. He felt strong too. "He's a neighbour."

"I know that. What's he like?"

"You remember the last time you were here?"

"You were having dinner with that good looking woman."

Ed nodded. "That's right. Well, that good-looking woman is Joe's wife."

That knocked him back a bit. Costello shaking his head, trying to get things straight. "You telling me this Faherty is married to Stella?"

"Is that so hard to believe?"

"The one I met here the other night?" Costello shrugged. "I just wouldn't have put them together. You know how you can sometimes pair people off, well Jesus not in a month of Sundays would you pick those two."

"Well, there you have it."

"Or I wouldn't have put him down as a guy who belts his wife. You know him well?"

"Not particularly."

"Were you surprised when you heard about it?"

Ed shrugged. "It's hard to surprise a copper these days, you know that. Who knows what goes on behind closed doors?"

"The reason I'm asking," Costello said, "is that I was sure we'd nailed Benner on Saturday night. That picture, it was the dead feck of him and you remember what he said about playing pool? That's how he got by. When he wasn't ripping places off, that is."

"So?"

"So I'm still not convinced it wasn't him."

"You're saying Joe lied."

"I'm asking you if it's possible."

Ed shook his head. Jesus, once Costello got his teeth into something. "You really think Joe let the guy walk?"

"Maybe. You ever see Benner before we picked him up?"

"No. I don't think so."

"Never around the area."

"Making some sort of contact with Joe?"

"That's right. And maybe Joe was scared to pick him out."

"No chance," Ed said. "Look at it this way. Let's assume it *was* Benner for arguments sake. He's going from house to house – isn't that what you said? – pretending to be a Mormon. If he sees someone he knows then he's just going to walk away, isn't he? Unless Joe was in on the whole thing."

Costello paused. "Is that so ridiculous?"

"It's worse than ridiculous. Joe Faherty's your average meat and two veg type who hit his wife once and even she admits she may have driven him to it. I'd know. I live across the road from the guy. He hasn't a criminal bone on his body."

Costello shook his head. "Maybe you don't know him as well as you think you do."

And what could you say to that? It was nuts thinking Joe Faherty was involved in any criminal activity: as Stella said, the guy hadn't enough imagination. But try saying that now, Costello standing there with that mad look in his eyes, reaching so hard he'd grab at anything – anything that might put Benner away. What exactly was happening here? Costello was a Grade A bastard, no argument there, but one thing about him – he was always the one in control. When Costello laid his fists into someone, you knew the guy wasn't going to end up in a coma. He had his undertaker and his garage and a way of organising things so that they wouldn't come back at him.

Now you couldn't even talk to him.

This obsession with Benner, it was crazy and if Ed wasn't careful it was going to land them both into trouble. So what if the guy had ripped off Costello's place? It was eight years ago. Some things you were better off forgetting about. Get over it, move on and start pulling in a few quid to share with the closest thing you had to a friend in this world.

What Ed wanted to say was, Grow up, for fuck sake!

Then he thought, Why not go down that road? "Benner make a complaint against you yet?" he asked.

That got a reaction. "Someone been talking?"

"Just asking."

"He did actually."

"An official one?"

"I got notification today. Can you believe it?"

"Oh, I can believe it all right. You know why?"

Costello taking a step back now. "Why?"

"Because he's dead fucking right to. You know as well as I do he'd nothing to do with those burglaries we dragged him in for. And now you're trying to pin some shit from London on him. On the basis of an identikit and Christ we both know what sort of a likeness you can get with those. Enough witnesses put their spoke in and you can end up with a picture of a bloody horse, but no, you have to go and keep hassling the guy and now we've both got some answering to do. You ever think about the shit you're bringing down on me? Now I've got to explain why all of a sudden this Benner character is the prime suspect for a couple of the crudest burglaries you ever saw in your life."

Yes, Ed thought, this was better. That business last Saturday night, it had knocked something out of Costello. He was different. Weaker or maybe just a little distracted but what he didn't need was for Ed to start laying into him. Why had he come here? To collect a few quid, sure, but also but also to let off about Benner. Or maybe just to throw his weight around since what was the point in having a whipping boy if you couldn't give him a kick when you felt the need?

Benner's complaint, it was a hassle but there was another way of looking at it. Costello had to be worried about what Ed would tell an investigator.

"What option did you leave him?" Ed said. "Look at it from his point of view, for Christ sake. You already kicked the shit out of him once and now you're harassing him. He thinks it's okay at first, maybe you've just got to get it off your chest. Once, twice down the station, that's fair enough. But then you have a shot at having him extradited for murder. On the basis of an identikit, for the love of Jesus. What option does he have? He thinks you're going to stitch him up – who the hell wouldn't? – so what's left for him to do but file a complaint against you."

He stopped there. Let Costello get in if he wanted to but no, he just stood. Amazed probably, that Ed was finally speaking up for himself.

Look at this, Ed thought.

He said, "What you'd want to do is forget about this shit…" hitting home now, Costello's expression changing, ready to strike back, "…because if I say the wrong thing to an investigator, we're both screwed."

Which stopped him.

After a pause, Costello said, "Maybe that's something we'd be best off discussing."

"I agree."

"Your end of the story."

"My end of a lot of things. This Benner business is way down the list," Ed said and he led him through it. Why was Costello here? To check that the collection had been made and to put his hand out. Which was fine with Ed – this time. Next time too, that'd be okay but after that Costello could go jump. Unless of course he either started to bring in his share or made the collection himself in which case Ed would call by with *his* hand out.

Another thing – if Costello intended harassing Benner any further, Ed would just as soon be left out of it.

Costello listened. He didn't like it but he listened, what choice did he have? That detective's badge, it had taken long enough to earn: run into a judge who liked Benner's face and it could be gone again. Ed knew it and Costello knew it.

Ed asked him if he'd got all that. Share the money, share the risk. And leave Benner the fuck alone, for Christ sake.

"Anything else?" Costello said.

"There is," Ed said. "You like to call around here, don't

you?"

"Sometimes."

"Well, telephone first in future. A little courtesy, it goes a long way."

Sometimes Paddy would take a look and think, Is this the one? His gaze would fix on a customer and he'd look for a sign, any sign, that maybe the guy wasn't a golfer. A bulge in the jacket, or a mannerism that might tell him something and he'd be ready to bolt, down behind the counter and out through the back door he always kept open. Which was crazy even thinking like that: a pro would have the place sussed, entrances and exits. A pro wait till the shop was empty and he'd walk in with the gun already in his hand.

Some nights, it was hard to get to sleep.

He was trapped here in this shop. It reminded him of when he was a kid and he'd dream he was creeping through a house at night, the folks safely tucked up, only Paddy wouldn't be able to find the door out of the house. He'd be panicking, moving through doorways that just led to other rooms, waiting for someone to wake.

And yet… it was hard to explain.

What was it the man said? – that you never felt so alive as when you were in danger. Today, he could smell Aoife's perfume on his jumper. If he closed his eyes, he could feel the side of her face against his shoulder as she linked him. It was a strange feeling – all those years he'd tried to remember her voice or picture her face, wandering from one place to the next, thinking, What's she up to now? Married, he'd presumed. Kids of course, but then again maybe not, but married at least. Or maybe just engaged, who the hell knew? Whatever else he'd always imagined that she'd have changed because that's what happened sometimes – you could spend years pining after an old girlfriend and then when your boat finally came in and you hooked up with her again, you found she was now a different person. All this time, you'd been in love with a memory, and where did that leave you?

Would this happen with Aoife?

Not if it hadn't happened already.

Yes, he felt alive. He was frightened, sure, – sometimes so bad that he could barely keep his food down – but he wasn't going anywhere, and now he'd come to another decision. He wasn't going to pay out a grand a month to someone he didn't know. All he really knew about blackmail was that once you paid the other guy had you by the goolies. It was that simple. Pay once and you'll pay again. Pay a grand and you'll pay two.

So the answer was No.

He'd be polite about it. He'd say, Sorry chum but you're not getting a fucking penny.

He'd sit back and wait. See what his new pal made of that.

30

Ricki Lake, Ed knew, used to be fat but all that was behind her now: these days she was a TV personality who talked about her weight loss and what a battle it had been. Or else she refereed between warring couples and offered them counselling after the show. Today's program was nearly over, Ed stretched out on the couch watching four fat women being led out after a makeover, the audience going nuts and disco music blaring from behind the stage.

He watched the screen split into two, the before and the after, both of which looked pretty much the same to Ed. Soon someone in the audience would stand up and say how it didn't matter what you were like on the outside, it was what was in your heart that counted. It was a banker – same thing every week – and it was all very well, Ed thought, unless you were twenty-five stone and couldn't get from one side of the room to the other. Programs like this, they were okay – Oprah, Sally Jesse, Geraldo and what was that other one's name? – Jenny Jones. Get yourself in the right mood and you could just lie there, let the hour waste away in front of you.

A lot of the women he went out with watched them. He wondered if Stella ever did and then hey, there she was at the end of his driveway.

On the doorstep, she said, "Guess what? Joe's violated the barring order already."

He led her inside, tossed the newspaper off the armchair so she could sit.

"No communication, that's what it says. Only today I get this cheque through the post. Enough to cover his share of the mortgage and a little left over. What do you make of that?"

Ed shrugged. "What do *you* make of it?"

"Remember what you told me the other day?"

"About?"

"About money."

"How if someone puts some in your hand, the thing to do is close your fist around it."

"Exactly. Only I'm not sure if this compromises my position. If I don't report it, what happens later on if Joe turns up at the door?"

"Simple," Ed said. "You pick up the phone and call the police."

"But then he's going to say that he was sending me money and well, there was no charge against him for that."

"It doesn't matter a damn what Joe says. You can take the money and then if he turns up some day you can have him charged. You can even have him charged with sending the cheque and you still won't have to give the money back."

She liked that: he could tell. She said no, she wouldn't have coffee but a cold drink might be nice. There was no Coke left. No mineral water either. Warm, early Autumn weather like this, it was hard not to go through the cold drinks.

He found a bottle of Robinsons Lemon Barley Water at the back of the press.

"Speaking of unwelcome visits," he said, "I had one of my own."

"Costello?"

"The very man." Saying it and then thinking: Where am I going with this? He wanted to tell her, boost his ratings after the hammering they'd taken from Costello first time round but if he was to tell the thing properly, really give her a feel for what happened, he'd have to mention the monthly collection. And that wasn't something you told to just anybody.

But then again: Was Stella just anybody?

He hoped not. She'd turned up on *his* doorstep this time, after all. And it was she who advised him to get the hell out from under Costello.

"Beginning of every month," he said, "Costello pays me a visit. We have this little thing going. Or at least we had until he went and got himself promoted. The way it works, you find a garage owner who might be willing to pay for a little extra business, and you put it to him that maybe you might be willing to send some business his way. Because we're in a perfect position to do it. Say there's a prang at a crossroads, two cars thump into each other, chances are at least one of them doesn't have a regular garage. Or if he does, it's probably half way across the city. So you just drop the name like you're doing the car owner a favour, tell him you know this reliable local garage. Maybe they suspect you're in for a cut but most of the time they don't give a shit. All they want is their jalopy towed off the road. They just want the whole thing sorted out."

"And at the beginning of every month, you get a payment."

"That's how it works. There's an undertaker who pays as well. But then Costello got promoted so he's not out on the street as much these days. And that's the problem. I'm dragging in the business and I'm doing the collecting. All he does is show up with his hand out."

She didn't seem surprised. Costello though, she'd thought he was a Senior Detective, up near the top of the force but Ed said no, he'd spent most of his career in uniform. A personality like that, it could either work for you or against you.

"He's had me over a barrel since I was the one who made the collection all the time."

"Why was that?"

"I wanted the money. I knew I wouldn't get promoted. Whatever chance Costello had, I had none."

"It sounds like he saw you coming."

Ed shrugged. "For a while there, he was the only one who would talk to me. The others were polite but they couldn't wait to get away."

"You think he picked you out?"

"To make the collection for him?"

"That's what I mean."

"Probably. I didn't think so at first. I thought it was just because he was on the outside as well since no one liked him. But I think you're right, he saw me coming. Keep his nose clean, let me do the dirty work."

Now they were silent. Ed was glad he'd told her; someone

he liked but not only that, someone he felt he could trust. If nothing else she was someone who knew the value of a pound. And if he was wrong, well so be it… He watched her settle into the armchair, sipping her lemon squash – thinking of her as a friend, sure, but also looking at that nail varnish and feeling something else.

"Now Benner has filed an official complaint and Costello's worried about what I might say. I could really sell him down the tubes if I wanted to. Not enough to get him fired, maybe, but he wouldn't fancy being back in uniform."

"And you're going to use it."

"I'd be a fool not to."

"What about the trouble you'd be bringing down on yourself?"

"You never know, I might get away with it. Just say I was following orders. No one knows how these things will go and Costello won't want to take the risk."

"This is what you told him when he called."

"I told him I'll make one more collection and then he has a choice. He can either stop putting his hand out or he can go make the collection himself. And he'd want to get the finger out and start pulling in a few quid himself."

She was nodding now. "That it?"

"And he's to stop dropping by uninvited."

"How'd he take it?"

"What do I care? That's his problem."

"Indeed it is," she said. "Know something, Ed? I'd say it's as well for you that Benner came home."

Joe looked at the Post Office Box in the GPO and wondered what was inside. If it was an envelope how thick would it be? Fifty twenty quid notes would make a nice tidy bundle. Unless it was a cheque, of course, only who would Benner make a cheque out to? Then again, why make it out to anybody? – he could just leave that line for Joe to fill in.

The box was empty.

Joe sighed and shook his head. Was the guy insane? Did he not realise that Joe held his life in his hands?

Then again: was Joe surprised? Looking at it now, he'd have been more surprised if there *had* been money in the envelope. Standing there emotionless in the line-up, Benner was the type who weighed things up. He was calm and he could hold his nerve. He was batting the ball back to Joe saying: No, I don't think I'll pay if it's all the same to yourself. He was saying: Let's see if you've got the guts.

And it was a fair question.

Joe wasn't going to the coppers; no point in even considering it. He'd come this far so, what the hell, he'd try again. He needed to put a tighter squeeze on Benner. The question was *How?* Another letter, he supposed, and if that didn't work, maybe a phone call.

What other options did he have?

He walked out of the GPO towards his bus stop. He'd go back to the flat, lie on the bed and try to figure it out.

One question still worried Stella: Why had Joe sent the cheque? Could it have been out of kindness or was there another reason? What if he wanted to come back, just move in again and pick up as though nothing had happened?

Anything was possible these days.

Or maybe he'd sent the letter *before* he'd received the court order. She could picture him standing there in his pyjamas, thinking about the mess he'd made of his life; seven years of marriage and what had he to show for it? Seven straight years shelling every penny he earned into a home he was now legally barred from entering. In which case there would be no more cheques. That would be fine, she thought, she'd make do. But there was a third possibility, one that sent a flutter down her spine. What if Joe had been talking to a lawyer? What if he was sending the cheque for the benefit of the judge who'd be making a settlement?

Yes, that was possible too – Joe and a lawyer plotting to turn her out of her home.

She walked across the room and looked out the window at the empty street. For the first time since Joe had gone, she was conscious of living alone. A shame, she thought, that Ed was a loser: he had plenty going for him.

She'd have to wait until next week. See if another cheque came through the door.

Every couple of days Paddy would hassle the old man about a raise. He'd ask was there no minimum wage in this country and Des would laugh and say, "Of course there is, what do you think you're getting?" Which pretty much summed it up, Paddy thought – easy job, lousy wages. But he had no rent bill, that was good, no tax either and as many frozen dinners as anyone could eat. All in all it was a reasonable short-term arrangement. Another month or so and he'd start looking for a flat: put the bite on the old man for a proper wage and see could he find something around the area.

If nothing else it would stop the old man picking up letters and saying, "You on someone's mailing list?"

The second note arrived on Friday evening. Same print, same notepaper, starting with the question – *You think I'm fucking joking?* Which he clearly wasn't. Then outlining the situation, how Louis Marks was dead and that it was time to start paying, that Paddy was free to walk the streets and well, there had to be a cost for that. This is your last chance, the note said. Take it or leave it.

Paddy took out his lighter and set the page alight.

It was a risk, yes, but so was paying. All he could do was go with his instinct.

Two days later, Joe checked the post office box and shrugged: this was getting him nowhere. It needed the personal touch. He needed to either telephone the guy or pay him a visit and see could he spell it out any clearer.

The truth, after all, was simple – refusal or no refusal, he still had Benner over a barrel.

31

What was it now – ten days? twelve? – since Sudds Donnelly had begun to ask around, starting with the regular haunts – pubs, pool halls, friends – all the while thinking, *Jesus, where the fuck is he?* Worried a little, sure, but knowing that Ray was able to look after himself. Someone like Ray, he had his routines. He had a tramp over in Croyden and another in Streatham, and if he wasn't with either of those, you could generally find him at the gym or hanging around one of the local bars. He wasn't a difficult man to locate.

Until now, it seemed. Now he was gone – phut! vanished into thin air. Nothing, not a trace, Sanderson telling everyone to stay calm: he'd put the word out across the city. Then a few days later, Sanderson saying: "Someone must know something, for Christ sake." But no one seemed to. Gone, that was the word, like he'd been whisked away into witness protection or a spaceship or something.

Sudds reckoned he was dead. One day, two – that was the most they ever went without seeing each other. Now it was twelve days without so much as a phone call. Yes, Sudds thought, something had happened to him. Someone had whacked him but the question was who?

They retraced his last steps – nothing.

Sanderson thought no way was it Benner. Benner was long gone, running like fuck as any sensible man would do. Why would he stay in London? To get himself killed? Or arrested maybe, since the word on the street was the coppers were after him too. No, Benner wasn't hanging around. He was gone, not as gone as Ray maybe, but well and truly fucking gone and he wasn't coming back to whack some guy he had nothing against in the first place.

Sudds was the one who knew Ray best so he'd have to think back. A recent argument maybe or was there some bugger who'd taken his time?

They'd have to be patient. They'd keep asking the right questions. Sooner or later someone would have something to say.

Ten o'clock Saturday morning, Des was waiting for his first lesson, making a nuisance of himself and wanting to know what a cracking girl like Aoife could possibly see in someone like Paddy. Grinning as he said it, Paddy grinning back but thinking, Jesus, he's right. Maybe he'd fooled her last time round. Eight months, after all, wasn't long. And it was hard to pin down exactly what had been so special about that period. The conversation mostly, he supposed; the way they could set off on a Saturday morning to drift around town and then, fourteen hours later, they'd be settled in a bar still talking. Paddy remembered liking himself when he was with Aoife Brennan. That was the biggest thing. He liked the way his mind worked. He wasn't shy as he was with other girls. With Aoife he was able to recognise the boy he'd been while his mother was still around. There were times when he could see the person he was about to become as soon as he got out of the habit of burglarising a house once a fortnight.

Could confidence really transmit itself so easily from one person to another?

Back then, same as now, he'd see Aoife leading him towards a conventional life, Paddy thinking this and looking up and yes, there he was – the witness, the one who'd let him walk. Standing at the doorway for a moment, then strolling through the shop wearing a nice friendly smile. Paddy thinking, *Jesus, anything could happen here*. But the guy seemed calm. Stretching out a hand now and saying, "I'm Joe Faherty, I'm a friend of your son's." Paddy calm too, hearing him say to Des, "I remember you from the television. You had some good years back when I had the time to be watching golf."

"Neither today nor yesterday," Des said.

"Not that long ago either," Joe said. "I met Paddy in London and he fleeced me at the pool table. We had a few pints only I lost the address. But I remembered him saying he was your son and that you were the professional here so I just decided to drop by. Keeping well, Paddy?"

"Not a bother. Want to buy anything?"

Joe shook his head. "I thought maybe you'd want to meet up sometime."

"I get out of here about six."

"You know *The Beachcomber*?"

"Sure."

"Well, come straight from work then." He smiled at Des. "Sorry to rush," he said and he disappeared again.

Joe worked six days one week, five the next, taking every second Saturday off which was fine only he could have done with the extra money. Or he might have preferred a week day but it never worked out that way. Today, he was home by eleven, lying on the bed and thinking about his next step – whether to sit back and play it cool or maybe stick a finger in Benner's face and tell him what was what. Also to reassess the situation. The note business hadn't worked and Joe still wasn't sure why. It should have worked. It was the best way to blackmail someone, he imagined – anonymously – just make your collection every month and without the worry that someone was going to do you in.

An arrangement like that, it could go on until one party died which was probably why Benner wasn't getting into it in the first place. So what was the situation now? Benner had won the first battle; he'd held his nerve. He'd said, Go ahead and do it – now Joe had to think of something else. But then again: why should the onus be on Joe, why not leave it to Benner to come up with a solution?

Joe slept for two hours in the afternoon; he felt good walking into *The Beachcomber* that evening. Nice and casual wearing a loose shirt and jeans, Benner waiting for him in the same outfit he'd been wearing earlier – grey chinos and a light blue *Des Benner Golf Hut* sweatshirt. Benner sitting in an alcove, smoking and looking without interest towards the bar, then turning around and saying "Can I get you a drink?"

Joe shook his head. "Not now."

"You sure?" Paddy said. "It won't weaken your position here."

"Well, that's lovely," Joe said, "but I still don't want anything." He sat down and began to unwrap the cellophane from a new pack of cigarettes. "We have a lot to talk about."

Paddy nodded. "I certainly hope so," he said "I'd hate to see you do anything rash."

"Want to know what I've already done?"

"Sure."

"I went to see my lawyer. He's got a letter telling how you were one of the Mormons who killed Louis Marks. It says we ran into each other a few weeks back and you threatened me and my family. Said you'd have us killed if I ever testified against you. Anything happens to me and that letter is opened."

"If you die, you mean?"

"That's right."

"What happens if you die and I've nothing to do with it. What happens then?"

"Then you go to jail, I suppose."

"I don't like the sound of that," Paddy said. "Maybe you should've asked that the letter only be opened if you die under suspicious circumstances."

Joe shrugged. "Well, that's your problem. It's in your interest that nothing happens to me."

"It certainly is," Paddy said. "Is that your real name, by the way – Joe Faherty."

"That's me. No 'L'"

"Well, Joe, I can't say it's been a pleasure so far but maybe we can work something out."

Yes, maybe they could. Joe was ready to tell him that was his problem too, that Joe himself had made the grand a month offer and now it was up to Benner to come up with something. But why push? Let Benner make the running. Joe felt confident. Not quite in control but not swamped either and pretty sure he'd made a good decision in setting up a meeting.

"It's an interesting one this, isn't it?" Paddy said.

"I think so."

"You have me by the goolies. Go to the coppers with that yarn about being threatened and I'm on the next flight to London."

"That's right."

"On the other hand, you've committed a crime too."

"Nothing compared to yours," Joe said.

"No. But I don't think you're a career criminal so it wasn't something that came easily. That's what I was banking on, that having put yourself through some soul-searching, you weren't going to run to the coppers immediately. You were going to want something out of it."

"I still do."

"Well, yeah, I understand that. But you've got to understand my situation here. I'm in a bit of a jam and paying you money is only going to get me further into it. You want a grand a month, right? I'm not going to earn that selling golf bags. So I get to work, taking risks all the time and then all of a sudden you want two grand a month. Which means that I have to take even more risks. Then, sooner or later, I'm going to take on the wrong job and I'll get nabbed because you've been getting easy money and want even more of it."

"Is that worse than going back to England?"

"No, it's not but it's not really much better either. All I'm doing is trading a murder or accessory to murder charge for a robbery one. And maybe that's not such a bad deal, but who's to say that if I do get out whatever number of years later, you're not going to pick up where you left off. And to be honest, I'd just as soon not do any time at all."

"What's your point?" Joe said.

"My point is that I think if I pay you, I'll end up going to jail anyway. It's just a question of when."

Joe stubbed out his cigarette, looked up again. He could see Benner's point but that's just what it was – Benner's point. Not his. So why should he care? He had his position and it was a position of strength. Louis Marks was six foot under and Benner was the one who put him there. Simple facts and did Benner really expect to walk away from them?

"So," Joe said, "where do we go from here?"

Paddy shrugged. “It’s a dilemma.”

“And you’re the one in the middle of it. I already made my suggestion.”

“The grand a month one?”

“That’s it.”

“And I’ve explained my situation.”

“Then it’s up to you to come up with something. You’re right, I’ve made a bit of a jump here and taken a hell of a risk with the coppers. So I want something out of it. But you’ve got a point of view too and I can see that. But what it comes down to is, like you say, I’ve got you by the goolies and you’d better come up with something. You able to meet me here, say Wednesday?”

“Same time?”

“No later. Make it eight. I work in town.”

“Sure. And you want me to have a suggestion.”

“Or a grand for me. Your choice. And don’t forget about the letter.”

“The one with your lawyer?”

“There are other copies too.”

“Terrific,” Paddy said, reaching for his cigarettes. “Maybe I should forget about the blackmail money and just hire you a bodyguard.”

Paddy spent Saturday evening in the Hollybrook with Aoife and then later on he lay next to her and listened to the quiet sounds of her sleeping. What now? he thought. When he was a kid and in a jam, he would pick a television character and ask himself, What would *he* do now? It was a matter of substitution. It was a matter of finding help where you could get it. The old man was generally busy and on the bad days his mother was so listless Paddy could barely get an answer from her. So he would turn to the television. Mannix or McCloud or Hoss from the High Chapparal, for instance. These were good solid down to earth folks, the type you’d be glad to have in your corner if you were in need of a little advice.

What would they make of this?

They wouldn’t get into this sort of a mess in the first place but that wasn't the point. The point was that he was screwed, well and truly quite spectacularly screwed, and he couldn't think of a way out of it. He knew what Michael Corleone would do. Michael would do a little research on the guy, find out that say he has a wife and a couple of kids. Then he'd have the wife shot. Get one of his boys to take her out, bang, and then go back to the guy and say, What do you make of that? Ask him if there was any letter to be opened if his wife got killed. Ask him about the kids – any letters if anything happens to them? And would the guy go to the coppers? Fuck, no – he'd crawl back into his hole and hold his kids tight and pray to Christ that one of them wasn't next on the list just for good measure.

There were some people who just weren't to be messed with no matter how many aces you held. But if sport taught you anything it was the need to reassess as you went along. Because that was what the weak couldn't do, they couldn't adjust – a bad start and well, it just wasn't their night. They were lazy. They were fatalistic. Flat table, round balls, the same as any other time only they'd know they were going to lose. Real players composed themselves. Real players forced themselves to concentrate on striking the ball. It was the difference between Christy O'Connor and Des Benner and it was the difference between a winner and a loser.

The point being that you had to block what had already happened from your mind. You had to look at the situation as it now presented itself. You had to find your way out of the shit.

Those nights alone – killers. Some nights Joe would stare at the luminous hands of his alarm clock and listen to the quiet next door. He'd feel the deepest ache inside. He'd watch the hours tick by and think of Stella or of Paddy Benner or of how he needed money. He needed enough to entice Stella back and allow them a new start together. Money was respect. Maybe it was loyalty and love as well. Joe needed Benner as much as Benner needed Joe but the trick, clearly, was not to let Benner know this.

Had he made the right decision setting up the meeting? Yes, he decided: he'd carried it off. He'd been firm. He'd looked

Benner in the eye and said, It's your problem, you sort it out. Which it was, Benner's problem, Joe nicely in the driving seat. Joe able to sit back and watch things develop but it was unnerving the way Benner had behaved. Where was the anger? Where were the threats and the lies? Where was the pleading? All the stuff Joe had expected – nothing. He replayed the scene in his mind – Benner saying all things being equal he'd just as soon not do any time. Then telling Joe he was thinking of hiring him a bodyguard.

Why wasn't he scared?

Because he knew that Joe wasn't going to the coppers, that was why.

Maybe Benner needed a nudge. Maybe it was time to play a little hardball.

Yes, he'd handled things well so far but now it was time to up the pressure. Wednesday night and Joe had his speech prepared, about how he didn't need the hassle or the worry so Benner could either pay up or go to jail. How long would he wait? A week, tops – and after that there'd be no more contact. Sure, the money would come in handy all right but the longer he let things run, the less likely he was to be seeing any.

So that was the deal. One week – take it or leave it.

Only he found it hard to find an opening. The first thing Paddy said was, "Go on. You might as well have a drink this time." And then when he got back from the bar: "Can you fill me in on this Louis Marks guy? What the hell was he thinking of?"

"He's my wife's cousin," Joe said. "Or *was*."

"I'd no idea which house he'd come from. It was one stupid thing he did."

Joe shrugged. "He didn't deserve to die for it."

"Not many people do something they deserve to die for, Joe. You know him well?"

"Not really. He had problems."

"Mental?"

"His nerves were bad."

"It's the one thing you can't legislate for in my line of work – the passer-by who decides to have a go. Coppers, unless you're unlucky you can generally predict the response time but some nutbag who wants to be a hero, he's the last thing you need."

Joe said, "I didn't even know he'd gone out. As soon as you moved on, I went back in to the telly. Then I heard this commotion a while later and there were cop lights flashing so I called to Louis and there was no answer. I presumed he was standing outside."

"Only he was dead."

"That's right. Shot in the face. What I don't know is why go through all this Mormon bullshit in the first place? Why not just knock on the door and produce the gun as soon as they open up?"

Paddy shrugged. "It's not really my style."

"You're a thief, aren't you?"

"There are different types of thieves."

"Costello said you were an armed robber."

Paddy laughed. "He really say that?"

"His very words."

"Well," Paddy said, "Costello is one prize wanker. Don't believe a word he says."

Joe watched Paddy reach for his cigarettes, then a funny thing – he must have assumed that Joe had none. He lit one, then slid the pack across the table. Like they were good friends or something – no need to ask.

It was a strange thing to do.

Benner said he was a burglar. He told Joe he'd burgled Costello's house some years previous and well, Costello was a slow man to forgive. And, by the way, had he rigged the line-up?

"He whispered the number in my ear. I wasn't sure if I'd heard him properly."

Paddy laughed softly and shook his head. "Well, no wonder he was disappointed. Your wife know you're here with me?"

Joe shook his head. "We're separated."

"Long?"

"Five weeks."

Paddy grinned. "Like to talk about it?"

"I'd rather not if it's all the same to yourself."

"Just being friendly," Paddy said. "Whatever your reasons,

that was a good turn you did for me so there's need for us to be at each other's throats."

Joe sipped his pint, three quarters way through it now, thinking he'd better buy a drink back. Pub rules still applied, didn't they? Even in a situation like this. Was Benner up to something? he wondered. Was he putting Joe at ease just to try something in a while? Or maybe he was thinking Joe might let up if they got to know each other a little better.

Whatever the case, he had a few questions of his own.

"Your partner, what was his name again?"

"Richard Hamilton"

"That's the one. He a friend of yours?"

Paddy shook his head. "That job was set up by a third party. I only met Hamilton a few weeks beforehand."

"So you're not exactly cut up over him."

"About as much as you are about Louis."

That got a reaction. "That's not fair," Joe said. "I didn't know Louis that well but Jesus, you wouldn't wish that on anyone."

"And that's why you're here."

Joe looked across the table. "You don't know anything about me. I've got my reasons."

"Sure you do. The same ones I had for going into that house in the first place. Or if I'm wrong and it's not money you're after, we might still be able to work something out."

That didn't sound too promising but Joe didn't want to push. The funny thing was: he was enjoying the conversation, trying to figure Benner out. Listening to him probe away with his questions and not quite sure why he was bothering. But Joe felt at ease with him. He was safe, still in the driving seat and whatever else about Benner, he was different to the average run of the mill type you were likely to meet.

A murderer? Joe was having trouble with that.

Standing at the bar while the drinks were being poured, Joe watched him light another cigarette, leave the pack back to Joe's side of the table. How could he be so relaxed? One leg folded across onto the other knee, just sitting there staring at the opposite wall, smoke rising slowly from his cigarette. Yes, whatever else about him, he was a study.

When Joe returned to the table he took another of the cigarettes. He said, “You didn’t kill Louis, did you?”

Paddy shook his head.

“But you’d do it if you had to. Am I right?”

“What makes you so sure I didn’t shoot him?”

“You wouldn’t panic like that. You’d hit him sure, with whatever you could lay your hands on, but he wasn’t a big guy. He wouldn’t have been able to stop two men.”

“Hamilton killed him.”

“Panicked?”

“Seemed to. It’s why the likes of me is better off without a gun.”

“You don’t carry one?”

“No.”

“But Hamilton did?”

“He wanted to kill me.”

“You serious?”

“No other reason for him to have it. He was going to shoot me as soon as I had the safe open. Only Louis came along and well the rest is history.”

Joe smiled. He took a cigarette from the box. “So Louis saved your life?”

“I doubt it’s much consolation to him.”

“Maybe not,” Joe said and laughed, “but sometimes you have to think of the family.”

Immediately, Joe felt bad about the crack. He liked it, thought it was a good one but Christ, Louis was a member of the family. Forty-one years old, gunned down thirty yards from his own front door and here was Joe making jokes about it. He was almost through the second pint already – one more and he’d begin to feel it. Or maybe he was feeling it already, that warm sensation kicking in.

Benner was talking about London, how glad he was to be out of there. Of all the places he’d been, London was at the end of the list. Right smack at the bottom. But Dublin, that was where he intended settling, so he needed to sort something out with Joe.

"I was waiting for you to get around to it," Joe said.

"My suggestion?"

"You got one?"

Sitting back in the seat. "I do actually. It's a beauty."

"I'm sure it is. Any chance you might be willing to share it?"

"One robbery," Paddy said. "We take our time, clean someone out good and proper and you take the haul. I'm in no rush so we can pick the right job."

Joe looked at him. "How much can I expect from it?"

"I was due a hundred and thirty grand for Downs Leaze."

Joe nodded. "That's not bad. But there's a problem."

"It still doesn't let me off the hook."

"That's right. How are we going to get around that one?"

"Simple," Paddy said. "I don't know why I didn't think of it earlier."

"I don't know why you're not telling me now," Joe said.

"Because you're coming with me," Paddy said. "That way we'll both be happy."

Paddy explained it – Joe would keep the proceeds while Paddy would keep some evidence of Joe's involvement in the robbery. It was the only way they could both walk away from this, he said, Joe with a wad of cash to help him adjust to life as a single man, Paddy staying out of jail for a murder he hadn't committed. It was simple and that was where the beauty lay.

"Hang on a sec here," Joe said. "I've never stolen a thing in my life. I don't know if I could."

"You're already a blackmailer, so it shouldn't be too great a leap. You know what you have to tell yourself?"

"What?"

"That whatever you steal is insured."

"What if I say no?"

"Then it's back to you."

"To make a suggestion?"

"Exactly. I've done my bit and if I do say so myself, it's a damn sight better than your offer."

"I kind of liked the first one," Joe said.

"You probably won't even have to come in with me. Keep watch maybe and then I'll photograph you with the stuff and we can each go our separate ways."

Joe looked across the table. "I'm going to have to think about this," he said.

"I thought you would."

"Same time next week, I suppose." Joe lit the cigarette he'd been playing with. "I never thought it'd be this complicated."

32

All this worry, maybe it was for nothing. Louise thought so and so did Eleanor. The other girls at work listened too but what interested them was the details – the angle of the blow, whether the fist was open or closed – and what exactly had led to the attack. Also Joe's previous form since stuff like that didn't just come from nowhere. It was in the blood, they said, or else it was what he'd seen growing up. They told stories about girls they knew who had been in abusive relationships. They related the advice they themselves had given, acting as friends and confidants, and what it all came down to, they told Stella, was one simple nugget: Get the hell out and don't even think about coming back.

She needed to practice some positive reinforcement. Thinking about whether or not Joe was after the house, that was letting the negative stuff in. It was counterproductive. It was allowing Joe to retain some control. The trick, they said, was to look to the future, to tell yourself that good things happened to good people and to rebuild your confidence. It was a matter of reconstructing the person, the complete person, the one who had been too strong for Joe to destroy.

All of which was damn all use to Stella. But it was better than bringing up the topic with her folks who would only start up about how they'd always known she was too good for Joe. That was *their* angle. And the house – what about the house? She'd never been happy there anyway. If she had to move, then so be it; it was a small price if it meant being rid of the likes of Joe Faherty. The real question was… Stella didn't give a shit what the real question was, she needed some indication of what Joe was planning. The friends she shared with Joe, they were keeping their heads down and that left Ed. She'd talk it over with

Ed. He might not know what to do but at least he wouldn't talk about negativity. Chances were that Ed didn't even know what positive reinforcement was.

Joe Faherty was pretty much as Paddy had expected – an ordinary punter who'd seen an opportunity and thought *Why the hell not?* A decent enough guy, it seemed; recently separated and maybe that had something to do with all this. What was it Faherty had said in London? – that he was over for an interview. Well, he was working now, putting the day in somewhere around town and looking to make a little extra on the side.

Would he take up Paddy's offer? Maybe, maybe not but there was no harm in looking around. Paddy took the DART out to Killiney to where the real money was: great big security gates and closed circuit cameras all over the place. Chris de Burgh lived in one of these houses – Paddy wasn't sure where he'd read that – and Bono owned another. Which was all very well but why rob a celebrity? What Paddy was interested in was some nice anonymous folks whose security system was there for a very good reason.

Go by the make of car, that was as good a place as any to start. Look for something ostentatious – a Merc or a Porsche or a vintage Aston Martin in the driveway. People like that owned expensive jewellery and they kept it close at hand in case there was somewhere they might like to show it off.

But then again: why aim so high?

Paddy wondered would Joe Faherty know the difference between a hundred grand job and a ten grand one. It was unlikely. So why not pick somewhere easier? Some comfortably alarmed place out in Booterstown or Sandymount – nice medium rich areas. Yes, maybe that was the way to go. Let Joe go through the proceeds, take a few photos and then later on if there were any complaints say: Sorry chum, that's the luck of the draw.

Why take unnecessary risks if the profits were going elsewhere?

Aoife was on the phone when he got home. She wanted to know about this new friend Paddy had been keeping secret. From

London, apparently, and a golf fan to boot.

"A bit of male company will do you good," she said.

"I don't really know him that well."

"I'm looking forward to meeting him," Aoife said, "but he'll find me a tougher nut to crack than old Des."

Tuesday evening, Ed was having what smelled like bolognese or chilli maybe, something spicy cooking in the large cast iron pot on the cooker. Ed still in his uniform, making a fuss; moving the newspaper so Stella could sit and asking what she'd have to drink. Or had she eaten yet? Telling her she was in luck, he'd just done the shopping so there was beer and wine or if she'd fancy something a little stronger there was that too. Stella telling him she'd manage a glass of wine if it was going, then saying, "I need your help with something."

She laid it out for him. Her worry now was that Joe was looking to contest the house, which technically he might have a right to but that wasn't her problem. Her problem was that she didn't want to move just yet. What she really needed to know was what sort of life Joe was leading now. He was working again, she'd guessed that much, but she didn't know where. Was he seeing anyone new? If so, was that something a judge might take into account?

Two cheques in two weeks – maybe somebody was putting him up to it.

Look at it this way, she said: a guy beats his wife and walks out of the house. Two weeks later a court order is handed to him and then, a few of weeks after that, he is seen with a new woman. What would that tell a judge about a person? Information, she needed good solid information – names, dates, times – the sort of stuff a solicitor could use.

"Maybe a private investigator. You know anyone reliable who won't cost me an arm and a leg?"

"Leave it with me," Ed said. "I'll give it some thought."

"Maybe I'm wrong," she said, "but I think he's up to something. And maybe there's someone pulling the strings."

"Good to see you're having a laugh," Paddy said.

And it was, Des and Aoife enjoying themselves, Paddy the butt of the joke. Aoife asking who the hell wanted to go out with a guy who had no friends. Someone like that, you'd never get away from him, always under your feet or on the other end of the phone. For Des it was the worry: why does no one like my son? The happiest day in any parent's life, he said, was when your kid finally found a friend. Only most parents didn't have to wait twenty-six years for it.

Yes, they were having a fine old time, Paddy knowing the evening was a write-off: no way would he get away to scout out a prospective house tonight. It was like the old days, he thought, Des and Paddy civil with each other if there was a third party present. Only it had always been different when Aoife was about. Aoife seemed to bring the best out of Des – it was still a performance, sure, but not such an objectionable one – and the evening would sail by. And these days they weren't above killing a joke, Des saying it was hard for parents not to blame themselves, Aoife talking about how it could hit a girl all of a sudden that she'd made a bad choice.

It had been easier to case the houses in London. All day to do it and no one expecting to see you.

"I wouldn't get too excited, folks," Paddy said. "He probably just wants to borrow some money."

Aoife walked to the back of his chair, draped her arms around his neck. "Now don't you be putting yourself down," she said. "That's our job."

Some nights lying in bed, Joe would picture himself opening the door to someone selling memberships to Greenworld. He'd stand there listening to the pitch and think, *Jesus, is this really happening?* And yes, it would be. Some smoothie, nice suit and tie on, just getting into his stride when Joe would say, "Why don't we talk this over inside."

Joe would offer him tea, and if he didn't want that, maybe a soft drink – blackcurrant squash or Ribena or peach juice. Something unusual. They'd be sitting opposite each other. "Right," Joe would say, "let's have it." Joe sitting back, chomping on a Goldgrain and thinking *You smug prick, how did you get this job?* Because that would be the question – how the hell had this clown been selected over Joe? Selling took skill. It took understanding and it took timing and in Joe's eyes, this guy wouldn't have much of either.

Indecision, that's what Joe would aim for, interested in the environment but not sure of the best way to show it. Concerned, yes, but not quite able to take the plunge. Stringing the guy along nicely. Asking him to repeat those carbon monoxide figures and then, when the new campaign being introduced in schools was mentioned, he'd say, "Hey, that's a good idea. Who came up with that one?"

He'd keep this up for an hour, then boot the guy out in his ear. No buts, no excuses, just tell him he wasn't hitting the right buttons.

What was it now – six weeks? eight? – since he'd had that interview. It seemed longer. A lot had happened in the meantime, practically all of it bad, leaving Joe with his grievances. Eoin and Evelyn were on that list, of course they were, but there were others as well. The crew who threw his CV into the bin, for instance. Stella's family, too, and Costello and what about the friends who never called? Where the hell were *they*? Siding with Stel, maybe, or else just lying low, none with enough consideration to track him down and pick up the phone.

Top of the list, though, Joe put his new workmates. The way it seemed, Joe had had his moment in the sun – now he was the houseboy again. And that's how it would be until someone else took off with a fur coat. On the monthly stock take there was a leather jacket missing which may or may not have been Joe's responsibility; he was only into his third week in the place. William was keeping an open mind on the matter. A team effort, he said, each with his own task and it was an open mind that kept everyone on his toes.

Whatever that was supposed to mean.

That night, Joe imagined himself and Benner ripping the place off. He pictured Brosnan and the others opening up some morning and finding the place well and truly rifled, Joe waiting a few minutes before saying, "That security consultant of yours, someone recommend him to you?"

He'd deadpan it, a nice gormless don't-know-any-better expression.

A moment like that would be something to savour.

Ed remembered Joe's address from the letter Stella had shown him. He spotted Joe coming out of the house – converted to flats, it seemed – and tailed him as far as the bus stop. Then he made his way back to the car. What buses went along that route? The 42, that was one, and the 42A as well. Maybe there was a B and a C but Ed couldn't recall ever having seen either. Not that it mattered. All the 42s as far as Ed knew ended up on Marlborough Street so the thing to do was drive into the city centre and wait. If Joe didn't appear, then he'd have to rethink things. Next time round he'd get on the bus and tail him properly.

He waited in the doorway of *Dolphin Discs*. Twenty to nine, Joe stepped off the bus.

It wasn't easy following someone who knew you: one quick turn and you'd be rumbled. And in a crowd like this – everyone on the way to work – you had to stick nice and close. Ed tailed him over O'Connell Bridge, along D'Olier Street and onto Grafton Street. Turning right now, Ed following, then thinking, *Where's he off to?* Watching him turn into one of the shops near the corner of George's Street.

A minute later, Joe appeared in a spiffy blue security guard's uniform.

A fur shop, no less. At least now Ed knew where to find him.

The idea was growing on Joe – what could be sweeter than to rip off William Brosnan, furrier and leather goods specialist? One thing about it, it would do away with the guilt. Rob a house and you were into someone's personal possessions – maybe some of the items had sentimental value – but a shop, that was different. A shop was a business. It was a profit-making enterprise. As Benner said, the stuff would be insured. Maybe Brosnan would even make a little on the deal but if he didn't, if he got stung, well so what? Brosnan was a prick. He was a shithead. A little jolt, a little lesson in humility, it would do him no harm.

Joe made sure he had cigarettes the next time he met Benner. They were sitting in *The Abbey Mooney – The Beachcomber* was too close to Clontarf Garda Station – Joe telling Paddy how he just might be interested in a deal. Depending of course on a number of things. First of all, how involved in the robbery would he have to be? The way he saw things there was no real need for him to set foot on anyone's property – that was Paddy's department – all he really had to do was sit back, wait, then allow himself to be photographed with the proceeds. After the stuff had been fenced, he could walk away with the profit. "You got anywhere in mind? he asked.

"Not yet. It takes time to find the right place."

"But you've been looking?"

Paddy nodded. "Southside."

"Whereabouts?"

"Sandymount, Booterstown – where the rich folks live."

Joe pushed his cigarettes across, just like Benner had done the last time. "If you pick a private house, how do you know what you might get out of it? This is pretty much a once-in-a-lifetime thing for me so I'd like to be sure of a decent payoff."

Paddy shrugged. "Well," he said, "that can be hard to guarantee."

"What about a shop?"

"What sort of shop?

"Try a jewellery shop? You ever rob a jewellery shop?"

Paddy shook his head. "I'm more of a home invasion specialist."

Joe took his cigarettes back, lit one. He blew the smoke away from Benner. "Say if you had some information about a place, you knew what type of alarm system there was. Would you be able to break in?"

Another shake of the head. "No."

"Why not?"

"Because the alarm is on the inside…"

"And you're on the outside."

"Exactly."

"You don't sound like much of a burglar," Joe said.

Paddy laughed and said, "Feel free to get somebody else if you want," and then he explained how alarms worked. As far as he was concerned, if a place was properly alarmed, you couldn't get in without someone knowing about it. Or if there were people who could manage it, Paddy had never met them. Most burglars, he was sure, worked pretty much as he did – they either went in when the folks were home or, if the place was empty, they might try to judge the coppers' response time and be away before they arrived. Or else they might set off the alarm, hide while the coppers checked things over, then go in. The only way you might get past an alarm was if there was a weakness in the system – a new unalarmed window or one without a sensor so you could take out the glass and climb through. Many jewellery shops, he said, doubled up; one alarm to stop you getting in, then infra-red beams scanning the inside. Find your way past that lot, he thought, and you deserved the goodies.

"Hmmm," Joe said. "that leaves us with another problem."

"Which is?"

"How do we know what the take is going to be?"

"We don't. Everything's a risk in this world."

Joe shrugged. "I'm afraid I'm going to have to think about this again," he said.

Putting an end to that tactic, Paddy thought. Joe was right to be wary – who wouldn't be? – but the thing was, it was practically impossible to estimate what the take would be. Not without inside information at any rate. The only guarantee Paddy had ever had was from Fynn, who usually wanted the return of an item he had sold. But without something like that, you were in the dark. Some houses were misleading; nice big car in the driveway and there was bog all inside. Or other times you could head in for a mooch around and come across something valuable.

Come to think of it, Paddy reckoned he was the wrong man for the job. Eleven years now he'd been breaking into people's houses and the top haul to date was twenty-eight grand. Which was fine for a night's work but not enough to get Joe Faherty off his back. For the past while he'd been looking for one big score – something no one else had noticed, something low risk but with a decent dividend. And what had he come up with?

It was nothing Joe Faherty needed to hear.

Only Joe seemed to have a few ideas of his own. A dark horse, it seemed, trying to case out the place where he worked – a fur shop situated off Grafton Street. Furs and leather goods and the odd expensive novelty item, the place doing better than anyone would think. Paddy let him talk. Why not? He was going nowhere. Thursday was bank day so Wednesday, Joe said, that was the time to go in. Wednesday night – or maybe Tuesday if Wednesday would look too much like an inside job.

What had they to lose by looking it over?

"I'll try to remember all the details of the alarm," he said. "Write it down for you and see what you think."

There was no chance, Paddy knew this. "Sure," he said, "I'll look it over."

33

Ed watched Joe turn into *Neary's* and he asked himself, Who was it that I met in there? And when, for that matter. It was hard to keep track of these things. Susan or Sarah, something like that, up from the country and wearing an inch of make-up. She'd kept putting her hand on his leg, he remembered that all right. And she was a nurse: yes, definitely a nurse, but the name? – it was a tricky one.

This was promising. Twenty past eight, Wednesday night, and Joe was meeting someone. Why else would he come back into town? He'd stopped at the chipper on the way home from work, Ed seeing this and thinking, what the hell, he'd give it a couple of hours. Ed watching from his car, not really expecting a result; ready to jack when hey, there he was. And now he was in *Neary's*. He was meeting someone; he had to be. And here Ed was, right behind him – how could Stella not be impressed?

He'd give it twenty minutes, then go take a look.

Or fifteen maybe, fifteen might be enough. Ed wanted to go home, put the feet up, see was there football on the telly. Or if there was no game, he might collect a video – watch Arnie or one of the boys shoot the shit out of a couple of hundred extras. Something light. Something to end a crappy day. Costello had dropped by this morning, wanting to know had anyone been by with a few questions. Which was typical Costello, Ed thought, thinking of himself. The thing to do now – Ed had talked it over some more with Stella – was to keep him at a distance. Play dead, that was the advice. Let the machine take the call. If it meant letting the little earner go for a while, then so be it – Ed could always find another garage, couldn't he?

One more collection, then the ball was back in Costello's court. Hopefully he'd do the decent thing and disappear.

Ed waited.

He looked at his watch: twelve minutes gone.

Standing here bored again. Yes, it had been a poxy day. Out on traffic duty this morning – the lights at the UCI Coolock were acting up – and then back to the station for a stint behind the desk. Pizza for lunch. Nothing to investigate, nothing to do. Nothing to even think about, for that matter – except Stella, that was – which had led him here to this doorway on Chatham Street, wondering, *How much longer can I go on like this?*

The first person he saw, right down the end of the bar was Paddy Benner – whatever *he* was doing here.

Then, Christ, it hit him.

Ed stood in the doorway and stared. He backed out onto the footpath again.

"What on earth are you getting yourself into, Joe?" he whispered.

It wasn't so much that Joe liked Benner – he did, but that wasn't the point – no, the important bit was that he liked himself when he was with Benner. Benner saw the funny side of things and Joe found himself responding. There was no bitterness between them. No aggression either. Louis was dead, nothing was going to change that, and now it was up to the living to look after themselves.

In some ways, it was hard to believe he was a thief. When Joe met him first on the doorstep in Down's Leaze he'd seemed a polite, earnest sort of a guy. A religious loo-la maybe, but refined and well-spoken. And then after Costello had put him in the know, what then? That he was some sort of spoiled rich kid turned bad? It was one possibility. Or a sociopath, maybe, whatever the technical definition for that was.

Now it was hard to know what to think. Each time they'd met, Benner was the same, the pressure never showing, confident that it could all be sorted out and well, what was the point in arguing in the meantime? The best thing about him: he and Joe had no history together. They didn't know each other, didn't know any of the same people. He had no expectations of Joe. As far as Benner was concerned, if you came by a certain type of information, you either gave it to the coppers or you put it to some use. Who was Paddy Benner to judge anybody?

"I don't see how you can guarantee me a payoff from a house," Joe said. "Not without some inside information."

Paddy shrugged. "You just get up to the bar," he said, "and let me do the thinking."

Stella could remember once when she was a kid, playing out front when a schoolmate passed by, her mother in tow. Someone had written BRITS OUT on the front wall. Next door the shop front was all boarded over.

You live *there*? the friend said. It's a nice garden, the mother said. And it was – a nice garden, well cared for and full of colour. A garden like that showed pride. The family who lived there were settled in the area. It showed that some people were happy to live where others wrote graffiti all over the front wall.

"Just for the time being," Stella said. They knew she was lying but who cared?

And since then each place had been temporary. Two flats – one in Fairview, one in Artane – and now this house. All temporary. A starter home, that was the term – somewhere to live while you sorted yourself out financially. All part of a journey to a house you could point to, one you could show someone and say, Yes, that's mine, you want to come in? But this wasn't it. This was a three bedroom semi-detached in Santry. This was the lower end of suburban life, counting the pennies and remembering to put the bins out on a Sunday night.

Maybe Joe really did want back into it. The letter, she read it again and Jesus, it was hard to decide.

She wondered had Ed started tailing him yet.

"You ever hit a woman, Paddy?" Joe wanted to know.

Paddy nodded. "Once."

"Why?"

"She was blocking the stairs."

"You were robbing her house."

"That's right."

"And how did it make you feel?"

"Hitting her?"

"That's what we're talking about."

"I couldn't give a fuck."

"Really?"

"She was in my way, wasn't she?"

"I hit my wife," Joe said. "Just once. Lost my temper, and whack! I belted her one. Over money, that's what it was. I was out of work at the time. Seven years, happy ones, and then it all just fell apart. Here, I want to tell you a story. You mind hearing a story?"

"As long as you keep it brief."

"Okay," Joe said, "short and sharp, they're the best ones. Well, once, a few years back – five maybe, or seven – my sister got involved with this bloke who started knocking her around. I didn't know at first – you wouldn't believe how nice the guy came across when you'd meet him – but behind closed doors, that was a different matter. Lots of punches to the body so the marks wouldn't show. Or else she'd tell lies to cover for him. He got inside her head, if you know what I mean, and Jesus she just couldn't think straight. Thought it was all her fault. He was one sick fucko, let me tell you. Well, anyway, when I found out about it I got this pal of mine and we paid him a visit. Big bruiser, this guy, you wouldn't want to tangle with him. Danny Kennedy, that's his name. And I tell you we beat the living crap out of this bastard. Took him unawares, kept things all nice and friendly until he'd got us a beer. Then we started into him. Battered him from one side of the room to the other. Held his face so close to the fire he's probably still marked from it. You could hear his hair burn." Joe looked across. "What do you make of that?"

Paddy shrugged. "It's not really my kind of story," he said. "I like a story with a nice dog in it. A Labrador or a border collie, something like that. A dog and a happy ending, now that's the sort of story I'd be interested in."

Joe shook his head, not quite sure what was going on. Here he was, spilling his guts out, trying to get to something important and Benner… well, he was taking the piss, wasn't he? Joe said it wasn't true, the story, it never happened. But that wasn't the point. The point was that it *could've* happened. Because that's what Joe would've done, he'd have beaten the shit out of the guy. He was the type who'd hear about a woman getting hit and Christ, it'd make his blood boil.

"What does that make me?" he asked.

"What'll you do with this money, Joe? The money I'm going to earn you."

Joe made a *who knows* motion.

"You think she's coming back?"

"It's why I'm doing this."

Paddy flicked his lighter in the air, caught it again. "Wallop your wife and see her walk out, that's one part of your life that's over. If she's any sense it'll take a lot more than I can earn to change her mind."

Joe shrugged. He looked across for a moment. "You got a better plan?"

Stella was doing the ironing when Ed turned up. She had it prepared, what she was going to say – about how she'd just been tossing the idea around and for God's sake, she'd never intended for him to take on the surveillance himself. Hadn't Ed already done more than enough for her? No, that wasn't the intention at all so if he'd just add up the hours, they could work out a rate and…

She didn't bother. She said, "*Benner*? What would Joe be doing with him?"

Then she said, hey first things first, was he absolutely one hundred percent sure it was Benner and that they were together?

"Holy shit," she said.

A moment later, she said, "Let's take this back to the beginning. Two guys posing as Mormons call to the door in London. Joe sends them on their way and a short while later Louis is shot. Joe goes to the police station to give evidence. He spends ages there making one of those pictures, what are they called?"

"Composites."

"Right. Composites. Then he comes home and tries not to think about it. In the meantime he thumps me and leaves and he sets up in his flat, wherever that is. Then he gets called into the

Bridewell to identify a suspect named Paddy Benner who's being hounded by your friend Costello. He says that the person he met on the doorstep in London isn't in the line-up. And why should he lie? But then you follow him and see that he's meeting this Benner character."

"That's about it," Ed said. "Is there any way Joe could have known Benner before London?"

"I don't see how."

"Me neither. He must have got in contact with him after the line-up."

"But why?"

"I can't think of a reason."

"A robbery?"

"Would you mark Joe down as a thief?"

Stella shook her head, then made a face. "I wouldn't have put him down as a wife-beater either."

Ed was pacing back and forth across the room. "It has to be. I've never heard of anyone striking up a friendship over an identity parade so there must be something at the back of it. And what other skills does Benner have? Costello said he was sure Benner was dead in the water for that business in London. Only he walked. Could Joe have let him walk so he could use him later on?"

"Maybe it wasn't Benner who shot Louis," Stella said.

"Had to be. Otherwise how would Joe know Benner was a thief? He must have recognised him in the line-up, let him walk, then tailed him."

"But why?"

Ed shrugged.

"That the best you can do?"

Stella watched him, the gears clicking into place in his head. "The fur shop," he said.

"What fur shop?" she said.

"The one where Joe's working these days," he said. "That fur shop."

Benner had left – off to meet his girlfriend, he said – and Joe was still sitting in *Neary's.* Still nursing his pint, readying himself for the walk home, thinking things over. A hypocrite, that's what he was. He was a decent guy, sure, a good neighbour, the sort of person most people would be happy to have living next door – all of this, as long as things were going *his* way.

Maybe most middle class, middle of the road folks were like that. Because that's where unemployment hit hardest, he imagined – in the middle classes. The rich, they were protected. Or if they did fall on bad times – a high level businessman, say, who goes bust – well, he always knew there was a risk involved, didn't he? He knew he was walking on a wire, that's how he made his money. Or someone who loses a crappy job cleaning out toilets or something, well he always knew it was a possibility, didn't he? Of course he did. As soon as things turn bad, he's the first to go. He knows this. But the guy in the middle – the salesman, the store manager, the quality controller – he thinks he's protected, he feels he's owed something. He's sacrificed excitement. He's sacrificed the prospect of real wealth. Excitement and wealth – the highs – he's sacrificed them both so that he'll be spared the lows when the bad times come.

But in a recession the lows could hit anyone. Joe understood this now. In a recession all bets were off; you looked over your shoulder and prayed to Christ you weren't next to go.

Nineteen years, Joe counted, going on twenty, moving between salons and supermarkets, filling up orders and keeping an eye on the figures. Nineteen years, most of it spent in traffic. Had he actually achieved anything? He couldn't imagine what. He'd sold one hell of a lot of shampoo, that was all. Tons of the fucking stuff. And for what? So he could have a little security? So he could sit down in the evening without the feeling that the chair might be pulled out from under him?

Someone had sold him out. Someone hadn't kept his half of the bargain.

It was one of the reasons Joe admired Benner. Eight years, apparently, moving from one place to the next, living off his wits. That was the phrase – *off his wits*. What a way to live! Playing pool mostly, he'd said, and why should he lie? Stealing sometimes – this was true and there was no condoning it – but at least he hadn't sold his life away for a little security.

Joe looked forward to the time when he'd be setting him free again.

"Maybe Benner wasn't involved in London," Stella said. "Here's a possibility: what about if Costello drags Benner in for Louis's murder? If he hates him so much he might tell Joe he's a thief – just so he'll be picked out. Then Joe would know Benner's the man he needs if he's looking for someone to rob the fur shop."

Ed didn't seem so sure. "What would Costello have to gain by it?"

"He's trying to harass Benner."

"But as soon as he gets to London he's going to walk."

"He was going to walk on the burglaries you were questioning him for."

Ed shrugged. "The thing is that Costello was sure Benner was the one. The composite, it was the dead feck of him and the London Met said they were looking for an Irish guy by the name of Paddy who spent a lot of time playing pool. That's Paddy Benner. I didn't think so before but Jesus, if he's hanging around with Joe, that's pretty strong evidence."

"So, okay, let's say it is Benner. We still don't know why they were meeting."

"No."

"Benner's a burglar. Is that right?"

"A creeper."

"Which is?"

"He'll go in while you're at home. At least that's what Costello told me."

"Would he be able to rob a fur shop?"

Ed sitting on the couch, staring across and thinking Christ, it was an odd situation. "I'll have to get back on to Costello. See exactly what Benner's track record is. I can't wait to see Costello's face when he finds out I'm the one who's nailed Benner."

Stella was sitting legs crossed in the armchair. "Maybe you shouldn't rush into anything," she said.

34

These days with Aoife – gravy. It was the best of Autumn weather. It was jacket weather, Paddy letting things move along, getting to know her again, the real Aoife, twenty-six next January and a schoolteacher now. She was busy these days. She was settled back into the new term. Four weeks until the October break, she said, and they might even go somewhere – a long weekend maybe, Paris or Amsterdam, somewhere like that.

There was no need to tell her he loved her. That was a given. Paddy talked about the things that mattered to him – sport, for instance, and the lessons it taught you – and Aoife talked about the books she was reading or those she was teaching to her classes. She talked about films, her favourites, and the module she was hoping to introduce into Transition Year as soon as there was an opening in the timetable. And maybe they might think of finding somewhere to live together. It was, after all, going to happen sooner or later. Kill or cure, she said – and so much for taking things slowly.

The thought of losing her now put a sharp chill in Paddy's heart. Make the wrong move, he knew, and he'd be a goner. No arguments – just gone. History. The issue would be trust. Loyalty too, that would be mentioned, but mostly the talk would be of trust – how could she ever again be sure that he was telling the truth? She'd cry, maybe, but she'd be strong too. Nothing would bring her back.

So, yes, he was deceiving her, but what option did he have?

Faherty didn't fancy a house job and this was a blow. Still, things were running Paddy's way. The trick, same as before, was to get out of this mess before his luck turned.

The weakness, Paddy saw it almost immediately. "See this

thing you've drawn here, that's a sonar. They use them on doors mostly. As soon as you open the door, the connection is broken and the alarm goes off."

"So?"

"See this other one, that's a sensor. It picks up vibrations to stop you tampering with a window."

"So you can't take out the glass."

"Exactly. There some sort of attic in this place?"

"Brosnan said there's a floor but he wouldn't want to go walking on it."

"What about a skylight?"

"I don't know what sort of alarm is on it. There's a window of some description on the roof."

"Well, that'll have a sensor. But it's this one here that I'm interested in. The door between the upstairs and this floor, the trapdoor, you're telling me there's a sonar alarm on it."

"I drew what I saw."

"Well, then it'll only stop you coming down through the trapdoor. You could cut down through the ceiling and there'd be nothing to pick up the vibrations."

Joe nodded, he was impressed. Hopeful too. "That's good, isn't it," he said.

"Not really," Paddy said. "There's still no way to get in. That's the main problem."

Aoife was a quieter person now. More restrained. She didn't pipe up in the cinema any more. Before, when Paddy was eighteen and she was seventeen, she'd shout something out in the middle of the film. 'No, don't go back there!' Or: 'No, don't listen to him, he's lying.' Of course the punter would go back – there would be no film if he didn't – but it never stopped her offering the advice.

Paddy loved that about her, the way she'd be so engrossed that she couldn't help herself.

Yet these days she was different. Less spontaneous, he supposed, which was fine: they'd both changed. Maybe that was what a broken heart did for you. Or maybe it was the university degree. Whatever the case, these days she kept mum through the film. One night, on the way out of the Savoy, Paddy could feel the nerves hit again, bad this time. "Jesus, Paddy," Aoife said, " what're you so jumpy about? Everyone who crosses your path, you look at them twice."

Paddy didn't know what to say.

"You've got to try and relax."

"I'm relaxed."

"What's the worst that can happen?"

"You tell me."

"It's Costello, isn't it? That's what has you so uptight. Well, he's not going to come near you now. You know that, don't you?"

Paddy took a breath. "You reckon?"

"Absolutely. He can back off or he can kiss his pension goodbye. A hearing hanging over him, he'd be nuts to risk it."

Of course it was easy to figure a way in. All you had to do was jemmy the skylight window during the daytime, while the shop was still open and the alarm was turned off. It was that easy – get in, sit and wait a few hours, then cut your way down onto the second floor. No problem. But there was a secondary alarm. From the looks of things it was one of those infra-red systems, a beam spreading across the room, angling down from about ten feet up the wall. Any movement below that height and the beam would pick it up. Or at least that was how they usually worked. Still, he was considering it, this fur shop. Maybe it was worth a look. Most jewellery shops were damn near impossible to crack – unless you tried a smash and grab, that was – and Faherty seemed set against a house job. There was a weakness, the skylight, and that was worth considering. A man on the inside and a weakness in the system, was he going to get a better opportunity?

Then again: he had no idea what sort of safe was in there. Would he be able to peel it?

It was hard for Paddy to concentrate. He felt closer now, closer to being free of this mess. One robbery, that was all. He needed to be patient. He needed to plan the thing properly. Some evening – a month from now, maybe, or two, whatever it took – and he would go in. He understood, in theory, how to immobilise an infra red system but he'd never done it before. First thing he'd do, he'd go check the layout of the shop himself.

Four o'clock, Friday afternoon, he didn't even glance at Joe. There were two sales assistants, a middle aged woman and a spivvy young guy, both occupied. Paddy looked at the furs. He lifted price tags and moved along the rows, watching the assistants and never looking back to the doorway. Joe was inexperienced. He was an amateur and amateurs always thought they could step in and out of character. They thought it showed how confident they were. A wink, or a nod maybe, between two people who shouldn't know each other – there were jobs that had been fucked up over far less.

The alarm had been installed by *Independent Systems*, a similar model to the one in the shop where Aoife had bought her denim jacket. How high was it set? Ten feet, maybe, eleven at the most, and angling down to the skirting board at the far end. An infra red system was sensitive to movement; it would pick up an intruder's body heat and then the racket would start. Unless of course it was a silent alarm linked to the cop shop. Did Joe know whether or not the alarm was silent? – he hadn't mentioned it.

That night in Neary's Paddy explained it. There was a certain type of glass you could get – or tin foil might do, he wasn't sure – that acted as a mirror; it reflected the beam back on itself. Because that was how this system worked: the beams were transmitted and then they were received back again. Any change in these beams – the slightest movement could cause this – and the alarm would go off. It was a simple principle. So the trick was to return the beams without allowing them do a circuit of the room.

Drill your hole in the attic floor, Paddy thought, then hang a sheet of this stuff down to block the beam. That was the plan. Then drill another hole and drop down through it.

Ed stepped through and thought, *Jesus, what's up with her?* Nothing, not even a nod – she just turned on her heels and let him follow her to the sitting room. It was Joe's sitting room too, this struck Ed as he stepped inside, the same Joe who wouldn't be coming back and who was making some sort of break in his life. Joe was planning a robbery, he had to be. The people who lived next to you, even the ones who held your spare key on a hook inside the front door, you just didn't know them. If there was a lesson to learned here, and Ed believed there was, then this was it.

"Joe confined himself to base this evening," he said. "Watching the box, most likely."

"If he has one," Stella said.

"That's right. If he has one. You okay?"

"Nothing wrong in this corner."

Ed looked at her back – a heavy sweatshirt but shortish, that tight pair of jeans underneath. "Still getting used to it, eh? Well, it's hard. In my line of business, you see pretty much everything. Scumbags, of course, there's no shortage of them, but for every ten of those there's your average bloke who gets in over his head. He sees an easy few quid and says why the hell not? The gifted amateurs – most of them haven't a clue and they end up getting three frees a day."

Stella turned to face him. "I don't really want to see Joe go to jail."

"And that's to your credit. It shows what sort of person you are."

"I don't suppose there's any way we could keep him out of it."

Now this was one to consider – something he wasn't expecting. "Keep Joe out of it?"

"Out of jail."

"On the robbery charge maybe, because Benner will go in alone. We follow him in and take him as he tries to escape. But there's a conspiracy charge to answer. Unless of course I don't bring Joe into it at all. Just say I got a tip-off about the robbery and I'm following it through."

Fixing her gaze on him now. "But why would you do that?"

"I'm not sure I would. It would mean letting Benner walk on the murder charge."

"That's right. Louis is dead."

"Louis shouldn't be forgotten."

"And there's you to consider in this. This could be a break for you."

Ed made a face. It was a break, yes, but what sort of break? By now, the initial excitement had worn off. Peanuts, that's what this really was – in the grand scheme of things at any rate. Ed had a chance to stop a burglary. The city turning nasty – rapes, armed robberies and now the drug gangs had started picking each other off – and here was Ed expecting big changes over a foiled burglary. Would he receive a promotion? It was unlikely. Or respect, which was what the real issue here, why should his colleagues respect him? All he'd done was strike lucky. He'd happened to walk into a pub where two guys were drinking and he'd put two and two together.

Still, it was better than nothing.

"Costello is the man to consider here," he said. "If a copper can pick it as an inside job, Joe's the one who knows Benner. Which means he's screwed even if Benner decides not to dob him in it." Ed looked across and shrugged. "I don't see any way we can keep him out of it."

Benner hadn't ruled out the fur shop but there were things to consider. He needed to buy some equipment, conduct a few experiments. He needed to see if it was possible to block the infra rays from the rest of the room. And he was concerned that he was already on tape, picked up by the security camera, since a copper who had any sense would take a look through the old cassettes.

Monday morning, Joe said, "That coat that's missing on the stock take, I've been thinking about it."

"Go on," said Brosnan.

"I was hoping it might be on one of the tapes. I could take a look through them."

Brosnan didn't seem interested. "I don't think so."

"How long do you keep the tapes for?"

"Two weeks. There's enough cassettes for two weeks and then they're taped over."

"Up to you," Joe said. "If you like I can take them home.

Just the daytime ones, that'll narrow it down."

Brosnan wasn't interested. That night, Joe telephoned Paddy from a call box down the road. Benner's voice sounded far away – Australia maybe, or somewhere in Africa, Joe imagined. A tinny sound with interference cutting in and out. Benner wasn't saying yes and he wasn't saying no. He was thinking it over. Give it a week, he said, and he'd let Joe know.

35

Where was Donnelly and where was the other hundred and fifty quid? Half now, half later, that was the agreement, Willie Byrnes sitting on his brother's couch and listing his expenses. Gas, electricity, TV licence – the usual stuff. Smokes, bus fares and a pint in the evening. On top of which, he had to eat, didn't he? Then last week his shoes had finally given out – just fell apart, Willie said, the sole flapping like crazy – which was another thing he didn't need. The money he owed, he was good for it. All he needed was a little more time – a month hopefully, two at the most – and he'd have turned the corner.

His brother looked across the room and said: "What about that shit you're pumping into your veins again?"

Willie about to answer when the brother said: "Not that I give a fuck any more. You tell me you're off the stuff and I say okay. I give you four hundred to help you out of a hole and then a month later I hear you're back on it again. So fair enough, you're an adult, it's your choice. But you get me my money back and you stay away from this house."

The brother said: "Clear your debts before you kill yourself."

Willie said he was working on a few things – irons in the fire, so to speak. But in the meantime, no later than Friday, he'd have a hundred and fifty. Maybe more but the hundred and fifty, it was as good as in his hand. There'd been a mix-up. He'd done a job for a big wheel in London by the name of Ron Sanderson and there was money due. Sanderson was straight. They'd done business before, when Willie was living in London and helping out at the race meetings.

A few days, that was all.

"See that phone book there?" the brother said. "Go look up

directory enquiries for England. Tell your pal to make the cheque out to me because if you get your hands on the cash, we both know where it's going."

Paddy had plans. A flat with Aoife for a start, see how that worked out, and then maybe a night course. The job market was a mess out there. He had no employment record – no experience and no references. No skills either, other than burglary and playing pool. He'd put the bite on the old man for a decent wage and firm up the details of the job. Then he'd think about a course, something practical, something he might at least be able to put on a CV.

He'd give up smoking, he decided. He was down to twelve or so a day, which was okay, but still he felt it in the morning. And he picked up colds too easily; five, six a year on average. It would be difficult, he knew this, but worth it – no cough, no shortness of breath, none of that sensation that someone had wiped ash on the inside of his mouth. And he might even try to eat properly, balance things out with a few vegetables and see if that made a difference.

All of which was in the not too distant future. Wednesday lunchtime, he borrowed Des's car and drove to Fairview. He bought a Passive Infra-red Detector for £12.99 and a lamp for £4.50. In the house he rigged the detector to the lamp. When he waved his hand in front of the detector, the lamp clicked on. When he held a mirror in front of the detector, the lamp clicked on. But the tin foil worked. He lowered it down slowly in front of the beam and the lamp stayed as it was. He tried his hand again. Click. He tried the mirror. Click. But the tin foil, it didn't seem to interfere with the beam; he held it there for a moment and smiled and now all he needed to worry about was the safe.

Stella said, "You ever think how you're just ploughing along and it never seems to make any difference? Every time you get a few quid in your pocket a bill appears the next day."

She said she didn't blame Joe for what he was doing; at least he was showing a little gumption, after all. There was other stuff she could lay at his door, not least the assault on her, but this… this was just taking advantage of a situation. And soon he'd be going to jail for it. Which seemed a pity, she said. Seven years, living under the one roof and sharing the same bed – it hurt her to think of him standing up in court to be sentenced.

She hadn't been easy to live with, she knew this.

The problem was that there were things she wanted from life – material things, yes, why lie about it? – and she needed someone to supply them for her. She wanted comfort. She wanted a decent house with a garden and some nice clothes to wear. She liked classy restaurants. A mentality like that, she said, it came from childhood. Some people grew up with nothing and they expected nothing, but there were others – and who knew the reason for it? – who grew up seeing nice things around them and hoped one day to have them.

Insecurity, she said, that's what it was.

She said, "Ed, there's an attraction between us, isn't there? It's why you're here tonight and it's why I called to you last night. But that's as far as it's going to go. Because I can't make another bad investment. If we get involved, romantically I mean, then another year down the line, or two maybe, I'm going to feel the same way about you as I did about Joe. And I'd hate for that to happen."

She looked across the room. She shrugged and gave a small smile. "Maybe we should stop this before it goes any further," she said.

"The Lotto," she said. "That's what we need. Give us a chance to set ourselves up together."

Plans, sure, the prospect of taking up a decent steady life – one with a mortgage and bills, with debit and credit and the trick of balancing the two. But something else was happening, something Paddy was unsure about. There was a part of him coming alive again. It felt good, deciding if there was a way into this fur shop and if there was, could he get back out again?

He made an inventory of the items he needed:

A ladder.

A jemmy for the skylight.

A battery operated circular saw to cut a hole in the attic

floor.

A hammer and a cold chisel to peel the safe.

He needed somewhere to store his stuff – Joe's flat was one possibility, or maybe a locker of some description. And a camera, he needed a camera. One of those Polaroid jobs would do, he imagined – something simple, something that gave you an instant picture so there could be no argument.

A detective would want the credit; it was something you could bank on. Ed would be permitted to come along but this would be someone else's show – maybe even Costello's – surrounding the place with as many coppers as he could get, then a triumphant swoop when the moment was right. Ed would be congratulated. A note would be put in his file and he'd be sent on his way, back to his reports and his traffic duty, back to the polite disregarding looks of his colleagues.

The Louis Marks murder, it hadn't even made the Irish papers. And this would be nothing more than a botched burglary that had been touted beforehand. So why had he been so excited about it? The surprise, maybe, or the fact that he knew the parties involved. Or the way Costello had had his nose rubbed in it, that may have been a factor. He knew what Stella was angling towards – the idea that someone might take the money away from Joe and Benner. Was she using him? It was a possibility. A bad investment, she'd said, and maybe she had a point, but things turned for people, didn't they?

That attraction she'd talked about, he'd been feeling that for a while and he knew there was something on her side too. And if she *was* using him, so what? What was the worst that could happen? He'd sleep with her and get a pile of cash for his trouble which, whatever way you looked at it, wasn't the worst deal in the world.

He was thinking this as he was led into her living room that night.

"You know that thing you've been thinking about?"

She turned to face him. "Yes."

He liked that; not even pretending to be Little Miss Innocent. "Well, it's crossed my mind too."

"And?"

"There's not much risk."

"You're the one who knows. You're the expert."

"Let's say we take the money. Who's going to object?"

"Benner, for one."

"No. That's where you're wrong. Benner won't give a shit where the money goes. He's got Joe off his back – if this is a blackmail situation which we think it is. Why should he care? He wasn't getting it anyway."

"Unless he's in for a cut."

"Okay, let's say he is in for a cut. Which I doubt since there's no reason for Joe to give him anything. But let's say he is. He's a smart guy. He'll write this off and think what the hell, he's walked away from another close scrape. And Joe will be the same."

"I wouldn't worry too much about Joe."

"Me neither. Joe can't say a word or he's up for blackmail or conspiracy to commit a robbery. Not to mention subverting the course of justice. Joe will write this off too."

"So everyone's a winner!"

"That's right. Especially us."

"You and me."

"You and me."

He was sitting on the couch now. He watched her move towards him, shifted slightly to allow her some space next to him. Only she sat into his lap. She draped her arms around his neck. "We'll be the winners. You have the know-how for something like this. And the experience. You'll need a gun, just to be on the safe side."

"One problem," he said. "How will we find out when they're going to rob the place?"

She pushed back her hair. "Joe'll be coming home soon," she said. "That's how."

What was it they said on the sites? – that there were two bad pays, early and late. Get paid early and you didn't want to finish the job; leave it run and you had to chase your money. Which was never an easy thing to do. The agreement had been for three hundred – a hit, Willie Byrnes presumed, only there had been nothing in the papers – and now Donnelly was light. Would Sanderson be willing to pick up the tab? It was unlikely but for the sake of a phone call…

On the sixth attempt he got hold of Sanderson's secretary.

He'd try again later, he said. Tell someone you were chasing him for money and you'd be waiting for the return call. A hundred and fifty quid, it wasn't much but why let it go? And if Sanderson came through, he'd let the brother have something. A hundred, maybe. Or seventy five. Half and half, that seemed fair since it wasn't as if Willie was without running expenses himself.

It wouldn't be easy, no, but it was far from impossible. What worried Paddy most was the silent alarm. Sometimes you could hear a click as the phone line was engaged to the police station but you couldn't rely on that. And Joe was a problem. Would he be able to carry it off? If the coppers suspected an inside job would he hold out through the questioning?

Thinking things through, lying on the bed and staring at the ceiling, then suddenly thinking, *Oh sweet fuck!* How had he missed it? The phone, all he had to was block the line. A mobile phone would do the trick. Bring in a mobile and call the shop number on that. Then answer the call and leave both phones side by side, just as if there was a conversation going on. With the line occupied – and it would stay occupied until the battery ran out on the mobile – the alarm call couldn't get through to the station.

It was simple.

Then when he was leaving, the alarm would be silent and the coppers wouldn't know a thing.

He lay back on the bed again. A safe, you couldn't be sure what was in it, but the stock, that was a different matter. Bring a truck to the back door and load up. Clean the place out good and proper. Paddy sighed. For years, he'd had his eyes open for one big payday.

Stella lay in Ed's king-size double bed listening to him tell how he'd be thirty-five next birthday and Jesus, where was the future in that? Did she know where ex-coppers went? Into the security business, that was where, the top men moving in as consultants with the big companies while the rest – Ed was talking about himself here – ended up outside discos telling folks to try again next week without the jeans. That was the story, plain and simple. Stella listened to it and thought, Maybe he's trying to justify it to himself. He was a copper, after all, sixteen years in the force, and he'd taken an oath to uphold the law.

Thinking this but also wondering, What will the take be? How much could she bank on? – that was the question. It was an inside job, that was good, so Joe would know the best day to break in. But even so. How many people used cash to buy a fur coat? Assuming of course that they were after the fur shop which she'd find out in time and now she was lying next to Ed, the back of his hand touching her hip. Ed was a terrific looking guy. He was experienced; he had the moves. But still she was disappointed, Ed having kept it slow for long enough to get her going but then losing the run of himself. Still it was the first time and there was promise. There was something to work on.

Now she said, "Let's make a list. Of things we need to worry about."

"Okay. Number one is Joe."

"Will he be able to carry it off?"

"Someone figures it's an inside job, he'll be number one suspect."

"Exactly."

"Then again," Ed said, "he fooled Costello. He let Benner walk. He must be confident otherwise he'd get Benner to rob somewhere else."

"Maybe that's what they're doing, robbing somewhere else."

"Maybe. But my guess is the fur shop. A man on the inside and an experienced burglar, they'd be stupid not to look at it."

"Who says they're thinking of one single job. Maybe Benner was just giving him a weekly payment."

Ed shook his head. "And hang around for a pint once he's made it? No, they were together. There was something going on between them, that much was clear."

Stella said okay, fair enough. So they were together and planning something. Maybe the fur shop, maybe not. She hoped so, it sounded like a lucrative one, but if wasn't, then that was fine. As long as they were robbing somewhere, that was. The best way, she reckoned, was to get them both together, explain the situation while they were looking down the end of a gun and tell them to hand over the proceeds. Ed could tell Joe to collect his things at the front gate. He could tell Benner to sit tight, maybe he wasn't off the hook just yet.

Ed moved his hand from her hip. "That's not such a good idea," he said. "Benner killed Louis Marks."

"Which is why he's in this situation."

Ed shook his head. "Don't give him an excuse to come after us. I don't think he's the one you want to tangle with."

36

"The stock," Paddy said. "What do you think it's worth?"

Joe shrugged. "Close to a million, maybe."

"And the resale value?"

"You talking about a fence?"

"Could be."

"Would you get half?"

"A quarter probably for something like this. Still, that's a quarter of a million."

Joe looked towards the counter. "You're taking it on then?" Paddy said well there wasn't a whole lot of choice, was there? On top of which maybe there was a way to lift the stock. Half and half, he said, Joe would keep whatever was in the safe but the stock, they'd sit on that for a year or so. "I can kill that alarm from the inside," he said. "We load up with whatever we want, bury it up the mountains and take our time finding the right fence."

Sitting back in the seat now, letting Joe take it in. Another pause. Then: "Why tell me this?"

"Why not stiff you?"

"Exactly. Get someone else with a van. Drop the stuff off and then deliver the cash to me."

"Because you'll want to be there when I come out. Otherwise I could stiff you with the cash. Give you a cut, then when you complain say, Tough shit, chum, off you go to the coppers if you want."

Joe said he'd thought of that. "What's the risk involved?" he asked. "The extra risk."

"A couple of minutes, that's all. I'll have the stuff in plastic sacks. Just a couple of minutes to load up and away we go."

Paddy watched him sip his pint, the wheels turning over. He was the type who took his time. "Why should you get fifty percent? From what I remember, I'm the one in the driving seat here."

"I do believe it's my idea. On top of which I'm the one going in."

"And you're the one who killed Louis Marks."

"I didn't have to tell you this. I could pay you off, then come back later. But go in twice and that's twice the risk. Twice the take as well, but I'm happy with half."

"Seventy-thirty," Joe said.

Paddy shook his head. "Look, put your mind at rest. Give me what I want and you can stop worrying about me. There's enough things to worry about without a disgruntled partner."

That seemed to strike a note. Joe shrugged. "Fifty-fifty," he said with a sigh. "Maybe this blackmail business isn't for me."

The first thing that struck Joe was, shit, he was within fifty yards of her; Stella turning in the gate as he was leaving the house, see could he shake off that restless feeling. Stella standing there in the navy overcoat he'd bought her last Christmas. Was this a good sign, her wearing the coat? Joe with that feeling in his stomach, like the one you got when the lift shot down unexpectedly.

"So this is it. Where you're living these days."

He nodded. "It's Jean's."

"I know. I knew it was around here somewhere. I got your letter."

"And the money?"

"It helped." She looked up and down the street. "You working?"

"Security. In a fur shop of all places."

"That's good," she said. "I knew you'd find something."

She followed him inside, the flat a tip but who cared? Dishes piled next to the sink, unwashed clothes on the chairs. What would she expect? Recently separated guy – seven years was a long time, remember – of course he'd struggle a little at first. She didn't pass comment. She lifted a shirt, placed it on the armrest. But she didn't sit down.

"You shouldn't be here," Joe said.

"The court order, I was still angry."

"It hurt, Stel," he said. "Almost as much as having to move out."

She nodded. "I know. We were both hurt. You paying rent here?"

"No. But I have to be out within a fortnight."

"Where to?"

"I'll find somewhere. Might have to pay for it, but I'll find somewhere. Stel, that stuff I put in the letter, I meant it. Every word. But that's not all. All I see in the mirror now is a man who beat up his wife. There's no way to explain how that feels."

"It happened, Joe. Show me the point in denying it."

"I know."

"And we can't pretend it doesn't matter."

"I know that too. Your face has healed. That's good. Good healing in the face, lots of blood flow there."

"Look, Joe," she said, "I have to be somewhere. I just wanted to see how you were. I was concerned about that."

"And I appreciate it."

He watched her for a moment. She said, "I was wondering if you want to come over for dinner some night? Tomorrow, if you like. We can talk then, catch up on things. Nothing special, whatever's in the freezer."

Joe didn't know what to say.

"I'll do enough for two. Something that'll keep in case you can't make it."

Yes, Paddy thought, he was taking it on. Because he was being blackmailed, that was the main reason, but there was something else. Pride maybe. Or because that was what he did, he burgled. Fourteen years now, always looking for a possibility, always with an eye out for the big payday. And now here it was! It was waiting for him. There were problems – that alarm for one, and maybe Joe would fold when questioned – but even so, an opportunity like this…

He lit a cigarette and watched Joe dig. Ray Donnelly was buried five hundred yards away and, a little beyond that, the revolver he should have used as soon as Paddy stepped through the front door. Why confuse things? – he was sticking to the area he knew. But all that was history now. And soon this too would be in the past. The robbery wouldn't change anything; once it was over Paddy would pick up the straight life again. He'd move in with Aoife. He'd find a new job maybe and see where that took him.

"That's terrific work you're doing there," he said.

He said, "Maybe you'd want to think about getting that letter back from your solicitor. Just in case old Stella clubs you to death with a saucepan tonight."

Joe was looking for signs. The coat she wore yesterday, the last major present he'd bought her, was that one? And the meal tonight – lamb chops, peas, potatoes – it was one of his favourites. But against that there was no candle or flowers in the middle of the table and Stella herself was just in an old pair of jeans with barely a trace of make up on. The flowers he'd brought were still in the wrapping paper next to the sink.

The trick, he knew, was not to get his hopes up. A line of communication had been opened and that was good. It was the first step. It showed that he'd handled things well so far; the letter, moving out of the house, leaving her the car – these were things that that clearly meant something in Stella's book. He'd taken responsibility. He hadn't made excuses or passed the blame. He'd respected Stella's right to get over this in her own way and maybe, just maybe, things were beginning to turn for him.

Still the conversation was stilted. He asked her how she was doing and she said fine and she asked about his new job. A real dead-ender, he said. Much worse than selling shampoo and his colleagues, they were nothing to write home about. But as Stella herself had often said, it was easier to get a job if you were already working. He hadn't stopped looking. He had responsibilities – the mortgage on this house, for one – and he intended to meet them.

He told her about the next door neighbours, how they'd told him to go fuck himself when he complained about the noise and how he'd gone in the next night and made shit of the place. Well not quite – but anything that might make a noise, he'd destroyed it. Why not tell her? What had he to lose? Crazy, he said, doing something like that but things had been getting away from him for some time now. Ever since he'd been let go. That was the start of it, he said, the slippery slope, and Jesus, it was good to see her again.

"I can't even begin to explain how sorry I am, Stel," he said.

She looked across the table, a piece of potato sitting on the end of her fork. "I've been doing a little thinking myself," she said. "I was pushing you too hard."

"It doesn't excuse what I did."

"Maybe not. But you were under pressure and all I was doing was adding to it. You remember that night I came home from *The Trocadero*?"

"I wasn't sure if *you* remembered it."

"I said things that night---"

"The pressure," Joe said. "That was the pressure. It builds and builds until you're both ready to crack. It was the worry, Stel. You having me hanging around the place; me seeing you bring in a wage and resenting it. It just kept building."

"I thought our marriage was stronger than that."

"So did I. Maybe we both learned something."

"The barring order," she said. "I'm going to get it withdrawn. I can do that, can't I?"

"You don't know what that means, Stel."

"Let's talk about something else," she said. "There was more to our marriage than a bad six months, wasn't there?"

"Plenty more," he said. "Seven good years, let's talk about them."

Where would a copper go to get a gun?

He could get a name, that wouldn't be too hard, just turn up at the guy's door and tell him he needed a shooter. And hear the guy say, Get the fuck out of it! With something like this, you needed a recommendation. You needed the dealer to be sure that you weren't a cop working a sting.

Eight o'clock, Saturday evening, Ed was standing next to Lar Reilly, a small time drug dealer and, according to Ed's sources, a man in the know. Reilly there with a sly look on his face wanting to know what Ed might need a gun for.

"You going to tell me who you get it from?" Ed said.

"Who says I'm getting one?"

"*If* you get one, you going to tell?"

"Like fuck I will."

"Well that's how it works. Don't ask and you won't be disappointed."

Ed waited. "It'll cost you," Reilly said.

"Three hundred, that's the offer."

"Five is the price. You can sell it back for two-fifty if it hasn't been fired."

Ed shrugged. Three? five? – what difference did it make? Still he said, "Five's high."

"It's the special pig rate. Take it or leave it. I can have it tomorrow if you want."

It was like talking to the old Stel. She was remembering the good times – walks, parties, Christmases spent with family – things Joe was sure she'd have forgotten. Those nights in Majorca, she said, had she ever been happier? And full of hope too. Things were good then, she said. They were younger, both pulling in a decent wage and there was an energy to them. Real prospects, that was what they had.

Joe hearing this and expecting her to say, Where did it all go wrong?

She said, "You remember that rain in Majorca?"

Joe remembered it all right; it wasn't the sort of rain you'd forget. Go for two weeks in the sun and run into the heaviest deluge the place has seen in sixty-six years. Or maybe sixty-eight – he wasn't sure. And it felt like it. Joe could remember the sight of the drops exploding off the cobble stones. He could remember squeezing out his shoelaces later on.

"Then, as soon as we got back to the apartment…" Stella said, smiling now.

"On the cold tiles."

"Those were the days," she said. "There was no holdin' us back then."

Hearing her talk like this Joe wished he could tape it for Benner. Benner who'd earlier in the day said, No disrespect to the woman, Joe, but she sounds like one thundering bitch to me. Which was a dreadful thing to say. Then he'd said, Jesus, you'd really want to like wedding cake to marry someone like that. These were things no man should ever say to another, Joe thought. But Benner had said them. Sitting there on a tree stump, too lazy to take a turn with the shovel, holding forth like he was an authority or something.

But maybe that was the impression Joe had given.

If so, he'd been disloyal. He'd given an outsider – a stranger, at least – the lowdown on their marriage. He'd offered intimate details. He'd betrayed this woman, his wife, and watching her move across the room to sit next to him on the couch he felt ashamed. Seven years, he thought. She wasn't perfect, no, but she was still special. She'd found it in her heart to forgive. She was able to look beyond her own hurt and maybe she deserved a little more than to be called a bitch by someone – a thief, let's not forget that – who had never even met her.

She looked vulnerable, he thought.

She looked tired too. Or disappointed maybe, as if the talk of old times was making her regretful. He wanted to reach out and touch her hand, hold it. He wanted to tell her he had no regrets. Seven terrific years, after all. The best seven of his life and if nothing else maybe they could carry him through the rough times.

She looked into his face, offered a tiny smile and a shrug.

"I still love you, Joe," she said, "and I'd be lying if I said I didn't want you back in the house. But that rut we were in, I'm not going back there again. I'm sorry but I need something to hope for."

Ed moved his armchair to the window and watched through the net curtains, seeing Joe arrive shortly before seven, a bunch of flowers in one hand, letting himself in with the key he must have held on to. Ed settling in for the evening, snacks and drinks at his side, not wanting to miss the show if Joe came roaring out again. But knowing that wasn't going to happen. Stella was good. She knew how to pace things. She knew when to speak, when to shut up. She'd worked her magic with Ed after all – Ed could see this now – leading him on, getting him to tail Joe and then once she had something to gain, leading him upstairs to her bed. Which was fine. He knew the score. It didn't mean she didn't like him or have feelings for him – it was just the way she was. Once this was over, once Benner had gone back to whatever life he was leading and Joe was on his way again, then they'd decide what they wanted to do. Stick together maybe or else divide the proceeds and say good-bye. Either would be okay. Ed, like Joe, was making a break in his life and that had to be good.

If he had a preference it would be to stick with Stella a while, see how things developed. But that was up to her.

He watched the house. Nothing, not a movement, Ed waiting for some sign of what was going on. He was thinking of what he might do with the money. A robbery like this, it was impossible to predict what you might come out with, but he was hoping for some sort of nest egg, something he could put by to supplement his pension, maybe even enough to allow him to retire a few years early. His tastes had never been expensive ones. Yes, that would be fine, he thought, to get out of the force before they squeezed the last bit of self-respect from him. That would be worth the risk.

At 11:35, he saw the light go on upstairs. He smiled. Stella was right, Joe was a loser. If he was upstairs, in her bed, it meant that Stella had found out what she wanted.

The following morning, he saw Joe emerge. He watched him move away up the road and then five minutes later, Stella appeared. Ed moved the armchair back to its original position. He took his time answering the door.

"Aren't you the smart boy!" she said. "You were right, it's the fur shop."

He led her inside. "Good. At least we know that."

"And it's going to be a Wednesday evening. Thursday's bank day and Benner says Tuesday would look even more like an inside job than Wednesday would. He's going in through the skylight while the shop is still open."

"Any idea when?"

"Soon. Maybe next Wednesday if he's ready. If not, the one after. You get the gun?"

"I'll have it later today."

"So we're in business."

"We'll need more information."

"They're taking the stock as well. They've a hole dug up the mountains."

"Jesus," he said. "That sounds good. Get him to show you the spot and we're almost there."

She grinned at him. "Slowly does it," she said. "He'll show me in his own time. He's dying to."

They sat in Sanderson's Jaguar, Sudds Donnelly listening and wanting to say, I fucking told you it might have been Benner, if only you'd fucking listen. And he'd been right. It *was* Benner. This Byrnes bloke – a gopher by the sound of things, and a junkie – had disappeared before Sudds had arrived on the scene. He'd tracked Benner down, got a hundred and fifty quid for his troubles and now he was looking for more. Benner must have surprised Ray, killed him – there was no other explanation for it.

At least now he knew.

"I'm sending Dave Robbins with you," Sanderson said. "You ever met him?"

"I can handle this on my own. I want to do this myself."

"I want Robbins. And a statement, something people will remember."

Sudds shrugged. Robbins or not – did it really matter? "When do we leave?"

"He's back middle of next week."

"What if Benner's gone?"

"Then we'll start looking for him."

"If he's there, it'll be a slow one."

"Slow is fine."

"I'm bringing Ray's body home."

"That's up to you. You ready for this?"

"I'm ready."

"A statement," Sanderson said. "Loud and clear."

38

5:00 pm, Wednesday, September 28, Paddy Benner jimmied the window on the roof of *William Brosnan, Furriers* and climbed inside, feeling with his feet, thinking, *Shit, am I going to have to jump here?* – then there it was, the floor, Paddy slowly easing his weight down. The light was good. He pulled his bag inside followed by two sheets of cardboard, two foot squared and covered with tin foil. The floor seemed solid. He laid the bag next to the wall. He closed over the Velux window and he could feel the dust in his throat.

This attic was properly floored – an extra room for a family living above a single story shop, Paddy guessed, only Brosnan had bought it over and changed the second floor into a selling space.

Paddy could hear voices below; nothing he could make out.

The past few days had been hectic, Paddy thinking well maybe this Wednesday or if that didn't pan out, then the following week. Telling Des he needed time off to get his name down in the jobcentres. And also to check out the night courses available. Just a few days to get himself organised, he said; things had been helter-skelter since he'd got home.

Monday night, he'd lifted a Ford van from a car park in Finglas. Then a three piece extension ladder from a building site on the way back. The rest of the stuff he'd paid for – the power drill, the flashlight, the extension cord, the set of punches and driftpins, a small sledgehammer and a cold chisel. The two mobile phones were stolen; bought from a dealer at the back of Capel Street.

All the while thinking, Maybe this Wednesday, but unlikely.

Only why wait if you were ready to go?

He felt that shiver, the excitement, same as he always did.

Joe left work at the usual time following the street to the side of the shop, lifting the ladder down and folding it again – everything nice and calm since that was how you did it, you looked like you were on the level and people just left you alone. A confidence trick, Benner had told him. Why would anyone notice a guy moving a ladder?

The van was parked no more than twenty yards away.

Driving out of town, Joe felt good. Nervous, yes – who wouldn't be? – but confident too. It felt good to be on the move. Benner was smart. He was capable and tough and he wasn't going to panic. The impression you got from Benner was that he was a survivor, that even if things didn't go to plan, if something went haywire, he'd still cope.

Joe had his own role to play, he knew this.

Firstly to get rid of the ladder. He was to wait in the flat for a call and when that came, he'd drive back into town. Then they'd load up and drive away. The tricky bit, maybe, would come tomorrow, when the staff – not just Joe, but Joe particularly – would be interviewed. Even if there was no suspicion of an inside job, someone would be talking to him. Simple routine questioning. And he was confident. He'd make it through, he was sure of it, because his life was coming together; because he had a wife and a home to return to.

His *own* home.

This new life, mind you, would be different. But he was ready for it. And Stella seemed ready for it too. She seemed upbeat. Since he'd moved back in, she'd been warm; little things like touching his arm as they passed on the landing or the way she draped her legs across his lap when she was reading on the couch. Intimacies, you'd call them, small gestures that really told you something. But it was the worry that most encouraged him. She was up the walls that something awful – she'd never met Benner, remember – was going to happen. Making him take her up into the mountains to the spot where the furs would be hidden.

Just so she'd know in case he didn't return.

Protecting her investment, he imagined, an investment in

her future.

Des made it home just after six, calling to Paddy and thinking, *Well, I wonder where he is.* With Aoife, maybe, that was most likely. When the phone rang, he said, "I thought he was with *you*." Then he said, "There's the doorbell, he'll call as soon as he gets in."

Immediately, as soon as Des pulled the door back, he knew it was trouble – two men, one a monster with scars on his face and the other well… you'd take him for somebody's accountant. Des about to front it out, ask what they wanted when, Jesus, they were in on top of him, the big one first, in and through the house and the other holding a revolver to Des's forehead.

Saying, "Nice and easy now, you don't want this to go off."

He led Des through to the kitchen, Des feeling himself being pushed into a chair now, feeling metal on his wrists, then the click of the handcuffs. Telling them to take what they wanted, then the tape being placed across his mouth. Then the big one back again, his face sort of swollen and misshapen saying, "No sign."

Outside, he could hear a car speed past.

Des watching, thinking, *Oh please Jesus no,* but yes it was happening, the smaller one, in his nice jacket and tie, lifting something from a hold-all. A container, a white plastic container, Des bucking in the chair now thinking *Christ, it's petrol.* And then the smell, yes petrol, feeling it on his face and chest and arms and legs.

Oh sweet God…

"You know where he is?" the small one said.

Des shaking his head, then hearing, "Well, at least we asked." Then the striking of a match. Des trying to talk now, grunting and bucking in the chair.

It was the big one who ripped the tape away.

"I'm telling you I don't know where he is… You have to believe me… He doesn't stay here every night and his girlfriend's just been on the phone and she doesn't know where he is either. I don't even know if he's coming back tonight."

"So where *might* he be?"

"I don't know. I just don't know."

"Oh well," and Des saw the match loop in the air, dropping short of the petrol.

"He's got a friend by the name of Joe Faherty. A good friend, he's probably with him. F-a-h-e-r-t-y – no L. That's the only one of his friends I know."

"Where can we find Faherty?"

"Jesus, how do I know! The phone book. Yeah, the phone book, I swear that's the best I can do. Please, I'm begging you, you don't want to do this…"

Des saw the flare of the match and then one of them, he wasn't sure which, was saying, "That's not enough, I'm afraid." He bucked and screamed and the chair toppled and then, from the ground, he could see the smaller one still with the match in his hand. The smaller one looking across as if to say, It's your gig…

"That your final offer?"

Des screamed. Sudds Donnelly shot him once in the side of the head.

Some of the old safes you could punch in thirty seconds flat – if you had the right equipment, that was – but this one was bright and shiny and new and Paddy knew from just looking at it that it wouldn't be easy. A lead spindle shaft, most likely, with lock nuts that were away from the shaft so you couldn't smash the shaft through the gut box and break the lock nuts that way.

Which was okay, what he'd expected. It was a matter of being patient.

He was ahead of time. The folks downstairs had left by a quarter to six and Paddy had started cutting, through the floorboards first, lifting them and placing them to one side, removing the insulation foam and then the tricky part, the ceiling – plywood, he reckoned – of the floor below. Paddy cutting half a square, taping it so it wouldn't fall in, then cutting the rest. The cardboard covered in tin foil was hanging on two lengths of twine. He taped each to the floor and gently lowered the sheet.

He waited.

Ready to bolt across the roofs if the coppers arrived.

By twenty past six he was in. He drilled another hole in the next floor, and hung down another sheet of cardboard. Then he plugged in the extension cord to the power drill and set to work.

Stella was explaining it to Ed, packing Joe's things and saying how it was like having someone constantly breathe on you, that sort of feeling where you wanted to scream and run or else shout, Just get away from me, will you! Following her around the house with his questions. Asking about the washing machine or the colour of the bedroom wall and whether or not they should get it painted. Endless, she said. Stella leading him along – having to – but thinking, Christ, just get the hell away from me.

Slow suffocation, she said, how else could you describe it?

Even small things, she said – his smoker's cough, for instance, or the way he'd make a production out of cooking the dinner. These were things she'd accepted, tried to ignore, when they were together because that's what you did, you made the best of things. You coped. And his body, it was a slab of meat and could just about make her skin crawl.

Yes, it was *that* bad.

And to think that she'd once been scared that she'd end up living alone.

She pressed the second of the suitcases closed. "That gun you've got there," she said, "don't be afraid to use it. Joe's got life assurance."

"Only joking," she said.

Jesus, it was slow! Paddy worked on the upper left hand corner of the safe using a high speed bit, feeling it slip, then trying again; trying to get a hole started in the outer layer of steel so he could get his chisel under it and begin to bend back the layers underneath. There was a quicker way, of course; just pound the shit out of a corner of the box until the plating was bent far enough out of shape to get a jimmy behind it. But why risk the noise?

Within fifteen minutes he had something he could work with. The drill quiet now, he could hear the traffic outside. With the hammer and the cold chisel he enlarged the hole, then used the jimmy to pry it back further. The chisel and the jimmy, using them alternately, prying back the outer layer and feeling the sweat cover his back. Knowing he was through the worst of it now. Ripping the rivets and the welds, prying loose a second layer of steel, and then a third – and suddenly he was through to the asbestos fireproofing. It took him seven minutes to chip out the concrete and the asbestos and to pry open the locking bar inside.

It was ten to seven.

He emptied the contents of the safe into a black plastic sack.

And looked around. If he hurried, if he had the furs packed within an hour, he could still make daylight. He wanted to be out before night-time. Someone sees two guys load up a van on a nice clear evening, he assumes it's overtime. Do it after dark and he thinks it's a robbery.

Early evening or the dead of night – two choices.

He cut the chain on a rack of furs and began to fill the black plastic sacks.

"You Joe Faherty?"

Ed had seen the two pull up, the little and large show, one who looked like a businessman and the other, well, Jesus, he was a big one. Ed telling Stella he'd see what they wanted. Now telling the two, "That depends on who wants to know," seeing the barrel of the gun point at his chest and stepping back inside.

Stella saying, "Hey, who the hell…" and seeing the gun too.

Ed watching her being pushed back into a kitchen chair, standing there thinking, Christ, he should do something. The gun was stuck in at the back of his trousers. Then hearing the click of a pair of handcuffs.

He watched the smaller one lift a white plastic container from a hold-all.

"Any idea what we want?"

Stella shook her head.

"Paddy Benner, that's who we're looking for."

Stella looked to Ed. Ed looked back.

He was just standing there.

"We'll take you to him," she said.

And that was the end of the talking. They were led to a red saloon parked on the kerb outside. The street was silent, nothing, not a sound apart from dead leaves moving with the breeze. Everything calm, early evening, not a movement from the neighbouring houses. Ed drove; Stella sat in the back next to the smaller man, moving down into Drumcondra and towards the city centre. Towards the mountains where Benner and Joe would be, Stella thinking, Oh please Jesus… This pair, she could tell, were stone killers. She could tell from the casual way they were going about things – stepping inside, taking her and handcuffing her to the chair. They were here to murder Benner, nothing surer, and why would they leave a witness?

Maybe they knew about the robbery.

Stella thinking this and wondering about Ed. The guy was a copper, for the love of Jesus; why hadn't he used the gun? Just pull it out, lead the big one to chair and handcuff him. Then keep it pointed at the other one while Stella phoned the police. Only Ed hadn't moved. Standing there, frozen like a dummy while that one, the little creepy one, was taking the container from the hold-all. About to cover her with something – acid maybe, or petrol – and all Ed could do was look.

As if to say, What'll we do now?

Stella stared out the window as they headed towards town. She was thinking, *Why didn't I take the gun?*

Paddy worked row by row, double bagging the furs to protect them from damp, taping each bag tightly at the top. The leathers he'd leave but the furs – coats, jackets, hats and scarves – he piled in rows next to the back door. He could feel the sweat cover his back.

It took him just under three quarters of an hour. He counted the bags – fifty one. The pit they'd dug in the mountains, maybe it would be big enough: if not they'd have to dump a few bags. He'd spoken to Joe about being discreet with the money; if he was stupid, if he flashed it about, there would be someone along to speak to him.

He sat for a moment and looked around, the empty racks

shining in the artificial light. Outside, the street had grown quiet.

At twenty to eight Paddy slipped one of the mobiles from his hold-all and dialled the number of the shop. On the first ring he answered the call and left both phones side by side.

With the second mobile he phoned Joe's flat. He let it ring three times, then disconnected. Then three more and he disconnected again.

Now it was just a question of waiting. Fifteen minutes, maybe, twenty at the most – depending on the traffic.

Ed could feel his breathing even out again, the dread still there and the fear… Christ, yes, the fear. But the panic, that paralysis, it was easing, Ed able to operate the controls properly, gently accelerating from thirty to thirty-five to forty until the smaller one said, "Don't speed." Ed drove along Pearse Street into Rathmines and on towards Templeogue, right past three Garda stations hoping something, *anything*, might happen. But knowing it wouldn't. Thinking maybe if he saw a cop car…

He'd already missed one chance, he knew this. Back in Stella's house, he could have acted. He could have taken the gun out and started blasting. Only he wasn't ready. The gun, he'd expected just to have to show it to Benner who'd shrug and say, Fair enough, and to Joe who'd be so shocked that he wouldn't be able to even speak. Especially if Stella was telling him what was what. Only all of a sudden these two arrived and Jesus, it had thrown him, leaving him standing there with that feeling like he just couldn't fucking move.

He'd bottled it, he could admit that. Just like the last time, standing there trembling, hearing Sean Linehan get the shit kicked out of him and wanting to move, *having* to, but too terrified to take a single step. Like he was fucking paralysed. And then once he'd got himself together, once the panic had passed, it was too late. Which was the difference today. Today he had a gun which only Stella knew he had. Today he had a second opportunity, one he had to take, and at least that was something.

Was this the chance he'd been waiting for?

He tried to clear his mind.

Why were these two here? The robbery maybe, but it was unlikely – they'd thought that Ed was Joe Faherty. Which meant that it was something else. They were English, that much was obvious, the big one with a strong London accent so Benner must have tangled with them over there. And the face – Ed could just see it out of the corner of his eye – somebody had really done a job on him. Could it have been Benner? Yes, it was possible; as he'd explained to Stella there was something about Benner that told you maybe he wasn't the man to cross.

So something had happened in London and these two had tracked Benner down. But how did they know about the connection between Benner and Joe? As far as Ed knew, it was a connection only he and Stella were aware of. And Costello of course, but he knew nothing of the robbery. So think about it! Two killers have come looking for Benner and somehow – Ed couldn't begin to imagine exactly how – they got Joe's name. They turned up at the house, mistook Ed for Joe and now they were on their way to see Benner, Stella giving directions from the back seat. And that was it. Benner was about to be murdered and Stella, Ed and Joe would all be witnesses.

Why would these two leave witnesses?

They left the streetlights behind. Ed felt calm now, felt as though maybe he was about to prove something to himself.

The van was backed right up to the door. Joe stood in the back, out of sight, catching the bags and piling them up. He was wearing the baseball cap Benner had given him – hair and eyes, apparently, were the strongest distinguishing features for a witness to latch onto. They kept a conversation going, also Benner's idea, discussing the week-end's football results and handing the bags from one to the other. Joe watched them pile up, thinking, Jesus, we're going to get away with this…

People passed by. No one said a word.

Twenty minutes later Benner closed over the back door to the shop and climbed into the passenger seat.

Now it was just a question of not getting pulled over.

Stella felt the nuzzle of a gun on her cheek. She heard the

big one say, “Where the fuck you think you’re taking us?” and heard Ed say, “You want Benner, then this is where he’ll be.” Which sounded more like the real Ed. Listening to him tell how Benner was robbing the fur shop he, Ed, worked in and that this place up ahead – a small clearing in the middle of some woodland – was where they were to meet up.

Stella for the first time feeling a little hope.

It was in his voice – calmness, or confidence maybe. Stella thinking maybe he was telling her something – that they weren’t dead yet, that he still had a gun that no one knew about. It was twilight now, Stella staring out the window at the vague shapes of the trees and hedges and beyond that the dull grey sky.

“Take this side road,” she said.

And they were almost there. Stella had been here twice already – once with Joe and then with Ed – and she knew the landmarks. A boulder just sitting there behind an old stone wall, a tree stump the size of a kitchen table. Telling Ed to slow down here, wanting to make contact with him.

Ed pulled up next to a clearing at the edge of some woodland.

“Benner’ll be here sometime tonight,” he said.

They stepped out of the car, Stella watching Ed point in the direction of the pit, hearing him say how that was where the stuff was to be buried and thinking, *What the hell are you waiting for?* Feeling herself shiver; the fear, yes, but the cold too, the breeze stronger up here. And then seeing him move, jerking the gun from the back of his trousers and bang! he’d shot the bigger one in the chest, ready to swivel, Stella watching and gasping and thinking *Yes go on, the other one*, seeing him swing his arm around when Christ it was like the side of his head had exploded. Ed’s legs buckled underneath him. The smaller man, standing over him now and firing once more into his forehead. Everything happening that fast, Stella standing there, too startled to even run, thinking about it now only she was being dragged by the wrist. He handcuffed her to the door of the car. He looked around and said, “Fuck it!”

Stella felt the need to vomit. She’d been slow, she knew this. Maybe she could have got away. Only it was the fright and noise, that sudden shock and then Ed was lying in front of her. She watched this man, someone you'd never take for a murderer, pace up and down in front of her. She could hear the scrunch of his shoes on the damp grass.

Was he going to take it out on her?

The other one was still alive. Stella could hear him gurgling. She heard him say something – she couldn't make out the words – then heard the other one say no, he was here for Benner. Heard him say, "Well, that's your problem. I get paid to do a job." She saw him reach inside the bigger one's jacket and remove a pistol.

For ten minutes, Stella watched a man die.

Standing there watching, hearing the breaths grow more shallow, wondering why the hell she was still alive. She had served her purpose. Benner would be here sometime tonight and this man, the one who had reacted so quickly to shoot Ed, would kill him.

So why not kill her now?

He could do it with his hands if he wanted, she was sure of it.

She waited. It was getting darker now. She could feel herself tremble. The car keys, they were in the pocket of Ed's trousers – she'd seen him put them there – and he was within reach. Only when would she get the chance? When this man went to murder Benner maybe. But surely that was too much to hope for.

They waited.

Stella said nothing. She felt the breeze cool on her face, saw the city in the distance. She watched him pace slowly back and forth.

Twenty minutes later they saw car lights. They watched them get closer.

"You tell me exactly what I can expect here and I won't burn you alive. Paddy Benner, what does he look like?"

So that was it.

Jesus, she thought, *he's never met Benner.*

Already Stella had it worked out. If she could get the keys from Ed's pocket she could reach around and roll down the window. Then maybe she could lower her head to the ground and swing her legs around and in the window. That would leave her right hand cuffed to the door handle, her left free to operate the controls.

It was going to happen. He was going to leave her to go kill Benner. And Joe, presumably, unless he got away in the dark.

"Two men," she said. She paused for a moment. "Benner's the older one," she said, "a heavy set guy just touching forty."

Paddy stepped out and felt the cool air sharp against his face. He closed the van door and listened. It was quiet up here, nothing except for the soft breeze and the sound of a car in the distance. Against the sky he could see the serrated edge of the trees. He bent down and rubbed his hand against the grass – yes, it had been raining – and followed Joe to the back of the van. An hour or so, he reckoned, and then they'd be on their way. He saw the figure emerge, heard the guy say, "Sorry, I'm a bit lost," a London accent and the slightest twitch under his coat. Already he was running. Head down, pounding across the earth, hearing the gun go off, once, then a second time, Paddy seeing the trees ahead and diving for them. Then another shot, a *thunk* in the wood next to him. Then the sound of a car starting up and more shots, one of them clanging off metal and the car roaring away. Paddy running like fuck, weaving between the trees, already knowing where he was headed. And knowing he'd make it too. This guy – a hitman, Paddy presumed – would follow him on the same line. He'd assume that Paddy would run straight, as fast as he could. Paddy turned left, towards the edge of the woodland.

In the half light now it was difficult to make things out clearly. He slowed to a quick walk. This was thick forest, you'd be doing well to find anything in here. He moved as silently as he could, through the trees, hearing his footsteps and his breathing, searching for the pathway he knew was there. If he kept walking, if he'd guessed the right direction, it had to be here somewhere. Then once he found the pathway, he'd move parallel to it in the shadow of the trees. It was just a matter of finding something he recognised – the gorse bush or the yellow stained stone he'd left sitting on top of another.

It was the stone he saw first. First of all thinking, No, that's not it.

But, Jesus, it was.

Next to a smallish cedar tree he began to dig with his fingers, feeling calm again, scooping the handfuls of earth and laying them aside. Stopping every few moments to listen, then digging some more until he felt the plastic bag.

With Ray Donnelly's 22 millimetre revolver in his hand he started walking back to where the van was parked.

Stella stayed in second gear along the dirt track, gunning the engine as hard as she could, scared to take her hand off the wheel in case she crashed. Checking the rear-view mirror for lights every ten seconds or so, expecting to see that van appear but no, nothing, Stella seeing the main road in front of her and thinking, God, I'm nearly there. Then the feel of smooth concrete under the car and she was driving down the mountain, knowing there would be headlights somewhere behind if she was being followed. But not taking any chances, keeping it steady, moving into third now…

Where was the nearest Garda Station? They'd passed a few on the way out, Ed taking a roundabout route, but she couldn't remember exactly where. Templeogue maybe, was there one in Templeogue? This side of the city she didn't know so well. She followed the road signs back in the direction of the city centre, holding her breath as cars passed her on the outside.

She wondered if Joe was still alive.

She'd tell the coppers two men barged their way into her house, Stella there having a coffee with Ed from across the road. Let them think what they wanted about that. Then how they were led up the mountains at gunpoint, the two saying nothing, not a word. Telling Ed to shut up when he asked what this was all about. She'd describe how Ed disarmed one and killed him and was shot by the other and how she herself was handcuffed to the door of the car. There was more shooting, she'd say, just as she was driving away.

Who were those men? she'd ask.

Garda O'Brien, she'd say, he was shot and I'm sure he's dead.

***

There was no mistaking it – two dead bodies. Paddy moved through the trees and yes, there they were, lying side by side on the edge of the dirt track, Paddy rolling the first over and it was Sudds Donnelly. He'd been shot in the stomach. The second one had half his head blown away but Christ, it looked like that copper, Costello's sidekick. O'Brien, was that his name? What in the name of sweet fuck was *he* doing here? Donnelly didn't surprise him – maybe the two boys had a falling out – but this copper? Paddy couldn't imagine what he might have to do with all this.

He moved on.

In the clearing, next to the van, he could see Joe lying motionless. If he was alive, which was unlikely, Paddy had to get him to a hospital. If he was dead, Paddy needed to bury the body. He needed to allow himself time before Joe's solicitor released that letter, the one Joe had written, his insurance so he could be sure Paddy wouldn't bump him off.

He'd be an easy target, he knew, trying to load the body into the van.

Paddy circled the clearing to get close to Joe. From ten yards away he could see the expression. Joe was dead, no doubt about it – lying there with his head at an unnatural angle, mouth and eyes wide open. Paddy lay on his front and moved forward. He crept past Joe and rolled under the van.

And waited.

He felt ready now, that same calmness like just before he'd break into someone's house. It suited him, this place, up here at night in the dark and the quiet because that's what gave Paddy an edge – the quiet. Everything calm and still apart from that light breeze. Eleven years now he'd been creeping through people's homes. He knew his own body and the sounds it made. He knew how to move silently. And this clown, whoever he was, was an amateur; he'd picked the wrong man to kill and then he'd fired at a moving car. Which meant that someone had got away on him.

It also meant there was a chance the coppers would be here

before long.

Paddy needed the van and he needed Joe's body.

He lay completely still. He could feel the dampness through his shirt.

He heard the footsteps and then Joe's body being searched. Then the rattle of keys and the footsteps moving closer, Paddy lying and waiting and then when the van door was opened, he slid out and up. A small neat man somewhere in his forties, stopping at though he was frozen, Paddy pressing the gun to the side of his head.

"Out," Paddy said.

He watched the guy step down, heard him say, "Hey, that was good, you were under the van, weren't you?"

And shot him. Once in the back, feeling the gun kick in his hand, seeing him slump forwards against the van. Then once in the in the back of the head. He wiped the gun clean in his shirt and let it fall.

He looked at the two dead bodies.

"Fuck it," he whispered.

It was almost fully dark now.

Paddy tossed five of the plastic sacks onto the ground. He tried to lift Joe's body – one arm under his back, the other under his knees – but Jesus, he was heavy, Paddy finally dragging him to the back of the van and heaving him in from there. He felt cold, the sweat beginning to chill on his back. He knew what he had to do; he had to bury Joe and get the fuck out of the country. He had to disappear, find a false passport somehow and try to start a new life somewhere.

At least he had cash. Joe wouldn't be needing it.

But first the body. He started the van and pulled away. This area would be combed, he'd have to move further up the mountains since the coppers were most likely coming from the city direction. He had his burglar tools in the back. He could use the jemmy to dig the grave and then just keep driving south, as far as he could before ditching the van. There was no point in trying to explain this to Aoife. She'd be worried at first but then the coppers would come calling and she'd understand. She'd know the truth of it, what sort of person Paddy really was.

Jesus, it was a mess – starting with Down's Leaze, with Hamilton and Malik. That was the part he regretted. Tim too and the Donnellys, he'd made some bad decisions there, but the robbery, that was where the fuck-up began. Getting involved with a pair of amateurs he didn't trust.

This time Aoife would be able to move on, make a life for herself. He was sure of it. What other choice would she have?

He was wrong about the coppers, they were coming from both directions. Paddy met them as he hit the main road, no sirens or lights but he knew they were cop cars, Paddy rolling down the window to ask what the problem was. Ready to play it cool, knowing he wouldn't have a chance on foot.

An armed detective said, "Out of the car and keep your hands where I can see them."

Paddy said, "Hey, sure, no problem.".

He felt the metal of the van hard against his face and then the cuffs going on. He was led by the arm. As he was pushed into the back of the squad car, he heard the back door of the van being opened. Another detective sat into the front of the car. Paddy sat quietly. He stared out the window. There'd be a delay, maybe; calling an ambulance, or waiting for the forensics boys to get here. Which was fine, Paddy thought; he was in no hurry. What hurry could there possibly be?

It was funny but he could feel his breathing ease, just sitting here now, watching the city lights in the distance. It was nice, the way they curved around the bay. The city, it was as if somebody had just turned it on.

He was still thinking about Aoife and how she'd react.

The old man too, and what he'd make of it all.